PENGUIN BOO

AN EPIC UNWRI

Muhammad Umar Memon was bor
migrated to Pakistan in 1954. He
University and later in the US, where he took a Master's degree in Near Eastern Languages and Literatures from Harvard and a Ph.D. in Islamic Studies from UCLA. He writes fiction and literary criticism in both Urdu and English and has also translated a substantial body of contemporary Urdu fiction. Six volumes have appeared to date, including *The Colour of Nothingness: Modern Urdu Short Stories* published by Penguin. His first collection of short stories was published in 1989. He has edited *Studies in the Urdu Ghazal and Prose Fiction*, and has authored a book on religious polemics, *Ibn Taimiyya's Struggle against Popular Religion*, which appeared from The Hague and Paris in 1976. He is the editor of *The Annual of Urdu Studies*, General Editor of the Pakistan Writers' Series (Oxford University Press, Karachi), and is on the editorial board of a number of professional journals.

At present he is Professor of Urdu, Persian and Islamic Studies, University of Wisconsin, Madison.

PENGUIN BOOKS

AN EPIC UNWRITTEN

Muhammad Umar Memon was born in 1939 in Aligarh and migrated to Pakistan in 1954. He was educated at Karachi University and later in the US, where he took a Master's degree in Near Eastern Languages and Literatures from Harvard and a Ph.D. in Islamic Studies from UCLA. He writes fiction and literary criticism in both Urdu and English and has also translated a substantial body of contemporary Urdu fiction. Six volumes have appeared to date, including *The Colour of Nothingness: Modern Urdu Short Stories* published by Penguin. His first collection of short stories was published in 1989. He has edited *Studies in the Urdu Ghazal and Prose Fiction*, and has authored a book on religious polemics, *Ibn Taimiyya's Struggle against Popular Religion*, which appeared from The Hague and Paris in 1976. He is the editor of *The Annual of Urdu Studies*, General Editor of the Pakistan Writers Series (Oxford University Press, Karachi), and is on the editorial board of a number of professional journals.

At present he is Professor of Urdu, Persian and Islamic Studies, University of Wisconsin, Madison.

Muhammad Umar Memon

AN EPIC UNWRITTEN

THE PENGUIN BOOK OF PARTITION STORIES FROM URDU

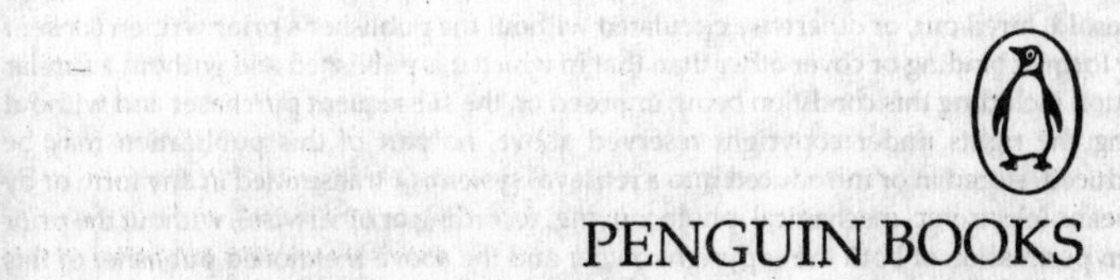

PENGUIN BOOKS

Penguin Books India (P) Ltd., 210 Chiranjiv Tower, 43 Nehru Place, New Delhi 110 019, India
Penguin Books Ltd., 27 Wrights Lane, London W8 5TZ, UK
Penguin Books USA Inc., 375 Hudson Street, New York, NY 10014, USA
Penguin Books Australia Ltd., Ringwood, Victoria, Australia
Penguin Books Canada Ltd., 10 Alcorn Avenue, Suite 300, Toronto, Ontario M4V 3B2, Canada
Penguin Books (NZ) Ltd., 182-190 Wairau Road, Auckland 10, New Zealand

First published by Penguin Books India (P) Ltd. 1998

10 9 8 7 6 5 4 3

Typeset in Palatino by Digital Technologies and Printing Solutions, New Delhi

Contents

. . . and After

To
Ralph Russell
Mahmood Ayaz (1929–1997)
Zeeshan Sahil

Love can also be a rabbit
whose two eyes
have been plucked out with a knitting needle.

Or a small bear
that goes on playing with hives
after the honey's run out.

Or a wheel of wood
turning its fashioner
all his life
along one particular roundness.

— From *Wheel* by Zeeshan Sahil
Translated by G.A. Chaussée

Preface

n May 1996 I accepted, with some trepidation, David)avidar's invitation to translate a volume of short prose iction works from Urdu dealing with the Partition of the ubcontinent in 1947. My trepidation arose for two reasons: he manuscript was required by May 1997 at the latest. A eries of prior commitments and my teaching job at the university made the deadline seem unrealistic, if I was ;oing to give it the effort it deserved—which inevitably has neant for me consultation with the original writers, or hose of them who are still with us, at any rate. The other, erhaps more important reason was that there have been n the past couple of years at least three other collections, in total of six volumes, from India alone which focus on the 'artition corpus, although, admittedly, each tends to be vider in scope than the present volume in that it includes naterial not just from Urdu but also a number of other outh Asian languages. What was there left to translate? In etrospect, however, I feel I made the right decision in aking on the assignment, even though the time constraint lid prove quite daunting at times.

As I read through the other collections, I realized that ontrary to what I had assumed, there were at least three ery good reasons for undertaking yet another selection. I hould perhaps make it clear at the outset that of the three ollections, I find the book edited by Saros Cowasjee and :.S. Duggal to be the most readable, as well as the least shrill n its ideological pronouncements.

One reason was my own bias. I happen to agree witl Milan Kundera that the realm of fiction is essentially meeting ground of opposites, of contraries—a space larg enough to accommodate competing versions of truth unlike the real world where each of these versions mus necessarily collide with the other, overpower and preferably, annihilate it. Fiction does not—at least, shoulc not—moralize. Rather it imparts a kind of wisdom— trans-empirical wisdom I'm tempted to say—felt dee inside the individual in something like a visionary flash Whatever lessons are to be learnt, are learnt in this quie space, without the need to prove that one has grown i stature in some measurable way. Had it been otherwise none of what is occuring today in South Asia would hav occurred as we would have been the wiser for our perusa of the fictional works written in the immediate aftermath c Partition. Again, if one were to write the history of the Wes mainly on the basis of the creative achievements of it writers, it would be difficult to imagine the same Wes capable of the Holocaust and the more recent Bosnia genocide. And again as Kundera has it, fiction does nc write the history of a society, but the history of th individual, indeed, it only articulates the existentia situation of the individual—as, for example, in the characte of Ishar Singh in Saadat Hasan Manto's short story 'Thand Gosht.'

What our writers wanted to say about the Partitio (unfortunately, with the single exception of Manto, I don think they have said enough) they already have sai through the protagonists that inhabit their fictional spac That they chose fiction and not political demonstration an speechification should be reason enough for us not to dra their creative work in a moral reformation of society. Ther s no such blueprint to be found there. Indeed, it was not neant to be there in the first place. As the narrator in Intizar Iusain's 'An Unwritten Epic' remarks aptly, 'literature is ieither constructive nor destructive; it's just literature.' ınd: 'What is this animal called "constructive literature?" . . I've never yet seen anything destructive in literature. If iterature isn't destructive, how can it be constructive?' Even in the unlikely event that literature could hammer nough sense into its readers, the task is well nigh mpossible in South Asia where the percentage of literacy s shamefully low, and practically insignificant where iterary readership is concerned.

I felt that the ideological underpinnings articulated in he learned introductions to the earlier selections worked s a sort of distorting filter against the material presented. n other words, I found them too intrusive for my comfort. Hence my decision to steer clear in my own presentation of ny such narrowly nationalistic aspirations on the one and, and of a kind of mealy-mouthed, neo-Gandhian numbo-jumbo on the other.

Another reason was the shocking—perhaps uninten-ional, but born of laziness nonetheless—inaccuracy and nwarranted deletion frequently found in translations of Jrdu short stories. Admittedly, some of the stories were oorly written: either the writer lacked a good grasp of the Jrdu idiom, as in the case of Rajindar Singh Bedi's Lajwanti,' or had only a tenuous grip on the technical onstraints of the genre, as in the case of Ahmad Nadim Qasimi's 'Parmeshar Singh.' But these inadequacies hardly ntitle the translator to distort, however noble his or her easons to do so might be. I also felt that in some cases the anslator didn't even know Urdu, and possibly worked rom a Hindi transcription or, in some cases, from earlier

English translations, so that the errors of one or the other were reproduced intact. Cultural references, in my opinion integral to the content of the work, as in the case of Ashfac Ahmad's 'The Shepherd,' were flattened out or glossec over in silence. Aside from the injury to the original implici in such an approach, it also raised some disturbing questions about the integrity and the intent of the translator Let me elaborate: We often see and reject the ease with which some Western 'scholars' speak so authoritatively about Third World countries, when, in fact, their acquaintac with the Third World is cursory, tentative, and sketchy. Thi is contrasted by the meticulous attention to the minutes detail they exhibit when they speak about the First World We ought to look at our own Orientalism sometimes: hov we exercise the same authority and arrogance vis-à-vi some of our own languages and literatures, how entir trajectories of feeling and thought are nullified by a singl stroke of cultural hubris. In the present selection, I hav therefore made every effort to preserve the integrity of th original Urdu material. While I'm at it, let me confess tha in one case, Bedi's 'Lajwanti,' I have had to excise, mos reluctantly though, a whole paragraph, which I've nonethe less indicated in my translation with '[...].' I say reluctantl because if it could have been somehow retained, it woul have provided us with an instance of Bedi's occasionall faltering technical hold on the short story. But th paragraph in question proved too intractable to be tamec even after prolonged and repeated attempts. It was not th language, but the allusions borrowed, I presume, fro some Greek or Roman material. I might also mention her that Bedi, who subsequently realized how misplaced thi paragraph was, himself excised it from his own translatio of the story, as has every other translator before and since

The third reason was even more important. This is the fiftieth year of India's and Pakistan's independence. A presentation of material dealing with Partition requires, inevitably, that one should account for things since it all began fifty years ago. How have we fared over the five intervening decades? How are things today? What have we made of ourselves since we became the captains of our own ship, the directors of our own souls? In 1997 it makes no sense to talk about 1947 and its massacres and simply stop there. I, at least, cannot conceive of the Partition minus the developments in India, Pakistan, and Bangladesh over the past half-century that separate us from the event itself.

The present volume therefore seeks to present a selection of short stories written in Urdu about the time of Partition and shortly thereafter, as well as those written in Pakistan and India since the Partition—stories which are anticipated by it and are therefore, in a sense, congenitally connected with it. These stories are grouped in two roughly equal parts, represented as 'Partition . . . ' and ' . . . and After.' The other two things I have consciously sought are fidelity to the original in rendering it into readable English, and to resist the seduction of personal comment—to stand between the writer and his reader. What we have gained through Partition, what we have lost as a consequence of it, is all there in the stories.

This has also led me to shun copious annotation. I cannot imagine the translation of a contemporary French or Russian novel or short story cluttered with notes. Hence I cannot imagine the same for a piece from any of the South Asian languages. An obscure allusion in a foreign text calls for some minimal effort on the part of its reader. This shouldn't be any different for a reader of South Asian material. And yet, at a point where the text risks total unintelligibility, a hesitant note may be the only answer. In such cases, readers are welcome to look at the end of the book 'Glossary and Notes.'

A word about the choice of the material. Why 'Sahae,' a medium-weight work by Manto, and not one of his masterworks, say, 'Toba Tek Singh?' Simply because these major works have all been translated already—some, such as 'Toba Tek Singh,' at least five times that I know of. I naturally opted for the more obscure 'Sahae.' And why nothing by Krishan Chandra? For one thing, although he has admittedly written half a dozen short stories on Partition, all of which appear in his collection *Ham Vahshi Hain* (We're All Brutes), he rarely manages to rise above the worst kind of effusive Progressive jargon and slogans in his Partition corpus; for another, he wears his socialist intent unabashedly on his sleeve.

Likewise readers and critics may find the stories of Syed Muhammad Ashraf, 'The Rogue' and Masud Ashar, 'Of Coconuts and Bottles of Chilled Beer' rather opaque, certainly oblique. How—they may ask—are these stories thematically linked to the event of Partition? Superficially they are not. But at a deeper level they are, if one is willing to admit that the effects of the cataclysmic event are very much with us today and continue to cast a pall over the corporate existence of the countries that emerged in the historical and cultural wake of Partition. I for one do not see Partition as something finished and done with, a moment frozen in time. It is true the two stories in question are not as transparent as Ilyas Ahmad Gaddi's 'A Land without Sky,' but few would deny that Ashar's story captures with remarkable realism and tragic clarity the tense character of Bengali-West Pakistani relations, the atmosphere of deep mutual distrust in the period just prior to the breakup of

Pakistan; a Pakistani partition that itself refigures in some striking ways the Partition of India. Even today many Pakistanis cannot believe that the Bengalis should have gone their separate way. This story, the only one of its kind, underscores with brutal frankness the falsity of such expectations. The hurt felt by the Bengalis, the depth of their alienation comes palpably alive in this work which is both even-handed and full of empathy. On the other hand, Ashraf's ṣtory is even more subtle. It powerfully evokes the atmosphere of distrust and paranoia among Muslims and Hindus following the resurgence of Hindu nationalism in recent times and portrays with engaging realism and sensitivity the collapse of mutual trust so essential for keeping a multireligious society together. Written in the aftermath of the Babri Mosque incident (1992), it shuns any notion of separatism and exclusion; rather, it invites reflection on the nature of the 'rogue', which is a state of mind, a mentality, and must be felled within the individual. Urdu and Hindi speaking readers will not miss the story's subtle inter-linguistic play of words. The 'rogue' is not just a mad beast, it is also the *rog* (the malady) within the self. Thus the roots of both stories are found directly in the event of Partition, and they are articulated in terms of the painful history that it set in motion. Seen in this light, they will not appear out of place in the present collection.

Although most of the translations were done especially for this volume, some were made at different times over the past twenty-five years and have appeared elsewhere. Here they are offered after substantial revision and with permission from their earlier publisher. They are: Hasan Manzar, 'Kanha Devi and her Family,' *The Annual of Urdu Studies* 10 (1995), Khalida Husain, 'The Wagon,' *Indian Literature* XIX: 6 (Nov.—Dec. 1976); Intizar Husain, 'An

Unwritten Epic,' co-translated by Leslie A. Flemming, *Journal of South Asian Literature* XVIII:2 (Summer-Fall 1983); and Ali Imam Naqvi, 'The Vultures of the Parsi Cemetery' and Muhammad Salim-ur-Rahman, 'The Thaw,' both in my *Colour of Nothingness: Modern Urdu Short Stories* published by Penguin. The two poems by Faiz Ahmed Faiz and Zeeshan Sahil are gratefully reproduced from *The Annual of Urdu Studies* 11 (1996).

I owe a debt of gratitude to my friends Tahira Naqvi and G.A. Chaussée. The former translated, at my request, Ismat Chughtai's short story 'Roots' especially for this volume. The latter meticulously went over the entire text and offered valuable suggestions for improvement of idiom and expression. His help has been immeasurable.

Madison — *Muhammad Umar Memon*
1 May 1997

Partition . . .

The Dawn of Freedom (August 1947)

These tarnished rays, this night-smudged light—
This is not that Dawn for which, ravished with freedom,
we had set out in sheer longing,
So sure that somewhere in its desert the sky harboured
a final haven for the stars, and we would find it.
We had no doubt that night's vagrant wave would stray
 towards the shore,
that the heart rocked with sorrow would at last reach its port.

Friends, our blood shaped its own mysterious roads.
When hands tugged at our sleeves, enticing us to stay,
and from wondrous chambers Sirens cried out
with their beguiling arms, with their bare bodies,
our eyes remained fixed on that beckoning Dawn,
forever vivid in her muslins of transparent light.
Our blood was young—what could hold us back?

Now listen to the terrible rampant lie:
Light has forever been severed from the Dark;
our feet, it is heard, are now one with their goal.
See our leaders polish their manner clean of our suffering:
Indeed, we must confess only to bliss;
we must surrender any utterance for the Beloved—all
 yearning is outlawed.

But the heart, the eye, the yet deeper heart—
Still ablaze for the Beloved, their turmoil shines.
In the lantern by the road the flame is stalled for news:
Did the morning breeze ever come? Where has it gone?
Night weighs us down, it still weighs us down.
Friends, come away from this false light. Come, we must
 search for that promised Dawn.

— Faiz Ahmed Faiz
Translated by Agha Shahid Ali

Sahae

Saadat Hasan Manto

'Don't say that one lakh Hindus and one lakh Muslims died; say that two lakh human beings died. That two lakh human beings died is not such a great tragedy after all; the tragedy, in truth, is that those who killed and those who were killed both have nothing to show for it. After killing a lakh of Hindus, the Muslims may have thought that they had finished off Hinduism. But it lives, and will live on. Likewise, after killing a lakh of Muslims the Hindus may have exulted that this will have killed Islam. But the truth is before you: this hasn't managed to put even a scratch on Islam. Those who think that religions can be killed by guns are foolish. Mazhab, *din, iman,* dharm, faith, belief—all these are found in our soul, not in our body. How can they be annihilated by butchers' cleavers, knives, bullets?'

Mumtaz was unusually excited that day. Just the three of us had come to see him off at the ship. He was leaving us for an indeterminate period of time and was headed for Pakistan—a Pakistan we hadn't imagined would come into being even in our dreams.

We were Hindus, all three of us. Our relatives in West Punjab had incurred heavy losses in both property and lives—presumably, this was why Mumtaz had decided to leave. Juggal had received a letter from Lahore telling him that his uncle had died in communal riots, which affected him in a bad way. Still under the impact of the news, he casually said to Mumtaz one day, 'I'm wondering what I would do if riots broke out in my neighbourhood.'

'Yes, what would you do?' Mumtaz asked.

'I might kill you,' Juggal said in all seriousness.

Mumtaz fell silent, dead silent. His silence continued for nearly eight days, and broke only when he suddenly announced that he was leaving for Karachi by ship at 3:45 p.m. that very afternoon.

None of us talked to him about his decision. Juggal was deeply conscious that the reason behind Mumtaz's departure was his comment: 'I might kill you.' Perhaps he was still wondering about whether in the heat of passion he could kill Mumtaz or not—Mumtaz who was his bosom buddy. That's why he was now the silent one among the three. But strangely enough, Mumtaz had become unusually talkative, especially during the few hours before his departure.

He had started drinking from the time he got up in the morning. He had his baggage packed as though he were going on a vacation. He would talk to himself and laugh for no apparent reason. If a stranger saw him he would have thought that Mumtaz was feeling overwhelming joy at the prospect of leaving Bombay. But the three of us knew well that he was trying hard to deceive both us and himself in order to hide his true feelings.

Many times I tried to talk to him about his sudden departure. I even gestured to Juggal to bring up the subject but Mumtaz never gave us a chance.

After downing three or four drinks Juggal became even quieter and went to lie down in the other room. Braj Mohan and I stayed with Mumtaz. He had quite a few bills to pay up, he had to give the doctors their fees, he had to fetch his clothes from the cleaners—all these chores he went through light-heartedly and easily enough. But as he was taking a paan from the stall next to the restaurant at the farther end of the street, his eyes began to well up with tears. As we moved away from the stall he put his hand on Braj Mohan's shoulder and said softly, 'You remember, don't you, how Gobind lent us a rupee ten years ago, when we were down on our luck?'

After this Mumtaz remained silent, but once we returned home he broke into another endless stream of small talk—all totally unconnected, but nonetheless so full of feeling that Braj Mohan and I found ourselves fully participating in it. When the time for his departure drew near, Juggal came in and joined us too. But just as the cab started for the docks, a hush fell over everyone.

Mumtaz's eyes continued to say goodbye to the wide, sprawling bazaars of Bombay, until the cab pulled into the harbour. The place was terribly crowded. Thousands of refugees, few of them affluent, most poor, were leaving—a crush of people. And yet Mumtaz alone seemed to me to be leaving, leaving us behind for a place he had never even seen before, a place which, no matter how hard he tried to get used to it, would still remain unfamiliar. This was my thinking at any rate. I couldn't tell what was going through Mumtaz's mind.

After his bags had all been taken to the cabin, he took us out onto the deck. For a long time he gazed out at the place where sky and sea came together. Then he took Juggal's hand in his and said, 'How perfectly deceptive . . . this meeting of the sky and the sea, and yet so incredibly delightful too!'

Juggal remained silent. Perhaps his earlier remark—'I might kill you'—was still tormenting him.

Mumtaz ordered a brandy from the ship's bar; that was what he had been drinking since morning. Drinks in hand, we stood against the guard rail. Refugees were piling into the ship with a lot of noise and commotion, and sea gulls were hovering over the water, which looked almost still.

Abruptly Juggal downed his glass in one huge gulp and said rather crudely, 'Do forgive me Mumtaz—I think I hurt you the other day.'

Mumtaz paused briefly and asked Juggal, 'When you uttered those words—"I might kill you"—was this exactly what you were thinking? You had come to this decision with a cool head?'

Juggal nodded his head, and then said, 'But I feel sorry.'

'You'd have felt sorrier had you actually killed me,' Mumtaz said philosophically. 'But only if you had paused to reflect that you hadn't killed Mumtaz, a Muslim, a friend, but instead had killed a human being. If he was a bad man, what you would have killed was not his badness, but the man himself. If he was a Muslim, you wouldn't have killed his Muslim-ness, but his being. If Muslims had gotten hold of his dead body, it would have added a grave to the cemetery, but the world would have come up one human being short.'

Stopping to think a bit, he resumed, 'Perhaps my co-religionists would have anointed me as a martyr, but I swear I would've torn through my grave and cried that I didn't accept the title, I didn't want this diploma for which I'd taken no exam. Some Muslim murdered your uncle in Lahore, you heard the news in Bombay and murdered me—Just tell me this: what medals do we deserve for this? What robes of honour do your uncle and his killer back in Lahore deserve?

'If you ask me, the victims died the miserable death of a pie dog, and their killers killed in vain, utterly in vain.'

Mumtaz became worked up as he spoke, but the emotional excess was matched by an equal measure of sincerity. His observation that mazhab, *din, iman,* dharm, faith, belief—all these were found in our soul, not in our body, and that they couldn't be annihilated by cleavers, knives, and bullets had made an especially deep impression on me. So I told him, 'You are absolutely right.'

This made Mumtaz think again. He said with some unease, 'No, I wouldn't say "absolutely right". I mean, yes, sure, this is all okay. But perhaps I haven't been able to say it all clearly, the way I want to. By "religion" I don't mean *this* religion, nor this dharm, which afflicts ninety-nine per cent of us. I rather mean that very special thing which sets one individual apart from all others, the special thing which shows that someone is truly a human being. But what is it? Unfortunately I can't put it on my palm and show it to you.' A sudden gleam appeared in his eyes and he said, as if to himself, 'But what exactly was special in him? A staunch Hindu, who worked the most abominable profession, and yet his soul—it couldn't have been more luminous.'

'Whose soul?' I asked.

'A certain pimp's.'

The three of us started. Mumtaz's tone was natural enough, so I asked him in perfect seriousness, 'A pimp's?'

Mumtaz wagged his head in affirmation. 'What a man! Amazing. And even more amazing that he was, as is commonly called, a pimp—a procurer of women—and yet had an absolutely clean conscience.'

Mumtaz paused for a few moments, as if refreshing his memory of past events, and then said, 'I don't remember his full name. Something Sahae. He came from Benaras. And he was extremely particular about cleanliness. It was a smallish place where he lived, but he had elegantly divided it in neat little sections. The customers' privacy was scrupulously maintained. There were no beds or cots, but instead mattresses and bolsters. The sheets and pillowcases were always clean and spotless. And even though he had a servant, he did all the cleaning and dusting himself. Not just cleaning; he did everything himself, and he always put his heart into it. He was not given to cheating or deception. If it was late at night and only watered-down liquor could be had in the neighbourhood, he would say straight out "Sahib, don't waste your money." If he had a suspicion about one of the girls, he'd let you know up front. He even told me that he had earned 20,000 rupees within a period of three years, taking two-and-a-half rupees as commission from every ten. He only wanted to make another 10,000 rupees. Why only 10,000? Why not more? He told me that after he had made his 30,000 rupees he would return to Benaras and open a fabric shop. I don't know why he was so keen on opening a fabric shop, of all things.'

At this point in the narration I couldn't hold back my surprise, 'What a strange man!'

Mumtaz continued: 'I used to think he was a fake right down to his littlest toe. A huge fraud. Who could believe that he called all the girls who worked for him his "daughters." He had opened savings accounts at the post office for all the girls. Every month he'd deposit all their income for them. It was just unbelievable that he actually paid out of his own pocket for the expenses of some ten to twelve girls. Everything he did seemed to me a bit too contrived.

'One day when I went to his place he told me that it was both Amina and Sakina's day off. "I let them go out one day every week so that they may go to some restaurant and satisfy their craving for meat. Here, as you know, everyone else is a Vaishnava." I smiled to myself thinking he was taking me for a ride. Another day he told me that the Hindu girl from Ahmedabad he had married off to a Muslim customer had written him a letter from Lahore, saying that she had made a votive request at the tomb of Data Sahib which had been granted. So now she had made another such petition on behalf of Sahae: that he may earn his 30,000 rupees soon and return to Benaras and open his fabric shop. I broke out laughing. I thought, since I'm a Muslim, he is just trying to please me.'

'Were you wrong about him?' I asked Mumtaz.

'Absolutely! There was no difference in his word and his deed. It is possible that he had some weakness, he may have slipped several times in his life, but on the whole, he was a very fine person.'

'And just how did you come to know this?' Juggal asked.

'At his death.' Mumtaz fell silent for a while. After some time he peered into the space where sky and sun had been gathered into a foggy embrace. 'The rioting had begun. Early in the morning one day I was passing through Bhindi Bazaar. There were few people around due to the curfew. Even the trams weren't running. I walked along looking for a taxi. When I arrived near J.J. Hospital, I saw a man rolled into a bundle by the large bin on the sidewalk. I thought it must be some labourer sleeping, but when I saw the blood and gore splattered on the cobblestones, I stopped. It was clearly murder. I thought it best to get out of there, but then I perceived a slight movement in the body. I stopped again. Not a soul was anywhere around. I bent over and peered down at the body. It was the familiar face of Sahae, but stained all over with blood. I sat down beside him on the sidewalk and looked closely. His twill shirt, which always looked spotless, was soaked in blood. The wound was perhaps in the area of the ribs. He started to moan faintly.

I carefully shook his shoulder, as one does to wake up somebody who is sleeping. One or two times I even called him by the only name I knew. I was about to get up and leave when his eyes opened. For a long time he stared at me with those half-opened eyes. Then his entire body started twitching and, recognizing me, he said, "You? You?"

'One after another I asked him all kinds of questions. Why had he come to that area? Who had wounded him? How long had he been lying on the sidewalk? The hospital was right across from us—should I let them know?

'He was too weak to talk. After I'd fired off all my questions, he groaned out these words with the greatest difficulty: "It was my time. This is how Bhagwan willed it!"

'Who knows what Bhagwan wanted, but being a Muslim, *I* didn't want to see a man I knew to be a Hindu die in a Muslim neighbourhood, feeling that his murderer was a Muslim, as was the man who now stood watching his life ebb away. I'm not a coward, but at the time I felt worse than a coward. On the one hand, I was afraid of being arrested for the murder, and on the other I was scared that even if I wasn't arrested, I could still be detained for interrogation. It also occurred to me that if I took him to the hospital he might implicate me to avenge himself. After all, he was dying, why not take me along too? Assailed by such thoughts, I was about to flee when Sahae called my name. I stopped. I didn't want to, but my feet simply froze. I looked at him as though telling him, "Get on with it, mister, I have to go." Doubling over with pain, he unbuttoned the front of his shirt with the greatest difficulty, put his hand inside, and then his strength gave way. At that point he said to me, "In the waistcoat under the shirt . . . in the side pocket . . . there is some jewellery and twelve hundred rupees. It . . . is Sultana's property . . . I'd left it with a friend for safekeeping . . . Today . . . I was going to send it to her . . . you know it's getting ever more dangerous these days. Please give it to her and . . . please tell her to leave right away . . . but . . . be careful about yourself!"'

Mumtaz fell silent, but I felt as though somewhere far away, where the sky and the sea were curled up in a foggy embrace, his voice was slowly dissolving into the voice of Sahae as it rose on the sidewalk pavement near J.J. Hospital.

The ship's whistle sounded. Mumtaz said, 'I did go and see Sultana. When I gave her the jewellery and money, she broke into tears.'

We said goodbye to Mumtaz and left the ship. He was standing on the deck by the guard rail, waving his right hand. I said to Juggal, 'Don't you feel as though Mumtaz is calling after Sahae's spirit—to make it his mate on his trip?'

Juggal said only, 'How I wish I were Sahae's spirit!'

Lajwanti

Rajinder Singh Bedi

Touch the leaves of the lajwanti,
they curl and wither away.
—From a Punjabi song

After the Partition, when countless wounded people had finally cleaned the gore from their bodies, they turned their attention to those who had not suffered bodily but had been wounded in their hearts.

Rehabilitation committees were formed in every neighbourhood and side street and the campaign to help the victims acquire business, land, and homes for themselves got underway with much enthusiasm. There was one programme, though, which seemed to have escaped notice. It concerned the rehabilitation of abducted women. Its rallying cry was 'Rehabilitate them in your hearts!' It was bitterly opposed by Narain Bawa's temple and the conservatives who lived in and around it.

A committee was formed in the Mulla Shakur neighbourhood near the temple to get the programme off the ground. Babu Sundar Lal was elected its secretary by a majority of eleven votes and the Vakil Sahib its president. It was the opinion of the old petition writer of the Chauki Kalan district—in which other well-regarded individuals of the neighbourhood concurred with him—that no one could be expected to work more passionately for the cause than Sundar Lal, because his own wife, Laju—Lajwanti—too had been abducted.

Early in the morning when Sundar Lal Babu and his

Early in the morning when Sundar Lal Babu and his companions Rasaloo and Neki Ram used to make their rounds through the streets singing in unison, *Touch the leaves of the lajwanti, / they curl and wither away!* Sundar Lal's voice would fade. Walking along in silence he would think about Lajwanti—Who knows where she might be? In what condition? What would she be thinking of him? Would she ever come back?—and his feet would falter on the cobblestone pavement.

But by now things had reached a point where he had stopped even thinking about Lajwanti. His pain was no longer just his; it had become part of the world's anguish. And to spare himself its devastation he had thrown himself headlong into serving the people. All the same, every time he joined his companions in that song, he couldn't help wondering at how delicate the human heart is. The slightest thing could hurt it. Exactly like the lajwanti plant, whose leaves curl up at the barest touch. Well, that may be. But for his own part, he had never spared any effort in treating his own Lajwanti as badly as possible. He would beat her on the flimsiest pretext, taking exception to the way she got up, the way she sat down, the way she cooked food—anything and everything.

Laju was a slender and agile village girl. Too much sun had turned her skin quite dark, and a nervous energy informed her movements, which brought to mind the fluid grace of a dew drop rolling mercury-like on a leaf: now to one side, now to the other. Her leanness, which was more a sign of health than its absence, worried Sundar Lal at first, but when he observed how well she could take all manner of adversity, including even physical abuse, he progressively increased his mistreatment of her, quite forgetting that past a certain limit anyone's patience is sure to run out.

Lajwanti, too, had contributed her share in obscuring the perception of such a limit. By nature she wasn't one to hold on to her anguish for too long. A simple smile from Sundar Lal following the worst fight, and she was unable to stop her giggles: 'If you beat me ever again, I'll never speak to you!'

It was obvious she had already forgotten all about the fights and beatings. That's how husbands treat their wives—she knew this truth as well as any other village girl. If a woman showed the slightest independence, the girls themselves would be the first to disapprove. 'Ha, what kind of man is he? Can't even keep his little woman in line!'

The physical abuse men subjected their wives to had even made it into the women's songs. Laju herself used to sing:

Marry a city boy?—No sir, not me.
Look at his boots, and my waist is so narrow.

Nonetheless, at the very first opportunity she had fallen in love with just such a city boy, Sundar Lal, who had first come to her village as part of a wedding party and had whispered into the groom's ear, 'Your sister-in-law is pretty hot stuff, yaar! Your wife must be quite a dish too!'

Lajwanti had overheard him. She took no notice at all of his large, heavy boots, and forgot all about her own narrow waist.

Such were the memories that Sundar Lal recalled during his early morning rounds with his companions. He would say to himself, 'If I could get another chance, just one more chance, I'd rehabilitate Laju in my heart. I'd show the people that these poor women are hardly to blame for their abduction, their victimization by lecherous rioters. A society which is unable to accept and rehabilitate these innocent women is rotten to the core, fit only to be destroyed.'

Sundar Lal would plead with the people to take these women under their roof and give them the same status which any woman, any mother, daughter, sister, or wife enjoyed. He would urge the families never to mention, even to hint at the things the poor women had to suffer, because their hearts were already wounded, already fragile, like the leaves of the touch-me-not plant, ready to curl up at the merest touch.

The Mulla Shakur Rehabilitation of Hearts Committee took out many early morning processions to put its programme into effect. The wee hours of the morning were the most feasible time for their activity: no human noise, no traffic snarls. Even the dogs, after an exhausting night-long watch, would be asleep at this hour, as they lay curled up inside the tandoors long since gone cold. And people, huddled in their beds, would wake up to mumble drowsily, 'Oh, that group again!'

People listened to Sundar Lal Babu's propaganda, sometimes with patience, sometimes with irritation. Women who had made it safely to this side of the border lay loosely in their beds, while their husbands, lying stiff beside them, mumbled protests against the noise kicked up by the morning rally, or a child somewhere opened its eyes for a moment and fell back to sleep, taking the doleful petition of 'Rehabilitate them in your hearts' for a lullaby.

Words which enter the ear so early in the morning rarely fail to produce an effect. They reverberate in the mind the whole day, and even if their underlying meaning is not readily apparent, one nonetheless finds oneself repeating them. So, thanks to this effect, when Miss Mardula Sara Bai secured the exchange of abducted women between India and Pakistan, some people in the Mulla Shakur neighbourhood willingly took their women back. They went to receive them outside the city at Chauki Kalan. For a while the abducted women and their relatives faced each other in awkward silence. Then with their heads bent low they returned to pick up the pieces of their lives and rebuild their homes. Meanwhile Rasaloo, Neki Ram and Sundar Lal rooted for them with cries, now of 'Long Live Mahendar Singh!' now of 'Long Live Sohan Lal!' They kept it up until their throats went dry.

But there were some abducted women whose husbands, parents, or siblings refused even to recognize them. As far as their families were concerned, they should have killed themselves. They should have taken poison to save their virtue. Or jumped into a well. Cowards—to cling to life so tenaciously!

Hundreds, indeed thousands of women had in fact killed themselves to save their honour. But what could they know of the courage it took just to live on? What could they know of the icy stares it took for the survivors to look death in the face, in a world where even their husbands refused to recognize them? One or another of the abducted repeats her name to herself: 'Suhagwanti'—she who has suhag, the affection of her husband. She spots her brother in the crowd and says only this one final time, 'Even you, Bihari, refuse to recognize me! I took you in my lap and fed you when you were small.' Bihari wants to slip away, but he looks at his parents and freezes, who steel their hearts and look expectantly at Narain Bawa, who in turn looks in utter helplessness at the sky—which has no reality, which is merely an optical illusion, the limit beyond which our eyes do not function.

Laju, however, was not among the abducted women Miss Sara Bai brought back in the exchange. Sundar Lal, balanced precariously between hope and despair, saw the last girl come down from the military truck. Subsequently, with quiet determination, he redoubled his efforts in advancing the work of his Committee. No longer only in the mornings, the Committee took out an evening rally as well, and now and then also held meetings at which the old barrister Kalka Parshad Sufi, the Committee's president, held forth in his raspy, asthmatic voice, with Rasaloo always tending his duties beside him, holding the spittoon. Strange sounds would pour out from the loudspeaker: '*kha-ba-ba-ba, kha-kha . . .*' Next Neki Ram, the petition writer of the Chauki, would get up to say something. But whatever he said or quoted from the Shastras or Puranas served only to contradict his point. Just then Sundar Lal would move in to salvage the situation. But he couldn't manage more than a couple of sentences. His voice would become progressively hoarser and tears would roll on his cheeks. He would give up and sit down. A strange silence would sweep over the audience. Sundar Lal Babu's two sentences, which sprang from the depths of his heart, affected them more than all the oratory eloquence of the old barrister Kalka Parshad Sufi. But the people shed a few tears then and there, which eased their hearts, and returned home, as empty-headed as ever.

One day the Committeewallahs started out on their preaching mission early in the evening and ended up in an area long known to be a conservative stronghold. Seated on a cement platform around a peepul tree outside the temple, the faithful were listening to stories from the Ramayana. Narain Bawa was narrating the episode in which a washerman had thrown his wife out of the house saying,

'I'm no Raja Ramchandar, who would take Sita back after she had spent so many years with Ravan.' Which led Ramchandarji to order the virtuous Sita out of the house even though she was with child.

'Can you find a better example of Ram Raj?' asked Narain Bawa. 'True Ram Raj is one in which a washerman's words too receive the utmost consideration.'

The rally had by now reached the temple and stopped to listen to the Ramayana story and pious hymns. Sundar Lal caught the last few words and retorted, 'We don't want Ram Raj, Bawa.'

Angry voices shot up from the throng of the faithful:

'Be quiet!'

'Who do you think you are?'

'Shut up!'

But Sundar Lal, undaunted, moved forward. 'Nobody can stop me from speaking!' he shouted back.

To which he received a fresh volley of equally angry words—'Quiet!' 'We won't let you speak!'—and from a corner, even the threat, 'We'll kill you!'

Narain Bawa said to him gently, 'Sundar Lal, my dear, you don't understand the rules and regulations of the Shastras.'

'But I do understand one thing, Bawa. And it is that even a washerman could be heard in Ram Raj, while its champions today won't even listen to Sundar Lal.'

The very people who a minute ago had gotten up determined to put him in his place quickly sat down, sweeping away the peepul fruit which had meanwhile fallen on their seats, and said, 'All right, let's hear him out.'

Both Rasaloo and Neki Ram spurred Sundar Lal on, who said, 'No doubt Shri Ram was our great leader. But why is it, Bawaji, that he believed the washerman but not his own wife, the greatest Maharani ever?'

Narain Bawa explained, putting a novel spin on it. 'Sita was his own wife. It would appear, Sundar Lal, that you have not realized the importance of this fact.'

'Yes, Bawa,' Sundar Lal Babu said, 'there are many things in this world that I don't understand. But as I look at it, under true Ram Raj, man wouldn't be able to oppress even himself. Injustice against oneself is as great a sin as injustice against another. Today, Lord Ram has again thrown Sita out of his house, just because she was compelled to live with Ravan for some time. But was she to blame for it? Wasn't she a victim of deceit and trickery, like our numberless mothers and sisters today? Was it a question of Sita's truth or falsehood? Or of the stark beastliness of the demon Ravan, who has ten human heads, but also has another, bigger one, that of a donkey. Today our Sita has been expelled once again, totally without fault, our Sita . . . Lajwanti . . .' He broke down and wept.

Rasaloo and Neki Ram raised the red banners on which the school children had that very day skillfully cut out and pasted different slogans for them, and the procession got going once again, all shouting 'Long Live Sundar Lal Babu!' in unison. Then someone yelled 'Long Live Sita—the Queen of Virtue!' and someone else 'Shri Ramchandar . . .'

'Silence! Silence!' a joint cry went up. Within seconds months of Narain Bawa's labour went down the drain, as a good portion of his congregation got up and joined the procession, led by barrister Kalka Parshad and Hukm Singh, the petition writer at Chauki Kalan, both triumphantly tapping their old walking sticks on the ground. Sundar Lal walked along with them. Tears were still streaming down his cheeks. His heart had been hurt very badly today. The people were shouting with great gusto:

> *Touch the leaves of the lajwanti,*
> *they curl and wither away.*

The song was still reverberating in the ears of the people. The sun had not yet risen and the widow in house number 414 in Mulla Shakur was still tossing restlessly in her bed. Just then Lal Chand, who was from Sundar Lal's village and whom the latter and Kalka Parshad, using their influence, had helped to set up a ration shop, rushed over to Sundar Lal's. He offered his hand from under his thick, coarse shawl and said, 'Congratulations Sundar Lal!'

'Congratulations for what, Lal Chand?' Sundar Lal asked, putting some molasses-sweetened tobacco in his chillum.

'I just saw Laju Bhabhi.'

The chillum fell from Sundar Lal's hand and the tobacco scattered on the floor. 'Where!?' he asked, grabbing Lal Chand by the shoulder, and shaking him hard when he didn't answer quickly enough.

'At the Wagah border.'

He abruptly let go of Lal Chand's shoulder. 'Must be someone else.'

'No, Bhaiyya, it really was Laju,' Lal Chand tried to convince him. 'She was Laju all right.'

'Do you even know her?' Sundar Lal asked as he gathered the tobacco and ground it between his palms. 'Well then,' he said, removing the chillum from Rasaloo's hookah, 'tell me, what are her distinguishing marks?'

'A tattoo on her chin, another on her cheek.'

'Yes yes yes!' Sundar Lal himself completed the description. 'And a third one on her forehead.' He didn't want there to be any doubt.

Suddenly he recalled all those tattoos on Lajwanti's body he had known so well, tattoos she had gotten as a little girl, which resembled the light green spots on the touch-me-not plant and caused it to curl up its leaves at the slightest hint of an approaching hand. Exactly the same way Lajwanti would curl up from modesty the instant anyone pointed at her tattoos. She would withdraw into herself and disappear, afraid that all her secrets had been let out, that she had been made poor by the plunder of a hidden treasure . . . and . . . Sundar Lal's entire body began to burn with an unknown fear, with an unknown spirit and its purified fire. He grabbed Lal Chand by the shoulder once again and asked, 'How did Laju get to Wagah?'

'There was an exchange of abducted women between India and Pakistan,' Lal Chand said.

'What happened then?' Sundar Lal asked, as he squatted down on the floor. 'Tell me, what happened then?'

Rasaloo too sat up in his cot and asked, coughing as only smokers do, 'Is it really true? Lajwanti Bhabhi's returned?'

Lal Chand continued. 'At the Wagah border, Pakistan handed over sixteen women and received sixteen in exchange. But an altercation developed. Our volunteers objected that there were too many middle-aged, old, and useless women in the contingent Pakistan was handing over. A crowd quickly gathered on the scene. Just then, volunteers from the other side pointed at Laju Bhabhi and said, "Here, you call her old? Have a look. None of the girls you have returned can match her." Meanwhile Laju Bhabhi was frantically trying to hide her tattoos from the people's probing eyes. The argument got more heated. Each side decided to take back their 'goods.' I cried out, "Laju! Laju Bhabhi!" But our own military guards beat us up and drove us away for making a racket.'

Lal Chand bared his elbow to show where he had been struck by a lathi. Rasaloo and Neki Ram remained silent, while Sundar Lal gazed far away into space. Perhaps he was thinking about Laju, who had returned, but then again had not. He looked like someone who had just crossed the scorching sands of Bikaner and now sat panting in the shade under a tree, his parched tongue hanging out, too exhausted even to ask for water. The realization struck him that the violence of the pre-Partition days still continued even after Partition, only in a different form. Today, people didn't even feel sympathy for the victims. If you asked someone about, say, Lahna Singh and his sister-in-law Bantu, who used to live in Sambharwala, quick and curt would come the answer: 'Dead!' and the fellow would move on, unaware of death and the difference it made.

Worse even than this, there were cold-blooded people who traded in human merchandise, in human flesh. Just as at cattle fairs prospective buyers pull back the snout of a cow or a water-buffalo to assess its age by examining its teeth, these human traders now put up for public display the beauty of a young woman, her blossoming charm, her most intimate secrets, her beauty spots, her tattoos. This sort of violence had sunk right down to their very bones. In former times, at least, deals were struck at fairs under the protective cover of a handkerchief. Fingers met, negotiated, and concluded in secrecy. Today, however, even that screen had been pulled up. Everybody was bargaining shamelessly in the open, with no regard for decorum. This transaction, this peddling, recalled an episode straight out of Boccaccio—a narrative depicting the uninhibited buying and selling of women: countless women stand lined up, baring themselves before the Uzbek procurer, who pokes and prods them with his finger. It leaves a pink indentation where it touches the body, a pale circle forms around it, and the pink and the pale rush to meet. The Uzbek moves on, and the rejected woman, crushed by humiliation and shame, sobs uncontrollably, holding the waistcord of her loosened lower garment with one hand, hiding her face from the public's gaze with the other. Later, even the feeling of shame departs. Thus she walks nude through the bazaars of Alexandria. [. . .]

Sundar Lal was getting ready to go to the border town of Amritsar when the news of Laju's arrival overtook him. Its suddenness unnerved him. He hurriedly took a step towards the door but, just as swiftly, stepped back. A sudden feeling to give in to his unhappiness overwhelmed him. He felt he wanted to spread all the placards, all the banners of his Rehabilitation Committee out on the floor and sit on them and cry his heart out. But the situation was hardly proper for such an expression of emotion. He bravely fought back the turmoil raging inside him and picked his way slowly toward Chauki Kalan, the venue for the delivery of the abducted women.

Laju stood straight in front of him, shaking with fear. If anyone knew Sundar Lal, it was she. She had forgotten none of how badly he had treated her before, and now that she was returning after living with another man, there was no telling what he might do. Sundar Lal looked at Laju. She had draped the upper half of her body in a black dupatta, one of its ends thrown over her left shoulder in the typical Muslim fashion, but only out of habit. Perhaps it made it easier to socialize with the Muslim ladies and finally to make her escape from her captor. Then again, she had been thinking of Sundar Lal so much and was so mortally afraid of him that she scarcely had the mind to change into different clothes or even to worry about draping herself with the dupatta in the right fashion. As it was, she was unable to distinguish the basic difference between Hindu and Muslim cultures—whether the dupatta went over the right or left shoulder. Right now she stood before Sundar Lal, trembling, balanced between hope and fear.

Sundar Lal was shocked. He noticed that Lajwanti was fairer and healthier than before; indeed she looked plump. Whatever he had imagined about her turned out to be wrong. He had thought that grief would have emaciated her, that she'd be too weak even to speak. The thought that she had been happy in Pakistan wounded him, but he said nothing to her, for he had sworn not to quiz her about such matters. All the same, he couldn't help wondering: why had she chosen to return if she lived a happier life there? Perhaps the Indian government had forced her to, against her wishes.

But he was quite unable to see the pallor on Lajwanti's tawny face, or to fathom that it was suffering, and suffering alone, that made her firm flesh loosen and sag from her bones, making her look heavy. She had become heavy with an excess of grief, though superficially she appeared healthy. But hers was the kind of plumpness which made one pant for breath after taking only a few steps.

His first gaze at his abducted wife had a disturbing effect on him. But he fought all his thoughts back with great manliness. Many other people were also present and one of them shouted, 'We're not about to take back these Muslim leftovers!'

But this voice was drowned out by the slogans of Rasaloo, Neki Ram, the old petition writer of Chauki Kalan. Above them all rose the loud, cracking voice of Kalka Parshad, who somehow managed to speak and cough at the same time. He was absolutely convinced of this new reality, this new purity. It seemed he had learnt a new Veda, a new Purana, a new Shastra, which he desperately wanted to share with others. And surrounded by all these people and voices, Laju and Sundar Lal returned home. It seemed that after a protracted moral exile, the Ramchandar and Sita of an age long past were entering Ayodhya, while the people both celebrated by lighting lamps of joy, and at the same time showed regret for having put the couple through such incredible misery.

Sundar Lal continued his 'Rehabilitation of Hearts' programme with the same ardour even after Lajwanti's return. He had lived up to it both in word and deed. People who had earlier taken his involvement for just so much sentimental idealism were now convinced of his sincerity. Some were truly happy at this, but most felt disappointed and sad, and many women of the Mulla Shakur neighbourhood, except for the widow, still felt uncomfortable stepping into Sundar Lal's house.

To Sundar Lal, however, it made no difference at all whether people recognized or ignored his work. The queen of his heart had returned and the yawning emptiness in his chest had been filled. He had installed the golden image of Laju in the temple of his heart and diligently stood guard at its doorway. Laju, who used to be so afraid of him, now began slowly to relax under his unexpectedly gentle and caring regard.

Sundar Lal no longer called her Laju, but 'Devi,' which made her go mad with unnameable joy. How much she wanted to tell him what she had been through, and cry so profusely that the tears would wash away all her 'sins,' but Sundar Lal deftly avoided listening to her. And so she still carried a trace of apprehension in her new-found ease. After he had fallen asleep, she would simply gaze at him. If he caught her watching him and asked for a reason, she wouldn't know what to say beyond 'Nothing' or 'I don't know.' Sundar Lal, exhausted from the day's gruelling work, would go back to sleep. Once, though, in the beginning, he did ask Lajwanti about her 'dark days.' 'Who was he?'

'His name was Jumma,' she said, lowering her eyes. Then, fixing her eyes on his face, she wanted to say something more, but couldn't. He was looking at her in a strange way, as his hands caressed her hair. She lowered her eyes again. Sundar Lal asked, 'Was he good to you?'

'Yes.'

'He didn't beat you?'

'No,' Lajwanti said, dropping her head on Sundar Lal's chest. 'He never hurt me. And yet I was very afraid of him. You used to beat me, but I never felt scared of you. You won't beat me ever again, will you?'

Tears welled up in Sundar Lal's eyes. He said, feeling deep shame and regret, 'No, never again, Devi.'

'Devi!' Lajwanti thought, and she too broke down in tears.

She felt overwhelmed by a desire to tell him all, holding back nothing, but Sundar Lal stopped her saying, 'Let's just forget the past. You were hardly to blame for what happened. Society is at fault for its lack of respect for goddesses like you. In that it doesn't harm you a bit, only itself.'

And Lajwanti couldn't get it all out. It remained buried inside her. She withdrew into herself and stared at her body for the longest time, a body which, after the partition of the country, was no longer hers, but that of a goddess. Yes, she was happy, indeed very happy, but it was a happiness marred by a nagging doubt, a misgiving. She would sit up in bed with a start, like someone surrounded by a surfeit of happiness who suddenly hears an approaching sound and looks anxiously in its direction, waiting.

Ultimately, the nagging doubt replaced happiness with a chilling finality. And not because Sundar Lal Babu had again started mistreating her, but because he had started treating her with exceeding gentleness. She didn't expect that from him. She wanted to be the same old Laju once again, the one who would quarrel over trifles and then make up in no time at all. Now, though, there was no possibility of even a quarrel. Sundar Lal had convinced her that she was in fact a lajwanti, a glass object too fragile to withstand the barest touch. Laju would look at herself in the mirror, and after thinking long and hard would feel that she could be many things, but could never hope to be the old Laju ever again. Yes, she had been rehabilitated, but she had also been ruined. Sundar Lal, on his part, had neither the eyes to see her tears, nor the ears to hear her painful groans. How fragile the human heart can be—this escaped even the most ardent reformer of the Mulla Shakur neighbourhood. The early morning processions continued and, machine-like, he joined in the refrain with Rasaloo and Neki Ram:

Touch the leaves of the lajwanti,
They curl and wither away.

The Shepherd

Ashfaq Ahmad

It was a long, cold winter night. I was sound asleep in my warm bed, with the quilt pulled all the way over my head, when somebody rudely shook me awake.

'Who is it?!' I screamed.

A large hand bumped against my head and a voice shot forth from the darkness, 'The police have arrested Ranu.'

'What?' I said, as I tried to push the trembling hand away from me. 'What is it?'

The ghost of darkness repeated, 'The police have arrested Ranu—Now, translate it into Farsi.'

'Damn you, Dauji,' I moaned, on the verge of tears. 'No peace even at midnight! Get out of here! I won't stay in your house any more. And I won't study either. Damn you, Dauji! You're a dog!' I broke down in tears.

Dauji made a kissing sound to calm me and said, 'How will you pass your exams if you won't study? And if you don't pass your exams you won't become a great man. Well then, how will people come to know about your Dauji?'

'May God just make everyone die . . . you . . . people you know . . . even me. Especially me.' The thought of dying so young made me weep so much that I choked.

Meanwhile Dauji caressed my head with great affection and said, 'Enough. That's enough. Be a brave boy, my darling son. Come on now, just translate this sentence, and I won't bother you any more.'

The stream of tears was beginning to subside. I said in a huff, 'The bastards have got Ranu today, tomorrow they'll whisk away somebody else. But your translations . . .'

'No, no,' he interrupted, 'I'll never wake you up at night again and ask questions. I promise. Now come on, be good and translate: "The police have arrested Ranu."'

'I can't,' I said, still sulking.

'Always quick to say "No,"' he said, removing his hand from my head. 'At least try.'

'I won't,' I said hotly.

He laughed a little and translated the sentence himself: *Karkunan-e gazma-khana Ranu-ra tauqeef kardand.* There. *Karkunan-e gazma-khana* stands for *Thanewale.* OK? It's a new word for you, a new construction. Now repeat it ten times.'

I knew he wasn't about to get off my back. Helpless, I started the litany of *gazma-khanas.* After I'd finished my ten repetitions, Dauji said, practically entreating me, 'Well now, repeat the whole sentence five times.' When the five-fold affliction, too, was over, he helped me back into my bed. Pulling the comforter over me he said, 'Don't forget it. I'll ask you the first thing in the morning.'

And then he left the room.

Every evening I would return home via the miller's lane after my Quranic lesson at Mullaji's. All sorts of people lived in that lane, but I was familiar only with the portly water-carrier whom we had nicknamed 'Kaddu Karela Dha'i Aane.' There was an enclosure for goats right next to his house. It was bordered on three sides by mud houses, and had a high fence in the front made up of thorny bramble and slap-dash pieces of wood nailed together. On the other side of the enclosure was an open square field, and beyond it the dingy one-room house of the crippled potter. Next to that was another small—but real brick—house with red ochre-framed windows and a door covered with ornamental brass nails. The lane slowly curved at this point and narrowed, and the farther one walked down it, the more its two sides seemed to draw together. It was, perhaps, the longest lane in our *qasba*. It was certainly the loneliest. Walking down it alone I was always overwhelmed by the feeling of walking down the barrel of a gun—the moment I'd come out of it, a deafening bang would go off and I'd fall dead. But in the evening I usually found someone or other passing by and felt my life had been spared.

One of the pedestrians I occasionally ran into was a tallish man with a snow-white moustache. He bore a strong resemblance to Mulkhi, who sang *barah-mahs*. He sported a large turban of fine muslin, a long khaki coat which loosely hung from his slightly bent back, narrow-legged pajamas of coarse cotton, and a pair of flat boots. A boy about my age, and outfitted every bit like the older man, often appeared in tow. The older man talked to him in soft tones, his head bent, his hands stuffed into his coat pockets. As they came up to me, the boy looked at me and I at him. We each turned our heads ever so slightly and moved along without stopping for a moment.

One day, after some unsuccessful fishing at Thathiyan's pond, as my brother and I were returning to our *qasba*, we saw the same man sitting on the bridge over the river. His turban lying in his lap, and his white *chutiya* looking as though it had been pasted on his head like a soiled chicken feather. When we came up to him, my brother raised his hand to his forehead and said loudly, 'Salaam, Dauji.'

The man nodded and replied, 'May you live long.'

I was delighted that my brother knew the man. A little later I too squeaked, 'Dauji, salaam!'

'May you live long, may you live long,' the man

acknowledged the greeting, raising both his hands in blessing.

My brother, however, whacked me hard on the face and thundered, 'You show-off! Dog! Why did you have to greet him after I did? Why do you have to poke your nose into everything? You wretch! Do you even know who he is?'

'Dauji,' I said, putting on a crying face.

'Dauji who?' my brother asked, flaring up.

'The man sitting over there,' I replied, fighting back my tears. 'He's Dauji.'

'Don't talk nonsense,' my brother said glaring at me. 'Imitates me in everything. Copycat! Dog! Show-off!'

I said nothing in response and followed my brother in silence. Actually, I was happy for having been finally introduced to Dauji. I couldn't care less about the abuse I had received. I was used to my brother hitting me. He was older and liked to show off.

Now that I had made my acquaintance with Dauji, I started timing my own passage through the lane to coincide with his. Greeting him pleased me, and receiving his greeting pleased me even more. He said 'May you live long' with such deep affection that I felt a strange exhilaration wash over me, and I had the sensation of walking slightly above the ground.

The exchange of greetings continued for about a year. During this time, all I could find out about Dauji was that he lived in the house with red ochre-framed windows, and the little boy who accompanied him on his walks was his son. I tried to tease more information about him out of my brother, but he was mean to me and always took exception to every little thing I said or did. Whatever I asked, he fired back his two routine answers: 'None of your business!' or 'Stop this nonsense!' But thank God, I didn't have to wait long to satisfy my curiosity.

After I'd passed my fourth class at Islamia Primary School and entered the fifth in M.B. High School, Dauji's son turned out to be my classmate. Through him, and without owing my brother anything, I learnt that Dauji was a Khattri by caste and worked as a petition writer outside our *qasba's* courthouse. The boy's name was Amichand. He was the smartest boy in class. He sported a turban larger than anyone else's and had a small face like a cat's, which prompted some boys to call him 'Meow,' and others, 'Mongoose.' I, however, called him by his real name, in deference to Dauji, I guess. Maybe that's why we became friends. We exchanged secret mementos and took an oath to remain close friends through thick and thin.

It must have been a week before the summer vacation when I visited Amichand's house for the very first time. The day was a scorcher, but the desire to acquire Shaikh Chilli's stories had so possessed me that I gave no thought to heat or hunger and accompanied him right after school.

Amichand's house was small but sparkling clean and well lit. A small *devrhi* immediately inside the door with the brass nails led into a rectangular inner courtyard, at the edge of which was a red veranda. Behind this was a room of similar length. One side of the courtyard was occupied by a single pomegranate tree, a few canna plants, and a small patch of coriander. On the other side was a fairly wide staircase, with a tiny kitchen situated under its arch. The red ocher-framed windows opened into the sitting room adjacent to the *devrhi*. The door of the sitting room was blue.

As soon as we stepped into the *devrhi*, Amichand shouted 'Bébé namaste!' Leaving me alone in the middle of the courtyard, he slipped into the sitting room. Bébé had spread out a large gunny sack in the veranda and was sitting on it working her sewing machine. A girl sat next to her, cutting fabric with a pair of large scissors. Bébé mumbled something by way of response and continued to work her machine. The girl, though, lifted her face and looked at me, and then turned around and said, 'Bébé, looks like Doctor Sahib's boy.'

The machine stopped.

'Yes, yes, of course,' Bébé said, smiling, and made a sign with her hand for me to approach her.

Twisting the strap of my satchel and taking uneven steps, I walked timidly over and stood flat against a pillar.

'What is your name?' Bébé asked me affectionately.

I lowered my eyes and told her my name very softly.

'He resembles Aftab quite a bit, doesn't he, Bébé?' the girl said as she laid the scissors down on the floor.

'Of course, he does. He's his brother, after all.'

'What about Aftab?' a voice came from inside the room. 'What was that about Aftab, my child?'

'Aftab's brother is here, Dauji,' the girl replied after a pause. 'He's come with Amichand.'

Dauji emerged from the room, shirtless, the legs of his pajamas pulled up to his knees, his turban still lodged securely on his head. He walked into the veranda carrying a small bucket of water. He looked at me closely and remarked, 'Yes, indeed, he does resemble Aftab quite a bit. But my Aftab is very skinny, while he is quite *gol-mol.*'

He put the bucket down on the floor, patted me on the head, pulled over a wooden stool and sat down beside me. He lifted his feet a bit, dusted them off, and then plunged them into the bucket. 'Does Aftab write home?' he asked, as he scooped handfuls of water and splashed them on his legs.

'He does,' I replied slowly. 'We got a letter from him

just the day before yesterday.'

'What does he say?'

'I don't know. Abbaji would know.'

'I see,' he said wagging his head. 'Well, you should ask Abbaji. One who doesn't ask, doesn't learn anything.'

I remained silent.

After some time, still splashing water onto his legs, he asked, 'Which *siparah* of the Quran are you learning these days?'

'The fourth,' I replied, confidently.

'What is the third one called?' he quizzed me.

'I don't know,' my voice sank.

'Tilka 'r-Rusul,' he said, pulling his hand out of the bucket.

For a while Dauji shook his hand dry in the air. Meanwhile Bébé continued to work on her machine, and the girl laid out food on the low wooden *chauki* in the veranda, while I continued to twist and turn the strap of my satchel. Amichand was still inside the sitting room, and I, pasted to the pillar, was sinking progressively deeper into my embarrassment. Abruptly Dauji turned toward me and said, 'Recite the *Surah Fatiha* for me!'

'I don't know it,' I said, utterly ashamed.

He looked at me with surprise and asked, 'Not even *al-Hamdu li l-Lah*'?'

'That I do know,' I said quickly.

He smiled a bit and said, as if to himself, 'It's the same thing, the same thing.' Then with a nod of his head he said, 'Recite it for me.'

As soon as I began, he pulled the legs of his pajamas down and spread the loose end of his turban over his shoulders. After I had said *'ad-dalleen,'* he joined in to say *'ameen'* with me. The thought occurred to me that he would now get up and give me a reward, because the first time I had recited the *al-Hamdu li l-Lah* before my Taya, he too had repeated the word *ameen* with me and had given me a rupee reward. But Dauji didn't budge. If anything, he seemed to have turned into stone.

Meanwhile Amichand appeared with the Shaikh Chilli book. As I was leaving, I said, somewhat less ardently than was my habit, 'Dauji salaam,' and still immersed in his thoughts, he responded softly, as was his wont, 'May you live long.' Bébé briefly interrupted her work and said, 'Come over and play with Amichand sometime.'

'Yes, yes, do come sometime,' Dauji chimed in, as if reminded of something suddenly, 'Aftab used to come too.' Then, bending himself over the bucket he added, 'Our Aftab—how we miss him!' and recited a couplet in Farsi.

Such was my first, formal meeting with Dauji. I concluded from it that he was a skinflint, too quiet for anyone's good, and, perhaps, a bit deaf as well.

That evening I told my mother about my visit to Dauji's and how he missed Aftab Bhai. She said with a note of bitterness in her voice, 'You should have asked me first. It's true Aftab took lessons from him and respected him a lot, but your father doesn't speak to Dauji. They had a quarrel some time ago and have been upset with each other ever since. If your father finds out that you've been to Dauji's, he'll be angry.' Then, feeling sympathy for me, she added, 'Don't breathe a word about it to your Abbaji.'

I was not about to. But, I kept visiting Dauji, and heartily enjoyed discussing all sorts of grown-up things with him. I would find him sitting on a mat reading some book or another. I'd go and stand quietly behind him. Sensing my presence he'd close the book and say, 'Ah, Golu, you've come. Good!' Then looking over his shoulder at me, he'd smile and say, 'Let's hear the latest gossip.' I'd dig deep inside, and with my limited ability and understanding would find something or other to say. He laughed hard—to please me, I guess, for, as I now think about it, the things I said were hardly interesting. Then, tearing a sheet of paper from his register, he'd have me do a question. I hated it. But the deal he proposed I found too seductive to resist: after one question I could shoot the breeze with him for the next fifteen minutes, then another question, then fifteen more minutes of talk. Invariably I'd give in. I'd take the sheet of paper and work on the question. But his made-up question turned out to be so frustratingly complicated that it ate up not only the gossip session but the next round as well. If, as luck would have it, I answered it quickly enough, he would point to the mat and ask, 'What is it?'

'Mat,' I'd shout.

'No, no,' he shook his head, 'I mean in Farsi.'

Irritated, I snapped, 'What, you think we're taught Farsi at school?'

'But I teach you, Golu, don't I?' he tried to calm me down. 'Here, listen: *boriya* in Farsi, *haseer* in Arabi.'

Mischievously I folded my hands before him and said, 'Mercy—please! Spare me your Farsi and your Arabi. I don't want to learn either. Please, I beg you!'

He pretended not to hear me and kept repeating: '*Boriya* in Farsi, *haseer* in Arabi.'

There was no stopping him after that, even if one poured lead into one's ears to block it out.

Amichand was a bookworm. Perched in the sitting room he studied all day long. Dauji rarely interrupted him, but that doesn't mean he escaped Dauji's assaults either, which were quick to come whenever the opportunity offered itself. When he emerged from the room for a drink of water, then and there Dauji, looking up from his book, fired off the question: 'Tell me the noun form of the verb "to do."'

'Deed,' Amichand answered, his lips still stuck to the tumbler. He tossed the tumbler under the pitcher-stand and slipped back into his room. Dauji resumed his reading.

Of all his family, Dauji was most fond of his daughter. To all of us she was Bibi; Dauji alone had christened her Qurrat. Now and then he called her and said, 'Qurrat Bitiya, when are you going to get rid of those scissors?' In reply, she merely smiled, but Bébé, who simply hated this 'Qurrat'-business, retorted loudly, 'By calling her "Qurrat," you've doomed her to stitching kurtas all her life. Even if one may not be pleasant, one should still say nice things.' And Dauji, taking a long, cold breath, remarked, 'How could the ignorant ever know what "Qurrat" means!'

This incited Bébé's anger, and she spat out whatever came to her mind—first name-calling, then curses, finally descending to galis. If Bibi tried to stop her, Dauji told her not to: 'Daughter, the wind has to blow, and galis have to rain down. Don't even try to stop her.' He would then gather his books, pick up his favourite *haseer* and quietly go upstairs.

Right at the beginning of the ninth class I fell into a particularly bad habit, which brought me great grief. The late Hakim Ali Ahmad was the only physician who practiced traditional Yunani medicine in our *qasba*. Only moderately interested in his practice, he was rather a fantastic storyteller. Stories of Sufi saints, of genies and ghosts, of the domestic life of King Solomon and Queen

Sheba—these were his sure-fire remedies. A few tins of confected drugs, a dozen or so bottles of different syrups, and a pair of magnifying glasses was all his dingy, dark clinic had for medical wherewithal. In addition to medicine, he treated his patients with his magical orations and special charms, handed down orally from Prophet Solomon. So patients even from far-flung villages flocked to him for treatment, and returned cured.

Within a couple of weeks of our acquaintance the Hakim Sahib and I worked out a deal: I'd swipe empty bottles and vials from my father's dispensary for him, and he'd lend me volumes of *Dastan-e Amir Hamza* to read. These books were so full of wonder that I read them on the sly in my bed all night long, with the result that I invariably overslept in the morning. This annoyed Amma a lot, and made my father worry about my health. But I assured them that I'd risk my life to clear the tenth class, and clear it well enough to secure a scholarship. Nights I spent roaming the magical palaces of *Tilism-e Hosh-Ruba*, and days standing on the classroom bench in punishment. I nearly flunked my quarterly examination. By the time the second quarterly exam rolled along, I fell ill. The finals I passed, but only through the influence that Hakim Sahib was able to use on my school teachers.

Sandalinamah, *Fasanah-e Azad*, and *Alf Laila* were my constant companions in the tenth class. I kept the first two books at home and *Alf Laila* at school, locked up in my desk. Sitting at my desk in the very last row, under my geography book, I'd strike out with Sindbad and roam the world over.

Around ten in the morning of 22 May the examination result arrived from the University to which M.B. High School was accredited. Amichand was ranked first not only in the school but in the entire district. Twenty-two boys had

een successful, and six had flunked. Hakimji's magic was
neffectual against Punjab University, which had heart-
essly included me among the failures. That very evening
His Reverence—my honourable father—thrashed me with
cane and threw me out of the house.

I went and sat on top of the Persian wheel, thinking well
nto the night about what I might do next and where I might
go. The land of God was by no means narrow, and I too was
well equipped with the stratagems of Amr Ayyar—Amr the
Trickster—and the devices of Sindbad the Sailor. Yet I
couldn't figure out a way. For some three hours I sat right
here thinking hard of a way that might enable me to live
n. Right about then, Amma, wrapped in her white chadar
nd frantically looking for me everywhere, wandered into
he area. She asked me to return home, promising that she
would persuade Abbaji to forgive me. I wasn't interested in
ny forgiveness; I had only one more night to spend at my
parents'. Come morning, I'd be on my way. So I followed
er back to the house without even a hint of regret and
stretched out on my bed as usual.

Next day I ran into two of my fellow flunkies, Khushya
Kodu and Desu Yabyab, sitting near the lumber store
ehind the mosque. They were cooking up a plan to go to
Lahore and set up some kind of business. Desu Yabyab told
me that Lahore was full of business opportunities, because
e had often heard his uncle mention a friend of his,
Fatehchand, who had done so well there that he bought two
cars in just one year. When I asked him about the nature of
Fatehchand's business, Yabyab said Lahore offered all
kinds of business. All you needed was an office with a big
signboard. People saw the signboard and they came of their
own and gave you more business than you could handle.
By 'business' he meant, at that time, 'currency notes.' When

I asked him once more to explain the business we'd get. Kodu flared up and said, 'Yaar, Desu knows everything. What we want to know is this: are you with us or not?'

He then turned towards Desu and asked, 'We'll set up our office in Anarkali, right?'

Desu thought for a bit and then replied, 'Either there, or outside Shah Almi—both places are equally good.'

'Anarkali would be better,' I said. 'It's more famous. All the newspaper ads give Anarkali as their address.'

And so we decided to leave for Lahore the next day by the 2 p.m. train.

I returned home and started to prepare for the trip. As I was polishing my shoes our servant walked in and told me with a mischievous grin on his face, 'Come, Doctor Sahib is asking for you.'

'Where is he?' I got up, putting the brush back down.

'At the dispensary,' he said, still grinning widely, since he, too, was present at the scene of my humiliation the other day.

I climbed the stairs full of fear, slowly opened the screen door and entered into Abbaji's room. Dauji was there with him. Still cringing from fear I greeted Dauji and heard, after a long silence, his familiar blessing, 'May you live long.'

'Do you recognize him?' Abbaji asked me sternly.

'Of course,' I replied in the manner of a polished salesman.

'Damn you, you bastard! I'll . . .'

'No, please, no, Doctor Sahib,' Dauji pleaded, raising his hand. 'He is a good child, he . . .'

But Abbaji rudely cut him short and said, 'Munshiji, you have no idea how this miserable wretch has sullied my honour.'

'Please don't worry,' Dauji replied, his head lowered.
He is even brighter than Aftab, and one day . . .'

This really made my father fly into a rage. He banged
is fist on the table and said, 'What kind of talk is that,
Munshiji? He doesn't even measure up to the dust on
Aftab's shoes!'

'He will, Doctor Sahib, one day, he will,' Dauji nodded
is head in affirmation. 'Please don't worry about him.'

Dauji got up from his chair, placed his hand on my
houlder and said, 'Look, I'm going for a walk. You come
long too. We'll talk on the way.'

My father continued to sit and fume as he nervously
urned the pages of his register, muttering all the while.
Slowly I walked over to the screen door and as I was
opening it, Dauji turned around and said to my father,
Doctor Sahib, please don't forget. Have it delivered right
way.'

'Yes, yes,' Abbaji said amidst all his banging. Dauji said
Khuda Hafiz' and left the room with me.

Taking me along through the town, and telling the
ames of different trees in Farsi, Dauji brought me to the
ame bridge where I'd first met him. He took his favourite
pot on the bridge, removed his turban and put it in his lap,
ubbed his head and beckoned me to sit opposite him. He
losed his eyes and said, 'I shall be your teacher from this
ay forward. And even if you don't come out at the top of
our class, you certainly will pass with a first division. This
assure you. I'm backed by *Khudavand-e Ta'ala* in whatever
resolve to do, and thanks to His mercy, I've never been
isappointed.'

'I don't want to study,' I interrupted rudely.

'Well then, what will you do, Golu?' he asked with a
mile.

'I'll go into business,' I replied. 'I'll make money. And when I come back here in my own car, you'll see.'

This time around it was Dauji who interrupted. 'May Allah give you not one, but ten cars,' he said with exceeding kindness. 'But I shall not ride in the car of an illiterate person, and neither will Doctor Sahib.'

'Who cares?' I retorted, flaring up. 'Doctor Sahib can live happily in his house, and let me be happy in mine.'

'You don't care even about me?' he asked, surprised.

I was about to say something when he sadly repeated 'You don't care even about me? Golu, not even me—really?'

I felt moved by the tone of his voice and said softly, 'I do care about you, but . . .'

But he didn't let me finish. 'Could such a word, such a word of *kufr* have ever escaped from my lips before my hazrat, my ustad?' He quickly put his turban back on his head and, joining his hands in reverential humility, added 'I, the lowliest of creatures in the durbar of the Prophet Humbler than the dust under the feet of Hazrat Maulana A mere servant, how could I have ever said such a thing to my Master? Wouldn't I have merited the collar of reproach of opprobrium?'

He then folded his hands on his chest, and, lowering his head all the way to his thighs, continued, 'I, a goatherd by caste, my father a milkman from Mundasi. I, a child of ignorance, my family the family of Abu Jahl. But how a single glance of kindness, a single gesture of the Master transformed Chintu into Munshi Chinta Ram. People call me Munshiji, but I say I'm merely a lowly servant of the Master—may God's mercy be on him! Fit only to carry his slippers . . . People think . . .'

Dauji carried on, sometimes joining his hands in humility, sometimes bowing his head low, sometimes kissing his fingers and then touching his eyes, and punctuating it all with the recitation of Farsi couplets. Perplexed and a bit regretful, I found myself touching his knees and pleading with him softly, 'Dauji, Dauji.' But Dauji was on with his own litany: 'My Master, my Hazrat Maulana, my Murshid."

When finally he emerged from his mystical absorption, he raised his eyes and said, 'What nice weather! When it's hot during the day, the evenings are always cool and very pleasant.'

He got down from the bridge wall and said, 'Let's go. I have to buy some things from the bazaar.'

Insolent and haughty as I had been when I set out with him, I was a good deal more ashamed and sorry when I returned with him. He bought a few items from the shop of Ghume Pansari (who was none other than Desu Yabyab's father), picked up the bags and started walking. Many times I wanted to take the bags from him and carry them myself, but I lacked the courage to ask. A strange shyness, an unfamiliar diffidence got in my way. Such was my inner state when we arrived at his house.

It was only then that I found out that henceforward I was to sleep and study at Dauji's, my bedding, with a hurricane lantern lying beside it, having preceded me.

It was not my fate to become a businessman and honk my way through the streets in a Packard car. And, it would appear, neither was it the fate of my friends who had fled to Lahore. Within three days of their departure, their parents hauled them back home. But who knows, had I been with them, what glorious year of success our office in Anarkali would be enjoying today.

Dauji made life a living hell for me. He practically destroyed it. I spent the day at school, listening to all that garbage, and the night—the incredibly short night of summer—answering all the questions he threw at me. His cot right next to my bed on the flat rooftop, he busily quizzed me about the rivers Moong, Rasool, and Marala. And although I'd given him the correct answer, he'd still ask me the same question. I gave him the correct answer once again, and once again he asked about the same rivers. I flared up and snapped at him, 'I don't know! I don't want to answer!' which made him fall silent and hold his breath. I closed my eyes and tried to fall asleep, but feel the sting of remorse in my eyes, like grit. So I called him softly, 'Dauji?'

'Yes,' he said in a grave voice.

'Ask me another question?'

'*Bahut be-abroo ho-kar tere kooche se ham nikle*—describe its syntactic structure!'

'It's a very long sentence. I'll write it down in the morning and do it then. For now, give me another.'

He lifted his eyes to the sky and said, '*Mera Golu bahut achchha hai*—there.'

After thinking a bit I started, '*Achchha* is an adjective; *hai* a copula; together they make up the predicate . . .'

Dauji sat up erect on the cot, raised his hand and said, 'Jan-e Pidar, haven't I told you to identify the subject first?'

To save myself from the torture of syntactical description I asked him, 'Why do you call me Jan-e Pidar? 'Why don't you call me Jan-e Da'u?'

'Bravo!' he exclaimed with delight. 'Now that's an excellent question. *Jan* is a Farsi word, and *dau* comes from Bhasha. You cannot join the two with a Farsi genitive. Those who write or say *din ba-din* commit a terrible mistake. One should either say *roz ba-roz* or *din par din*. Likewise . . .'

Obviously the trick had backfired, I was dragged into a

roblem more daunting than syntactical description. And o I yawned and tried to say sweetly, 'Dauji, I'm very leepy.'

'But the syntactical description?' he asked abruptly.

No matter what excuses I now used, or the things I said o deflect his attention, he remained unyielding, sitting igid and expectant on his cot. And if my response didn't ome quickly enough, he picked up the turban lying on the hair and replaced it on his head. There was no getting away rom his questions.

After Amichand went away to college, I moved into the itting room previously occupied by him, and gradually lso replaced him in Dauji's affections. The fact is, I too had rown exceedingly fond of Dauji. Which doesn't mean I iked the way he treated me. I found it atrocious, and I still lo. Even more atrocious today. Perhaps because I'm now a sychology student, a rather bright student, and Dauji had een schooled in the rigid environment of *maktabs*. Two of is worst sins were: to assault you with questions without etting up, and to stop you from any kind of play or liversion. Study, study and study—he'd settle on nothing ess, and when your time was up, you'd die hunched over pile of books. He had only one prescription to keep ourself bodily fit: long walks, and early in the morning at hat. Two hours before sunup he walked into the sitting oom and woke me up. He shook me by the shoulder and aid, 'Get up, Golu! See, you've grown fat.'

Every other parent woke you up with a sweet, 'Come n son, wake up, it's morning' or 'the sun's risen.' But his umiliating catch phrase was 'You've grown fat.'

If I whined, he'd try to sweet-talk me, 'If you become o fat, how will you tour your district mounted on a horse?'

Unwilling to stir from my warm bed, I'd join my hands

and plead with him, 'Dauji, please, not so early in the morning. Kill me, take my life, but for heaven's sake don't wake me up! Please!'

This never failed to get to him. He quickly pulled the comforter back over my face and walked out of the room.

Bébé, it would appear, bore some old grudge against Dauji. And he feared her very much. She stitched clothes for the neighbourhood women all day long and kept up a steady barrage of curses against him. Her name calling and invectives infuriated me, but living in the river I couldn't very well get on the wrong side of the crocodile. Now and then, when her abuses became particularly nasty, Dauji sought refuge in my room. He sat himself down in the chair and put his hands over his ears to block out the relentless stream of maledictions. After some time he remarked, 'I know it is a great sin to speak behind someone's back, and God forgive me for that, but your Bébé is a perfect *bhatyaran* and the three of us—my Qurratulain, I, and to a degree even you—are merely hapless sojourners in her inn.'

Bébé did, in fact, look something like a *bhatyaran*. Very dark, with intensely white teeth, she had an arched forehead and narrow eyes. She padded her way around stealthily like a cat, sniffing out gossip like a go-between. She targeted poor Bibi for such name calling that it sent her weeping for days. She got along well only with Amichand, perhaps because the two resembled each other quite a bit or perhaps because, unlike Bibi, he didn't love his Dauji all that much. I liked Bibi all right, but getting along with her was something else again. I'd be upstairs in the barsati doing a math problem, while Dauji sat downstairs. If Bibi came upstairs to pick up some firewood, she stopped briefly to look at me and then peered down the short wall and shouted, 'Dauji, he isn't studying; he's playing instead —making cots out of sticks.'

I made a face at her like an angry child and snapped, 'None of your business! Okay, I'm not studying—what's it to you anyway? Behaving like some thanedarni?'

Whereupon Dauji called out to me from below, 'No, Golu, no. One doesn't fight with sisters.'

I yelled, 'She's plain lying! I *am* studying!'

Meanwhile he came softly up the stairs. Seeing the cot I was fashioning out of sticks half concealed under my notebook, he said to Bibi, 'Qurrat, my child, you shouldn't tease him. I've had quite a time bringing this genie under control. If he slips out again, there is no way I can bring him back in line.'

Unmoved, Bibi said, 'Just pick up the notebook, Dauji, and see for yourself.'

I glared at Bibi, but she gathered the firewood and went back downstairs, leaving Dauji to reason with me. 'All this that Bibi says, it is for your own good. Why else would she bother to tell me? Whether you pass or fail, it makes no difference to her. But she has your best interests at heart. She wants you to succeed.'

I just couldn't understand Dauji's logic: how could she have my best interests at heart by complaining about me? By squealing on me?

Back then, my routine went something like this: I'd leave Dauji's at about ten in the morning for home, eat my breakfast and then go to school. My lunch would arrive from home at midday recess. After school I'd return home, fill my lantern with kerosene and come over to Dauji's, where in time my dinner would arrive from home.

When the courts weren't in session, Dauji came and sat in the school's playground waiting for me. On the way home I had to face a gale of questions. He asked me the details of what all I had been taught at school that day. He escorted me to my house and then took off for his evening stroll. The judge set up his court in our *qasba* for ten days a month; the other twenty days he presided at the district court. Those ten days Dauji regularly sat outside the courthouse. Now and then somebody came along, Dauji wrote out the petition for him, and thus earned a couple of rupees. The rest of the time he spent reading books—even here.

Bébé's work, on the other hand, was rather more steady, and her stitching and socializing with the neighbourhood women produced a more profitable result. For some years now the major part of the house's expenses was covered by the money she earned from stitching. As a result, she had come to dominate Dauji even more.

One day, contrary to the routine, I went to the courthouse to meet Dauji. Court was over for the day and Dauji was lounging on a bench inside the thatched shed of the baker's shop sipping tea sweetened with raw sugar. I quietly reached down and picked up his mat and bag, and then, throwing my arms around his neck, said, 'I've come to fetch you today. Let's go.'

He downed the remaining tea in a few big gulps, took an anna coin out of his pocket and gave it to the baker, and quietly walked out with me. A streak of mischief danced through me and I said, 'Just wait until we get back. I'll tell Bébé how you help yourself to tea on the sly.'

To evade his embarrassment, Dauji smiled some and said, 'He really fixes excellent tea. Besides, raw sugar tea relaxes the nerves. And he gives a full glass for just an anna—not bad! But please don't tell your Bébé. She'll kick up a huge fuss. She'll become more violent with me.' And then, somewhat fearful and somewhat sad, he added, 'She can't go against her nature.'

I felt a surge of tenderness well up in me for Dauji that day. I felt I wanted to do something for him, indeed, I wanted to do a whole lot. But at that time, the promise that I wouldn't tell on him was already a whole lot. When I told Mother about the incident, she began to have me or the servant carry gifts of milk, fruits, sugar, etc., over to Dauji's now and then. But poor Dauji, he never saw any of these provisions himself. But it did catapult me in Bébé's regard, and she started treating me somewhat more preferentially.

I vividly remember walking into Dauji's with a pitcher of milk one morning. Bébé had gone away with her friends to bathe in Baba Sawan's pond, and only Dauji and Bibi were at home. Spotting the pitcher of milk Dauji chuckled, 'Let's make some tea. I'll go and get some raw sugar from the shop. Meantime you put the kettle on.' Right away Bibi started to get the fire going. I went and brought water in a pan. The two of us sat down on the *chauka* and started chatting. Dauji promptly returned with some raw sugar and said to us, 'You go and do your work. I'll fix the tea.'

So Bibi started working the sewing machine and I busied myself with the direct and indirect speech exercises. Meanwhile, Dauji kept blowing into the fire and, after his habit, kept instructing me loudly, 'Galileo said that the earth moves around the sun. It was Galileo who discovered that the earth revolv*es* around the sun. Make sure that you don't write, "revolv*ed* around the sun."'

The water had come to a boil. Dauji was happy, joyously swaying his head back and forth and repeating the song he'd just improvised, 'O Golu! O Golu! Don't forget what Galileo said, what Galileo said, O Golu ' He added the tea leaves to the boiling water. The pan was still on the fire and

Dauji, like a small child, was trying to synchronize his 'Golu Galileo, Golu Galileo' with the *'gul-bul, gul-bul'* of the boiling water. I was laughing as I did my grammar exercises, and Bibi quietly smiled as she worked the sewing machine. The three of us were very happy in our small home, it was as if the joys of the whole neighbourhood, indeed, of the entire *qasba,* had alighted on our house like fairies with large, colourful wings.

Just then the door opened and in walked Bébé. Dauji turned around to see and, instantaneously, his face blanched. Steam was rising from the boiling pan, in which small bubbles were furiously chasing each other. The old man was caught red-handed at his forbidden game. Bébé took a few steps towards the hearth, and Dauji, rising from the *chauka,* intoned apologetically, 'It's just tea.'

Bébé gave him a whack and thundered, 'Have you lost all your shame? May you be damned! May death take you away! What, you really think you can drink tea at your age? I wasn't home, so you thought you could take advantage. You couldn't care less if I died, indeed, you'd rather I died today, so that you could be happy, make all your wishes come true. Damn the woman who brought you into this world! Damn the fate that's stuck me to you. Why don't you die? Why would you . . .'

Frothing and foaming away, Bébé jumped over the *chauka* like a she-wolf, picked up the pan with a piece of cloth, and threw it on the floor. Boiling tea splashed over Dauji's legs and feet, who fled like a child, screaming, 'May God help you, may God help you!' and sought refuge in the sitting room.

Bibi and I couldn't help but break into a laugh at his departure, rather at the manner in which he had fled. We laughed so loudly that, for a second, the whole house resounded with it. I somehow escaped Bébé's wrath, but Bibi had to bear the full brunt of her assault. She pounced on her, grabbed her by the hair, and screamed, 'My saut, tell me what you think you're doing with this old coot? Come on, out with it, or I'll strangle you this minute! Why did you give him the key to the pantry?'

Poor Bibi started to sob. I got up and slinked into the sitting room. Dauji was ensconced in his favourite chair and was slowly rubbing his feet to soothe the pain of the scalding. He looked so comic that I again started to laugh, but I stuck my head into the closet to muffle the sound. He beckoned me to come over and said, *'Shukr-e kirdgar kunam keh griftaram ba musibati na keh ma 'siyati!'* (Thank the Creator that though I'm in trouble, I haven't sinned.) After a brief pause he added, 'I'm lowlier than the lowest slaves of him on whose blessed head the old hag of Mecca used to dump her garbage.'

When I gave him a perplexed look, he explained: 'Should I, the meanest slave of *Aqa-e Namdar*, complain about a few splashes of hot water, then may my life be cursed. May God save me from the fires of hell through His love of the Prophet Muhammad. May the God of Ibrahim grant me strength. May the God of Ayyub bless me with the gift of patience.'

I asked, '*Aqa-e Namdar*—who's he, Dauji?'

This pained him, but he said with his usual affection, 'Jan-e Pidar, that's no way to ask. Don't make the spirit of my ustad, my hazrat angry with me. He was not only my *aqa*, he was also my father and my teacher. In fact, he stands in the relationship of a grandfather to you. Your grandfather teacher . . .' He quickly folded his hands over his chest in extreme reverence.

I owed my very first exposure to the phrase *aqa-e namdar*

and the compound *kotahqismat mujawwizah* to Dauji. He took his sweet time in relating the incident in which these occurred, following up every sentence with Farsi couplets extolling the Prophet of Islam, again and again sending the reward for them to the soul of his dear departed ustad.

After he was done narrating, I asked him with great politeness, 'Dauji, why do you love your ustad so much? Why do you always join your hands when you say his name, and why do you call yourself his servant?'

Dauji smiled and said, 'A man who can transform an ordinary donkey like me into one addressed as Munshi Chinta Ram, as Munshiji, what would you call such a man if not a Messiah, an *aqa?*'

Slowly I inched my way from the edge to the center of the cot, wrapped the quilt securely around myself, and fixed my gaze on Dauji. He sat with a drooping head, now looking at his foot, now gently rubbing his calves, laughing some and then slipping back into silence. Finally he said:

'It's amazing. What I started out as, what I became! . . . The first words Hazrat Maulana uttered to me! Lifting his blessed face to me he said, "Shepherd boy, come here." I walked over to him, leaning upon my staff. Boys from Chhatta Pathhar and other villages were sitting in front of him in a semi-circle memorizing their lessons. It seemed I'd walked straight into a darbar: no one dared even look up at me. When I approached the Huzur, he said, "My dear, aren't you the one I see herding goats around here everyday? Maybe you should let the animals graze on their own and come over here and study with me a bit." He didn't wait for my answer and instead asked, "What's your name?" "Chintu," I replied, in the coarse manner of a country boy, which prompted His Eminence to smile, even laugh a bit. And then he asked, "What is your full name?"

Again, without waiting for my response, he proceeded to say, "Must be Chinta Ram." I nodded my head. His students were now stealing glances at me. I was wearing a long *khaddar* shirt and a loincloth in place of a proper pajama. On my feet I had a pair of coarse half-hide shoes; my head-covering improvised from an old pair of red shorts. "My goats . . ."

I interrupted him and asked, 'You used to be a shepherd? Really, Dauji?'

'Yes, yes indeed I was,' he said with pride, 'I was a shepherd. My father owned a dozen goats.'

My mouth fell open in surprise. In an attempt to get to the bottom of it all I rushed to ask, 'And you used to graze them near the school?'

Dauji pulled his chair over to my cot and said, stretching out and resting his feet on the edge of the bed-frame, 'Jan-e Pidar, back in those days, even the cities didn't boast of schools, and I'm talking about just a village. Who'd heard of your M.B. High School seventy-four years ago? It's just that my *aqa* was fond of teaching. So people living in the neighbourhood sent their boys over to him to learn their ABC's. His entire family was adorned with the jewel of knowledge and enjoyed a surfeit of spiritual blessings. His father had the rare distinction of being the only hakim in the entire district, and a top-notch preacher to boot. And his grandfather was the Mir Munshi in the employ of the Maharaja of Kashmir. A veritable river of learning flowed in their home. Farsi, Arbi, algebra, Euclidean geometry, medicine, astronomy—they were the maids they employed in their house. I never had the good fortune of meeting Huzur's father, but I was fortunate enough to hear the stories of his great erudition. He was good friends with the poet Sheftah and the poet-physician Momin Khan Momin, while he, Hazrat Maulana himself, had been educated in Delhi under the close supervision of the late Mufti Azurdah.'

Afraid that Dauji might be tempted to leave his main story and strike out on some tangent, I quickly asked him, 'So you started to study with Hazrat Maulana?'

'Yes,' Dauji began, as if reminiscing to himself. 'What a wonder he was! What a discriminating eye he had! Whoever he singled out for his attention, he transformed him from a humble servant into a master and lord. He could charge a speck of lowly dirt with the most astounding power of cure . . .

'Then and there I laid down my club and took a seat near him on the bare ground. But he commanded, "Go and sit with your brothers on the mat." To which I replied, "All my eighteen years I've spent on the bare earth. What difference would it make now?" He smiled again, took out a scroll of *abjad* letters from a wooden chest, and said, "Repeat after me: *Alif, be, pe, te* . . ." What a lovely voice he had—God be praised! With what affection, what tenderness he spoke: "*Alif, be, pe, te,* . . ." Chanting the alphabet Dauji lapsed into his past.

A while later he raised his right hand and said, 'Over here was a Persian wheel, and a pond of fish right beside it.' He waved his left hand in the air and added, 'And over there, the brick houses of peasants who worked the fields. The space in between was occupied by Huzur's garden, and facing it was his magnificent haveli. He set up his school in this very garden. The gate of munificence was open; everyone was welcome. Religion offered no barrier; difference in creed was of no consequence.'

After thinking for some time and fashioning a sentence which would do justice to the decorum imposed by the lofty memory of his revered teacher, I inquired, 'What was the *ism-e girami sharif* (honourable and noble name) of Hazrat Maulana?' Whereupon Dauji first corrected my construction and then said, 'Hazrat Ismail Chishti, may God's mercy be upon him. He used to say that his father always called him "Jan-e Janan," but sometimes "Mazhar Jan-e Janan" too, because of the correspondence of the two.'

I was eager to hear more of this fascinating story when Dauji abruptly stopped and said, 'Explain the Subsidiary System to me.'

Damn these British! Whether they came in the guise of the East India Company or as bearers of the royal edicts of Queen Victoria, they always managed to spoil things for us. Anyway, I explained the whole structure of the Subsidiary System to Dauji, like the multiplication table of one-and-a-quarter. Subsequently, he picked up the grammar book from the table and said, 'Go and see if your Bébé's anger has subsided.'

I stepped out into the veranda, pretending to add some water to my ink-well, and found Bébé busy at her sewing machine and Bibi cleaning the *chauka*.

The greatest sore spot of Dauji's life was Bébé. Whenever he perceived relative calm inside the house, whenever Bébé looked to be in a better mood, he would call out to us, 'Come, all of you, and recite a *she'r* each.' Invariably, I was asked to go first, and I almost always obliged with these lines:

Lazim tha keh dekho mera rastah ko'i din aur
Tanha ga'e kiyun ab raho tanha ko'i din aur

(You should have waited for me a while longer
You wanted to go alone—well then, stay alone a while longer.)

He would break into applause and then lay down his terms 'Good. But give me a fresh couplet, and make sure it isn't in Urdu, nor from a longer poem.'

'Okay, but give me time to think,' I said. 'Meanwhile, Bibi can recite hers.'

Bibi too had a favourite couplet she usually began with

Shunidam keh Shapour dam dar kasheed
Chu Khusrau bar ismash qalam dar kasheed
(I've heard that as Shapur breathed his last
Khusrau struck out his name.)

Once again Dauji shouted 'Order! Order!' And Bibi, putting down her scissors, recited a different one:

Shori shud wa az khvab-e adam chashm kashodim
Didim keh baqist shab-e fitnah ghunudim
(A tumult awakened us from our sleep of non-existence
We dozed off again seeing that the night of commotion had not ended.)

Even as Dauji complemented Bibi, he would still point out, Daughter, you've already recited that one several times before.'

Then, looking at Bébé, he said to us, 'Well, today, even your Bébé will recite a couplet.'

But Bébé had only one answer, a stale one at that: 'I don't know any *sher-geet*.'

'Well then, sing some *ghoriyan* instead,' Dauji tried again. 'The ones you sang at your sons' weddings.'

Bébé's lips made as if to smile, but somehow couldn't. Instead, Dauji himself started singing *ghoriyan*, exactly mimicking the manner of women, inserting sometimes Amichand's and sometimes my name into the festive verses. Then he declared, 'When my Golu Molu gets married, 'I'll flaunt a bright red turban. I'll walk with the Doctor Sahib in the wedding procession, and I will sign my name as a witness on the papers.'

At this I would lower my eyes with the customary shyness of a young boy. He would continue: 'Who knows, my little bahu must be in the fifth or sixth class somewhere in the country today. Girls are taught housekeeping one day a week, so she must've already learnt to cook quite a few dishes. She'll be very bright, not like this blockhead who can't even remember whether *madiyan* means mare or hen. She, of course, will have all this at the tip of her tongue. *Far-far*, just like that. I'll teach her Farsi. I'll start with basic calligraphy, and then I'll teach her the *shakistah* style. Our women usually don't know how to write *shakistah*. But my bahu will, I'll teach it to her. Which means—listen Golu—that I'll be living with you. My bahu and I will speak to each other in Farsi, and while she will elegantly say *Befarma'id, Befarma'id'* all the time, you'll just stand there like an idiot and gawk at us.'

Dauji would then fold his hands on his chest, bow slightly in a gesture of deference and respect, and rain down a torrent of *Khele khub, khele khub, Jan-e Pidar, chira in-qadr zehmat mi-kashi, . . . Khub . . . yad daram'* and God knows what else. Poor Dauji! He'd set up his little world on his little mat, and he kept it going by issuing edicts in ornate Farsi.

Sitting one day sunning himself on the rooftop, after he had ordered just such an imaginary world into being, he said to me softly, 'God has granted you a virtuous wife and me a dutiful bahu. May He, by His generosity, also grant just as good a wife to my Amichand. His ideas don't sit well with me. All this Seva Sangh, this Muslim League, this Belcha Party—I don't like them at all. You know, he's learning how to use lathis and clubs these days. He's not likely to listen to me. But if the Venerable and Sublime God could grant him a pious and *momin* wife, she'd surely talk some sense into him.'

The word *momin* bothered me quite a bit, but I decided to remain silent. Anything I would have said would only have hurt Dauji.

While Amichand's and my marriages were mere talk at his point, Bibi actually did get married, on 12th January. Dauji had already filled me in about jijaji Ram Partab: what a fine boy he was, how he measured up to Dauji's prior consultation with the Quran, so on and so forth. But what pleased him the most was that his samdhi was a teacher of Farsi and belonged to the Kabir Panthi sect.

That evening, when the time came for Bibi to leave her parental home for good, the whole house was thrown into a commotion: Bébé wept inconsolably, Amichand shed his tears quietly, and the women from the neighbourhood whispered among themselves. I stood leaning against the wall, and Dauji stood right beside me with his hand on my shoulder, repeating now and again, 'Why do I feel so wobbly today? Seems I can't keep my balance.'

When the bridegroom's father came over to Dauji and asked for permission to leave, Bibi suddenly fell backward and fainted. She had to be moved to a cot, and the women dutifully started fanning her. Just then, still leaning on me for support, Dauji walked over to her cot. He helped Bibi sit up and said, 'This is no way to behave, my child. Get up now! Isn't this, after all, the very first hour of your new and independent life? Come on, don't make it inauspicious!'

Bibi hugged him, still crying loudly. He stroked her head gently, lovingly, and said, 'Qurratulain, I'm a sinner, for I couldn't give you the education you deserved. I'm ashamed that I'm unable to send you off with knowledge as your dowry. I know you'll forgive me for this, and perhaps even barkhurdar Ram Partab will too. But I'll never be able to forgive myself. I'm at fault and I stand before you with my head bowed in shame.'

This made Bibi cry even harder, and copious, fat tears rolled out of Dauji's eyes and fell on the ground. The groom's father quickly moved forward and reassured him, 'Munshiji, please don't worry. I'll teach her the *Karima* myself.'

Dauji hurriedly turned around and said as he joined his hands deferentially, 'That I've taught her already, as well as *Gulistan* and *Bostan*. But, to my deep regret, that's not nearly all I wanted to teach her.'

Whereupon the other man laughed and said, 'Well, well—Even I haven't studied the whole *Gulistan*. Whenever I came to a passage in Arabic, I just skipped it.'

Dauji stood quietly for some time, his hands folded as before. Bibi thrust her hands out of her embroidered red silk shawl and patted first Amichand and then me on the head, and, supported by her girlfriends, picked her way slowly toward the *devrhi*. As Dauji, still leaning over me, also made to move, he hugged me tightly and said, 'What, are you crying too? Were you not supposed to give me support?! O, Golu, . . . the apple of my eye . . . what's the matter with you? . . . Jan-e Pidar, why are you . . .?'

His voice choked and my tears too came fast. The groom's party were riding in tongas and ikkas, followed by

Bibi seated in a rath, while Amichand and myself, with Dauji between us, walked along behind them. If a cry escaped from Bibi's lips, Dauji quickly moved forward, lifted the screen of the chariot, and advised her, 'Say *La-haul*, daughter, say *La-haul*.' The loose end of his turban that he had placed over his eyes had by now become completely wet.

Ranu was the coarsest individual who lived in our neighbourhood. Evil and meanness seemed to have been pounded right into his bones. The enclosure I referred to earlier actually belonged to him. He kept a couple of dozen goats and a pair of cows there, and sold their milk in the mornings and evenings in the open field right next to the enclosure. Just about everyone in the neighbourhood bought their milk from him and, because of his propensity for making mischief, sort of yielded to him. As he walked past our house, just for the fun of it he'd rap his lathi on the ground and greet Dauji with '*Pandata, jai Ramji ki!*' Time and again Dauji told him that he was not a pandit but only an ordinary man. As Dauji saw it, a learned man alone was entitled to be called a pandit. But Ranu wouldn't buy it. He'd chew on his moustache and say, 'Listen to this! Whoever sports a *bodi* on his head has got to be a pandit.'

Anyway, Ranu was friends with all the petty thieves and playboys of the area, who came together in the evening at his enclosure for gambling and poetry full of sexual innuendo. One day, after Bibi had been married, when I went to buy milk from him, he winked at me and remarked, 'Still living there, eh? But the morni's already flown away.'

When I didn't react to it, he stirred the frothy milk with the tin measuring cup and said, 'The Ganga was flowing right inside the house—tell me, did you take a dip?'

Anger flared up inside me. I swung the pitcher I'd brought along for milk and brought it down on his head with all my strength. The tremendous blow, even if it failed to produce any blood, almost knocked him out. As he collapsed on the takht, I ran back home. After recounting the incident to Dauji, I hurried to my own home and told Abbaji what all had happened. Thanks to my father's intervention, Ranu was immediately summoned to the police station, where, after a mild rebuke and a stern warning, he was released by the Havaldar Sahib.

From here on out, Ranu, whenever he ran into Dauji, made him the butt of his biting taunts, the nastiest ones reserved for the small tuft of hair, the *bodi*, that Dauji wore on his head. And truth be told, that flattened width of hair really didn't look at all good on Dauji's learned head. But he used to say, 'This is a memento of my deceased mother, and it's as dear to me as life itself. She'd put my head in her lap and shampoo it with yogurt, then massage it to a sparkling shine with a bit of mustard oil. Although I never dared remove my turban before my Hazrat Maulana, he knew that I had a *bodi*. When I returned home for vacation after working for a year at Dayal Chand Memorial High School, His Excellence asked me, "I hope the city didn't make you get rid of it." I shook my head "no," which made him very happy. "Few mothers can boast of a more dutiful son than you," he complemented me, "and few teachers can have the good fortune, as I have, of teaching a student like you." I touched his feet and said, "Huzur, please don't put me to shame. Whatever I may be, it's all due to the grace of your feet." He laughed and said, "Chinta Ram, please don't ever touch my feet. What good is the touch which I can't even feel?" Tears surged in my eyes. I said, "If only someone could tell me where to find it, I'd spare nothing to bring you the remedy. I'd offer even my own life, if its vitality, its warmth would return life to Your Honour's legs, but I'm helpless."

'He fell silent. After some time, he looked up at the heavens and said, "If such is God's will, then let it be. May you live long. Thanks to your sturdy shoulders I've managed to see the whole village once again after ten years."'

Dauji, going further back into his memory, down to the farthest reaches of days past, resumed: 'Every day at the crack of dawn I'd arrive in the *devrhi* of his grand mansion and call out, "Your servant's here!" After the ladies had withdrawn to one side, His Honour would call me from the courtyard to come in, and I'd approach him, my hands joined in obeisance, complementing myself over my good fortune. After touching his feet I waited for his command. He'd bless me and inquire after my parents' health and the affairs of the village, after which he'd say, "All right then, Chinta Ram, you may now lift this bundle of sins." I'd take him onto my back, as though he were a basket of flowers, and exit the mansion. Sometimes he asked, "Give me a tour of the garden!" Another time he commanded, "Take me straight to the Persian wheel!" And still other times, with touching tenderness, he'd request, "If it won't tire you, would you please take me to the mosque?" I told him repeatedly that I could take him to the mosque every day, but he always declined, saying, "Whenever I feel like going there I ask you, don't I?" Anyway, I'd sit him down on the ablution platform, remove his delicate shoes and, after securing them in my sack, sit snug against the wall. From the platform His Reverence would drag himself to the prayer rows. Only once could I endure seeing him labour in this fashion. Never again. My courage wouldn't hold. After I'd removed his shoes I'd quickly cover my face with the bottom of my shirt, raising it only after he called out for me.

'On the way back, I took him home through some of the longer lanes of our *qasba*. At this he never failed to remark, "You take a meandering route, Chinta Ram, only to please me. I suppose you don't think that I notice. But it pains me to see how you have to lug me around like this, to waste your time."'

'How could anyone have told him, "But, Aqa, this period is the high point of my life; this inconvenience, the very purpose of my being. You say I have to lug you around. Hardly! I feel I'm carrying the phoenix, whose auspicious shadow falls on me alone."

'The day I learnt the *Sikandarnama* and recited it from memory, he became so overjoyed it seemed as though the sovereignty of the seven climes had been bestowed upon him. He showered me with his blessings, for this world and the next, patted my head affectionately, and then rewarded me with a rupee. I considered it as precious as the Black Stone of the Kaba, kissed it, touched it to my eyes, and tucked it into my turban as if it were Sikandar's very own diadem. Meanwhile he went on blessing me, raising both his hands and saying, "You've accomplished what even I couldn't. You are a pious man, and God has granted you this distinction. You may be a shepherd, but you're like Moses. You're a true follower of the Lord of Batha. That's why God has blessed you. And He will bless you even more. You will see much, much prosperity."'

Dauji put his head on his knees and fell silent.

Exams were approaching and Dauji was getting stricter with me. He made sure that I'd be occupied with one thing or another even in my free time. After I'd finished work on one subject, he'd be ready to assault me with the books of the next. Even if I got up to have a drink of water, he pursued me like a shadow, using the time to quiz me about important historical dates. He had made it his routine to be present at the school gate in the afternoon. One day I slipped out through the boarding house door, so he now started to take his perch right in front of my classroom. Not only had I grown irritable and stubborn, but also foul-mouthed as well. *'Dauji ke bachche!'*—had become my catch phrase. I wouldn't even hesitate to call him a dog when I felt put out by the relentless manner in which he put his questions to me. If this made him unhappy, he never said anything more than 'Watch it, Domni. Is this any way to talk? When I find you a wife, the first thing I'm going to tell her is: "Jan-e Pidar, he used to call your father-in-law a dog."'

'Domni!'— that's as far as he went in retaliation to all my insults and name calling. Or, if he felt slightly more hurt he'd call me 'Munh-carhi Domni.' That was the limit of his anger and distress. He never called me by my real name. Whenever my older brother was mentioned, he referred to him as 'Son Aftab' or 'Barkhurdar Aftab.' But he coined a new name for me every day. Among these 'Golu' was his favourite, with 'Tanbura' a close second, followed by 'Mister Hawannaq' and 'Akhfash Square'. 'Domni' was reserved for times when his anger got the better of him. At times I really gave him a hard time. He'd be sitting on his mat reading something, having already served me with an algebra problem, which had taxed my patience to its limit. I'd kick the pile of books and notebooks lying in front of me nd start singing loudly:

'Tere samne baith ke rona te dukh tenun naiyyun dasna.'
(I'll sit in front of you and cry
But I'll never tell you the reason why.)

auji would look at me mystified, and I'd promptly start nging a *qawwali*, clapping out the time: *'Naiyyun, naiyyun, aiyyun dasna te dukh tenun naiyyun dasna dasna, dasna, dasna, asna tenun, tenun, tenun, tenun . . .'*

He'd peer at me over his eyeglasses, smiling, then walk ver to me, pick up my notebook, open it to a fresh page, ick his big hand between my clapping palms, and say with reat tenderness, 'Look, son, this isn't really a difficult roblem.'

But as soon as he removed his hand to explain the roblem, I'd start clapping again.

'Look, son, am I not your Dauji?' he'd ask with great ride.

'No, you're not,' I'd say curtly.

'Then who's your Dauji?' he'd ask, disappointed.

'Voh sachchi sarkar,' I'd point towards the sky and say ischievously. 'He's the true Master, He's the true Provider everybody . . . Come, come goat, tell me now, who's the rovider of everybody?'

He'd get up and start to leave. Just then I'd curl my arms ound his waist. 'Dauji, you're not angry, are you?'

He'd break into a smile. 'Let go of me, Tanbure! Let go me, son! I was just going to get a drink of water. I'll be ght back.'

I'd pretend to be hurt and say, 'Just when the time came explain the equation, Dauji suddenly remembers that 's thirsty.'

He'd promptly sit down and open the notebook.

'Akhfash Square, when you could see very well that it wa a $4x^2$, why didn't you apply the third formula? And eve if . . .'

After all this, God alone knows how long Dauji wen without a drink of water.

It was the second week in February. Only a month and half remained before the final exams. The fear of doomsda had taken hold of me like a ghost. Without any urging fror anybody, I had stepped up my studies and had becom quite serious. But I just didn't get the geometry problem: Try as hard as Dauji might, nothing seemed to work. So i exasperation one day he told me, 'There are fifty-tw propositions in all. Just memorize them. There's no othe way.' So I started cramming. But any proposition I' memorize the night before would be forgotten by th morning. I became disheartened, and felt beaten. Or evening, after he had finished making me draw a assortment of geometrical diagrams and had drilled me i a number of exercises, Dauji too became anxious. I' faltered many times, and he felt quite crushed. When he ha left, after ordering me to bed right away, I took out m notebook and pencil and wrote like mad, cramming unt one-thirty in the morning. But whenever I'd try to wri down a proposition without looking at the book, I'd g stuck after only a few words. I nearly cried, imaginir Dauji's crestfallen face and my own hopeless condition. went out into the courtyard and sat on the stairs ar actually broke into tears. Huddled with my head on m knees, I cried and shivered from the cold at the same tim An hour or so later it struck me that the only way to sav Dauji's honour was to open the door and leave for goo

Having made my decision, I raised my head to begin acting on it, and who did I see but Dauji, standing in front of me wrapped up in a blanket. He pulled me to himself and hugged me with great affection, and I broke into sobs which resounded throughout the courtyard. He gently kissed me on the forehead and said, 'Well now, Tanbure, what's this? I didn't think you'd give up so easily.'

He then wrapped the blanket round both of us and led me back to my room. He sat me on the bed, carefully wrapped the comforter around me, and himself sat down in a chair, tucking his legs underneath himself.

'Euclidean geometry,' he remarked, 'is a hard nut to crack. It's made you miserable. Well, it used to make me miserable too. But in a different way. I had already gone through and taken notes from all the algebra and geometry books I could find at my Hazrat Maulana's. Nothing in them seemed inaccessible. I thought I'd mastered mathematics. One night as I lay in my bed thinking about a certain problem which had to do with isosceles triangles, I got confused. I lit my oil lamp and drew the diagram and thought about it deeply. The "given" seemed OK from an algebraic point of view, but I couldn't come up with a geometric proof. The whole night I kept working on the problem, but I didn't cry like you. Early in the morning, when I appeared before the Hazrat, he drew the problem on paper and started explaining it to me. But the point where I'd got stuck was precisely the point where his otherwise penetrating intelligence also felt some resistance. And he said, "Chinta Ram, we can no longer teach you. At the point where a student's and a teacher's learning coincide, the student is well advised to look for another teacher."

'I gathered my courage and said, "If anyone else had

suggested it, I'd have considered it out-and-out *kufr*. But, Huzur, since you say it, your smallest word is like a Divine command unto me. How can Ayaz, a mere slave, dare say a word before Mahmud, his Ghaznavi master?! I accept what you say, but I feel terrible."

'He said, "Come now. Don't be so sentimental. Hear me out."

'I bowed my head and said, "Please go on."

"In Delhi," he said, "Hakim Nasir Ali Sistani is considered a great expert in geometry. Since you like geometry so much, maybe you should go and study with him. I'd be happy to write him a recommendation for you."

'I expressed my willingness. But he said, "Go and ask your mother first. If she agrees, then come back to me."

'Ask Mother to let me go? There was no chance of this ever happening, so I didn't ask her. When the Huzur inquired about the matter, I told him some lie, like I was busy whitewashing the house and would ask her when I was done.

'The next few days I spent in great nervous tension. Day and night I struggled with myself to find a way out of the problem, but it proved quite intractable. Its unyielding severity made me more confused and flustered. I wanted to go to Delhi, but I couldn't hope to get either the Huzur's permission or his reference letter, at least not without proof of my mother's consent. Which she, at such an advanced age, was not likely to give.

'One night, when the entire village was asleep, and I was feeling as despondent as you feel today, I took half the money, a total of two rupees, from the savings my mother kept in a small basket, and slipped out of the village. May God forgive me for this, and may He keep the souls of those two elders forever pleased with me. Really, I'd committed a great sin. My head will remain bowed before them with shame and guilt until the end of time.

'I came to the place behind the haveli where the Huzur used to sit and teach. I fell to my knees, kissed the ground, and said in my heart, "I'm indeed an unfortunate man. I'm leaving without your permission, but I'll forever need your blessings. And if you don't forgive me, I'll die at your feet."

'With these words, I picked up my staff, laid it on my shoulder, and set out . . . Are you listening?' Dauji looked at me intently.

Huddled inside my comforter I sat still as a porcupine. I blinked my eyes quickly a few times and said in a hushed voice, 'Yes.'

Dauji resumed: 'Providence really was on my side. They were laying the railroad tracks for the Jakhul-Junaid-Saras-Hisar line in those days. This was the most direct route to Delhi, and one could also get work along the way. So I'd work one day and walk the next two. Thus, with the assistance of the Invisible, I made it to Delhi in sixteen days. But while I had reached the place of my desire, the object of my desire still eluded me. I was unable to locate the house of Hakim Nasir Ali Sistani. Nobody seemed to know where he lived. I searched for two days, without any success. Luck, however, still hadn't abandoned me. New houses were being built for the British. I found work there. In the evening, I'd look for Hakim Sahib's quarters, and at night spread out my *khes* in a dharmshala and sleep soundly upon it. Finally one day—as the saying goes, "He who seeks, finds"—I found out where Hakim Sahib lived. His house was in one of the dingy, dark alleys of the stone-workers' neighbourhood. I presented myself to him that evening. He was sitting in a small room talking to some friends in a loud voice. I removed my shoes and stood at the threshold. One of the gentlemen asked, "Who is it?"

'I greeted them and said, "I've come to see Hakim Sahib."

'Hakim Sahib sat surrounded by his friends, his head bowed and his back towards me. Without altering his posture he asked, *"Ism-e girami?"* (Your respected name sir?)'

'I joined my hands and replied, "I've come from Punjab and . . . "

'Before I could finish he said in a loud voice, "Oh, so you are Chinta Ram!"

'I didn't know what to say. But he went on. "I got a letter from Ismail. He writes: 'Chinta Ram might visit you. He's run away from home, without telling us. Help him.'"

'I remained standing in silence. This prompted him to say in his sweet, strong voice, "Miyan, come on in. What's this—have you sworn not to speak?"

'Even when I took a few steps toward him, he didn't bother to look at me and continued to sit huddled like a new bride. Then, in a commanding voice, he said, "Barkhurdar sit down."

'I promptly sat down where I was. He said to his friends "Give me a minute. Let me settle with him first." He then asked me, again in a commanding voice, "All right, what's the geometry problem you don't get?"

'Timidly I told him. Without changing his posture he reached for his shoulders, pulled his shirt up so that his back was completely exposed, and said, "Come on, use your finger and draw the isosceles triangle on my back."

'I went into a daze, unable to move. After a minute, he said. "Come on, miyan, hurry up. I'm blind, so this is my paper and pen."

'I took a timid step toward him and, shaking all over

started to trace the triangle on his broad back. After I'd drawn the invisible figure, he said, "Now draw a perpendicular line b from point s to point *j*."

'I was completely flustered to begin with. And on top of this, there was nothing there to see. So I took a guess, placed my finger on a spot, and just as I was about to draw the perpendicular, he said sharply, "What're you doing? That isn't point s!" And then, "Well, you'll get used to it, in time. Six finger-widths below the left shoulder is point s, draw the line from there."

'*Allahu Akbar! Allahu Akbar!* I can't even begin to tell you how learned he was! What an incredible voice he had! What sharp intelligence! He was explaining while I sat wonder-struck. It seemed that right then, with this last sentence of his, the isosceles triangle was about to appear on his back in lines of pure light.'

By now Dauji had drifted off into a recollection of his time in Delhi. His eyes were wide open. He was looking at me. Then again, he was not. I asked impatiently, 'What happened then, Dauji?'

Getting up from the chair he said, 'It's late. Go to sleep. I'll tell you some other time.'

But, like an unruly child, I wouldn't leave him alone. So he said, 'All right, but you must first promise not to let despair get the better of you. That you will consider these trifling geometrical propositions to be just like so many *batasha* sugar drops.'

'I'll consider them pure halva, don't worry.'

Still standing, he draped the blanket around himself and said, 'The long and short of it is this: I remained in Hakim Sahib's attendance for a year and washed my blind eyes with the few drops I could gather from that Ocean of Knowledge and Learning. When I got back, I went straight to the presence of my *aqa* and placed my head at his feet. Whereupon he said, "Chinta Ram, I'd pull back my feet if I had the strength to do so." I broke into tears at this, and he said, passing his hand lovingly over my head, "I'm not angry with you, but one year is an unbearably long time. Next time when you decide to go away, don't forget to take me along."'

Tears surged into Dauji's eyes as he repeated these words. He slipped out of the room, leaving me stupefied and still.

The exams were just around the corner now. The very thought gave me the shivers. But, strangely, my body was getting fatter, which became a source of great consternation for Dauji. He'd often grab my chubby hands and retort, 'Be a thoroughbred Arabian charger, don't just sit around like a tethered donkey!'

I'd take great umbrage at this remark and in protest I'd stop speaking to him. Even my constant threats of fast-unto-death failed to move him and his worry turned into full-fledged anxiety. One day he woke me up before his morning stroll and, despite my kicks and screams, my pleas and curses, pulled me out of bed and stuffed me into my coat. Grabbing me by the arm he practically dragged me out of the house. It was a winter morning, around four o'clock, not a soul anywhere in sight throughout the alley, completely dark all around, and Dauji was taking me for a stroll! I was talking nonsense. To which he responded, 'He's still groggy! The Tanbura's still tuning up.' Adding, now and then, 'Come on, Tanbure, play in tune! What's this strumming off-beat!'

Dauji let go of my arm only after we'd gotten far outside

the village and the icy gales of the morning had forced my eyes open. We passed the Persian wheel belonging to the Sardars and left it behind, then the river, then even the cemetery, but Dauji kept walking on as if possessed, reciting what sounded like verses from the Quran. When we reached the rubble mound, I practically dropped dead from fright. People avoided walking through that area even in broad daylight, because it was believed to be the site of a city buried long ago, haunted by the victims' ghosts who ate the heart of anyone who happened to wander through. When I began to tremble with fear, Dauji carefully wrapped a warm muffler around my neck and ordered, pointing to the two acacia trees up ahead, 'Run around them as fast as you can. Ten times. Then breathe deeply a hundred times, and then come back. I'll wait for you here.'

To get away from the haunted hill, I took off toward the trees. First I sat down on a rock to catch my breath, and figured I had sat long enough to have run six of the ten rounds. I got up and ran the last four laps around the trees at the slow pace of a camel and then sat down on the same rock again, taking my deep breaths. Meanwhile, strange animals started howling near the trees, and an excruciating pain shot through my ribs. I thought it best to return to the hill, wake up the drowsing Dauji, and after we had returned home, to let him have it. Filled with anger and shaking with fear, I picked my way to the hill. And what did I see but Dauji kneeling on the rubble, as he thrashed his head like a mad man, loudly reciting his favourite couplet:

Jafa kam kun keh farda roz-e mehshar
bah pesh-e' ashiqan sharmindah bashi
(Don't be so cruel, lest tomorrow at Resurrection
you may come to feel small in the company of lovers.)

He'd strike the ground with his palms, look up and wave his index finger in the air, as if saying to somebody who stood before him, 'Come, think it over. I'm telling you . . . I'm telling you . . .' Then he'd lunge and throw himself on the rubble, repeating over and over again, on the verge of tears, '*Jafa kam kun, jafa kam kun.*'

For a while I stood frozen. Then I screamed and, instead of the *qasba*, ran back toward the acacias, as the realization hit me that Dauji—there can be absolutely no doubt about it—knew the *ism-e a'zam*, the sovereign charm, and was presently trying to bring a genie under control. What I'd seen with my own eyes standing before him was none other than a genie—exactly like the one in the illustrated edition of the *Thousand and One Nights*. But Dauji, unable to subdue him with the charm, had himself fallen before him, screaming again and again, '*Jafa kam kun, jafa kam kun.*' The genie, however, wouldn't let go of him.

I sat down on the same rock and started to cry.

After some time Dauji appeared, back to his normal self, and said, 'Come, Tanbure, let's go,' and I, smitten with fear, meekly followed him. On the way, he seized the two loose ends of his turban, now come undone and hanging from his neck, and started to sing, rocking his head to and fro:

> *Tere lamme lamme val Farida turya turya ja.*
> (Walk along briskly, Farida
> Your long hair streaming behind.)

As I was walking behind this magician, with my own eyes I saw his head change its shape: his serpentine curls began to hang down past his shoulders, his entire body became covered with long, matted hair. Past that day no amount of threat, not even being hacked to pieces, could induce me to go out with him for a walk again.

Just a few days after this, big clods of earth and pieces of brick began to fall into our courtyard. Bébé raised hell with her yelling and screaming. She stuck to Dauji like a bitch with pups. She pounced on him, hitting him so hard that he fell to the ground. She was screaming hysterically all the while, 'You old warlock, look what your spells have done, your Farsi, your black magic! It's all backfired! The evil spirits you've let loose are throwing bricks at my house! They want to destroy it! They want death!'

She started to scream even harder. 'He's killing me! He's burnt me alive, people! This old fool has cooked up a plan to take my Amichand's life! He's cast a spell on me! He's broken every bone in my body!'

Amichand was as dear to Dauji as his very own life. How could he be out to kill him? But it is also true that all that ghostly brick-throwing had been set in motion entirely on account of Dauji. When I backed Bébé up on this, Dauji, for the first time in his life, spoke harshly to me: 'You're an idiot. And your Bébé, *Umm-e Jahileen*— What, you've started believing in *jinn-bhuts?* After I've been teaching you for a whole year? Oh, how you disappoint me! What a pity, instead of placing your trust in knowledge, you've come to believe in women's superstitions. What a pity!'

Leaving Bébé to her screams and Dauji to his moans of regret, I climbed up to the rooftop and sat down in the sun.

That very evening, as I was returning to Dauji's from my house, Ranu, squinting as usual, asked me, 'I hear rocks are coming down at your Pandit's house. Hope you didn't get hurt—did you, Babu?'

I didn't want to tangle with the low-life, so I quietly stepped into the *devrhi*. That evening, as Dauji listened to me go over the geometry propositions, he suddenly asked, 'Son, do you really think that *jinn-bhuts* and *pari-churels* are real?'

When I said that I did think so, he chuckled and said, 'You really are very naïve. I'm sorry I snapped at you today. Why didn't you tell me before that *jinns* existed, that they could throw bricks? I wouldn't have gone through the trouble and expense of having Wali, the mason, and Phatte, the labourer, build the rain portico for us; I could have just as easily asked one of your *jinns* to do the work—and for free, to boot. But tell me this, do the *jinns* only throw bricks? Or do they also know how to lay them?'

'Laugh as much as you want, Dau, but the day a brick cracks your head open, you will know.'

'Not in a million years, and certainly not by a brick one of your *jinns* hurls. You know why? Because a *jinn* just doesn't exist. He can't pick up a brick, so there's no question of it hitting my head, or for that matter yours, or your Bébé's.'

After a pause he added: 'Listen. It is a basic law of physics that a material object just can't be moved by something non-material. You follow me?'

'I understand,' I said hotly.

While our *qasba* did have a high school, it had no facility for taking the high school exams. For that we had to go to the district center. So, when the day arrived for our class to leave for the exams, parents and such like gathered around our lorry. Dauji was not one to stay away. While the parents and relatives of other boys were sending them off with blessings and prayers, Dauji, having jotted down the summary of the main points of a year's worth of instruction, was bombarding me with one question after another, answering them himself along with me. From a question on the reforms introduced by Akbar, the Mughal emperor, he'd next jump to a question about the causes of weather changes, and thereon to: 'Then came along another king who, by his comportment, resembled a Hindu. He was dead drunk, and a woman . . .'

'Jahangir,' I answered.

'And the woman?'

'Nur Jahan,' both of us answered together.

'What's the difference between *sifat-e mushabbah* and *ism a'il?'*

I dutifully explained the difference.

'Examples?'

I gave him a few examples.

The rest of the boys had by then already boarded the orry. Somehow I pried myself free from Dauji and darted nto the vehicle. But he was not about to let me off the hook o easily. He swung around and walked over to the window nd threw yet another question at me: 'Make sentences ısing "break in" and "break into."'

I made the sentences.

The engine started and the lorry began to move. Dauji ept coming along and shouted, *'Tanbure, madiyan* means *hori* and *makiyan* means *murgi.* Remember: *madiyan—ghori, nakiyan—murghi, madiyan—ghori, makiyan—murghi . . .'*

It took me a whole year to get this drum-beat repetition ut of my head and begin to breathe freely.

The first day, I did well in the history exam. Still better he next day in the geography exam. The third day was a unday. The math exam was scheduled for the following day. On Sunday morning I received a page-long letter from Dauji crammed full of nothing but algebraic formulas and mathematical laws.

After the exam I came out to the veranda and compared my answers with some of the other boys. I'd done well enough to score 80 out of a total of 100 points. I went wild with joy. My feet scarcely touched the ground, exclamations of joy pouring out of my mouth. As soon as I stepped out of the veranda, I saw Dauji. He was standing with his *khes* thrown around him, looking intently at the math exam he had borrowed from one of the students. I hugged him, screaming 'Eighty points! Eighty points!'

He grabbed the paper from my hands and asked with bitterness in his voice, 'Show me, which ones did you get wrong?'

'The one about the four walls,' I said, still swaying with exhilaration.

He become irritated and said, 'You must have forgotten to subtract the area of the windows and doors.'

I hugged his waist and shook him like a tree. 'Yes, yes To hell with the windows!'

'You've ruined me, Tanbure,' Dauji said in a sinking voice. 'All those three hundred and sixty-five days—how cried myself hoarse warning you to be extra careful when you attempted the question about surfaces. But you weren't careful. You just let yourself forget it. You wasted twenty points . . . an entire twenty points!'

And looking at his face, my eighty per cent success was so overshadowed by my twenty per cent failure that it seemed to have no reality at all. On the way back, he kept muttering to himself the entire time, 'If the examiner turns out to be a charitable man, he'll at least allow for one point The rest of your exam is correct.'

Dauji remained with me there till the end of exams. He'd stay in the *sarae* where our entire class was housed and instruct me clear up to midnight, after which he would leave, as he said, for a friend's. He'd be back at eight in the morning to accompany me to the exam hall.

The exams over, I dropped Dauji from my life as if I never knew him. I'd spend the entire day roaming around with my friends, and my evenings reading novels. In between, if I had the time and inclination, I'd drop in to say 'Hello' to Dauji. He was insistent that I spend at least an hour with him every day so that he could prepare me for college. But I was not about to walk into his trap. Flunking a hundred times in college was infinitely more agreeable to me than studying—or even talking—with him. It still is. Even if I only casually asked him something, he'd tell me to translate it into Farsi. When I did so, he'd tell me to break it up syntactically. Somehow, as we were talking, the Havaldar's cow barged into the house; I tried to drive it out with a stick, but Dauji could only think to ask me, 'Is "cow" a noun or a verb?' Even an idiot with a fifth class education knew that it is a noun. But Dauji's verdict: it's both. A noun as well as a verb. 'To cow' means to harass, to threaten.

All this went on after I'd taken my exams and was waiting for the results. One day some of my friends and I decided to go hunting. I begged my friends not to go by way of the courthouse, because Dauji was sure to be there. He'd stop me and start asking about all those idioms which have to do with hunting, guns, and cartridges.

If I spotted him in the bazaar, I'd quickly slink into a side alley. And on those rare occasions when I did go to greet him, out of courtesy to be sure, I'd spend more time with Bébé than with Dauji. He'd often say, 'You're abandoning us just as Aftab did.' And out of pure mischief, I'd respond, '*Khele khub, khele khub!*' and start laughing.

The day my results were announced, Abbaji and I visited Dauji with a small basket of laddoos. We found him sitting on his *haseer*, with his head bent low. But he got up the minute he saw Abbaji, went inside the room and promptly returned with a chair, which he placed next to his gunny sack mat. 'Doctor Sahib,' he began, 'I'm genuinely ashamed. Fate works in strange ways. I was expecting a first division for him. Unfortunately it couldn't be. He started with a weak foundation . . .'

'But I missed it by only a single point!' I chimed in.

He looked at me and said, 'You have no idea how that one point has broken my heart. But, I must consider it God's will.'

Abbaji and he began to talk and I went over to Bébé and started to chat with her.

In my first days at college, I always wrote back to Dauji promptly; later, only sporadically. Gradually, our correspondence practically ceased.

Back home on vacations I went to greet Dauji just as I would any other of my former school teachers. Now, though, he no longer threw questions at me. He felt happy seeing me all dressed up in *kot*, *patloon*, and *ta'i*. He wouldn't let me sit on the cot. 'If you won't let me grab a chair for you,' he'd say, 'then at least bring it yourself.'

I'd pull a chair up beside him and sit down. He'd express his desire to look at the books I'd checked out from our college library, and in spite of my promise to bring them over to him, he'd show up at our house the very next day to have a look.

Amichand, for reasons best known to himself, had meanwhile dropped out of college and left for Delhi to work in a bank. Bébé still stitched clothes for her neighbourhood customers, and Dauji still sat outside the courthouse, though he brought hardly any money home. Bibi wrote home now and then. She was living a happy, contented life. A year's worth of college life had managed to put a lot of distance between Dauji and myself.

The girls, who until a couple of years ago freely played all sorts of games with us boys, had now become self-conscious and shy. Throughout my second year at college I tried, and to a degree even succeeded, in spending my vacations away from home. The long journey to Abbotabad seemed considerably more appealing and satisfying than the short trip home.

It was during this time that I bought myself a lovely pink writing pad with matching envelopes—my first ever. Obviously not the kind on which one wrote to Abbaji or Dauji. Dasehra vacations came and went, as did the Christmas break, and Easter afterwards. The days just rolled on.

As the time for the country's independence drew near, a series of clashes broke out and fast deteriorated into violent attacks and bloodshed. News of communal riots started to pour in from all over. So Amma promptly had all of us return home. This was still the safest place for us. Banias and rich merchants began to flee, leaving their property behind. But other Hindus and Sikhs had not yet made a move. Shortly thereafter refugees from across the border started to stream in, bearing the news that the country had finally become independent.

One day a few houses were torched in our *qasba*, too,

and on at least two street corners fierce battles took place. The police and military declared a curfew. When it was lifted, all the Hindu and Sikh residents of our *qasba* fled.

In the afternoon when Amma sent me to find out about Dauji, I saw all kinds of strange faces in that familiar lane. An ox stood tethered in the *devrhi* of Dauji's house, with a gunny-sack curtain hanging behind it. I rushed home with the news that Dauji and Bébé too had fled, and choked as I said the words. I felt as though Dauji had left us for good, that he was not going to come back. Ever.

But Dauji was not as faithless as that.

Three days later at the local mosque, long after sundown, after I had taken down the names of the freshly arrived refugees and promised to have blankets sent to them, as I was walking through that same alley, I saw a crowd of perhaps two hundred men gathered in the open field. *Muhajir* boys, brandishing lathis, were shouting slogans and abuses all at once. I made an attempt to tear through the throng and penetrate to its center, but the ominous, bloody look in the eyes of the *Muhajirs* held me back. A boy was telling an older man:

'He'd gone away to the neighbouring village. When he returned, he just went straight into his house.'

'Which house?'

'The one the refugees from Rohtak have claimed,' answered the boy.

'So?' the elderly man asked.

'So nothing. They seized him. Found out he was a Hindu.'

Just then someone from the crowd yelled, '*Oai* Ranu, run! Come quickly! This one's yours. The Pandit. Just the one for you!'

Ranu, at the time, was driving his goats back to the

enclosure. He halted them, asked a lathi-wielding boy to keep an eye on them, and himself lunged into the crowd.

My heart skipped a beat: was it Dauji they had grabbed? Without even looking at the accused man, I pleaded with the people nearest me, 'He is a good man. A pious man. Don't hurt him, please! He is . . .'

Several pairs of hate-filled eyes glowered at me, and a young man, brandishing his chopper, threatened me, 'Maybe I should let you have it too! Supporting him like the devil's own advocate! You weren't there, that's why!'

Others in the crowd heaped abuse on me and concluded, 'Must be an *Ansar*.'

Scared, I ran to the other side of the crowd and tried to blend in. Ranu, along with a contingent of his friends, stood surrounding Dauji. He was tugging at Dauji's chin and mocking him, 'Come, son, what do you have to say?'

Dauji just stood there in silent immobility. Suddenly a youngster snatched the turban from Dauji's head and yelled, 'His *bodi!* First, clip off the *bodi!*' And Ranu dutifully obliged, clipping it off with the sickle he used for pruning twigs and branches.

'Should we let him have it now?—what do you say?' the same youngster asked.

Ranu replied, 'Nah! Let him go. He's far too old. Maybe I can use him to tend my goats.'

Seizing Dauji by the chin and lifting his face up, Ranu ordered, 'All right, Pandata, let's hear you recite the *kalimah!*'

'Which one?' Dauji asked, softly.

Ranu struck Dauji's now bare head so hard that he nearly fell down. He fumed, '*Salé*, bastard, you make fun of me? You think there are five, six, seven *kalimahs* or what?'

After he was finished reciting the *kalimah*, Ranu shoved

his lathi into Dauji's hands and said, 'Get going, you coot, the goats are waiting for you.'

Bareheaded, Dauji started off behind the goats, as though he were Farida, the one with the long flowing hair.

Banished

Jamila Hashimi

Birds flap away overhead. Daylight, turning a ripe shade of yellow, has descended to the steps of Achchal's large tank, and the ebbing rays have given the Gurdwara's spire a golden-white tint. The fair beyond the vast field is beginning to wind down. Dasehra effigies will be set on fire before long. People will shout and scream, flee in mock dread, and the shower of sparks will look like fireworks in the bluish haze of the encroaching evening. The fire's embers will burn and jump for a long while, giving nearby faces a grotesque look, as if every last face, a veritable image of Ravan, has come to watch with glee Sita's ordeal of separation, her gruelling banishment all over again.

Banishment is a hard thing to endure. But does one have control over anything? Anything at all? Who wants to suffer knowingly?

Bhai used to say, 'What is it with you, Bibi? Always dreaming. This love lavished upon you today, the gaiety that engulfs you, all this will slowly end. Time diminishes everything, but so slowly that we get used to it.'

Where is Bhai today? If the breeze, dipped in the scent of my homeland, which chases me like a spy, could somehow backtrack and find him, I would beg it, 'Go, ask him why the pain doesn't diminish. Toiling for years under oppressively heavy burdens and trudging along difficult paths, why does man still dream, longing for happiness? Why does he love light incurably'?

Why did Sitaji, after her exile had ended, pray for only

one thing: to meet her Ramchandraji again? Doesn't misfortune harden the substance in man that longs for happier days? Why can't one come to love the dark? Yes, why not?

The pear tree has blossomed every year since Munni was born. When the seasons change, its branches are filled with flowers, the tree bends over heavy with fruit, deepening its bond with the earth. Its roots burrow deeper into the soil. No one can rupture that bond.

Munni has grown now. How quietly the years have padded past me!

Today Bari Ma asked Gurpal, 'Kaka, take bahu and the children out to see the Dasehra fair. She hasn't stepped out of the village once in so many years.'

Gurpal snapped, 'When did you ever ask me to take her out, Ma? If she hasn't set foot outside the village, how am I to blame for it?'

Yes, how can anyone be blamed for that, really?

Whenever anyone calls me bahu, I feel insulted. I have been hearing this word for years, ever since the evening when Gurpal dumped me in this courtyard and cried to Bari Ma, who was sitting on a *chauki*. 'Look, Ma, I've brought you a bahu. A real beauty! The best of the lot!'

Bari Ma, raising the wick of the earthen oil lamp, strode over to me. My eyes were glazed over with hunger and dread. I had walked barefooted for miles and had no strength left even to raise my hand. I just collapsed at her feet. A single cow and a few buffaloes tethered in the courtyard stared at me for a while, then got up, leaving the fodder untouched.

Bari Ma sized me up from head to toe, again and again and then said to her son, 'If you had behaved like a responsible young man, I wouldn't have been in such straits today. I've practically gone blind from blowing into the fire to keep the hearth going. Even the *kaharis,* who helped out earlier, keep away from us, because we cannot give them any grain at harvest time. Just tell me, how much longer do you expect me to manage this house without any kind of help? If you could only put your heart back into farming, I could see some relief.'

Gurpal said, 'But at least look at her. You don't have to put up with the airs of the *mahris* and *kaharis* anymore. Here, I've brought you a bahu. She is your maid. She will do whatever you tell her to do—grind grain, fetch water, anything you want. I won't meddle.'

Many such 'brides' were brought to the village of Sangraon, but without the customary fanfare: no festive music, no racy songs to the beat of drums, no comic antics or spins or hip-thrusts of nautch girls.

No one oiled my dust-coated hair. No *na'in* was sent for to make me up. I became a bride without a single piece of jewellery, without any sindur for the parting of my hair.

Bari Ma heard Gurpal and looked at me as if I were some kind of calamity her grandson had picked up from the street. Still holding the lamp in her hand she quietly walked over into the kitchen. Nobody said a word to me. Oh, what a welcome this new bride was offered!

Since that day I too felt like Sita, enduring her exile, incarcerated in Sangraon.

At the fair the shopkeepers are taking down their wares, yelling obscenities at each other, puffing away at their biris. They are dumping their gear on the pack donkeys with such cruel force, as if the animals were made of wood and had no feeling. The chariots used in the Ram Lila show are standing at one side, and the boys who staged the performance are gobbling milk fat qulfis and pakoras with spicy hot sauce, unmindful of the stains the snacks have left on their colourful costumes, stains that look like a leper's open, ugly sores. Munni is so fascinated that she just stands and gawks at them. She doesn't even care that she could get lost. But what has care ever accomplished? One destined to be lost will be lost, even in a house full of people.

Gurpal tugs at her. My two boys are tired and grumpy. Every time they see a vendor, they tearfully insist on buying something from him. This is, after all, a fair. Here mothers, unmindful of their little ones, just forge ahead, carried forward by shoves and pushes. Their little lost children gaze in panic at every approaching face, and then bolt, crying. But when do those separated at a fair ever come together again? The separation stands like a wall between people who meant a world to each other once. Faces for which we are willing to sacrifice everything, on the faint hope that we might see them just once, vanish irretrievably. Paths, like the watery webs etched on the waves by minuscule crawling marine life, dissolve behind us. We can never backtrack on the paths we have already taken. Nothing ever returns. And the milling, jostling crowd at the fair can only move forward.

'Time lost is never regained,' Bhaiyya would say, whenever he spotted me neglecting my studies or playing doll house with my girlfriends after school. 'Bibi, you must know that every moment past is erased. It turns to dust.'

That doll house was a gift from my Baba, who had bought it at an exposition.

Munni is daintily holding her large rag doll with both her hands. Again and again she bends over and looks at it while Gurpal is peering into the crowd above. The two boys, holding on to the clay replicas of Ravan, look at every passing face with astonished eyes. There is so much affection for her doll in Munni's eyes—a hideous face made of some rag over which the eyes and nose have been drawn with some odd colours, a ring in its nose. Her head covered with a goldfringed chunri, holding on to her laihnga, this cheap little nautch girl would whirl into a dance any minute. So it seemed.

The path back to Sangraon leads along the edge of Achchal's watertank and through some fields. Life's caravan moves along. Even if there is nowhere in particular to go as one meanders through life's straight or crooked paths, one still must go on, never stopping, on and on, even if one's feet are bruised, one's heart totally empty.

The bluish haze has descended still further over the landscape. Evenings make me sad; I wonder why. A solitary star throbs forlornly in the sky, like the flickering flame of an earthen lamp. In the blue, empty space its loneliness reminds me of my banishment. In this human wilderness I am like a lonely tree which neither blossoms nor bears fruit.

The star calls back to mind the ship in which Bhai had sailed across the seas to a far country. With his improbably large baggage, as he was getting ready to leave, my mother's voice was overcome by grief. And yet she held back her tears, as she took care of his things and prayed for him silently in her heart. Outside the house, Baba was busy taking care of the arrangements. Bhaiyya was visibly sad. And Aapa was padding back and forth in the courtyard as if in a stupor. Only I was chirping about everywhere in the house. After all, unless you're wounded yourself, you don't know how badly it hurts.

All of us went to the port to see Bhai off. While Bhaiyya was busy going up and down the gangway taking care of the travel papers and personally overseeing the loading of Bhai's bags, I bent over the guard rail. Peering into the greenish muddy waters below I fired one question after another at Bhai: 'What's wrong with this water? Why are there oil slicks all over it? Why are there boats? Oars? And doesn't one feel scared when a boat pitches on tall waves?' The barrage of questions exasperated him and he answered impatiently, 'All these things, Bibi you will come to know on your own when you grow up.'

Today, I do know. I know how a boat without oars capsizes and sinks. But it doesn't always have to sink in the water. It can sink just as easily on the shore. Often a single wave is enough to send it to the ocean floor. Now that I'm grown up and have come to know things, Bhai is nowhere near me anymore.

The ship's siren sounded. Baba hugged Bhai, affectionately patted him on the head and said, 'Well then, may God be with you!' Bhaiyya, overcome with emotion, threw his hands around Bhai. Aapa, sensitive and faint-hearted, broke down in sobs. Bhai comforted her, 'Just look at Bibi, how happy she is. What's there to cry about? I'll be back in two years. I'm not going away forever—am I?' And then he hugged me and said, 'Bibi, I'll bring you presents from—guess where?—Paris. Just keep writing to me—you will, won't you?' And I had nodded my head vigorously.

When the final whistle sounded, Bhai walked away so casually, as though he were only going somewhere nearby. We kept waving our handkerchiefs until the ship disappeared from view.

The port lights swayed on the waves, and the light of the receding ship flickered like a lonely star and then faded away. And with it, whatever lights my life had known also faded away forever. Not even a stray gleam ever came up from the waves.

How I hugged Amma and sobbed. I heard somebody whisper into my heart, 'Never! You shall never see Bhai's face again!' My heart was throbbing fitfully, like the lonely star trembling with apprehension above the blue mist in the clear western sky.

The dark of the evening is spreading over the orchards in the distance. Gurpal has hoisted the two boys up on his shoulders, walking ahead of us on the white trails snaking through the fields. Munni is trailing along slowly. Ten fields up ahead, after crossing beyond the water ditches, he would wait until we caught up with him, meanwhile telling the boys the story of Ravan. But how would he ever know that Sita is trailing behind him, that he is Ravan himself?

Munni tells me: 'Ma, Swarup's Mama has sent her colourful clothes for Dasehra. All silk. They feel very nice. But, Ma, I don't have a Mama to give me such beautiful gifts. What's the matter with you, Ma? Why don't you say something? Didn't you like the fair? Are you tired?'

'Yes, Munni, I'm tired. I've grown old. I've had to walk far.'

'No, you're not old,' Munni said, full of youthful confidence, as she looked at me. 'You look just like the image of a goddess. Bari Ma says the same thing.'

How could Munni ever know how far I've had to walk? The immense distance from one life to another. When man's body shrinks and turns rigid, his heart is emptied of all hope. Then he's fit to be worshipped like a god. I've waited so long on the paths leading into Sangraon for those long separated from me that my eyes have glazed over. My heart is empty. I'm Lakshmi. And yet, the bonds of suffering endure. They are deep, strong, unbreakable.

Munni is asking again, 'Ma, don't I have a Mama?'

What shall I tell her? What answer shall I give? I just

stand at the crossroads, lost in my thoughts.

How much I loved Bhaiyya. But I also used to be so afraid of him. No sooner would he enter the house than the end of my chunri would slip automatically up over my head. My gait would become more measured and I'd find myself restraining my laughter. Standing next to him, it seemed nobody in the entire world was taller than him. How I loved my Bhaiyya—who bore himself with restraint and dignity, who talked with an innate sense of decorum. He wrote in perfectly straight lines, never soiled the pages or smudged his fingers with ink. He'd say to me, 'Bibi! When you grow up, you too will write just as neatly.' What if he saw me today? What would he say? So much black ink has been spilled over my fate that you can't see a single straight line on the entire page! Oh, I never did learn to write neatly!

Back in those days I'd set up my doll house and think: We can all live in it—Amma and Baba and I, Bhaiyya and Bhabhi and Aapa. All of us. In here. Life is a sweet song. We need nothing. We lack nothing.

When Bhaiyya got married, I said, 'Our house is a paradise. A perfect heavenly abode.' If I were to have raised my hands back then in prayer, I wouldn't have known what to ask for. Today, too, I haven't asked God for anything. The end points of suffering and joy are not very far apart in this dizzying business called life.

Bhai sailed across the seas, and my dreams of paradise were shattered. The jagged splinters of my broken life have scattered like glass, wounding everyone who comes near me. So no one does. Nor is there anyone going over to the other side, as though the path runs through a cremation ground. It's desolate. Who has the time or inclination to listen to Sitaji's lament in this country? The pain of loneliness is hard to bear. And life so difficult.

Standing up ahead, Gurpal is calling me. He's calling Munni. Both of us are walking very slowly. Only dried stalks stand in the cotton fields now. People gather and walk away, as they always do, with the smiling flowers. The wheat fields are still too young, without ear or grain. Supple, soft plants bend over in the wind. One has to bow to the wind. Everyone does.

Bari Ma must be feeling very impatient. Anxious. An unknown fear on my account troubles her all the time. The pathway to the country, she suspects I might flee to, is fraught with incredible hardship. And besides, I've travelled with Gurpal far too long to have any strength left to strike out in another direction. After all, all walking must cease at some point. One just can't go on forever. Especially when there is nowhere to go. Where can I go—with my wounded heart, my darkened fate? Munni stands in my way. She is the great distance that separates me from my own family. How can I dare look beyond her, beyond that distance?

Parties of minstrels are coming behind us singing bhajans. The fair has wound down and the fair-goers have spilled out on the many paths leading out. Children cry and whimper and sulk as they walk. Labourers, talking loudly, walk past Munni and me, followed by fast-walking barefooted women clad in bright clothes, holding back their veils just a little over their foreheads, packets of sweets bought at the fair in one hand, supporting their children on their shoulders with the other. Their slippers, tied to the ends of their dupattas, are dangling over their backs. An inexorable bond exists between the body and the earth. Nothing can come in between.

People are receding into the distance like a fading blur.

A sadhu, strumming on his iktara, walks past us and turns onto the path to Sangraon. His song is so full of sadness. What he says is right: When hope for light persists . . . I don't hear the strum of his instrument. Only a snatch of the song itself, carried by the wind, reaches my ears.

'Why are you so quiet, Ma? Why don't you say something. I'm scared.' Munni, trying to clutch my hand in the thickening dark, is unable to hold on to her doll. She sobs; her voice is hoarse with tears. She can't think of anything else.

When she grows up, she will know it's useless to fear the dark. Once it has the upper hand, it is practically invincible. Bhai used to say, 'Bibi, there's incredible force in water. It makes its own way.' At the time I couldn't understand the secret of that force. Now I know how circumstances force us each to find our own way. Whenever Bari Ma calls me these days, I cover my head with my embroidered dupatta and answer softly, 'Yes.' I try to finish all my work efficiently, so that I can keep myself busy with more, just to spare myself the feeling of oldness, the assault of all these thoughts.

When I had the time, I had nothing to think about. Now there is something to think about, but I have no time. I feel something is lacking. Try as hard as I might, I can't shake this feeling. Things happen. Then there are days when nothing happens. Today, when I close my eyes, my heart whispers, 'My family will visit me any minute. The moment Bhaiyya sees me, he will say, "What's this, Bibi? Embroidered dupatta? It doesn't become you at all. Come on, take it off. Here, look, what I've brought for you. Forget about your chores. Come, sit with us. Vacations are always too short. When I visit you, don't even think of going anywhere else, of doing anything. Just be with us."'

We would sit on sofas in the big sitting room, talk and look at the framed portraits of the family, sip tea, warm ourselves near the fireplace, and laugh. Amma would call out to us drowsily, 'You can talk in the morning, children. Now go to sleep.' At which Bhaiyya would shout back, 'The whole year I live away from home. I always go to sleep feeling sad and nostalgic. What's the big hurry, Amma? Let's enjoy. We'll go to bed, don't worry.'

And I used to think: Could all this crumble away like a dream one day? The little paradise we had fashioned from love and affection—would it be so covered over with dust that I'd look in vain for even a hint of freshness anywhere? Like photographs, are we merely shadows of reality? It was a crazy heart I had. A heart predisposed to think the oddest thoughts. An impossibly foolish, naïve heart!

I dream of impossible things and feel the excitement take hold of my heart. When I try to reason with it, it retorts, 'So what of it, Bibi? What have you got to lose? When did you ever hear of anyone having power over dreams? And besides, what's so wrong if the one you have been waiting for so long walks straight over to you one day?'

I reply, 'Only darkness is left for me.'

To which it says, 'Despair is the greatest sin.'

What can I possibly hope for? And from whom?

Munni tugs at the edge of my dupatta and asks, 'Ma, tell me, why doesn't Mama come to our house? Are we not going to his place on Diwali? All the other girls are going to see their uncles. Ma, I don't like it here any more. I didn't even like it at the fair. I'm sad. I want to go to my Mama's house.'

Who could tell me where her Mama lives? Outside Sangraon, all other villages look like doll houses to me, devoid of reality. Perhaps Sangraon too is unreal, a mere shadow. Perhaps everything is just a shadow.

And yet my soul keeps looking, for things that could never be found anywhere, hoping to hear voices that will never be heard again.

For some months now, as I carry the basketful of cowdung, churn milk, or clap out and spread dung cakes on the ground, my heart beats in a peculiar way. A familiar fragrance wafts through the air, and I feel sweet melodies, played on different instruments, draw near me. All this makes me lose myself. Still, I know well enough now that those dear to me live in a country I cannot possibly hope to reach. Like the pathways leading to Sangraon, all other paths criss-cross each other so often that they confuse and make one lose one's way. Besides, what is to be gained from searching for a place which now exists only in stories?

Lights from earthen oil lamps flickering through the open doors of well-settled houses call to mind some fairyland picture.

Gurpal, the boys, Munnị and I are now walking together, all side by side. Tall, soft reeds sway in the wind, and arch over to caress my hair with their fuzzy, silken tops, as the breeze, holding the edge of its brocade veil, begins to fall asleep.

It becomes easier if you have companions along the way.

Munni says, 'I'm tired, Ma. I can't walk anymore.' The boys too are whimpering and crying. They're so groggy they can hardly keep their eyes open, or even hold on to their toy Ravans. We leave the path and sit down on the raised trail around a field to catch our breath. Munni drops her head into my lap. Gurpal says: 'You know, lots of children were lost in the fair today. And all because women are so stupid. They lose themselves, forget to hold on to their children. They're so taken in by the Ram Leela, they just gawk at the show and lose sight of their children.'

'Not just at fairs. Children become separated from their mothers even outside fairs,' I say without looking at him, gently patting Munni on the head.

'Can't you ever bring yourself to forget that incident? That was a different time.'

How can I make him understand that time never changes. Man suffers because man cannot forget. *That* time lives on in my memory, just as it was. Flames were going up everywhere. The country had gained its independence. It had also been partitioned. Both Amma and Baba said, 'All these people who're afraid, they are mad. Look how they're fleeing to another country. How can pain, how can suffering even touch you here among your own people?' How naïve they were. Pain always comes from one's own people. Sorrow caused by strangers mean nothing. Life, the whole of it, had lost its beauty. The face of everything was covered with blood. The very people who did charity in the name of Bhagwan, Guru, and Allah slaughtered each other; those who readily laid down their lives to save the virtue of their sisters and daughters considered a woman's honour no more than an illusion. Independence and Partition broke our fetters, yes, but they also gave the lie to the age-old words of brothers and compatriots—words trampled in the dust under the feet of marauding bands of thugs.

Amma said to Baba, 'Maybe we should take the girls and leave. I'm terrified. It makes no sense to trust anyone these days.'

Baba, as collected as ever, tried to comfort her, 'Bibi's mother, you're worrying for no reason at all, just like everyone else. Nobody's going to bother us. Partition was inevitable. All this commotion will die down in a few days.

Don't worry. Everything will be back to normal. Everything.'

In ordinary circumstances this would have been enough to reassure Amma. But not that day. She said, 'It's not just our lives that I fear for. Don't forget, we have grown-up girls. Listen to me, send us to my brother's.'

Baba replied, 'Everywhere roads are infested with village hoodlums. They're butchering entire trains. This is not the time to leave. You just stay put in the house. God will protect us.'

Conditions had certainly made Baba worried, but as time rolled on, he asked us to put our trust only in God. Little did he realize that it was already too late. He sought refuge in the old life and its values. That was his mistake, a mistake for which he paid dearly. As Gurpal was dragging me out of our house, I saw Baba's body lying outside in the ditch, his face with its grey hair lying on the edge of the ditch. Forgetting his closed eyes and bloodied head, he was still praying, to whom only heaven knows. Could this be the time for any prayer to be heard? A shining spear had gone through Amma's chest and she fell on the spot where she had earlier prayed to God for the protection of her honour. And Aapa's screams—I can hear them even today sometimes in the howling gusts of wind. But I was just as helpless that day as I am now. What could I have done? Gurpal was dragging me away. My head was without its customary covering, but then I wasn't expecting to run into Bhaiyya along the way, either. Had he been with me, who would have dared touch me? Drag me so dishonourably in the streets of my birth place, every particle of which I loved with all my heart? Where is that country? My Baba's blood was spilled over it. His grey head was dragged through its dust. If I could so much as snatch a glimpse of that dust, I'd touch it reverentially to my forehead. It certainly was more fortunate than I.

I had a whole slew of things I still wanted to say to Baba. How much I had bothered Amma and teased Bhai and Bhaiyya. And when my body was dragged all the way over to Sangraon, rather than ceremoniously borne in the bridal palanquin, I didn't have a brother there to complain, 'What, as I leave the parental home there isn't anyone even to say goodbye?'

Pain becomes easier to bear if there is hope—just a glimmer of hope—of better days ahead. I never was able to work through it all. What should I erase from my memory? And what should I retain? Gurpal! You never did allow me to look back.

Bari Ma's beatings, Gurpal's abuses, the pangs of hunger—I endured them all seeking strength from the dim light of a lamp flickering somewhere far away, in the hope that one day Bhai and Bhaiyya would perhaps wander into Sangraon looking for me. I'd smile at Bari Ma and without so much as looking at Gurpal I'd just walk away with Bhaiyya. The wind would rustle through the neem leaves and sing and the entire village would celebrate and rejoice. Why does man consider himself the center of the universe? Why, indeed? Unless the eye is used to darkness, one keeps straining for light, dreaming. Hopes keep circling the heart like vagrant thoughts.

Munni's birth loosened my ties with my dreams, and the assembly of hopes around the heart scattered. I learnt to wake up from dreams and take my present for real.

When the two countries made peace, sadness swept over Gurpal. Apprehension, anxiety burrowed inside him. Bari Ma and he would sit on *chaukas* and whisper God alone knows what between themselves. But they never felt the need to tell me anything. Munni had by now started to walk and stammer a few words. All kinds of rumours circulated around me and then subsided like a dust storm. No army ever came to reclaim me.

Subsequently I heard that soldiers from the other country visited a nearby village to seek repatriation of their abducted young women. Repatriate them to what country? Where? To whom? The thought crossed my mind that perhaps Bhai and Bhaiyya too would come looking for me. They must have waited long for me outside the gates of the magic city. I must go. I really must. Everyday I'd tie my hopes into a bundle and peer with anticipation and longing at the bend in the lane.

That winter, soldiers did come to Sangraon to take me back home too. I thought: apart from being a sister to Bhai and Bhaiyya, I was also a mother to Munni. I wondered: who were these soldiers? And what would that country be like? For the first time I felt unsure of myself. My dreamland turned into dust and vanished. I realized that my roots had sunk deep in Sangraon. Decimation, withering, and ruination—who likes them, after all? And besides, every girl must one day leave her parental home to join her in-laws. Well, maybe Bhai and Bhaiyya weren't present at my wedding—so what? Hadn't Gurpal rolled out a carpet of corpses for me? Painted the roads red with blood? Provided an illumination by burning down city after city? Didn't people celebrate my wedding as they stampeded, screaming and crying? It was a wedding, all right. Only the customs were new: celebration by fire, smoke, and blood. He had carried me to Sangraon. The rest of my life was to be spent here in the small dingy room of a mud house surrounded by grain fields. A house filled with the thick blue smoke of cowdung cakes.

Years later when Gurpal brought a book to teach Munni the alphabet, I kept staring at the letters. The words came alive for me. I remembered all the stories that both Bhaiyya and Bhai would tell me, adding, 'Bibi, there are still more wondrous stories in books. You'll read them when you grow up.'

When the army did come to secure my release, I hid myself, just like the princess in the fairy tale. I wasn't about to leave with strangers. Why didn't Bhaiyya and Bhai come to take me away? I felt hurt by both of them. And I've remained angry with them ever since.

Sometimes, when Munni lies down beside me, she asks, 'Ma, you don't visit Mama even on Diwali. Why doesn't anyone ever send us sweets?'

Your Mama never came looking for us, Munni. He never came to take me away. Nobody has so much time in life to go looking for someone. Love finds new crutches. Slowly. Bhaiyya's children must be about as old as Munni now. They must ask their mother all about their Mama. And when they do, I'm sure she isn't forced to remain silent, or to so deftly evade talking about her brother. But there are times when the heart overflows with stories, and yet one remains tongue-tied. All these brides in the neighbourhood sit in the shade of the neem tree spinning their wheels and singing, but I remain quiet. What an aura of joy surrounds them! How sweet songs of their parental homes sound! Seasons change. Every year a father or a brother comes to take one or another woman back home. You should see then how Asha, Rekha, Poroo, and Chandra seem to walk on air. They hug everyone before leaving. Their words sound like pure music.

When the young women climb to the rooftops to make the crows take wing so that they may judge from their flight the direction from which their dear brothers would come, my heart begins to pound in my throat, so violently that I feel it'll burst. When I raise my hand to make a crow fly away, it just falls back limply to my side.

With time Bari Ma grew fond of me. Our bonds became stronger and deeper as I severed my last remaining links with my past. I'm her prized daughter-in-law now, her Lakshmi. She shows off the yarn spun by me to everyone she meets. When other women complain about their daughters-in-law, she praises me to high heaven just to rub it in.

What if the fragrance of grain and wheat mixed with the smoke rising all around turned into a sweet song! The sky arched over them slowly filling with stars; the water of the canal twisting in tiny waves—its notes! What if one day a young man coming along behind the peasants carrying bales of hay on their heads were suddenly to dismount from his horse right in front of my open doors, and I, dropping whatever I was doing, were to run up to him and hug him tightly, shouting 'Bhaiyya!'

Oh, who do I wait for standing in the doorway? How long am I condemned to carry the corpses of my hopes, long since dead? Why have my eyes brimmed over with tears as I stand staring into these serpentine village pathways? If my tears were to fall on Munni she would wake up worried and surely ask, 'Ma, why are you crying?' How would I tell her what ails me? Suppose she asked: 'Ma, why are there tears in your eyes? You cry even on the night of Dasehra. Are you tired?'

Gurpal has put the two boys on his shoulders. Munni and I are bound for Sangraon. Rather than embrace a second exile, Sitaji has accepted a life with Ravan. Where would I find the strength to step out of the darkness with ıothing but uncertainty for support?

All that was bright in my life has stayed behind, like the :ity. And yet, God knows why, I can't bring myself to love his darkness.

I must keep walking. Fatigue has spread throughout my ›ody like pain. All the same, I must keep walking. Exile or ıot, one is compelled to move on in life's fair. As I move ıhead, I cannot help wondering whether Bhai and Bhaiyya :oo sometimes miss me.

It's Munni that I'm most afraid of. Tomorrow, she'll ıgain ask that question. Of that I'm sure. But none of us will ›e able to answer it—not me, not Gurpal, not even, perhaps, 3ari Ma.

Why are some questions so hard, so difficult, that ıobody is able to answer them?

In the long wintry nights, suffering starts up a bonfire, ;ummons old dreams, and listens to stories. How can ;tories ever be true! But the heart is very stubborn. It keeps 'emembering the past. Why?

I want to know: Are there anxieties beyond Sangraon?

The stench of cowdung and urine, mixed with the ragrance of grain, flows on like the stream of life through he uneven village lanes.

Another day has ended. And days do get away from 'ou, like gusts of wind. How far do I still have to go?

Tableland

Upender Nath Ashk

'You seem to be an open-minded person, so I thought I might ask,' Seth Sahib said.

'Please be rest assured,' Dina Nath tried to allay Seth Sahib's fears. 'I'll make sure that the money gets to the Hindu refugees from Punjab.'

'How much do you suppose a blanket costs?' Seth Sahib asked.

'To someone of your means, even a fine, hundred rupee blanket may not seem very nice,' Dina Nath began, feeling a degree of glee within, 'but these are afflicted people. They need warmth more than they need softness. When I was in the sanatorium, Narain, our ward boy, brought one for ten rupees. It was a little coarse, but quite warm.'

'All right, put me down for three blankets.'

Three blankets, meaning thirty rupees. Dina Nath's face lit up with exhilaration. When he had first thought of visiting Seth Hiramal Viramal Advani at the latter's special cottage in the sanatorium complex, he wasn't expecting a donation of more than five rupees. But even that, right at the top of the list of donors, would provide sufficient inducement for the other patients to donate at least a half, maybe even a full rupee. He might just be able to collect enough money to buy a couple, or even as many as four, blankets and send them to help the refugees from Punjab. Within a few days of his stay at the sanatorium he had found out that although patients contributed liberally for entertainment, rummy nights, or no-host parties (to spend a few hours with the beauties at the tables, no doubt), only a few were willing to give for a worthwhile cause, while everyone else bowed out with one excuse or another. This, more than anything else, had prompted him to put down Seth Hiramal Viramal Advani's name at the very top of the list. He was a religious and generous man. But Dina Nath hadn't even imagined that he would give so much at one go. So when the Seth Sahib took out three ten rupee notes and placed them in his hand, the latter smiled courteously as he entered the figure on the list and said, 'Exactly what I had hoped for from you. That's why I started the drive with you.'

'Tell me, have your brother and your other relatives arrived?' Seth Sahib asked.

'They have, in Delhi, but in a very bad way. They had to leave everything behind,' Dina Nath replied sadly. 'Both our houses were torched, and our belongings looted. But thank God, at least nobody died.'

'Had it not been for this damned TB,' Seth Sahib said, coughing up some phlegm and spitting it into the spittoon, 'I myself would have sent fifty or a hundred Muslims packing off to the other world.'

A venomous smile swept for a brief second over his deathly pallid face as he uttered these words. Just this much conversation had so tired him that he fell back on his bed.

Dina Nath, too, had felt this same horrifying wish continually assault him over the past several days. The Seth Sahib, at any rate, had been a prominent figure in the Hindu Mahasabha, but Dina Nath was not one who made any distinction between Muslims and Hindus. He was a freelance actor who worked for any number of Bombay film companies; he took work wherever he could get it. Lately the poison of communalism had begun to spread even among the film companies. All the same, Dina Nath had no trouble finding regular work in films produced even by Muslim directors. And among his friends, Muslims were the more numerous by far. Then, after contracting TB, when he came to the sanatorium here in Panjgani and stayed for six months, he became good friends with another Bombay artist, Qasim Bhai, and a number of other Muslim patients too. He spent the greater part of his time in their company. Today, however, so much bitterness had been engendered in the heart of this same Dina Nath that he felt, as strongly as Seth Hiramal did, that if it were only within his power he'd slip off to Punjab and send as many of those woman- and child-brutalizing Muslims to the other world as he could.

Partly because he had recuperated some, and partly because he was short of cash, he had checked out of the sanatorium two months earlier and found himself a place to live. Many times the terrible news coming from West Punjab had made his blood boil, and many times he had seen himself in his dreams making short work of Muslims with a sword or a handgun.

Although the riots had been going on for a whole year now, he had been experiencing this sort of agitation in himself only for the last two months. The fire ignited by the Muslim League's demand for Direct Action twelve months ago at Calcutta had now reached all the way to Bombay. But Dina Nath had scarcely paid any attention to it. Just as a protracted illness makes the care-givers as much as the patient himself indifferent to it, so had Dina Nath become indifferent to the long-standing disease of communalism. How many Hindus were killed daily, how many

Muslims?—he had no interest in this sort of news. He lived in Malad, which was a good twenty miles away from the nearest riots in Bombay. Aside from any of this, he was far too busy to spare any attention. He was an actor, and even if no longer a mere bit-player, he was still not exactly famous. The constant struggle to look for fresh work after an assignment had ended, to keep a firm footing on the constantly shifting ground of the cinematic world, left him no time to indulge in this sort of 'foolishness' (yes, that's what he thought of the riots and disturbances). Then there was the greater consideration that all this rioting had occurred in Calcutta, Noakhali, Bihar, Bombay, and some cities in West Punjab, while his own Lahore had been spared its murderous flames. As far as Dina Nath was concerned, no other Indian city was more dear to him than Lahore, nor as worthy of his attention. Lahore was neutral. And so Dina Nath remained neutral too.

But then overwork, lack of rest, and a poor diet caught up with him in the form of TB. He had to leave Bombay and come to Panjgani, which ended both his work and his neutrality.

The situation in the country was fast deteriorating. The patients in the sanatorium participated en masse in entertainment programmes, rummy nights, or no-host parties. True enough. But if ever discussion veered toward an argument over Pakistan or India, a hush fell over them all. Qasim Bhai alone saw the hand of both the British and native reactionary forces behind all the disturbance and communal rioting, and cursed them roundly. Others, Muslims and Hindus, just blamed each other.

Dina Nath heard all this heated argumentation, which would later revisit him and rage inside his head every time he lay down to rest. His earlier indifference had by now vanished into thin air.

No sooner had he left the sanatorium two months ago than a veritable volcano exploded in Lahore, which made the Calcutta, Noakhali, Bihar, and Bombay riots look like mere firecrackers.

Dina Nath's neutrality was finished. The flames had made it to his beloved hometown. Indeed, they had, in a manner of speaking, stolen from him everything he held dear. As soon as the Boundary Commission was announced, the Muslims had set fire to Akbari Mandi. Dina Nath became concerned about his elder brother and other relatives. In response to his telegram, his brother wrote back from Lahore:

> Lahore is burning even as I write these lines. Hindu houses in Mohallah Sarban, Katrah Purabiyan, Bhati, and inside Dilli Darvazah as well as Shah Almi and Papar Mandi have been gutted by fire. Over a hundred houses were burnt down in the Papar Mandi fire alone. The fire was set at 2:30 in the morning, right in the middle of the curfew hours. Whoever came to put it out was gunned down by the police. Lahore is not known to have witnessed a greater conflagration. Its biggest wheat market, Akbari Mandi, had been burnt down only recently.
>
> As for the Old City, only owls hoot in Anarkali, and Civil Lines appears hushed like a frightened child. It's calm now, but it's the kind of calm that comes before the storm. Everybody, from the magistrate down to the ordinary policeman, has become a communalist. Our business at Lahore is finished. I'm thinking of selling off the two houses as fast I can and getting out of here. But properties everywhere just lie vacant and there are no buyers. People are fleeing, from the city, from Civil Lines, Sant Nagar, Rishi Nagar, Ram and Krishan Nagar, Bharat

> Nagar, and even Model Town. It's only a matter of days before Lahore will be completely emptied of Hindus.

The contents of the letter set off a whirlwind in Dina Nath's heart. It was not Lahore, he felt, but his own heart which was going up in flames. The packed, bustling bazaars of Shah Almi swirled before his eyes. Krishan Nagar, Sant Nagar, Ram Nagar, Rishi Nagar, and God knows how many other new neighbourhoods set up by Hindus had once all looked like so many stars set in the scarf of Lahore. Today, Dina Nath felt, the cruel hand of barbarism was methodically plucking each one of these stars out.

He received no more letters from his brother. But the news of Lahore's destruction, of the confused flight of its embattled population, and of the unspeakable brutalities against Hindu women, children, and old men in West Punjab reached him even in this remote area. The news took away his peace during the day, and his sleep at night. He was ill. The doctors had prescribed complete rest, both physical and mental. He had stopped reading the newspapers just to spare himself the torture they wrought in his mind. But try hard as he might, the heart-rending news reached him nonetheless. He was also terribly worried on account of his elder brother and other relatives—a worry he couldn't shake off, no matter how hard he tried. Just as he had given up hope of hearing from his brother ever again, having sent him a letter by air, followed by an express telegram, he received his letter from Delhi:

> I can't tell you how worried I've been lately. You are ill, so I didn't think it proper to write to you earlier; it would only have made your condition worse. My worry has

> eased a bit, hence the letter. If I'm less worried, it's not because my trials are any less. Really, they're just beginning. But having endured this calamity's first onslaught, when I look around, I realize that I'm not in it alone. Countless other refugees are my companions, and indeed some of them have suffered far worse than I. This gives me the courage to go on.
>
> Many have perished for all time in this calamity thrown at us by the unfeeling hand of barbarity (and for that reason are, perhaps, better off). Others have taken a nasty fall, and now lack the strength to gather themselves and get up. Still others can get up, but are unable to stand straight. Yet others, who can stand, have no energy left to walk. I, however, count myself among the fortunate few who have managed to stand up in spite of the fall, who have the strength necessary to move on.
>
> Here Mahatma Gandhi and other leaders are making every effort to enable the greater number of refugees to get up and walk. In spite of constant appeals for money, blankets, medicines, and other necessities, the fat-cats are concerned, even in this dreadful situation, only with adding more flab to their already bulging bellies. That's why prices are skyrocketing. Everything is expensive. Bribery is rampant. Life here in Delhi isn't easy. But don't let yourself worry. At least we have escaped with our lives. Man is pretty stubborn. He just doesn't give up his fascination with life no matter how bitter, how painful the situation. These days all of us are proving just that: our stubbornness. Those who had any self-respect chose to leave this world.

The bitterness of the concluding sentences tore at Dir Nath's heart. The happiness that his relatives' lives ha been spared, the grief that countless people had bee crippled, brought tears to his eyes. Just then the thoug crossed his mind: What if he could help even a few of th disabled to rise up again and take their place in the onward march of life! The Indian government's appeal, 'One blanket saves the life of one refugee,' flashed across his mind. Then and there he decided that not only would he send a blanket to the unfortunate refugees himself, but he would also approach his Hindu fellow-patients at the sanatorium for contributions. The thought to solicit donations from his Muslim friends just didn't occur to him. His former neutrality was by now finished. So when Seth Hiramal Viramal, handing him the thirty rupees, expressed his dreadful desire to make short work of Muslims, Dina Nath felt in that desire an echo of his own longing.

'Hey Brother, where are you headed with your notebook and pencil?' Qasim's voice startled him just as he exited the Seth's special cottage, proudly staring at the figure thirty, on his way to the Jubilee Ward. What should he tell him? He was at a loss. 'Oh, nothing,' he finally said, 'just collecting donations for the Punjabi refugees.'

'That's good work you're doing,' Qasim said. 'Just four days ago Bombay writers and artists held a rally throughout the city. Maybe you read about it in the papers. Prithvi Raj and Nawab stood holding hands in the leading truck. Behind them were a dozen or so trucks full of other famous artists, writers, and actors. Both men and women, Hindu and Muslim. The rally went through Hindu as well as Muslim areas and was welcomed by both. They all listened to their speeches and slogans against communal rioting. I'm myself thinking of collecting money here for the Anti-Riots Fund and sending it to support the efforts of the Bombay artists. Because important as it is to help the refugees, it's also important to stop peacefully settled citizens from becoming refugees. But no one here listens. You know what? They've just collected three hundred rupees for the Diwali celebration. I even reminded them of Mahatma Gandhi's words, that it didn't seem right to celebrate Diwali when lakhs of people were wandering around homeless. I suggested that they send the three hundred rupees to save Bombay from erupting into riots, or, if not that, to spend it on blankets for the refugees. Well, here's a good one: a Punjabi friend of mine quoted this saying from your part of the world: *Koi mare, koi jiye, Suthra ghol batashe piye*. People here are every bit like that Suthra. But I'm really glad you didn't just sit back. I'm an artist myself. I want to help my friends' efforts to ease the horrible situation our country's facing. But as a patient here I can't solicit. Not you, though. You've left the sanatorium. You can freely ask your patient friends for contributions. And you don't even need to ask for the R.M.O.'s permission. Come on, I'll go with you. Put me down for five rupees.'

Qasim sputtered out all this in what seemed like one long breath. Then he set out for his own ward with Dina Nath in tow.

'But let me tell you up front, I'm taking donations only for the Punjabi refugees,' Dina Nath said hesitantly.

'Why would I object to that? Hindu and Sikh refugees from Punjab must be feeling outraged inside. Unless they're resettled soon, they won't stop taking it out on Muslims who are no more to blame than they are. As I look at it, helping them is like helping my own brothers.'

What could Dina Nath say now? He quietly set off with Qasim for his ward.

Qasim first took Dina Nath to his own room. He

unlocked the closet, took out a five rupee note and put it in Dina Nath's hand, who couldn't help but take it. He thanked Qasim and offered his hand with the intention to leave.

Qasim Bhai took the extended hand in his, asked Dina Nath to wait a minute, and said, 'Friend, listen to me. Change your appeal just a bit. Say that you're seeking contributions for both Hindu and Muslim refugees.'

'But the Muslim refugees have left for Pakistan.'

'Not all. Quite a few still remain.'

'But, brother, I'm collecting only for the Hindus. And forgive me for being so direct. You're my friend. So I feel I can be open with you. You can have your five rupees back if you want.' Dina Nath held out the hand holding the five rupee note.

Qasim laughed. 'Like the general Hindu population, maybe you feel no sympathy for Muslims here either. You think that their suffering's been brought on them by their own sins. But my friend, if they're at fault, it's no different than the gullibility of an innocent child who lacks the intellectual resources to gauge the true significance of what his elders pass on to him. There is no difference between common people, especially those of our country, and children. Let's leave the common people aside, let's talk about the Hindu masses specifically. There was a time when they elected Subhash Babu a second time as the Congress president, without knowing exactly the wishes of Mahatma Gandhi. But when Gandhiji equated Patabi Satya Ramya's defeat with his own, the very same Subhash Babu was removed like a fly from a glass of milk. The very people who had elected him started talking ill of him. Dishonoured and risking his life, Subhash Babu somehow got out of the country and founded his I.N.A. And look what happens, the very janata who had forced him out now began to praise him to high heaven all over again. So much so that a time came when this very Congress had to beat his and his cohorts' drum just to win the election. Have a look at the common people some time. You'll find their naïveté shocking. Most don't even know what hand Jesus's followers, the British, have played in the calamity which has befallen them. The seed of Hindu-Muslim hatred which the Angrez planted in 1909 has grown into a flourishing tree and is oppressing the land with its venomous sap. They don't know that what we are witnessing today is simply the climax of the satanic politics of Hindu-Muslim enmity. Don't you see? In Punjab, riots broke out only in the cantonment areas, directly under British control. If an impartial tribunal were set up to investigate these bloody riots, the world would know how these followers of a peace-loving Isa used their cool, calculating intelligence, how they had lakhs of Hindus and Muslims massacred in Punjab in order to further their imperial interests.

'But what's done can't be undone. The least we can do is to uproot the poisonous tree whose seed was planted by the British. And thus let the sapling of freedom grow in safety, come to maturity, and bear fruit in the two countries of India and Pakistan. This isn't easy, and I know that. But don't you suppose we at least must know our responsibility at a cataclysmic time like this?'

Qasim Bhai suddenly stopped and then added, 'Well, it seems I've started to lecture you. Anyway, keep the five rupees. I said all that I did simply because there are more Muslim, Christian, and Parsi patients in the sanatorium than there are Hindu. If you had widened your appeal a bit, you could've collected more. Afterwards, you alone would have decided who to help out: the Hindu refugees or the Muslim refugees.'

Qasim's words sounded every bit as convincing to Dina Nath as Seth Hiralal's had earlier. But Qasim's words seemed to carry an echo of Dina Nath's own conscience. Which of the two was correct? More true? He was having difficulty deciding. Frustrated, he let out: 'I can't very well collect from Muslims and send it to Hindus. I just can't.'

'All right,' Qasim said, 'then do this: collect for the Anti-Riots Fund. Surely, helping the Hindu refugees is the same as stopping riots from spreading. Until they're resettled, they won't stop victimizing the Muslims to avenge themselves. Helping them is like helping the Muslims. Come on, I'll go with you. Remember, our appeal will be: "Stop the Riots! Help the Refugees!"'

Taking Dina Nath's silence for his approval, even if only a half-hearted one, Qasim set out with him.

Three hours later, when Dina Nath thanked Qasim Bhai and shook his hand, he had a full two hundred rupees in his pocket.

For the next seven days Dina Nath kept collecting donations without cease. The success of the first day, thanks no doubt to Qasim Bhai's help, had given him an unexpected boost. Where earlier he had not expected a collection of more than ten-twenty rupees, he now vowed to send no less than five hundred. As he still hadn't recovered fully, he went out only as far as the market very close to his hotel in the morning and evening. But in the past seven days he had ventured—albeit in a taxi—farther away to some of the other sanatoriums reserved for Parsis, Khojas, or Hindus, as well as combed through the neighbouring houses, bungalows, and bazaars. Today, on the eighth day, as he was walking along the main road, his pocket was only ten rupees short of the five hundred he had aimed for. He'd heard that Dr Merchant ran a private nursing home where he kept a few patients. Dina Nath was hoping to make up the difference there. After remitting the money, he'd take complete rest for a week and concentrate on regaining the weight he had lost in the frantic activity of the last seven days.

Over to the right, on the slope above Ring Road and its sprawling houses, a dark stone wall stretched out for quite some distance along the tops of the silver oaks. A month ago he had gone to see this wall with some friends. Winding its way along the serpentine road and passing by the Convent School, after the taxi had arrived at the wall, he was genuinely surprised to see that what he had earlier taken for a stone wall wasn't a wall at all, but rather the rocky face of a perfectly flat plateau stretching out for miles. How had such a large piece of flat earth, elevated so high, come to rest on its rocky sides?—he wondered. But then he was drawn away from his thoughts by the incredible beauty of the Tableland. Up ahead, perfectly level ground rolled out as far as the eye could see, where the winter chill had turned the grass to the colour of earth. The sky above looked like an inverted crystal bowl covering the Tableland, and the light, white wisps of cloud looked like foam in an upturned, emptied wine glass.

Dina Nath walked over to the side of Ring Road and stood there gazing. Panjgani, cropping up amidst the surrounding red rust hills like an unexpected and enchanting oasis in an awesome expanse of desert, appeared to him breathtakingly beautiful. Looking down from the Tableland's elevation,* the view, with its tiny roads

---

* Cf. the first sentence of this paragraph. The logical inconsistency is in the original text. - Translator

shaded by tall silver oaks, its miniature gardens, toy-like bungalows, and tiny men and women, took him completely in. He felt like just standing there and gazing forever at the paradisiacal, exhilarating beauty of Panjgani.

But he had been walking in just those beautiful Panjgani gardens and bungalows for the past seven days. The place, so indescribably beautiful from the Tableland, looked utterly ugly in reality. Not counting the dwellings of the local residents, he rarely walked into a house which didn't have a TB patient or his grief-stricken relatives.

As he walked along looking at those beautiful bungalows covered with silver oaks, a sigh escaped from Dina Nath's lips. The wealth of the affluent patients convalescing in those bungalows sharply contrasted with the dire poverty of those who fought the killer disease in cottages no bigger than chicken coops below the bazaar all the way to Jason Road. Suddenly two events accompanied by two faces flashed across his mind.

He had rapped on the door of just such a chicken-coop on Jason Road the other day when somebody, coughing away, had asked him to come in. The door was not bolted, so he walked in. It was a dingy small room with space just enough for a cot, a dirty old chair and a tea table. A frightfully lean and feeble patient lay on the cot with the quilt pulled all the way to his chest and a scarf securely wrapped around his neck and head. Dina Nath told him the purpose of his visit, stressing that although he was himself still ill, he nonetheless felt compelled to do his duty at a time when the country was facing its worst calamity. The eyes of the sick man brightened. With shaking hands and much effort he groped under the pillow, pulled out a small dirty looking wallet, and removing two one-rupee notes from it, he offered them to Dina Nath, saying, 'It's good work you're doing. I can't even sit, doctor's orders, otherwise I myself would join you in your good work. I'm a poor man. Please forgive me for contributing so little.'

Dina Nath felt a lump in his throat. He was overwhelmed and said, 'Two rupees, no, they're like two hundred. The tremendous encouragement your words have given me count for a lot.'

Then he asked for the man's name.

'Name, for just two rupees . . .'

Dina Nath interrupted, 'Please, let me write down your name. Just for my own satisfaction, so I know I didn't leave anybody out. Besides, it will also help others to know that members of every community participated with them in their good work.'

'All right then, Nasir M. Abuwalla,' the sick man complied.

Directly above the pallid, withered face of Nasir Bhai loomed, in Dina Nath's mind, the face of Champak Lal Ram Ratan Gharekar—a rotund face, over which layers of flab had put a smooth gloss, with its two prominent boils.

He owned a big store in Panjgani. Dina Nath visited it in the morning. The man behind the counter told him that he'd have to ask his partner; only then he could make a contribution.

'Give whatever you can,' Dina Nath said. 'I'm a sick man.'

'I can't. I mean without asking my partner, I can't. Come back in the evening.'

Dina Nath went back in the evening. This time around there was a different man behind the counter—an elderly man. In the manner of a sanyasi, he informed Dina Nath hat he'd turned away from all this *moh-maya* business years ago. 'My share in the store has now passed on to my son, Champak,' He said. 'It's him you should ask for a donation.'

The next morning he met Champak Lal. Call it good luck, but both partners were present at the time. Champak Lal was a young man of fair complexion and medium height. All dressed up in a suit. His smallish cheeks looked like a pair of puffed up loaves of bread. They were shinning from a generous application of facial cream, saturated with a sense of affluence-induced ease and satisfaction. After Dina Nath had told him for the third time why he'd come, he asked two questions of Dina Nath: Who had given him the right to collect donations, and what is the guarantee that the donation will in fact reach the refugees?

Dina Nath resorted to the little trick Qasim Bhai had taught him and said, 'I'm an artist and I'm taking contributions to support the rally Bombay writers and artists held on 2 October to stop the rioting. I'll send the money to the office at Devdhar Hall. And I'll show you the receipt if you want.'

He grabbed the notebook from Dina Nath's hands and glanced at it. Satisfied, he returned it and asked, 'How much do you want?'

Dina Nath, feeling already pretty testy at the man's rudeness, said nonchalantly, 'You've looked at the list. Surely you've seen contributions ranging from as much as thirty rupees to as little as four annas. Give whatever's right.'

The young man took out a four anna coin from the drawer and tossed it on the counter in front of Dina Nath. Then turning to his partner, who probably was an uncle, he said, 'Four annas for the fund. Make a note.'

Above him stood the Tableland in all its seductive beauty firm and unalterable. And below, Panjgani, with its bungalows, stores, and dingy houses no bigger than chicken-coops, and its people who had handsome faces but ugly hearts, or ugly faces and good hearts. Dina Nath wondered: In the shadow of this eternal beauty of the universe, the entire civilized world and its people . . .

Just then Dr Merchant's nursing home came into view. Dina Nath drifted out of his thoughts and approached the gate.

The facility included a bungalow in front and two blocks standing immediately behind it. The bungalow itself had four blocks, one of which was used as a dispensary with an A.P. room. The other three, as well as the blocks at the back housed the patients.

As luck would have it, Dina Nath collected five rupees from the very first block. A liberal-minded wealthy young man was staying there with his sick wife. He was happy because just that morning the doctor had told him that his wife was doing much better now.

Dina Nath was able to rake up another two rupees from the second block, and a single rupee from the third. All he now needed was another two rupees. He started out for the blocks in the last row.

He was still some distance away when he saw a girl standing with an older woman at the back, in front of what must have been the kitchen. From the women's garb, Dina Nath guessed that they were from the northern part of the country—the UP, or maybe Punjab. Both women ran back inside as soon as they saw him. But even in so brief an instant, he could see how lean and emaciated their bodies vere, and he could also see clearly the sadness that spilled rom their eyes. Their pained looks went straight through ıis heart like an arrow. He was quite familiar with that grief, or he had seen something of its reflection in the eyes of the ›atients and their loved ones who just arrived in Panjgani. The patient who's come with these women is perhaps ncurable, Dina Nath thought. Then he stepped forward ınd knocked at the first door.

He got a rupee from the place. He was now only one upee short of the five hundred. Caught between hope and lespair he advanced toward the other block. For some trange reason he wanted to collect the remaining rupee ight here, in Dr Merchant's nursing home. He rapped on he next door.

The girl who opened the door and disappeared before Dina Nath could come inside was probably, he felt, the ame girl he had seen earlier standing outside with her nother. Inside on a cot lay a frightfully emaciated man of ıbout fifty or so. Seeing a stranger, he sat up. His sunken, allow cheeks, the shadow of fear in his eyes gave away the ecret of the pain he had seen in the faces of the younger ınd older woman. He'd guessed right.

When Dina Nath explained the reason for his visit, a aint smile full of pain swept across the man's lips, and he aid in a feeble voice, 'We're so poor ourselves, I wish we could help.'

'Give whatever you can. Some gave thirty rupees, others only four annas.'

The middle-aged man groped in his pocket with his crawny, wood-like hand. He then called out, 'Afzal!'

The little girl came over and stood behind the door for a moment. The manner in which she said, 'Afzal's gone out', nade Dina Nath involuntarily ask, *'Ki tusin Punjabi o?'* (Are you Punjabis?)

'Ji asin bad-nasib Jalandhar se rahan wale an.' (Yes, we poo souls are from Jalandhar.')

'Did any Muslims there come out alive? Or were the all ruined, like the Hindus of West Punjab?'

'Everybody perished,' the middle-aged man said, a grief caught in his throat. Then, taking him for a fellow-Muslim because of the clothes he was wearing, h started to tell Dina Nath the story of his affliction.

All Dina Nath had heard so far were the stories o incredible cruelty to Hindu and Sikh women and childre in Pakistan. How young girls were raped and robbed o their virginity. How they were stripped and parade naked. How the breasts of old women were sliced off. Ho daughters were raped in full view of their parents. Ho parents were slaughtered before their children. Stories o murder, pillage, and bloodshed, all of which had brough Dina Nath's blood to a boil. But what the middle-aged ma now told him of the decimation of Jalandhar's Musli population made Dina Nath's hair stand on end. Was ther any kind of cruelty which these followers of Ram, Krisha Nanak and Gobind had not visited upon Muslims? An when the man told him how two huge fire pits had bee dug right next to the train station, into which Muslims wer dumped alive like sacrificial goats, and how the Brahmin after the offering to the god of revenge, shouted 'Jai! Jai! like someone possessed, it became impossible for Din Nath to remain in his chair. He got up and started pacin nervously back and forth inside the small room.

Two of the middle-aged man's young sons and a daughter and her husband had first been tortured and the made prey to the fires of revenge. His younger son ha somehow managed to escape to Pakistan. The man ha himself been overtaken by the events while in Delhi with his wife and their littlest daughter, where he had come to consult a hakim about his illness. When the riots broke out even there, they somehow made it to Bombay, with nothing but the clothes on their backs. He was already ill. The doctors diagnosed TB. Some Muslims helped out and he was admitted here in Panjgani. When his son, who'd escaped to Pakistan, heard about his illness, he risked his life and crossed over to Bombay, and therefrom to Panjgani.

'The fires of revenge spare nothing, whether it is the body or the heart,' the middle-aged man said. 'When my son tells us about the cruelty to which Hindus are subjected in Pakistan, we fall silent and think our own suffering is brought on by our own sins. We've been staying here for the last two months. Dr Merchant may be a Muslim, but he is not a Qarun. How long can he go on giving aid like this?' He tapped his forehead and concluded, 'Whatever God wills . . .'

Tears gushed forth from the middle-aged man's eyes by the time he finished narrating his story. Just then, God knows what happened to Dina Nath, but he completely forgot his promise to Seth Hiralal. He took out the entire amount of the donations—notes and change adding up to one rupee short of five hundred—and put it before the middle-aged man on the bed.

The man lifted his moist eyes in complete surprise.

'Baba,' Dina Nath began, 'I am a Hindu. Our house, our property, everything we owned has been looted in Pakistan. The cruelty to which the believers of the Rabbul Alamin have subjected innocent Hindus in Pakistan, and to which the worshippers of Bhagwan have subjected innocent Muslims in Hindustan—they will not be able to atone for it even in seven successive births. I only pray that

Bhagwan guide them to goodness. I was collecting this money for the relief of the suffering refugees in Punjab. You, too, are a refugee from Punjab, and no less suffering. It's not a lot. Perhaps it will help some, though.'

Before the middle-aged man could say anything, Dina Nath, wiping his eyes with his handkerchief, walked out of the room.

Surrounded by dry, rocky, rust-coloured hills, the flat stretch of the Tableland, grazing the very tops of the lofty silver oaks, rolled out in its incredible beauty, as the last rays of the sun seemed to kiss it goodbye.

Parmeshar Singh

Ahmad Nadim Qasimi

Akhtar was suddenly separated from his mother, like a coin falling from the pocket of someone in a great hurry—there one moment, gone the next. A search was made of course, but it amounted to little more than a commotion at the tail end of the ragged train of refugees—stirred up like soapsuds, only to die down and disappear. 'He's got to be coming along *somewhere,*' someone said. 'There are thousands of people in the caravan.'

Bracing herself with just such hope, Akhtar's mother trudged on toward Pakistan, thinking again and again, 'He must be coming along. He probably wandered off chasing after a butterfly. Surely he must have missed me at some point, cried some, and—he must be coming along. He's a smart boy. More than five years old. He'll show up. After we've arrived in Pakistan, I can search for him more carefully there.'

But Akhtar had lost the big caravan some fifteen miles from the border—whether chasing after a butterfly as his mother had speculated, or losing track of time as he forayed into a sugarcane field to pick himself a stalk. Anyway, as he ran screaming and crying inconsolably in one direction, a party of Sikhs closed in on him. The boy yelled at them angrily, 'Keep away, or I'll shout *Allahu Akbar!*' The words were barely out of his mouth when he blanched with fright.

The Sikhs, all of them, burst out laughing. But one of them, Parmeshar Singh, didn't find it at all funny. His tousled *kes* poked out of his loosely wrapped turban, which left his topknot at the back completely exposed. 'Don' laugh, *yaaro*,' he said. 'After all, the same Vahguruji made this child as he made you and your children.'

A Sikh youth, who had meanwhile bared his *kirpan* retorted, 'Wait a minute, Parmeshar, let my dagger pay its dues to its religion, then we'll worry about paying ours to our religion.'

'Don't kill him, *yaaro*,' Parmeshar Singh pleaded. 'He's so small! Just look at him. The same Vahguruji has made him . . .'

'Well then, let's ask him,' another Sikh said. He came over to the frightened boy and asked, 'Tell us, who's made you—Khuda or Vahguruji?'

Akhtar made a valiant attempt to swallow the terrible dryness that had spread from the tip of his tongue down to the pit of his stomach, and he blinked the tears from his eyelashes, which had accumulated there like grit. He looked at Parmeshar Singh as though he were looking at his own mother. He spat out a tear which had run into his mouth and said, 'I don't know.'

'Listen to this!' one of the Sikhs said. He swore at Akhta and started to laugh.

The boy, who hadn't finished, resumed, 'Amma say that she found me lying on a pile of hay inside a little barn.

The Sikhs burst into laughter. But Parmeshar Singh beside himself with anguish, broke down in tears, leaving his companions absolutely stunned. He started to wail, 'All children are alike, *yaaro*. Exactly the words of my darling Kartar. Wasn't he too found by his mother lying on a pile of hay inside a barn?!'

The bared *kirpan* was put back into its sheath. The group withdrew to one side. After whispering among themselve for a bit, one of the men stepped forward, grabbed the boy' arm and led him over to Parmeshar Singh, who was sobbing quietly. 'Here, Parmeshare, take him. Let him grow his *kes*, make him your Kartar. Here, take him!'

Parmeshar dashed forward and picked the boy up with such impatience that his turban came completely undone, allowing his hair to hang down loosely. He kissed the boy like someone possessed. He hugged him tightly and gazed into his eyes, thinking of things that lit his face up with joy. He then turned around and looked at the other Sikhs. He quickly put the boy down and rushed past them, toward the bushes up ahead, where he started to caper about like a monkey, his flowing *kes* matching the wild movements of his body. The rest of the party just gawked at him. Finally, he ran back to them, his hands joined together in a hollow ball. There was a smile on his lips, deep inside the thick mop of his sweaty beard, and his red eyes were shining with unusual brilliance. He was out of breath.

He came over to the boy and squatted down on folded knees and asked, 'What's your name?'

'Akhtar,' the boy answered, his voice no longer ragged with fear.

'Akhtar, my son,' Parmeshar Singh said with great tenderness. 'Come, have a look.'

Akhtar leaned forward a little. Parmeshar Singh opened his balled hands a crack, just long enough for the boy to get a peek.

'Aa-haa!' Akhtar clapped jubilantly and joined his hands into a hollow ball, just like Parmeshar Singh, and smiled through his tears. 'A butterfly!'

'Would you like to have it?'

'Yes,' Akhtar rubbed his hands in excitement.

'Here,' Parmeshar Singh opened his hands. Akhtar tried to catch the butterfly, but it swiftly flew away, leaving fine flecks of colour on the boy's fingertips.

Disappointment was evident on the boy's face.

Parmeshar Singh looked at the other Sikhs and said 'Why are all children alike, *yaaro*? Kartar too would draw a long face whenever his butterfly flew away.'

'Parmeshar Singh's gone half-mad,' the Sikh youth said with disgust. And the entire group started to head back.

Parmeshar Singh picked Akhtar up and sat him on his shoulders, and then started out behind the party. But the boy began to cry uncontrollably, 'I want my mother! I want my mother!'

Parmeshar Singh lifted his hand to pat the boy, but he pushed it away. When he told him, 'Yes, yes, son, I'm taking you to your mother,' the boy stopped sobbing, though now and then he still cried some, barely tolerating all the patting and caressing.

Parmeshar Singh brought the boy to his house, which formerly had belonged to a Muslim. After he'd lost all his possessions in his native Lahore and come over to Amritsar, the villagers had allotted him this house. The moment he'd stepped into the house with his wife and daughter, he froze and his eyes glazed over. He whispered in a mysterious voice, 'Something's reciting the Quran in this place. I hear it.'

Which had made the Granthiji and other village folk just laugh. His wife had already told them that ever since Kartar Singh's disappearance, her husband was no longer his usual self. 'God knows what's happened to him,' she'd said. 'Back there, and may Vahguruji not make me lie, he used to beat Kartar up and down like a donkey ten times a day. But while I've come to accept the disappearance of our son, after much crying and screaming, to be sure, he can't accept it, even after crying himself silly. There, I wouldn't dare give

›ur daughter Amar Kaur even an angry side-glance. It was enough to send him flying into a rage. He'd always say, 'Don't be harsh with her. Daughters are meek, vulnerable creatures. They are like travelers who have stopped a while to catch a little breath at one's house, and will move on when the time comes." But now, look what he does. She makes the slightest mistake and he hits the roof. He doesn't even think twice before screaming, "Abduction of daughters and wives—yes, *yaaro*, that's nothing new. But when did you ever hear of five and six-year-old boys disappearing?"'

Parmeshar Singh had been living in this new house for about a month now. Every night he would go on tossing and turning, then mumble something and sit up with a start. 'You hear it, don't you?' he'd whisper to his wife, as if he'd seen a ghost. 'Something is reciting the Quran in the house!'

His wife would say something vague and dismissive, then roll over and go back to sleep.

But Amar Kaur would be unable to go back to sleep after that. She would see shapes everywhere in the darkness, intoning the verses of the Quran. In the wee hours of the morning she would involuntarily stuff her fingers in her ears.

Back in Lahore District their house was located near a mosque. It was a delight to hear the muezzin call out the *azan* early in the morning. One had the feeling that the light filtering in from the east had itself suddenly started to sing. But all this changed after her neighbour Pritam Kaur had been gang-raped by some young men who later dumped her dead body on the garbage heap like an old discarded rag. Now whenever the muezzin issued the call to prayer, all Amar Kaur heard were the pathetic screams of Pritam

Kaur. Indeed, quite forgetting that she was no longer living next to a mosque, the very thought of *azan* made her tremble with fear.

With her fingers stuffed in her ears, she'd eventually fall asleep. Having stayed awake the whole night, she usually got up late in the morning. Which was as good a reason as any for Parmeshar Singh to get mad at her. 'Yes, that's all she *can* do—sleep, sleep, sleep! Girls—useless layabouts. That's what they are! Had she been a boy, *yaaro*, who knows how much work she'd already have finished!'

But when Parmeshar Singh entered the courtyard of the house today, he was uncharacteristically all smiles. His untucked hair was hanging loose and dishevelled over his shoulders and back, the comb still stuck in it, and he was lovingly patting Akhtar's back. His wife sat to one side diligently working the winnowing fan. Her hands froze in mid-air and she just gawked at Parmeshar Singh. Then she leapt over the winnowing-fan, ran to him and asked, 'Who is he?'

Still smiling, Parmeshar Singh said, 'Don't be afraid, silly woman! He's so much like Kartare. Do you know, he too was found by his mother on a pile of hay in a barn? And he too loves butterflies. His name is Akhtar.'

'Akhtar!' Her expression changed completely.

'Well, OK, Akhtar Singh, if it bothers you.' After a pause he explained, 'Don't worry about the *kes*. It'll grow long before you even know it. But you must slip a *kara* and *kachhera* on him right away. We'll give him a comb to wear in his *kes* after it's grown long enough.'

'Fine, fine. But whose child is he?' she pressed him.

'Whose child?' Parmeshar Singh repeated his wife's words as he gently took Akhtar down from his shoulder. He ran his hand tenderly through the boy's hair and replied

Why, he's Vahguruji's son. Our own. Darn it, *yaaro*, this woman can't even see that this tiny mole on Akhtar's forehead is exactly like the one Kartare had on his, exactly in the same spot. Well, I know, Kartare's was a little bit bigger. We used to kiss him on that very spot, didn't we? Akhtar's earlobes are pink like a rose blossom, and Kartare's were the same. A bit thicker perhaps. Can't she see that, *yaaro*? And . . .'

Akhtar, who had sat still so far out of sheer befuddlement, suddenly screamed, 'I don't want to stay here! I want to go to my mother! My mother!'

Parmeshar Singh took the boy's hand and gently nudged him towards his wife. 'There, take him into your arms,' he said. 'He wants to go to his mother.'

'Well then, let him go.' She appeared possessed by the same apparition that had taken hold of Parmeshar Singh when his gang had come upon Akhtar in the field—an apparition he'd had the hardest time shaking off.

'Look at the big hero!' the woman yelled. 'He went out to rob. And what does he bring back? This brat, barely a handful! Why couldn't you kidnap a girl? At least she'd have fetched a couple hundred rupees. We could have bought a few things for this decrepit house. Oh, you've gone off your rocker! Didn't you see this is a Musalla boy? Go, dump him where you picked him up. And make sure he doesn't set foot in my kitchen.'

Parmeshar Singh pleaded, 'Kartare and Akhtar were brought into the world by the same Vahguruji. Surely you understand that.'

'No!' she screamed, 'I don't understand that! Nor do I want to! I'll slash his throat at night and hack him to pieces and throw the pieces out! Why did you have to bring him here? Take him away! Throw him out!'

'Better yet, why not throw *you* out?' Parmeshar Singh said hotly. 'Maybe I should slash your throat instead.' He took a step toward his wife, who promptly ran off screaming and beating her chest. Amar Kaur came running from the house next door, followed by some of the women who lived in the same lane. A group of men also rushed to the scene, thereby saving Parmeshar Singh's wife from a thrashing.

The people reasoned with her: Parmeshar Singh was doing a good thing. Making a Musalman into a Sikh was not an everyday occurrence. If it were the olden days Parmeshar Singh would already have become famous as a 'Guru.'

That gave her some comfort, but she still cried on huddled in a corner, her head bent over her knees.

All of a sudden Parmeshar Singh let out a thunderous scream that shook the entire crowd. 'Where's Akhtar? My Akhtar, where did he go? You butchers better not have taken him, *yaaro*.'

Then screaming 'Akhtar! Akhtar!' at the top of his lungs he searched every conceivable place in the house, and then dashed out.

The neighbourhood kids trailed behind him out of sheer curiosity. Women climbed up to the rooftops to watch. By then Parmeshar Singh had already crossed over into the fields, babbling, 'I was going to take him to his mother wasn't I, *yaaro*? Where has he run off to?'

'Akhtar! Akhtar!' he yelled.

'I'm not going with you!' taunted Akhtar, who stood crying at a bend in the raised mud path along Gyan Singh's sugarcane field. 'You're a Sikh.'

'Yes, that's right, son,' the helpless Parmeshar Singh confessed. 'I am a Sikh.'

'So I'm not coming along with you,' Akhtar wiped his drying tears, clearing the way for the new ones forming in his eyes.

'You're not coming, then?' Suddenly Parmeshar Singh's tone changed.

'No!'

'You're sure?'

'No, no, no!'

'We'll see about that!' Biting his lips Parmeshar Singh grabbed Akhtar's ear and slapped the boy hard on the face. 'Now let's go!' he snapped.

Akhtar turned pale with fear, as though all his blood had been wrung out of him. Suddenly he threw himself down on the bare earth and started to thrash and scream, kicking up a cloud of dust. 'No, I won't! I won't! I won't! You're a Sikh! I'm not going anywhere near a Sikh! I want to go back to my mother! I'll kill you!'

This time it was Parmeshar Singh's turn to cringe. He too blanched, as if all his blood had been drained. He dug his teeth into his hand. His nostrils flared. He broke down in tears, screaming so loud that it froze some of the neighbours and children coming up behind them.

Parmeshar Singh folded his knees and squatted down in front of Akhtar. He started to sob like a child, hard and long, his lower lip out-thrust. In a voice overcome with emotion, he begged the boy, 'Please forgive me, Akhtar. I swear by your God, I am your friend. If you try to go back alone, somebody will kill you on the way. And then your mother will come after me from Pakistan and kill me too. Listen, I myself will take you back to Pakistan. OK? If you run into a boy there named Kartar, promise that you will bring him back here. You will, won't you?'

'All right,' Akhtar made the deal as he wiped his tears

with the back of his hand.

Parmeshar Singh hoisted him onto his shoulder and started to walk, but stopped suddenly. Up ahead a group of village children and some neighbours had been watching him closely. A middle-aged man among them said, 'Don't cry, Parmeshre, don't cry. A month isn't such a long time after all. His *kes* will grow long and he will look exactly like Kartara.'

He said nothing and walked away with quick strides. At a point along the way he stopped and looked back at the crowd and said, '*Yaaro*, you couldn't be more cruel. You want to make Akhtar into Kartara. What if somebody over there made Kartara into Akhtar? Wouldn't you call such a person heartless?'

Suddenly his voice boomed, 'This boy, I'm telling you, *will* remain Muslim. I swear by Darbar Sahib. I'll take him to Amritsar first thing tomorrow and get him the English haircut he wears. What the hell do you think I am? I am a Khalsa, in case you didn't know. I have a lion's heart in my chest, not a chicken's.'

Parmeshar Singh had just entered his house and was ordering his wife and daughter to treat Akhtar with the utmost deference and hospitality when the village Granthi, Sardar Santookh Singh, stepped in and barked, 'Parmeshar Singh!'

'Yes,' Parmeshar Singh looked over his shoulder. Granthiji had brought the entire neighbourhood along with him.

'Look,' the Granthiji said very gravely. 'Starting tomorrow, the boy will wear a turban, in the proper manner of Khalsas. As well as a *kara*. Also, he will come to the dharmshala and partake in the prashad. And yes, his hair will not come in contact with a scissors, ever. If it does, you will have to vacate this house at once. You understand?'

'Yes,' Parmeshar Singh said quietly.

'Very well then,' the Granthiji drove in the last nail. .

'As you say, Granthiji, as you say,' Parmeshar Singh's wife answered instead. 'As it is, he keeps hearing the Quran being recited at night all through the house. Looks like he was a Musalla in his previous incarnation. Our daughter Amar Kaur is quite beside herself. Ever since she heard that a Musalla boy has come into the house, she's been huddled in a corner crying. She fears something terrible is going to happen to us. If Parmeshar fails to carry out your command, I as well as Amar Kaur will both come to stay in the dharmshala. Let him just stay with his darling boy if he wants. Good for nothing! He has no regard for Vahguruji.'

'You stupid ass, what do you mean? Who has no regard for Vahguruji?' Parmeshar Singh yelled at his wife, taking the sting of the Granthiji's words out on her. He mumbled obscenities under his breath for some time, and then got up and came directly before Granthiji. 'All right, I hear your words,' he said in such a way that Granthiji promptly departed with the rest of the neighbours trailing behind him.

In just a few days one could scarcely tell Akhtar apart from the other Sikh boys—the same turban tied tightly around his head to the earlobes, the same bracelet worn on his forearm, and the same *kachhera*. Only at home, after he had removed the turban, could one see that he was not a Sikh. But his hair was growing fast. Whenever Parmeshar Singh's wife touched it, she felt a sense of satisfaction and happiness take hold of her. 'Hey, Amar Kaure, come over here!' she would call her daughter. 'See how well it's growing! Before long it'll grow long enough to roll into a bun and put a comb in it. And he will be called Kartar Singh.'

'No, Mother,' Amar Kaur replied from where she sat. 'Just as there is only one Vahguruji, and one Granth Sahab, and one moon, so was there only one Kartara, one and only one, my sweet little brother.' Amar Kaur would then break down in tears. 'No, Mother,' she'd pout, 'you can't distract me with this toy. You just can't! I know he's a Musalla. And Kartara just can't ever be a Musalla!'

'When did I say that he's the real Kartara? My darling son, my moon!' Parmeshar Singh's wife too would break down in tears.

Then leaving Akhtar alone, the two women would sit in a corner and cry their hearts out, commiserating with each other all the while.

Akhtar cried for his mother for a few days; but now he cried for something else. Whenever Parmeshar Singh brought home a little grain or a piece of cloth from the Panchayat that had been set up for the relief of the refugees, Akhtar would run over to him, wrap himself around his legs and say between sobs, 'Tie me a turban! Make my hair grow fast! Buy me a comb!'

Parmeshar Singh would draw him to his chest and hug him tightly. In a voice choked with emotion he'd say, 'Yes, yes. In due time, child. All in due time. Everything'll happen as you say, hair and all the rest. But one thing will not happen. Never. I shall never do that. You understand, don't you?'

Akhtar recalled his mother only rarely now. He would stick to Parmeshar Singh the entire time he remained at home, and when he had to go out, the boy looked at Parmeshar Singh's wife and Amar Kaur, as though begging them for a little love. Parmeshar Singh's wife bathed him, washed his clothes, and broke into tears as she combed his hair. She would go on crying for a long time. Amar Kaur, on the other hand, never looked at the boy without thumbing her nose at him. In the first days after his arrival, she had even whacked him once or twice. But when Akhtar complained about it to Parmeshar Singh, he became furious. Mouthing obscenities, he pounced on his daughter in such a fury that, had his wife not thrown herself at his feet, he surely would have physically picked the girl up and thrown her over the wall into the alley. *'Ulloo ki patthi!'* he roared at her. 'Who said only girls were being kidnapped? How come this slut is still hanging around here then? And who gets kidnapped instead?—a five-year old boy who doesn't even know how to wipe his nose! For heaven's sake, *yaaro*, what an outrage!'

From that moment forward Amar Kaur never dared hit the boy again, but she started hating him twice as much.

One day Akhtar started running a high fever. Parmeshar went out to consult the village vaid. Shortly thereafter his wife too went out, to borrow a little bit of fennel seed from one of the neighbours. Meanwhile, Akhtar, feeling terribly thirsty, asked for a drink of water. After a while, having received none, he opened his swollen red eyes and looked around. 'Water!' he moaned loudly. When nobody responded, he threw off the quilt and sat up. Amar Kaur was sitting in the doorway straight in front of him, weaving a basket of palm leaves.

'Give me some water!' he ordered hotly.

Amar Kaur knit her brows and stared at him. Altogether ignoring his request, she went on with her work.

'Give me water,' he screamed, 'or I'll beat you up!'

This time Amar Kaur didn't even bother to look at him. She screamed back, 'Just try it! You're no Kartara that I'd take your beating lying down. I'll hack you to pieces!'

Akhtar started to weep bitterly. For the first time in a long time he suddenly remembered his mother. After Parmeshar Singh and his wife had returned, he with medicine, she with fennel seed, Akhtar was crying his heart out. 'That's enough,' he began, sobbing. 'I want to go back to my mother. This Amar Kaur, the bitch, doesn't even give me water! I want to go back to my mother!'

Parmeshar Singh glowered at Amar Kaur. She had started to cry and was telling her mother, 'Why should I? Somewhere Kartara must be begging someone for water. If nobody takes pity on my brother, why should I take pity on him? Why should I?'

Parmeshar took a step toward Akhtar and said, pointing at his wife, 'Son, she too is your mother.'

'No, she's not!' Akhtar screamed angrily. 'She is a Sikh. My mother offers *namaz* five times a day, and when she gives me water to drink, she never forgets to say *bismillah*.'

Parmeshar Singh's wife quickly filled a cup with water and brought it over. When she offered it to the boy he smashed it against the wall and shrieked, 'No, not from your hand! You're the mother of this bitch, Amar Kaur! I'll drink only from Parmun's hand!'

'But this man is the father of a bitch like me,' Amar Kaur snapped, burnt up.

'So what? Let him be!' Akhtar screamed. 'It's none of your business!'

Parmeshar Singh's face was beset by strange, conflicting emotions. Akhtar's demand to drink water only from his hands made him smile and cry at the same time. He gave the boy his drink of water, kissed him on the forehead patted his back, and having eased him into bed, he went on gently massaging his head. Only toward the evening did the boy stir. By then his fever had subsided and he was sleeping peacefully.

That night, for the first time in a long time, Parmeshar Singh once again started in his sleep. He woke his wife up and whispered to her, 'Hey, you hear it, don't you? Something's reciting the Quran in the house.'

First dismissing it as one of his old hallucinations, she then quickly got up mumbling something, reached out for the cot on which Amar Kaur was sleeping, shook her gently and said, 'Daughter!'

'Yes, Mother, what is it?' Amar Kaur sat up.

The mother whispered, 'Listen—something really *is* reciting the Quran!'

The ensuing moment of silence was frightening; and even more dreadful was the scream from Amar Kaur's throat that followed. Akhtar's scream after that was more terrible still.

'What's the matter, son?' Parmeshar Singh jumped out of his bed and rushed over to Akhtar's bed. Hugging him he asked, 'Has something frightened you?'

'Yes,' Akhtar poked his head from the quilt and said, 'I heard a scream.'

'It was Amar Kaur,' Parmeshar Singh explained. 'We all thought we heard something reciting the Quran.'

'That was me,' Akhtar said. 'I was reciting it.'

A muffled scream escaped from Amar Kaur's lips once again.

Parmeshar Singh's wife quickly lit an oil lamp and sat down on Amar Kaur's cot. Both mother and daughter now gawked at the boy as if he would turn into a wisp of smoke any moment and escape from the cracks in the door, calling back at them in a dreadful voice, 'I'm a jinn! Tomorrow I'll return and again recite the Quran!'

'Won't you tell us what you were reciting?' Parmeshar Singh asked.

'You want me to recite it for you?'

'Yes, yes,' Parmeshar Singh said, eagerly.

Akhtar started to recite: *'Qul huwa 'l-Lahu ahad!'* Finishing with *'kufuwan ahad,'* he quickly poked his face into his collar and breathed on his chest. Then he smiled at Parmeshar Singh and asked, 'Want me to breathe on you too?'

'Yes, yes,' Parmeshar Singh quickly flung open his collar, and Akhtar breathed on his chest too.

This time around Amar Kaur had the hardest time suppressing her scream.

'You couldn't fall asleep—is that it?'

'Yes. I missed Mother. She said that any time you couldn't sleep, just recite the *Qul huwa' l-Lah* three times, and sleep will come. I was just getting drowsy when Amar Kaur shrieked and frightened me.'

'Well, recite it once again and try to sleep,' Parmeshar Singh told the boy. 'You should recite it every day. Loudly. Never forget it. Or your mother will spank you. OK, now go to sleep.'

He laid the boy back down and tucked him into the quilt. Just as he made to put out the lamp, Amar Kaur shouted, 'No, Baba, no! Don't put it out! I'm scared!'

'Scared?' Parmeshar Singh asked, surprised. 'What's there to be scared of?'

'Oh, it won't hurt to let it burn,' his wife said.

But Parmeshar Singh did put it out. 'Crazy women!' he laughed in the darkness. 'Absolute asses!'

Akhtar softly went on reciting the *Qul huwa' l-Lah* in the darkness. After a while he began to snore. Parmeshar Singh also went back to sleep, as did his wife, but all night long, n her incomplete sleep, Amar Kaur remained afraid, magining that she heard the *azan* coming from the neighbourhood' mosque.

Akhtar's *kes* had by now grown quite long, long enough o be rolled into a tiny topknot and hold a comb. Like everyone else in the village, Parmeshar Singh's wife too had egan to call him Kartara and treated him with considerable ffection. But Amar Kaur always looked at him as though e were an imposter, who at any minute would discard his urban and comb, and disappear reciting *Qul huwa' l-Lah.*

One day Parmeshar Singh barged into the house, uffing and puffing, and asked his wife, 'Where is the hild?'

'Who? Amar Kaur?'

'No, no. Not she.'

'Kartara?'

'No.' But after a moment's thought he said, 'Yes, yes, Kartara.'

'He's gone out to play. Must be out in the alley.'

Parmeshar Singh darted back out. Once in the alley, he tarted to run. When he came to the fields, he ran faster. Far n the distance he spotted a few boys playing *kabaddi* near Gyan Singh's sugarcane field. As he approached, he peered round the cane stalks and saw that Akhtar had pinned one f the boys to the ground with his knees. Blood was oozing rom the boy's lips but he diligently kept up the litany of *abaddi, kabaddi, kabaddi.*

The boy, finally admitting defeat, stopped the epetitions. After Akhtar had let go of him, he asked, 'Hey Kartaro, why did you hit me in the mouth with your knee?'

'I'm glad I did,' Akhtar shot back, haughtily, meanwhile ying his loose hair into a knot and sticking the comb into

'Is that what your Prophet has taught you to do?' the boy mocked him.

For a moment Akhtar was totally confused. Then, after some thought, he replied with a question of his own. 'And what has your Guru taught you?'

'Musla!' the boy cursed Akhtar.

'Sikhra!' Akhtar cursed back.

All the other boys then ganged up on Akhtar, but a single roar from Parmeshar Singh sent them running every which way. Parmeshar Singh tied Akhtar's turban back on, took him to one side and said, 'Tell me, son. Do you want to stay with me or do you want to go back to your mother?

Akhtar was fazed, unable to decide. He stood staring into Parmeshar Singh's eyes for a while, and then smiled and said, 'To my mother.'

'You don't want to stay here with me?' Parmeshar Singh's face turned so red that he seemed about to cry.

'I'll stay with you too,' Akhtar replied, offering what looked like a good solution.

Parmeshar Singh picked him up and hugged him. Tears, which had been born of disappointment, now streamed down his face as tears of joy. He said, 'Listen Akhtar, my son. The army is coming here today. They're coming to take you away from me. You understand? You go hide yourself somewhere. When they leave, I'll come and get you.'

Just then Parmeshar Singh spotted a spiralling cloud of dust far in the distance. He climbed up the raised mud trail around the field and looked closely at the spiral, which was getting bigger by the second. He said with a shiver, 'The army truck is here.'

He stepped down from the raised trail and ran around the sugarcane field shouting, 'Gyan, O Gyan Singh!'

Gyan Singh emerged from the field. He had a sickle in one hand and some grass in the other. Parmeshar Singh took him aside, explained something to him, and then both men returned to Akhtar. Gyan Singh snapped a cane stalk from the field, shaved the leaves off with his sickle, and gave it to Akhtar. 'All right, Kartare, come. You sit with me and enjoy the sugarcane until the army men have gone back. Look at them! What audacity! They've come to grab such a fine Khalsa boy. Huh!'

'Is it all right with you if I leave now?' Parmeshar Singh asked Akhtar for permission.

Akhtar, holding a long piece of the sugarcane peel in his teeth, tried to smile. Parmeshar Singh ran back to the village, as the cloud of dust drew progressively nearer.

At home, he explained the situation to his wife and daughter, then took off for Granthiji. Having explained the matter to him too, he tried to do the same with some of the other people.

The army vehicle stopped in a field beyond the dharmshala. The soldiers, accompanied by the village *nambardar*, came straight over to Granthiji. They asked if the village folks were keeping any Muslim girls. Granthiji gave them his word that there wasn't a single Muslim girl in the entire village, and backed it up by swearing on the Granth Sahab.

'Boys are something else again,' someone whispered into Parmeshar Singh's ear, which made him and some of the other Sikhs around him smile to themselves.

One of the army men then treated the villagers to a speech, stressing how the maternal affection of those mothers whose daughters had been stolen away from them had now turned into a torrent of pain. He also drew a touching picture of the plight of those brothers and husbands whose sisters and wives had been forcibly taken away from them. 'And what is religion, my friends?' he concluded. 'Doesn't every religion teach man to be truly a human being after all? Now look at your conduct. In the name of religion you take away from man his humanity. You trample on his dignity. You call yourselves Sikhs, you call yourselves Muslims. You say we are followers of Vahguruji, we are slaves of the Prophet.'

After the speech the crowd began to disperse. The army officer thanked Granthiji, shook his hands, and the vehicle moved along.

Promptly thereafter Granthiji congratulated Parmeshar Singh. The rest of the people crowded around him and started to offer their congratulations. But Parmeshar Singh, scared out of his wits before the arrival of the army vehicle, seemed utterly lost after its departure.

He walked outside the village and came to Gyan Singh's field. He hoisted Akhtar onto his shoulder and brought him home. After feeding him he put him to bed and caressed him with such affection that the boy fell asleep right away. Parmeshar Singh sat on the boy's cot for a long while. He would scratch his beard now and then, look around, and drift off into his thoughts. A boy playing on the rooftop of the house next door suddenly grabbed his heel and doubled over with pain, screaming bitterly, 'Oh, I've got such a big thorn in my foot! It's sunk all the way in!' The boy's mother ran up the stairs without even bothering to cover her head. She picked him up and took him in her lap. Then she called out to her daughter, telling her to bring a needle. She deftly removed the thorn, kissed him madly, and then leaning down from the edge of the roof she shouted, 'Hey, throw me my dupatta. I can't believe I did it—so shamelessly running up the stairs without a head cover.'

Parmeshar Singh, after a while, started and asked his wife, 'Listen, do you still miss Kartara?'

'Listen to this!' she blurted out, and then suddenly broke into tears. 'Parmeshare! Kartara is the wound in my heart which will never heal.'

Hearing her brother's name mentioned, Amar Kaur came over and sat at her mother's knee, crying herself.

Parmeshar Singh jumped up, as though he had dropped a tray full of glass dishes on the floor.

In the evening after supper, holding the boy's finger he led him into the open courtyard and said, 'Today you've slept plenty, son. Let's go out for a walk. It's a beautiful moonlit night.'

Akhtar agreed right away. Parmeshar Singh wrapped a blanket carefully around the boy and put him on his shoulder. When he reached the fields, he said, 'This moon you see rising in the east, son, it will be morning by the time it's directly overhead.'

Akhtar looked at the moon.

'The moon which is shining here, must be shinning back in your mother's country too.'

This time Akhtar leaned over to look at Parmeshar Singh.

'When it reaches straight above our heads, it will also be straight above your mother's head.'

Akhtar asked, 'Would my mother also be watching the moon just as we are watching it here?'

'Absolutely.' There was a loud resonance in Parmeshar Singh's voice. 'Would you like to go to your mother?'

'Yes, very much,' Akhtar said. 'But you never take me to her. You're bad. Very bad. You are a Sikh.'

'No, son,' Parmeshar Singh said, 'I will. Today. You can be sure of that. A letter came from your mother. She says "I miss my Akhtar very much."'

'I miss her a lot, too,' Akhtar said, as if remembering something suddenly.

'Actually, I'm taking you to your mother right now.'

'Really?' Akhtar began to jump up and down on Parmeshar Singh's shoulder. 'I'm going to my mother! Parmun'll take me to her! When I'm there, I'll write Parmun a letter!'

Down below, Parmeshar Singh wept silently. He wiped his tears, cleared his throat, and asked, 'Would you like me to sing you a song?'

'Yes.'

'But first you should recite the Quran for me.'

'OK.' Akhtar intoned the verses beginning with *Qul huwa' l-Lah*. When he concluded the recitation with *kufuwan ahad*, he breathed into his chest and said, 'Come, let me breathe on your chest too.'

Parmeshar Singh stopped walking, unbuttoned the front of his shirt, and looked up. The boy hung down and breathed into the open collar. 'Your turn now.'

Parmeshar Singh shifted the boy onto his other shoulder. Since he didn't remember any children's songs, he started singing all kinds of other songs, picking up his pace as he went along. Akhtar listened to him quietly.

Banto—her hair is like a dense forest.
Banto—her face is like the moon.
Banto—her broad hips flow sweetly.
O hey, O hear, people,
Banto—her broad hips flow sweetly.

'Who is Banto?' Akhtar interrupted.

Parmeshar Singh laughed. After a pause he said, 'You

know, my wife, Amar Kaur's mother. She is Banto, and so is Amar Kaur, and so must be your mother too.'

'Why my mother?' Akhtar was angered. 'She's not a Sikh.'

Parmeshar Singh fell silent.

The moon had risen well into the sky. The night was perfectly calm. A few jackals howled near the cane fields now and then, followed by the same absolute silence. At first the howls frightened Akhtar, but Parmeshar Singh's assurances calmed him. After a long silence, he asked, 'Why aren't the jackals howling now?'

Parmeshar Singh laughed. He recalled a story. The story of Guru Gobind. As he told it, he deftly changed the Sikh names to Muslim names. Akhtar kept asking, 'And then what happened? . . . And then what happened? . . .'

The story wasn't yet finished when Akhtar suddenly shouted, '*Arey*, the moon—it's right above our heads!'

Parmeshar Singh broke his stride and he too looked up. He then climbed up a small hill and peered into the distance. 'Who knows where your mother's country is,' he said.

He stood on the hill for a while. Suddenly the sound of *azan* came floating in from afar. Akhtar, beside himself with a rush of excitement, jumped so awkwardly that Parmeshar Singh had the hardest time holding on to him. He put him down and himself sat on the ground. Then, putting his hand on Akhtar's shoulder, who was standing beside him, he said, 'Go, son. Your mother's calling you. Just follow the sound.'

'Sh-shshsh!' Akhtar put his finger to his lips and whispered, 'One doesn't talk during the *azan*.'

'But I am a Sikh, son.'

'Sh-ṣhshsh!' This time Akhtar, feeling piqued, glowered at him.

Parmeshar Singh drew the boy closer and sat him in his lap. He gave him a long kiss on the forehead. After the *azan* was over, he wiped his eyes with his sleeve and said in a voice crumbling with emotion, 'This is as far as I can come. You go on ahead.'

'Why? Why can't you?'

'Your mother's orders. She writes that you should come alone.' Parmeshar Singh wheedled. 'Now, keep walking straight, until you come to the village up ahead. There, tell them your name. Remember, not Kartara, but Akhtar. Then tell them your mother's name, and the name of your village. And don't you forget to write me a letter.'

'I won't,' Akhtar promised.

'And, yes, if you find a boy there called Kartara, send him back over to us. You will—won't you?'

'All right, I will.'

Parmeshar Singh kissed the boy on the forehead once again and, swallowing the lump in his throat, said, 'Now go!'

Akhtar took a few steps, turned around, and walked back to the older man. 'Why don't you come too?'

'No, I can't,' Parmeshar Singh explained. 'Your mother didn't say that I should come too.'

'But I'm scared,' Akhtar said.

'Recite the Quran and you'll be okay,' Parmeshar Singh suggested.

'All right,' the boy agreed. He broke into a litany of *Qul huwa' l-Lah* as he walked away from the older man.

The soft, faint light of the dawn was struggling with the darkness on the horizon. And the little boy Akhtar, like strapping Sikh youth, was walking briskly away on th foggy foot trail. Parmeshar Singh, his eyes trained on the receding figure, sat on the hilltop, coming down from it only after the receding dot had become indistinct in the space up ahead.

Akhtar had barely reached the outskirts of the village when two soldiers rushed toward him. They stopped and asked him, 'Who are you?'

'Akhtar!' he said, as if the entire world knew who he was.

'Akhtar!' The soldiers looked, now at his face, now at his Sikh turban. Then one of them stepped forward and jerked the turban from the boy's head. Akhtar's *kes* came undone and cascaded down.

The boy became furious and snatched the turban back from the soldier. He felt his head with his hand, lay down on the ground, and wept bitterly. 'Give me back my comb!' he shouted. 'You've stolen my comb! Give it back, or I'll kill you!'

Instantly the two soldiers dropped to the ground with a thud, their rifle butts against their shoulders, as if to take aim.

'Halt!' one of the soldiers shouted and waited for a reply.

In the breaking daylight they both looked at each other, and one of them fired.

The report made the boy jump. Seeing the soldiers run off, he too followed them, shouting and crying.

Coming to the spot the soldiers stopped. By then Parmeshar Singh had wrapped his turban tightly round his thigh. But the blood was gushing out even through the innumerable folds. He was saying: 'Why did you have to shoot me?! I just forgot to clip Akhtar's *kes*! I only came to return Akhtar to his dharm, *yaaro*!'

In the distance, Akhtar was running over to them, his *kes* flowing in the air.

An Unwritten Epic

Intizar Husain

In Qadirpur, too, such a fierce battle broke out that people put their hands over their ears in denial when they heard it. Confusion was rampant. Human lives everywhere went for a penny a pound, give or take a few ounces. One person was killed taking two steps back, another taking four steps forward. One was hit in the back, another the chest. How could Qadirpur, insignificant as it was, stem the tide that had shaken even the roots of mountains? But thanks to Pichwa's presence, Qadirpur became the scene of a memorable feat. Knowing they were facing death, friends put on their shrouds, asked their mothers' blessings, committed their wives to God, and marched into battle with such valour and majesty that they revived the memory of wars fought in ancient times. A fierce battle broke out, with incredible bloodshed—heaps of corpses everywhere. Nor were the Jats wanting in character and ceremony. They came out mounted on caparisoned elephants, lighting up the night with their torches. Qadirpur's entire fame rested on Pichwa, so the bravest of the Jats were gathered from far and near. The elephants were lined up, the cannon, gunpowder, arrows and swords arranged, and the Jat army, weighed down with equipment, set off to conquer Qadirpur. In the branches of the banyan tree near the Eidgah, Majid sat guard. Seeing light beyond the trees further away, he pricked up his ears and very carefully studied the situation. Listening attentively to all the noises and focusing his eyes, he tried to analyse the light. Finally certain that the expected moment had at last arrived, he thundered out the news on his drum. As soon as the drum was struck, chaos broke out in the houses of Qadirpur. Asleep on the roof, Naim Miyan's two sons, Owais and Azhar, lost their senses when they heard the slogans and drumbeats. Owais was speechless. Azhar, unable to do anything else, got up and leapt headlong over the roofs coming at last to the roof of the Weavers' Mosque. There was a gap between the roofs here, and Azhar was stopped in his tracks. He had no idea what he should do next. Keeping guard below, Rahmat now thumped his club and challenged, 'Who's there?' Azhar pulled himself together with great difficulty and somehow managed to identify himself. Rahmat laughed and said, 'Miyan, you have disgraced the name of Aligarh College.' Despite Rahmat's opinion, both Azhar and Owais were alumni of Aligarh, and in the pre-Partition days whenever they participated in political rallies and enthusiastically shouted the slogan, 'India will be divided; Pakistan will be created,' their voices resounded with an unusual note of determination. After the Partition of India, however, they had begun to talk senselessly and extravagantly.

When Naim Miyan woke up, Azhar's cot was empty and Owais was standing speechless. Confused, he grabbed his rifle and cartridge case, but the people at the meeting place suddenly raised the cry *'Allahu Akbar!'* with such gusto that the cartridge case fell from his hand. There had been a vigil at the meeting place. People were now coming out, each one holding up his weapon.

Straightening his turban, Jafar put his javelin in position and started to draw on the hookah as he went out. Behind him Pichwa straightened his waist cloth and called out, 'This is no time for the hookah, my friend!' Jafar put down the hookah and went out thumping his javelin on the ground. Pichwa tightened and knotted his waist cloth with great satisfaction and arranged the silver-coated amulet on his neck. Then he rolled up his shirt sleeves, spat on his palms and weighed his club in hand. On his way out he called for Mammad. Annoyed at getting no answer, he called out again, 'Hey Mammad, you son of a bitch, where the hell are you?'

Throwing his vest around his neck, Mammad leapt out of a corner. 'Here I am, Ustad.'

'Hey, you son of an Ustad, are you coming out or not?' Reaching him, Pichwa's tone softened, 'Now look, you hang on in the Weavers' Mosque trench, and I'll take care of everything here.'

After he had instructed Mammad, he left the meeting place followed by a few of his young wrestlers. As he came out, he glanced at the haveli. Kalwa was leading the unit posted there. As soon as he saw Pichwa, he came to attention and shouted, 'Don't worry, Ustad, I'll break anyone who comes here in half.'

Pichwa was most worried about the haveli entrenchment. And he had reason to be. All the women of the Qadirpur settlement were gathered in it. Although there was a dark well inside the haveli and each woman had been clearly told what her duty required in the eventuality, a few nooses had also been set up for good measure. Pichwa had stationed several of his brave young men at the haveli and had told them, 'I'll roast anyone of you bastards alive who shows the slightest weakness.' Confident of Kalwa's bravery and satisfied with what he had said, he went on, weighing his club. A feeling of urgency had now become noticeable in the drumbeats, and far into the distance the conch shells had begun to sound as well. Pichwa quickened his steps. People were beginning to pour out of the other houses. Qurban Ali came out of his house brandishing the side rail of a cot. When the noise arose he hurriedly searched everywhere in the house but could not find even an ordinary piece of wood, let alone a regular weapon. First anger, then the pressure exerted by man's instinctive inventiveness, he fell upon a cot and tore it apart in a flash. Although Saiyid Hamid Hasan had several beautiful walking sticks brought from Nainital and Dehra Dun as gifts, he had nothing resembling a club. Hurriedly scrambling around, however, he and his wife finally managed to unearth a rotten, old sword stick. Munshi Sanaullah did not have to face this problem at all. In the front courtyard lay a piece of bamboo used to clear out cobwebs from the rooms; he picked it up as he rushed out. Nor did the Subedar Sahib have to worry about a club. He had a match-lock gun which he always kept clean. In the crowd of clubs, the raised barrels of a few other rifles were also visible. His vest pocket loaded with pellets, Hamid held in his hand a shiny black slingshot of shisham wood. A few steps behind Pichwa stood Rasula and Bhallan carrying on their shoulders an entire arsenal, including fireworks shaped like pomegranates, horns, and swords. Allah Razi's party came behind them, dragging an odd-looking cannon. Now this cannon had been fired once before, unfortunately in the direction of Allah Razi's companions. Allah Razi had not had the foggiest idea how the damned thing worked. So, several men were badly wounded and a few others were arrested by the police in connection with the incident. Now, however, Allah Razi was sure that it would not be his companions but his enemies who would be beaten to a pulp. Normally armed with clubs, Pichwa's companions, responding to the demands of time, had made a small modification to their weapons. No longer plain clubs, theirs now had short spears attached to them. Pichwa's, however, was the same as it had always been, except that, having soaked it in oil for three days, it was a little more slippery than usual. So what? The slipperiness that comes from oil makes a club shinier; it does not, however, affect its 'clubness'. It is the spear that destroys the 'clubness' of a club. With a spear attached to a club, it is no longer a club but a spear. Mammad's, Kalwa's, Rahmat's and Jafar's clubs had thus been reborn as spears. Pichwa's, however, was still just a plain old club—to modify it would have meant for him to change his whole mode of thinking. This club had become an inextricable part of his being. In a way it had given up its separate existence and become an indissoluble part of his own personality. Pichwa's club, consequently, was not merely a club; it was Pichwa's club. Nor was it like the staff of Moses, for that staff had a power of its own apart from Moses; and in a sense, although Moses needed the staff, the staff had no need of him. Pichwa's club was, at any rate, Pichwa's club. And although it too had performed many miracles, the miraculous power was in Pichwa's arms, not in the club itself. The best proof of this was the time Pichwa was accidentally forced to fight without his club. Seeing him unarmed, Tidda the wrestler's companions thought they could at last finish him off. Without hesitating a moment, Pichwa immediately took off his head cloth, tied a coin up in it and started showing his skill. Within five minutes he had three of them lay their clubs down in sheer helplessness—the many wrists he broke may be considered extra. And then he let them have it, banging their heads with their own clubs. Tidda's companions were not so brave that they could stare down an opponent: a few cracked skulls and off they went.

Tidda's poor young men, of course, were small fry. Pichwa was always ready to take on an entire village. It so happened that Pichwa was there when the people of Lachmanpur had angrily surrounded the Subedar Sahib. No doubt he had enraged them by firing at peacocks when he could not find any ducks. Anyway, a commotion had broken out everywhere. Lachmanpura was nearby and country bumpkins rushed up carrying cudgels. Hardly one to stand around at such a time, Naim Miyan was off like a shot as soon as he heard all the noise. Hamida, at his wits' end, darted off into a nearby cornfield. Only Allah Razi had apparently escaped unharmed, but as luck would have it, he landed in a field where a farmer was ploughing. The peasant whacked him in the face first and asked questions later. Saiyid Hamid Hasan's slowness proved his undoing. Lacking any other alternative, he tried to sweet-talk them into letting him go, but his peasant captors knew better than that. The Subedar Sahib just stood there—utterly befuddled, unable to think or do anything. Pichwa was incensed. With a *'Ya Ali,'* he took up his club and beat them mercilessly, killing several peasants, smashing countless wrists, and spraining many more. And when the Subedar Sahib and Pichwa arrived back in Qadirpur, they brought along, in addition to the slaughtered peacocks, a whole pile of very fine, heavy clubs.

It was only a coincidence that Pichwa and Tidda were at odds then over the hillwoman Billo. Although Pichwa was not averse to female company once in a while, he was not particularly one for running after women, as his real interests lay elsewhere. He and Tidda had already locked horns before over the affair with Nasira. Nasira had been legitimately accepted as a member of Tidda's wrestling group, although other people were not willing to accord him that status. Pichwa was never one to hold his tongue, and when he sat at Allah Razi's pan shop, put the pan in his mouth and took a puff of his biri, he became even more boastful.

As he sat there one day, seeing Nasira he lost control of himself and shouted out, 'Pay attention to me, not others!' Nasira was very embarrassed. When Tidda found out about it, his blood began to boil. Anyone else he would have slaughtered, but here it was a case of a camel against a mountain. Still he was so incensed that he took this boldness of Pichwa's as an act of war. The quarrel festered for several months; several skirmishes took place, but Tidda ended up humiliated every time. Not just this one quarrel; Tidda and Pichwa could never get along with each other.

Although Tidda was proud of his expertise, Pichwa refused to admit he had any. Whenever anyone mentioned Tidda, Pichwa would blow up. 'Bah, that son of a barber, that bastard, what does he know about expertise? Miyan, his party always puts up the poorest show in the wrestling matches at the *taziyas*.'

'But, Khalifa,' Allah Razi replied mischievously, for the sake of continuing the argument, 'now he's training very hard.'

Pichwa grew even more heated, 'Oh, to hell with his training; what'll it get him anyway? It's razors he's worked with. What does he know about wielding a club?'

Mammad was now warmed up. 'Ustad, this son of a barber must really want to get beaten up again. He thinks he's the great Gama, but one slap and all the stuffing will come out of him.'

'Miyan, I've already beaten that moron's brains in, but just look, the stupid fool still comes back for more.'

Mammad was not the kind to be content with great deeds of the past. He immediately retorted, 'Ustad, that was a long time ago, and soon it'll be forgotten. I swear to you, Ustad, I'll beat those jerks till they can't stand up.'

'Now wait a minute, boy. I'm itching for a fight with him myself. I'd clip the moron's wings, but he keeps avoiding me.'

Pichwa's excuse was partially correct. Although Tidda's group was not all that weak, nor were they short of words when it came to talking big, the fact is that whenever the chance to confront Pichwa presented itself, Tidda always managed somehow to skirt the disaster.

People with common sense in Qadirpur knew that Pichwa was a master of the art of *banaut*, but the superstitious kind circulated all sorts of stories about him. They would say that Pichwa knew magic. And Bhallan suspected this more than most. He had openly expressed his feelings several times: 'Miyaṇ, whatever it is, Pichwa must have something in his power.'

Rasula not only vehemently confirmed this, but also provided the proof: 'By God, the thing that baffles me is that Pichwa once threw a jinn down to the ground. Now, I've seen a lot of *banaut* in my time, but, Miyan, I don't care what you know about moving the stick, no one can win against a jinn. You take it from me, he knows some spell!'

Allah Razi's suspicions were aroused by the amulet Pichwa wore around his neck, but Hamida swore saying, 'I saw it with my own eyes. Behind the Eidgah, in a broken-down grave, Pichwa was standing on one foot reciting something. There's no question that some fakir has given him a charm, and that charm is where his power comes from.'

Jafar's story, however, was different. He would say

'Miyan, the thing is that Pichwa showed such great courage when those bloody Hindus wanted to tear down the Weavers' Mosque. Miyan, you should've seen the way he moved his stick; he made the fools lose their wits. Well, that night what did Pichwa see in a dream but that Maula Ali was patting his back. So you see, this is all through the grace of Maula Ali's feet; otherwise poor Pichwa and his *banaut* would not mean much.'

But these were all differences of opinion about cause and effect. That Pichwa was brave had been proved beyond doubt. Pichwa never gave people sufficient time to think twice about his bravery. Every now and then he would pick a fight with some group on some pretext or other and thus show off his powers. Never concerned about how things would turn out, Pichwa fought without any stab of fear or of thoughts of loss or gain. Moreover, purposiveness had never stained his art. Rather, it was the fight itself that mattered to him, and his club-fighting was free of any self-serving. Consequently, when the storm of communal riots began, Pichwa put all other considerations out of his mind and concentrated on the fact that he would now have a chance to display publicly his skill with the club. With both authority and excitement, he ordered his band, 'Tighten your belts, lads. After a long time dear Almighty God has finally heard us. We're going to have the time of our lives—God be praised!'

When the members of the group heard this, they could not contain their happiness. Mammad burst out, 'I swear by the Master if Qadirpur doesn't win, Mammad is not his father's son.'

Kalwa boasted, 'It's true, my club has seen better days. But now I'll dye it red again and bring out its true colour.'

Pichwa's companions made the same elegant and

showy preparations for the forthcoming fighting and bloodshed that people make for Eid. But all the elegance was wasted, for the tide of the fight turned before their very eyes. Then it was a question not of Qadirpur conquering, but of remaining undefeated. It took Pichwa a long time to feel the change in the wind. Offensive campaigns were all he had ever known, but what defensive action meant he came to learn the hard way only then. When he heard about the creation of Pakistan, he received the news with a feeling of immense chill. He wrung his hands in disappointment and said with deep regret, 'Miyan, while we sat here rotting, they won the battle over there.'

Then he lost his temper and roundly cursed himself and all the people of Qadirpur for having been unaware. Certainly Pichwa was glad that the battle had been won, but he was also grieved that it was not his blood that had helped buy this empire. After he had lamented enough, he said, 'Miyan, what was to be has happened. Come on, let's go to the peepul tree by the Eidgah and at least put up a Pakistani flag.' The other people of Qadirpur fainted when they heard Pichwa's idea. They tried hard to reason with him and explained where Pakistan actually was. Pichwa was flabbergasted. He could not understand how Qadirpur, where he lived, could be outside of Pakistan. After hearing what people said, he gave up the idea of flying the Pakistani flag, but then, on the urging of Mammad and Kalwa, he decided that, as Pakistan had excluded them from its brotherhood, they would make their own separate Pakistan. Consequently, they decided to fly on the banyan tree by the Eidgah an Islamic flag representing Pichwa's group, and not the flag of Pakistan. People were even more upset when they heard this. Already in bad shape, poor Naim Miyan lost his senses altogether when he heard Pichwa's idea. He tried hard to explain to Pichwa and made every attempt to dissuade him. All Pichwa answered was, 'Now you listen to me, Miyan, no Congress flag is going to fly in Qadirpur; we're going to put up the flag of Pichwa's wrestling group.' Naim Miyan was extremely worried and upset, but what could he do? Pichwa was no longer under his control. He had been very obedient and respectful before, but for several days now Pichwa had begun to complain about him, announcing his rebellion openly. Actually, even Naim Miyan was no longer what he had been before. Although he was still called the leader of the Muslim League, he no longer had anything to do with it. He had been very proud before and would get very irritated if anyone so much as mentioned the Congress. He felt it beneath his dignity to talk to a Hindu.

As soon as the Partition was announced, however, there was a change in his behaviour. With the creation of Pakistan, poor Naim Miyan was suddenly terribly confused and started to avoid even the mention of the Muslim League and Pakistan. But, anyway, what he did in the end saved him. Before August was over, he had gone to Pakistan. As they were leaving Qadirpur he said, 'We're just going to Delhi,' but about a fortnight later, the Subedar Sahib received a letter from him from Lahore. He had written: 'Brother, all the higher-ups I met in Delhi told me that the lives and fortunes of Muslims are no longer safe in India, and that we must go to Pakistan. We had a very hard time getting here, but, thanks be to God, we reached our country safe and sound. Azhar Miyan got a job in the Rehabilitation Department. God willing, Owais Miyan will also find a job soon. There's nothing left there now in Qadirpur. You should try to come too. By God's grace, I have some influence here, and we can work something out.'

When Pichwa heard the contents of the letter, he got up at Allah Razi's store and cursed Naim Miyan. But what good was it to beat the trail when the snake had already slunk away? Perhaps Naim Miyan may have lingered on a few more days, but, in fact, it had been Pichwa himself who had given him the push. Although Naim Miyan had explained the situation over and over to him, once he had taken it into his head, he had to go and put his flag on the peepul tree. Although the invasion would eventually have taken place, initially the Jats had hesitated because of Pichwa. But this action of his was especially provoking, and, as the Jats acted on the principle of not putting off for tomorrow what could be done today, they attacked Qadirpur. Now it is true that Pichwa's companions had beaten the hell out of the Jats in the fight, but Naim Miyan was not so stupid that he could not see what was brewing. He knew that the calamity had been averted—but only for a while longer.

Panic broke out in Qadirpur as a result of Naim Miyan's letter. Three days later Munshi Sanaullah folded up and left for good. On market day that week people found attractive bargains in household goods at the second-hand dealer's shop. Especially noticeable were Saiyid Hamid Hasan's Nainital walking sticks, Qurban Ali's shisham wood cots, and Munshi Sanaullah's china.

3 April 1950

How could I have known several months ago when I started writing this story that it would be ruined? If I had, I would have finished it immediately. As I wrote the story, I realized that the character of Pichwa could not be contained in a short story. Justice could only be done to him in a full-length novel. Moreover, I thought, no epic poem has yet been written on the riots. Now, I am no poet—so let me try writing a prose epic. And then, this is not the time for writing great poetry. Now, when we have no great epic heroes, I am surely very fortunate to have a character like Pichwa fall right into my lap. But how could I have known then that after the first riot was over, another would break out and Pichwa would come to Pakistan? How could that same Pichwa, who confronted the riot with his own body, have staggered and been pushed out? What terrible thing happened to Qadirpur? Where did Kalwa and Mammad drift off to? I have no idea. How could I have had the nerve to ask Pichwa about all this? I'm just sorry that the design of my novel is ruined. Pichwa and I are both unlucky. He was not fortunate enough to become the hero of an epic, and I am fated to treat the lives of insignificant people in worthless two-penny stories. People may look down their noses at this. It's true that Pichwa wasn't a great general or a splendid and glorious king; nevertheless, he had a certain dignity and greatness. And I never said my novel had to be called a *Shahnama*. An epic can also be called *Jumhurnama*. Anyway, there's no use arguing about it; it's all just a thought now.

7 April 1950

I can't figure out how to write about living things. I write about dead things. How can one possibly write about living things? There's a certain amount of definiteness about them. They don't have hidden corners and evocative shadows. You can write reportage or political poetry about living things, but not short stories or lyric poetry. I feel very nervous when I see living things. The critic who said that a writer should always keep a window open while writing is a fool. Who said you should keep a window open during a windstorm? I'm just amazed at how people can write with their eyes open. I have to write with my eyes closed. I take up the pen only after the subject comes to permeate my mind totally. The trouble is, though, as long as I can still see it, it doesn't settle down in my mind. As long as I lived in Qadirpur, it never occurred to me that Pichwa had it in him to become the subject of a story. When I came to Pakistan, my ties with Qadirpur were broken, and its life and people became a story for me. I didn't care whether Pichwa was alive or dead. As far as I am concerned, he was dead. Out of sight, out of mind. I started to write thinking him dead, but here he is, a living, breathing picture, moving around in front of me, and consequently, the character that had settled down in my mind has vanished like horns off a donkey's head. Down with *real* life: it's stolen from me the hero of my novel.

12 April 1950

Day and night I've been haunted by the question of whether or not I should write my novel. Sometimes I decide to start writing. After all, people do write about living subjects. Everyone is naked in this bath, if I take off my clothes, will a riot break out? Still, I just go on thinking. My head is with me, but my heart is on strike. To hell with writing—the character I had constructed with so much care and difficulty is no longer intact, to say nothing of the living personality. In Qadirpur Pichwa's living personality looked more like a character in a short story, but now that he's come to Pakistan, new twists are coming out in him. I thought of Pichwa as experiencing unrequited love, and this is the way I imagined the hero of my novel. Now I see more than unrequited love, he's experiencing an unrequited desire for employment. When I met Pichwa this morning, he said, 'Miyan, get me some kind of work. I have no damned place even to put my feet in. Babu, if I can't get any work, at least have a house allotted for me.'

I was greatly astonished when I heard these words from Pichwa's mouth. He was never worried about daily necessities in Qadirpur. Here he begs for food and wants a roof over his head. Where and how can I get him a house and job? All I can do is make him the hero of my novel. Originally I thought I would cast him as a twentieth-century Tipu Sultan, but now that he's come to Pakistan and wants a place to put his feet and something to fill his belly, all the height and grandeur of his character are destroyed.

Pichwa is wandering around looking for work. Today he went to see Naim Miyan about this problem, but he is scarcely the Naim Miyan he was—he won't give a black man the time of day now. He scolded Pichwa, 'Everyone just marches to Pakistan expecting to get something, as if his old man had buried a treasure here. They just don't realize that there isn't that much room in Pakistan.'

Pichwa complains that Naim Miyan has put on airs now that he's come to Pakistan. What's he complaining about? Naim Miyan is at the top of the heap—if he can't boast, who can? Obviously, in Qadirpur, Pichwa would never have stood for such harsh words, nor would Naim Miyan have had the nerve to look askance at Pichwa. He was always tongue-tied in front of Pichwa. In its own home, however, even the ant becomes a tiger. Clearly Pakistan is Naim Miyan's home and not Pichwa's.

20 April 1950

You can't teach an old dog new tricks. Pichwa may have lost everything he had but he still has his poetic temperament. Even in his unrequited desire for work, he looks like he's feeling unrequited love. His eyes burst out of his head when he saw the farmland of Pakistan. He told me, 'Miyan, if I could just get a *bigha* of land, what a change you'd see in Pichwa. Now, I'd put in a mango grove and I'd have a wrestling arena dug on one side where we'd have tests of strength. If you came here in the rainy season, Miyan, I'd give you such mangoes that you'd forget Malihabad.'

I answered, 'Look, you day-dreaming fool, who's going to give you a *bigha* of land? This land doesn't belong to you or me—it belongs to the zamindars.'

But when Pichwa is caught up in what he's saying, his feet don't stay on the ground. He answered, 'The zamindars, too, are our Muslim brothers. You just watch: Whoever I'll beseech in the name of Allah and the Prophet Muhammad will not hesitate to give me a morsel of land.'

You see Pichwa's strange logic—that zamindars too must start to be Hindus and Muslims.

22 April 1950

I feel as if the desire to create is decreasing in me. Sometimes I blame myself for this and sometimes external events. Every time I take up my pen, the slogan, 'Long Live Pakistan,' goes up with such force that I drop the pen. The cry goes up everywhere for 'constructive literature'. I can't hear anything else in this noise. What is this animal called 'constructive literature'? Things are recognized by their opposites. I've never yet seen anything destructive in literature. If literature isn't destructive, how can it be constructive? Literature is neither constructive nor destructive; it's just literature.

After one of my friends had gone on and on about constructive literature, I was just broiling, and I said in no uncertain terms that I wanted to write about homosexual love. He was incensed and said, 'That's a very sick love.'

'OK, you give me a healthy subject,' I replied angrily.

'Write about Pakistan,' he said.

I can't figure out what I should write about Pakistan nor how I should write it. Pakistan is a living reality, a fact—and I don't have the power to turn fact into fiction. Pakistan is a reality, while Qadirpur has become a story, a story I can tell. I don't have the power to paint the land of Pakistan, but Qadirpur doesn't need to be painted; it's a story in itself. Its earth is reddened with the blood of its devoted sons. The reddened earth there, the air full of cries for help, the charred houses, the demolished mosque, the ruined wrestling arena—all these things are telling a story eight hundred years old. I can tell this story with all the pain and sorrow that's in it, and I can describe with full feeling the deeds of the vanquished Arjuna of this Mahabharata, but this Arjuna—he's the real problem now. How can I write the Mahabharata of Qadirpur? The Arjuna of this Mahabharata is now the picture of failure and he wanders around the streets and lanes of Pakistan looking for a house and a job. He doesn't get these two things and he continues falling from his true place.

2 May 1950

'Miyan, what kind of order is this?' Pichwa was becoming ferocious, and I felt as if he could take a bite out of me. I shuddered. Then it entered my head that this wasn't Qadirpur but Pakistan, and that Pichwa didn't have the same power here.

Surprised, I asked, 'What order?'

Pichwa spat out the words. 'The order that any refugees that have come here can damn well go back to India.'

I didn't know what to tell him. I calmed him down with difficulty, explaining, 'Brother, let go of your anger. It's just that Pakistan is full to the rafters now. Where will these new refugees fit? Moreover, some higher-ups went to Delhi and they say all the Muslims in India are doing fine.'

At this Pichwa was even more incensed, 'Miyan, would I lie to you, I, who've come from Qadirpur?'

I know Pichwa is not a liar. He may have a thousand faults, but lying isn't one of them. So what if I know that, the world believes only what the big-shots say.

3 May 1950

How the land shrinks, how food becomes scarce—the reason is simple enough, but I can't help it if Pichwa is too thick-skulled to understand it. They say there was once a king. He went a great distance hunting. He began to pant, and his throat was parched. Then he saw an orchard. He stopped in the garden to catch his breath and asked the gardener for water. The gardener's daughter picked a pomegranate and brought it to him. She squeezed half of it into a glass, and the glass was full to the brim. The king drank the pomegranate juice and was refreshed. Then he set off again to hunt. On the way he thought, 'Not only are so many pomegranates produced in this orchard, but only half of one fills a glass. Why not tax them?'

By and by the king came back to this orchard and asked

the gardener for water. The gardener's daughter squeezed a whole pomegranate into a glass, and then another, but still the glass wasn't full to the brim. She involuntarily cried out, 'Father, our king intends evil!'

Surprised, the king asked, 'Just how do you know the king intends evil?'

The gardener replied, 'Maharaj, when the king intends evil the crops begin to fail.'

You don't need a great brain to understand a simple thing like this. Both the ignorant gardener and his daughter understood it, but Pichwa—his head is full of cowdung.

Pichwa says, 'Miyan, make me the king of Pakistan for just one day and then I'll show you how I make those friends who own lots of land, big houses and several factories jump up and down. I'd beat them black and blue and give a share to every one of the refugees.' Snapping his fingers, he says, 'Look, Miyan, I'd take care of everything just like that.'

But I don't believe him—he's always boasting. What he doesn't seem to understand is that if he really were made king of Pakistan, he too would change. The only people with a sense of responsibility are those without it. It is too many responsibilities that produce what is called irresponsibility. What's irresponsible is not a person, but a chair.

5 May 1950

The farther I run from politics the more it pursues me. Until Pichwa came to Pakistan he was a genuine fictional character. But now that he's here, he's become an important political issue. Now whenever I think about him I end up in a political morass. Why isn't he allotted a house? Why can't he get a job? Why is he being sent back to India? In short, I get caught in the maze of politics however I think about him. It's not that I can't talk about politics. I can say quite a lot about things like refugee rehabilitation, minority agreements, and abandoned property arrangements. Nor have I kept my mouth shut out of politeness. But why should I poke my nose into politics? Although I feel strongly that my creative talents are being ruined, that doesn't mean I should hold my nose and dive into the cesspool of politics. A frustrated singer should stay a frustrated singer; he has no business becoming a reciter of elegies. I wouldn't interfere even if someone sprinkled this whole terrestrial ball with kerosene and set it on fire.

I'm afraid of external life, the most disgusting aspect of which is politics. Politics makes me tremble just as the butcher makes the cow tremble, and, in fact, politics brings the same doomsday for the writer as the butcher does for the cow. The joke is that politics not only slaughters both literature and the writer, it's the one that eventually gets all the plaudits as well.

6 May 1950

My creative desire continues to cool, and whatever magic there was in the fictional potential of Pichwa's personality ebbs away. He no longer seems like a person at all; he seems more like a chess piece. First he's in this square, then he goes to that one, then he's shoved back again to the first one. The characters of a novel are supposed to be human beings—how can I make someone like him the hero of my novel? If I really sweated and ground out a novel with chess pieces for characters, would anyone respect it? Could a novel about chess pieces be called anything but a chess game?

7 May 1950

I thought it was just so much bravado, but he did really go back for good. What men call conscience is really a shameless thing. It never dies completely but remains half-dead or pretends to be dead, and can come to life any time at all. Pichwa asked me with some heat, 'Will the leaders go with us too?'

I laughed and answered, 'If they went, who would lead Pakistan?'

This made him angrier and he cursed Naim Miyan up and down.

I had told Pichwa to take it easy if he really had to leave and not to be in a hurry, that the government itself would take care of all the arrangements for the trip. This made him furious. 'Should I take money for a shroud here and make my grave in India? I don't want a charity shroud.'

8 May 1950

Pichwa's departure has revived the plan for my novel. But who knows, he might suddenly come back and mess up the plan. Is it inconceivable that death might take him? After all, human life doesn't endure for long. A person can die in a split second. It is entirely conceivable that the heat of Sind might finish off this man from the Doab, or that someone might throw him off the train, or that the train he's riding in might be attacked. In short, death just needs an excuse. What couldn't happen if God willed it, and slaughtering people is certainly an amusing sport, but . . . but why would He ride the horse at the bidding of others?

20 May 1950

It's been nearly a fortnight since Pichwa left. I don't know who else is left now in Qadirpur, but I've heard that the Subedar Sahib is still hanging on there. I fired off a letter to him but there's no answer yet. I have no idea where Pichwa ended up after gulping down the sands of Sind. I'd hesitate to say he even got across the border. I wouldn't be surprised if he took a liking to the dust of Sind. Or perhaps the land of Pakistan was offended and hugged the departing guest to her bosom. Isn't it true that the earthly heart of a country throbs for its people even if the hearts of fellow-countrymen do not? Both this new country and its uninvited guests are fantastic: the uninvited guests gripe about the indifference of their former compatriots, the latter complain that the former lack foresight and have no feeling for the hosts' difficulties. Regardless of whether there's room in the country, Pichwa left because there's no longer any in the hearts of the people here. And Pichwa left defiantly. He said it was dishonourable to stay any longer. Where has the truthful watchman of his false honour wandered off to? I have no idea. How much he preferred individualism too, this person, how concerned he was about guarding his personal honour. I don't know if he was able to guard his personal honour or not. All I say is this: when the whole nation is being disgraced, does the honour of an individual count for anything? What difference does it make?

21 May 1950

I wait for the postman every day. I keep looking at the door. When he comes, he brings several letters at a time but not the one I'm waiting for. What's happened to the

Subedar Sahib that he doesn't answer? Has he also passed away? A person's breath is fragile to start with, and the Subedar Sahib was even then sitting with one foot in the grave. And what happened to that daring fellow Pichwa? Did the earth swallow him, or the sky devour him? Did the winds carry him off, or the snake bite him? Man is no more than a bubble, but proud Pichwa went to fight the wind with a lamp.

23 May 1950

Yeh daur-e jam, yeh gham-khana-e jahan, yeh raat
Kahan chiragh jalate hain loog aye saqi
(This round of the cup, this sorrowful world, this night
Where do the people light the lamp, O Cup-bearer?)

So that person has gone for good and not only that, he has ended up miles from Pakistan. He has crossed the borders of both Pakistan and India and has entered the country which isn't marked by any borders, where countless refugees arrive every day and are settled in no time at all. The Subedar Sahib's letter—should I call it a letter or an elegy—has come. I didn't realize the Subedar Sahib, in between hunting geese and deer, would start writing elegies. He writes:

> Your letter arrived late, but I am thankful it came. It was late in coming for two reasons. First because the address was written in a language that everyone else here except me denies knowing, and second, because Qadirpur is no longer Qadirpur. Now its new residents call it Jatunagar. You have fired off questions one after another. Which ones should I answer and how? The times you talk about, brother! Where is Qadirpur now? As the poet says, *Ek dhup thi jo sath gai aftab ke*! (The sunlight has vanished with the sun!)

Here there is no longer a Tidda, nor an Allah Razi, nor people flying their own flag on the peepul tree by the Eidgah. When the land of Qadirpur became too narrow for its people, some sank into it, and the rest were driven off. You ask what condition the wrestling arena behind the Weavers' Mosque is in, and I doubt there is even a mosque any more. The mosques would gladly mourn the loss of their worshippers and the wrestling arenas the loss of their young men—but where is there a mosque or an arena today? Allah Razi's store? Your asking brought it to mind—Hindu butchers sell *jhatka* meat there now.

Your country had no room for Pichwa, but the earth of his former country clasped him to her bosom. I was not able to meet this fortunate person, but, yes, one day the whole village got excited, and I saw on the same branch of the peepul tree by the Eidgah where Kalwa and Mammad had flown the flag of their party, their master's head was now hanging.

I felt very strange reading your letter. Whatever the reason, you remembered us. Do continue to remember us with scraps of letters. We are not strangers:

Vaj'h-e begangi nahin ma'lum
Tum jahan ke ho van ke ham bhi hain
(Why do you think us strangers?
We are from the same place you are.)

I am getting old and pretty soon the lamp of my life will be snuffed out. Who will you write to then in Qadirpur? Do remember the two things I said about the address.

What a strange letter the Subedar Sahib has written. I[s] it a letter or the concluding sentences of some epic tale? [I] think I'll end the novel I'm writing, i.e., my Qadirpu[r] Mahabharata, with this letter. And what a death indeed thi[s] crazy Pichwa found! His life was a drama, and so was his death. The one undramatic event in his life was his flight to Pakistan. If only he hadn't come to Pakistan. Pichwa disgraced himself by coming to Pakistan and threw a monkey wrench into the works of my novel.

25 May 1950

Pichwa is dead, but my novel is still not coming together. My hands start to shake whenever I take up my pen. Sometimes I feel as if I murdered Pichwa. What devil got into my head wanting him dead? If novels and stories got written this way, writers would be tried for murder every day.

27 May 1950

Every day I resolve to, but I haven't started to write the novel yet. I pick up my pen and put it back down. I wonder why I'm writing this novel. People don't care about human emotions here—the mention of human emotions is still an afterthought. Appreciation of literature comes from concern for humanity. My nation doesn't value a human being; how can it care about literature? Why should I debase my creative talent and disgrace my pen?

I have definitely decided not to write my novel. But how long can I just sit at home and do nothing? I thought I ought to start moving around. I'm so disinclined to shocking people that I wouldn't want to do anything spectacular. I would be content even to go into the despicable slave trade, but it's not permitted privately now—the governments have taken it over. Naim Miyan says, if it hadn't taken me such a long time to come to my senses, he would have had me allotted some big factory. Now he has promised to have a flour mill allotted. I have to work somehow—if not a factory, let it be a flour mill.

29 May 1950

Naim Miyan has sure turned out to be a useful person to have around. Somehow he had a flour mill allotted to me. As the owner of a flour mill, I see a strange kind of change in myself. As long as I was stuck in the web of literature, I felt cut off from my nation. Remaining wedded to literature would have meant being neither here nor there: I wouldn't have written the novel, nor could I have done any other kind of work. Now, however, I consider myself a responsible citizen—a dutiful member of a rising nation.

1 June 1950

I'm writing in my diary for the last time today. From tomorrow on I won't have enough time for it. Keeping a diary is something to do when you're unemployed. The arrangements for the mill have been taken care of. God willing, it will start up tomorrow. Since the going price in the city for grinding flour is five paise for five *sers*, I thought at my place I would charge only four paise so that people would patronize the new mill right away.

Co-translated by Leslie A. Flemming

Do You Suppose it's the East Wind?

Altaf Fatima

The enormous weight of three hundred and sixty-five days once again slips from my hand and falls down into the dark cavern of the past.

The windows in this desolate room are wide open. How improbably strange the sky, draped in a sheet of dense grey clouds, looks behind the luxuriant green trees. It seems someone has filled space itself with a sweet, melancholic beauty. A cool breeze has finally started to blow, after much heat and sun.

Could it be the east wind?

Papers and books lie in a disorderly pile before me on the desk. I suddenly stop writing, screw the cap back on the fountain pen and clip it to my collar—not because the weather is absolutely delightful and the grapevine is maddeningly beautiful and one simply cannot write a book on dairy-farming in a setting so entirely out of this world. One cannot discuss the significance of the chemical components of milk any more than one can expound on the proper proportion of corn husk and mustard oil-cake in the cattle feed. All right, not another word about cows or water buffalo.

My problem is that I'm very absent-minded. I search for my pen everywhere, while it's clipped to my collar all along. I look at faces I have seen so often and wonder who they might be. I have never seen them before. And my memory is so bad I can hardly remember who has hurt me and who I have decided to hold a grudge against. Worst of all, the day I'm supposed to take care of some enormously important matter, I seem to end up spending it in some atrociously silly programme. Well, that's what it's come to with me. My one abiding fear is that the landscapes of my memory might become a yawning wasteland—derelict, empty, blanched. That I may lose my grip on familiar things and no longer recognize them at all. That's why I have pushed aside the sheets of paper and clipped my pen back on. Just so that I may lean back and squint into the far horizon and not let my eyes waver. After all, trekking back on the past's interminable highways, *that* time may twist around and look back. It just might.

What! It really has! There, look, the past is calling me. All scenes before my eyes are beginning to dissolve, and a long lost horizon is forming in space. This gigantic gate, here— It's the very same gate whose wrought iron bars we would hug tightly, swinging for hours on end. Tickets would be improvised and sold; the guard would wave the green flag, and the passengers, planting their feet on the bottom railing and grabbing on to the grillwork, would enjoy the train ride, as the others energetically swung the gate out into the street. Directly across the street from the gate the blacksmith's furnace would be ablaze, the clank-clank of red-hot iron being beaten into shape resounding through the air. And inside the gate small and large gardens opened to view—hedges of *nirbisi* and delicate trellises draped with rose vines. We would make believe that our train was now chugging along beside jungle and farmland. To bring the train into a station, we would stick the thumb under the chin, run the index finger along the ridge of the nose all the way to the forehead, and would cry with all the power our lungs could muster:

Koo-ooo! It felt as if the train actually were entering the station.

The entire summer vacation was thus spent swinging from the gate and playing violent games inside the summer house. There would be bloody skirmishes between robbers and cops, the robbers would be finally caught, they would repent, and right away set up stands where they would sell guavas and mulberries. Clay flowerpots would be broken, the shards then rubbed smooth into *ser* and half-*ser* weights and all kinds of coins. And suddenly one day the vacation would end and school would start the next day. But on that next day I would pretend I didn't know, and would manage to stay in bed until nine o'clock. The school bus would come and leave without me. But this couldn't go on. The very next day I would be violently shaken awake at four in the morning.

Every time the school reopened, a fresh calamity awaited us. This time, though, it came in the form of a new teacher: a portly woman draped in a borderless sari and wearing eyeglasses. She put a Hindi primer in the hands of each of the Muslim students and ordered them to learn it on their own. When I saw the primer I was offended. We were in the fifth class, weren't we? Then why were we being forced to learn it? We had already been through a similar primer once before. All the pictures were exactly the same. Anyway, she informed us that Hindi was compulsory in the fifth class. I carefully put the primer away in my satchel, and it stayed right there. Two days later when she showed up, I easily rattled off the lesson: *alif* for *anar*, *be* for *bakri*, *he* for huqqa, and *dal* for *dhol*. Crazy! Idiot! She was beside herself with anger, and ordered me to learn it all over again.

What misery! But who could I ask for help? The rest of the girls were quite a bit older than me and spent free class periods crocheting lace or knitting red and green woolen sweaters. I, who still played with marbles and broken glass bangles, felt shy in their presence. So I took the primer back and thought the teacher was crazy herself. They were pictures of hubble-bubble and she-goat all right. Bright and clear. Anybody could see that. Yet she must get angry When she yelled at me over and over again, I had to ask Mother for help: The teacher doesn't teach but keeps telling me to learn from somebody at home.

'Go ask Robby Dutt. He'll teach you,' Mother suggested

So I begged the boy whose father—whom we used to call Maharaj—lived in the quarters outside in the compound.

Robby Dutt—his big eyes smeared with a thick application of kajal, wearing a gigantic black tika in the middle of his forehead to ward off the evil eye, a gold amulet strung on a black thread round his neck—rolled his eyes and spelled out his terms:

'You won't pull my braid, right?'

'Right.'

'Let me swing on the swing?'

'Yes.'

'Push the swing twenty times for me?'

'Yes.'

'And give me *gosht-roti* to eat?'

At this point I faltered. If I gave him meat to eat as he wished, Mother's displeasure was sure to follow. She had expressly warned me, 'Don't you ever give him meat—understand?'

'All right, don't,' he said. 'I won't teach you.'

'I will, I will. OK, I'll give you meat.'

And when His Majesty came in to teach, he would straightaway crouch all of himself under a cot or a settee

I'd pull him out of there somehow, and then, in a voice calculated to overwhelm me, he would command: 'Read! *Chota* "a"! *Bara* "uu"! "Ee"!' All those pages with pictures on them—he had made me learn in no time at all.

Then one day he taught me: '*Mohan achcha larka hai. Bhor bhae jagta hai aur ashnan karta hai.*' ('Mohan is a good boy. He gets up early in the morning and takes a bath.') I couldn't believe that such familiar words could possibly come out of such a strange alphabet.

'You miserable ass! You aren't teaching me properly.'

'*Parhae to rahe hain. Aur kya tumra sar parhaen*?' ('I am too! What did you think I was doing?')

'Liar! Fraud! English sounds come out of English letters. And here you are teaching me Urdu in Hindi!'

'Go to hell! I'm done teaching you!'

He would throw in the towel and flee, because the matter was beyond him. He himself couldn't figure out how Hindi letters managed to emit Urdu sounds.

It took me a long time to make my peace with the idea that the letters of this weird and totally unfamiliar alphabet produced exactly the same sounds as the Urdu script I was familiar with.

Now the writing drill got underway. 'And what's this—the silly squiggly thing stuck to it?' I'd ask, pointing at the *matra* for the vowel 'o.'

Which would throw him off once again. '*Yeh eme hi hai. Tum is se mat bolo. Apna kam karo.*' ('It's just there. Don't meddle with it. Do your work.')

In short, he wasn't counting on explaining the vowel marks, and explain them he did not.

But something like anxiety nagged at my heart. Sheer deception, this! It didn't make sense that you read in the strange looking Hindi script exactly what you read in the

Urdu script. Surely it was a plot to confound the reader. Out of sheer stubbornness, I took it to heart that there was no point in slaving over this. Robby Dutt, too, seemed to have become fed up with my daily bickering and nagging. So I put the Hindi *qaidah* to one side. There was another reason too: I was soon going to attend a school where there was no such nonsense. And so that was the end of his teachership and my discipleship.

He was now scarcely seen all day long. He'd go to school, and when he returned he'd dart out to wander around. Or else he would stay home and talk like hoary old men. He had no siblings and all his close kin were back in his hometown.

Yes, Robby Dutt, you were really something else. Even now, I can see you vividly against the background. The truth is, you're never far from view. Whenever the rains come—and with them the thought that back on the old house dark rain clouds would be pouring down in a torrent, letting rivers of water gush noisily along the eaves, and people would be celebrating Saluno, the festival of raksha-bandhan—how can I not remember you? When the ties of teacher and taught broke off between us, you quickly forged another bond. You stood behind the door and kept repeating in your muted voice: '*Tum kesi behni ho, tum hamre* rakhi *bhi nahin bandhat ho.*' (What kind of sister are you? You don't even tie a rakhi on my wrist!) And yet again: '*Auron ki behnen to bhayya logan ke rakhiyan bandhat hain.*' ('Other sisters tie rakhis for their brothers.')

The whole day long you kept showing up behind the door, hurling taunt after taunt at me for not tying a rakhi, until Mother finally relented. She sent for a few rakhis from the bazaar and gave them to me. Next time when you sneaked behind the door, I grabbed your hand and tied the whole lot on your wrist. Seeing not one, not even two, but three separate rakhis on your wrist, you became overjoyed and sprinted off, reappearing only in the evening, clad in a sparkling white dhoti, a lacework kurta, a Gandhi cap on your head, holding a brass tray, with rice, *andarsas*, bananas, and coins amounting to about half a rupee. Then, extending your hand from behind the door, you set the tray down and said, 'This is your *dacchana*.'

Oh, you really were something. When did I have the mind, when was I eager to tie rakhis? But every year, well before Saluno, you would keep reminding me, 'Rakhi *mangali hamri*?' ('So, have you sent for my rakhi?')

Deep inside, how much you valued being made my brother. When Bibbi came from Shimla for the first time after her marriage, you lugged her bedroll inside the house yourself, practically doubling over under the weight. When told you didn't have to, that Jabbal could have just as easily carried it in, you replied quietly, 'Why Jabbal? After all, didn't Aapa's groom tease Aapa, saying what kind of brother you've got—he can't even carry your bedroll for you!'

And that wasn't all. You were pretty strange. You would fight over the swing, and when I gave it a push, you would say in your quivering voice, 'Not so fast! Easy! I'm scared!'

'Why are you scared? I'm not.'

You would say quietly, '*Tum gos-roti khati ho, ham dal-roti khate hain*.' (Because you eat *gos-roti* and I eat *dal-roti*.)

And if anyone ever asked you whether you were Hindu or Muslim, you replied with great equanimity, 'Me? My clan and caste is the same as Begam Sahib's. Why, I'm Begam Sahib's son.'

In fact, you were a Brahmin, and a Brahmin of the most

elevated rank; indeed, so elevated that your doctor grandfather had no qualms about giving his daughter's hand in marriage to a confirmed idler such as your father.

Anyway, whenever a little free time came your way, you would quickly make *wuzu*, unroll Mother's prayer mat on the settee, and start performing one *ruku* after another, dropping your forehead in *sijdah* after *sijdah*, mumbling a prayer under your breath and quickly passing your open hands over your face. And if anyone laughed, you felt hugely offended.

If a Hindu reproached your mother, the Maharajan, saying that you always hung out with Muslims and mimicked their ways, she would just laugh off the matter good-naturedly, saying, 'Just as well. Let him live as a Muslim. This way, at least, he might live. My two other boys both died.'

Well, the high point of the story came when a craze to hold *milads* swept through the entire neighbourhood. We did it too, and that did it. Nobody could reason with you. You fought with the Maharajan and kept insisting on holding a *milad* too, and she, a simple woman, consented. She prepared the floor, spread cotton rugs and sparkling white sheets borrowed from our house; she sent for flower bouquets; she burnt incense sticks; and she begged Pathani Bua to come and perform the *milad*, because 'My *lallah* wouldn't have it any other way.'

And guess who turned out to be the M.C. at the event? You, of course. Who else? You'd dole out paans to everyone gathered there, then daub them with *attar*, sprinkling rose water from the dispenser every five minutes, dying from worry that you might have missed a detail that was part of the *milad* ceremony at your Begam Sahib's.

On winter nights, when everyone tucked themselves

nto heavy cotton quilts and sometimes listened to stories, /ou too would burrow into somebody's quilt and hang out here.

And then it'd seem the earth grew both weary of its veight and impatient with familiar faces and voices. It was ike somebody had violently thrashed the grain in a vinnowing fan. One flew and landed here, another omewhere else. But grain and seed, no matter where they and, invariably set up fresh worlds for themselves, sending heir slender roots, like a leech, deep into the earth. They ling to it, and, in time, tear open the earth's bosom and ome out.

Well, Robby Dutt, it's like this: I ended up here. You nust still be there, grown into an honourable man, esponsible and wise. Once again the rainy season has rrived. It must be pouring back where you are. Farmers, vearing folded gunny-sack shells for raincoats, must be usy digging ditches and taking care of the fields. Flocks of erons and parrots must be zooming back and forth verhead. Brahmin women must still saunter out during aluno carrying rakhis for their brothers, draped in snappy ed and green saris, bindiyas on foreheads, feet stained with enna, black and green bangles strung up the length of their lashing white, plump arms.

Your arms must be filled with rakhis, and you must still ffer *dacchanas*—but openly, though, not from behind the loor.

So what? What do I care? I wasn't exactly dying to tie a akhi, you practically forced me to. Then again, the time for hose insignificant little nothings is well past now. Mankind ow thinks only of big things, of things that matter, and espises everything that is small or looks diminished. And tell you the truth, you or I or anyone who thinks about the past does wrong. Why must life stay fixed in one place? Life's ship must pitch and rock forever on the restless waves of time. What if we had gotten stuck on the beach?

On life's ocean one ship sails east, another west. Favourable winds push them on, and fate determines their destinations.

The ships of your life and mine also sailed to shores destined for us. And yet why does this desire suddenly overwhelm me?—to fly off quietly to where you are, sitting grand and dignified, to sneak up behind you and whack you and ask, 'Want to have me tie a rakhi? And, tell me, which tray of *dacchana* is for me?'

Why are all these long-lost matters returning to me, like an old pain suddenly come back to life? It's because after much smouldering heat and burning sun, a cool breeze has finally started to blow.

Do you suppose it's the east wind?

Roots

Ismat Chughtai

Everyone's face was ashen, no food had been cooked. It was the sixth day the children had been out of school and at home, making their own and every family member's life miserable. The same old scuffles, wallops, wrestling and somersaults, as if 15th August had never come. The fools didn't realize that the British were gone, leaving behind as they departed a deep wound that would not be healed for years to come. The surgery on Hindustan has been performed with crippled hands and blunt scalpels so that thousands of arteries have been slit, a river of blood is flowing, and no one has any stamina left to stich the wounds up.

If this were any other day the wretched children would have been told to go outside and blacken their faces there and make a riot. But of late the atmosphere in the city had been so oppressive that the Muslims were feeling as if they were under house arrest. On the doors were padlocks and outside the police were patrolling. The dear, sweet children were being allowed to pound grain on their elders' chests. Actually there was relative calm in the area of the Civil Lines. This kind of filth spreads more where there is overpopulation, where there is poverty, that being also the place where putrid heaps of ignorance, stacked with piles of so-called religion are slowly rotting. To make matters worse, the increasing numbers of arrivals from Punjab were striking fear into the hearts of the minorities. The heaps of filth were being raked with rapidity and, creeping slowly, the stench was now approaching the clean, well-kept streets. In some areas there had been open demonstrations. But the social characteristics of the Muslims and Hindus in the states of Marwar are so similar that outsiders will not be able to identify them even by their names or clothes. Those who could be easily identified as different had left for Pakistan as soon as they got a whiff of 15th August. As for the original residents of the state, they lacked the proper intellectual resources to figure out the intricacies of the Pakistan and Hindustan issue on their own, nor were they placed high enough socially that someone would sit them down and explain the matter to them. Those who could understand had already done so and had gone into safety, while those who went to Pakistan after hearing that four *sers* of grain and a half-foot long loaf of bread could be had for four annas, were returning, because on arrival they discovered that a rupee was needed to buy four *sers* of grain and a whole four anna bit had to be spent to buy a half-foot long loaf of bread. And they didn't find the rupees or annas at any shop or growing in the fields, and realized it's just as difficult to obtain them as it is to engage in the struggle to exist.

Subsequently, when it was suggested that minorities be asked to leave certain areas, a great deal of commotion ensued. The Thakurs openly stated that well, the population is so closely enmeshed that a special staff would be required to weed out the Muslims, which is just so much extra expense. However, if you wish to buy some land for the rioters, we can arrange to have some areas vacated. There are animals living here already, the jungle can be made available whenever you want.

Only a few families remained now, some of them the 'toadies' of the Mahārajah and hence in no way expected to leave, and a few others who were determined to go. Well, bedrolls were being prepared. Our family was also included in this group. As long as Baré Bhai was in Ajmer there was no special hurry, but as soon as he returned everyone became apprehensive. Still, no one paid too much attention to what was happening. Had it not been for Chabba Miyan's unexpected manoeuvre, quite possibly things would have continued in this manner and the luggage would not be packed for ages. Baré Bhai was leaving anyway and he was tired of telling everyone else it was time to go when Chabba Miyan suddenly decided to write 'Pakistan Zindabad' on the school wall. Roopchandji's children contested this slogan and distorted it by writing 'Akhand Hindustan' over it. A scuffle ensued and an attempt was made to destroy each other completely. The matter became so serious that the police had to be called in and the few Muslim children who had been left were piled in a lorry and sent home.

Now here's what happened. As soon as the children got home, the mothers who always heaped curses of death and disease on them, were overcome by maternal instincts and, running toward them, clasped them to their breasts. If this had been another occasion and Chabba had come home after a fight with Roopchandji's children, Dulhan Bhabhi would have treated him to such a licking that God help us! And he would be dispatched to Roopchandji so he could make him drink a mixture of castor oil and quinine. Roopchandji was not only our family physician, he was also Abba's oldest friend. He was friends with Abba, his sons were friends with our brothers, his daughters-in-law and our sisters-in-law were friends, and the youngest generation could not stand being separated from one another. The present three generations of the two families were so close to each other that no one would have guessed that after the division of Hindustan their love would be threatened with discord. There were those who supported the Muslim League, Congress, and Mahasabha in both families and heated debates on the topics of religion and politics frequently took place, but it was all like a game of football or cricket. Abba was a Congressi, Roopchandji and Baré Bhai were Muslim Leagies, Gyanchand was a Mahasabhai, Manjhle Bhai was a communist, and Gulabchand was a socialist. And the wives and children were supporters along the same lines. Usually when there was a battle, Congress generally came out on top; the communists and socialists suffered defeat, but ended up by throwing their lot in with the Congressis. The only ones who remained would be the Mahasabhais and the Leagies and they rushed to each other's aid; although they were opponents, they still combined their resources and attacked the Congress together.

But for some years now the Muslim League and Mahasabha had been gaining in strength. The Congress was almost deflated. The youngest generation, except for one or two non-partisan type Congressis, stood their ground under the leadership of Baré Bhai while Sewak Singh's little heart opted for Gulabchand's leadership, but despite all this their friendship and love remained unchanged.

'I'll marry my Lallu with Munee,' Gyanchand the Mahasabhai would say to Munee's Leagie father. 'And I'll bring gold anklets for her.'

'Friend, make sure it's not just gilding.' Bare Bhai would attack Gyanchand's workmanship.

And in the meantime the National Guard would write 'Pakistan Zindabad' on the walls, and Sewak Singh's heart would distort it so that it read 'Akhand Hindustan.' This was in the days when the question of Pakistan was merely a matter of amusement.

Abba and Roopchandji would hear and see all this, smile, and would start making plans to unite all of Asia.

Amma and Chachi, far removed from politics, chatted about coriander, turmeric and dowries for their daughters, while the daughters-in-law kept a close watch on each other's fashions. Along with salt and chillies, medicines were also sent for from Doctor Sahib's house. The moment someone sneezed he was dispatched to Doctor Sahib's and if one of us took ill Amma immediately started preparing lentil-filled roti or *dahibaré* and sent Doctor Sahib a message that if he wanted to eat he should come over. His grandson's hands clasped in his, Doctor Sahib would arrive without delay.

'Don't eat there, do you hear?' his wife would say as he left his house.

'I see, well then how will I get my fees? Shall we send Lallu and Chunee instead?'

'*Hai* Ram! You have no shame,' Chachi would mutter.

The fun would really start when Amma didn't feel well. She would tremble fearfully.

'No no, I'm not going to be treated by that joker.' But who would ignore the doctor at home and go looking for someone from the city? So the moment Doctor Sahib heard Amma was unwell he came running.

'Well, if you're going to eat all the pulao and zarda by yourself you will get sick,' he teased her.

'You think everyone is as greedy as you are!' she would grumble from behind the curtain.

'I say, the illness is just an excuse. Bhabhi, why don't you just send for me, I'll come. Why do you carry on this charade?' His eyes twinkling mischievously, he would smile and, cursing him, Amma would pull her hand away angrily. Abba would merely smile.

He would come to check on one patient and everyone would crowd around him with various ailments. Someone had a stomach ache, another one a bleeding pimple, an ear here was infected, while over there someone's nose was swollen.

'What is this Deputy Sahib! I'll surely poison one or two persons. All these animals coming down on me, do you think I'm a veterinarian?' He would examine each patient and continue to grumble at the same time.

And the minute there was news of a new pregnancy, he would begin to curse the entire apparatus of creation.

'Huh! This doctor comes without a cost, keep producing babies to grind grain on the wretch's chest!'

But no sooner would the pains start than he would start making rounds from his veranda to ours. Screaming and shouting, he made everyone nervous. The women from the neighbourhood couldn't show their faces and the fathers-to-be were slapped and reprimanded for exhibiting empty bravado.

Then, as soon as the baby's cry fell into his ears he would walk across the veranda to the door and from the door into the room, and Abba, feeling baffled, would accompany him. Muttering and slapping their foreheads, the women retreated behind curtains. With a hand on her pulse he would pat her on the back and say, 'Well done, my lioness!' Completely flustered, Abba would nervously act the part of a poorly trained nurse. Just then Amma would start screaming.

'For God's sake, these wretched men, what are they doing barging in here in the delivery room!'

And, sensing the delicacy of the matter at hand, both

darted from the room like scolded children.

Roopchandji had already retired from the hospital and his entire practice was limited to our family when Abba suffered a paralytic stroke. There were other doctors treating him as well, but Doctor Sahib was the one who stayed awake with Amma and the nurse. And after he buried Abba, a sense of responsibility was added on to the love he had for our family. He would make innumerable trips to the school to get the children's fees remitted; he forced Gyanchand to keep his mouth shut when it came to compensation for the jewellery made for the girls' dowries. Nothing important was done without consulting Doctor Sahib first. The idea of demolishing the western side of the house to add on two new rooms was abandoned at Doctor Sahib's suggestion.

'It's better to add two new rooms upstairs,' he suggested. And that's what was done. Mujjan didn't want to take any science subject as part of his F.A. degree; Doctor Sahib went after him with a shoe and the matter was resolved. When Farida quarrelled with her husband and went back to her parents, her husband approached Doctor Sahib and the following day Farida returned with her husband.

But today when Chabba came home after the fight he was showered with favours as if he were a heroic soldier who had won a battle. Everyone asked for the details of his courageous act and in the clamour of the other voices the only voice that remained mute was Amma's. It wasn't just today, it was since 15th August, when the tricolour had been hung at Doctor Sahib's house and the Muslim League flag had gone up on theirs, that she had lost her voice. A deep chasm, many miles long, had formed between these two flags and she gazed with sorrow at the frightful depth of this chasm, and trembled. And then the rioters had come on the scene. When, after having lost everything to looters, Bari Bahu's parents arrived with much difficulty from Bahawalpur, the mouth of the chasm widened. And when Nirmila's in-laws came from Lyallpur nearly half-dead, serpents began to hiss in this chasm. When Choti Bahu sent her son to have his stomach looked at, Sheela Bhabhi shooed the boy away.

And no one discussed this matter. The ailments in the house suddenly halted. Forgetting her hysterical attacks, Bari Bhabhi began packing her luggage.

'Don't touch my trunk,' Amma finally spoke and everyone was dumbstruck.

'You won't go?' Baré Bhai asked tartly.

'My goodness, may I be cursed! Why should I go to die among the Sindhi women? Those wretches, flapping their wide pajamas as they run about.'

'So go to Sanjhle in Dhaka.'

'I say, why should she go there? Those strange people, they gulp down rice with their fingers.' Sanjhle Bhai's mother-in-law, Mumani Bi spoke up sarcastically.

'Then go to Rawalpindi, to Farida's,' Khala said.

'May God forgive me! May God save everyone from the Punjabis, it's the language of hell they speak.'

Today my soft-spoken Amma's tongue was loosened.

'I say sister, you remind me of that story . . . *ai bi*, like Katto the squirrel who made such a fuss when the king sent for her, look, he sends a shiny elephant and she complains, oh it's black, and when he sends her a horse she complains, oh it kicks . . .'

Even though the atmosphere had become somber, laughter broke out. The expression of disgruntlement grew darker on my Amma's face.

'What is this childish talk?' The leader of the National Guard spoke irately. 'No one is making any sense. Do you want us to stay here and be killed?'

'You people go. There's no reason for me to go. These are my last days.'

'So you'll submit to brutality at the hands of unbelievers in your last days?' Khala Bi kept counting the bundles which contained items ranging from gold and silver jewellery to bonepowder, dried mustard leaves, and Multani clay. She was carrying all this clasped to her breast as if Pakistan's foreign reserves in sterling pounds would be reduced without these things. Thrice Baré Bhai had discarded her bundles containing wornout cotton from old bedding, but she screamed as if Pakistan would be reduced to poverty without them. And finally he was forced to allow the children's urine-soaked bed pads to be stuffed into bags and large containers. The wooden legs of the bedsteads were removed and tied up with rags, and in a short while a well-organized house took on the semblance of varying bundles of different shapes and sizes; it seemed as if the luggage had feet and had been skipping about, and resting momentarily now, it would soon be up again to commence dancing.

But Amma's trunk remained untouched.

My simple-faced Amma's restless gaze was riveted to the darkened sky, as if she were asking herself, 'Who will kill me, and when?'

'Amma is senile, her wits aren't about her at this age,' Manjhle Bhai whispered in his brother's ear.

'What does she know about the cruelty that's being inflicted on innocent people? If it's our own country at least we won't feel that our lives or our belongings are in danger.'

Had my soft-spoken Amma possessed a sharp tongue,

she would definitely have said: 'What is this strange bird called "our own country?" People, tell me, where is that country that was ours, whose soil gave us birth, the soil in which we rolled about and grew up? If that isn't our country, then how can a place where you live for four days become our country? And who knows, someone might tell us to leave that place too, we might be told, "Go, found a new country." I'm like a sputtering candle, a tiny puff of air and the question of country will cease to exist. And this game of destroying and founding a country is no longer intriguing. There was a time when the Mughals left their country to settle in a new land, today let's go and found a new country again. Is it a country or a pair of shoes, which if they are a little tight are discarded in favour of another pair?' But she remained silent and her face looked more careworn than before, as if after a centuries-long, futile search for a country, she had given up and had sat down, her own self lost in that search.

Every effort was made, but Amma did not budge from her place, she was like the roots of a giant oak that remain standing in the face of a fierce storm.

But when the caravan bearing her, all her sons, daughters, daughters-in-law, sons-in-law, and grandchildren, began boarding the lorries under police supervision, her heart broke into a million pieces. With a restless gaze she looked at the other side of the chasm; the house so close to the road seemed so far, like a minute spot on the distant horizon. Roopchandji's veranda was deserted. Once or twice children came out but they were dragged back in immediately. But Amma's tearful eyes spotted behind the door openings and bamboo jalousies, the eyes that were slowly filling with moisture. When the lorries departed leaving swirls of dust in their wake, a deadened sensibility showed signs of life on the left side of the house; the door opened and Roopchandji walked out, sneaking a surreptitious look at the empty, solitary house as he trudged forward with heavy steps, and for a short while he searched for faces lost in the clouds of dust. Then, his thwarted stare drifted guiltily over the desolation before him and returned to earth.

After entrusting her life's savings to Allah's care, she stood all alone in her courtyard, her aged heart, trembling like a small frightened child, wilted, and she felt as if there were evil spirits leaping from all directions, waiting to seize her. Teetering, she steadied herself by holding on to a post. When she lifted her gaze her heart jumped into her mouth. This was the very room whose threshold she had crossed in the loving lap of her bridegroom. In this room the veil had been lifted from the moonlike face of the young, innocent bride with frightened eyes, and a life of bondage had been stamped on it. In that room, on the side, her first daughter was born, and suddenly the thought of her oldest daughter cut through her heart like a sigh. In that corner her daughter's umbilical cord was buried. Not one but ten cords were buried here, ten souls had taken their first breath of life in this room, ten images of flesh-and-blood, ten human beings had been brought forth from the sacred womb which they had all abandoned today—as if it were an old snakeskin; they had left it to be tangled among thorns while they scrambled off, in search of peace and tranquility, after grain that was four *sers* a rupee, and the room still echoed with the lovable cooing of those cherished beings. She darted toward the room with her shirt front spread before her, but her lap was empty, the same lap which was once touched reverently by married women to bring them fecundity. The room echoed with the sound of desolation.

Struck with fear, she recoiled, but her fantasy, let loose, would not be held back; it staggered into the next room. Here her life's partner had turned his face from her after fifty years, here in front of the door his shrouded body had lain, surrounded by all the members of his family. How fortunate he was to be in the lap of his beloved family when he breathed his last, but he left behind his life's partner who, like a body without a shroud, had no one to call her own. Her feet were giving up on her; she sat down at the spot where for ten years she had lit a lamp for the dead man with her trembling hands. Today there was no oil in the lamp and the wick was also burnt up.

And across the road Roopchandji was vigorously pacing up and down in his veranda. He was swearing. He was swearing at his family, his servants, the government, the long, silent road before him, he was swearing at bricks, at knives and daggers, at the whole world, which trembled in the face of his attack, but mostly he was swearing at that empty house in front of him which seemed to be mocking him, making him feel that it was he who had caused it to disintegrate, to fall apart. He wanted to dismiss something from his mind, he wanted to use all his force to wrench it away, but he failed and became agitated. He wanted to pull out with all his might the thing that had taken hold inside him like the roots of rancour, but he felt as if his very flesh were being pulled along with it and, groaning in pain, he had to stop. Then, suddenly, his swearing ceased. He got into his car and drove off.

At night, when silence fell over the street corner, Roopchandji's wife entered slowly like a thief from the back door carrying two food trays, one on top of the other. The two old women sat across from each other in silence. Their tongues were still, but their eyes were conversing. The food n both trays remained untouched. When women indulge n backbiting their tongues move with the swiftness of cissors, but when assailed by emotions, their mouths are ocked.

Who knows how many distressing thoughts, finding er alone, fell upon her all night without warning. Will all f them be killed along the way? Not just one or two, all the rains were being attacked and their passengers cut down. 'he crop that she had irrigated with her blood for fifty years ad gone into exile today, staggering and falling as it went n search of a new field. Who knew if the new field would rove fertile for these plants? Would they wither and die, hese poor, exiled plants? Her youngest daughter-in-law, y God's grace, was close to term. Who knew in what jungle he would deliver? They had left their home, jobs, their usiness, everything. Had the vultures and crows left nything for them in the new country, or would they have o return with empty hands, and when they came back, vould they have the opportunity to put roots down all over gain? And who knew if this old, dying tree would still be live when spring returns?

Clinging to the walls of her rooms like standing water n a deep well, she ranted and raved until she finally ollapsed in exhaustion. But sleep, where was it? All night er old, fragile frame shivered as she confronted images of he lacerated, wounded bodies of her grown daughters, nvisioned her young daughters-in-law naked in a rocession, and imagined her grandsons dismembered, cut nto pieces. Who knows when slumber overtook her.

Suddenly it seemed as if the whole world were hundering at the door. True, life was no longer precious, ut even in a lamp without oil the flame quivers for a second efore it is extinguished, and isn't death cruel enough in all its simplicity, without the added complexity coming in the guise of a demon with a human form? It was said that these demons will take even old women by the hair, dragging them on the road until their skin is peeling and the bones begin to show. And finally all those worldly torments will come to pass, the very thought of which would make even the angels of hell turn pale.

The pounding on the door was getting louder. The angel of death was in a hurry, was he not? And then suddenly, all the bolts were released, the lights were turned on and, as if travelling from the bottom of a faraway well a voice fell into her ears. Perhaps her oldest son was calling her—no, these were the voices of the younger two sons coming to her from some unknown corner of the next world.

So did they all find a country already? So soon? The third son, behind him the youngest, she could see clearly that they were there, the daughters-in-law holding their babies in their laps, and all of a sudden the whole house came to life—all the souls were awakened and gathered around the sorrowful mother. Hands, big and small reached out to touch her, all at once tiny new buds erupted from roots that had dried, and agitated by the force of her new-felt joy, her senses, surrounded by darkness, eddied as they drowned.

When she opened her eyes she realized there was a familiar touch upon her pulse.

'*Arey* Bhabhi, I will come if you send for me. Why do you have to undertake this charade?' Roopchandji was speaking from behind the curtain.

'And Bhabhi, today I must have my fee. Look, I've brought your good-for-nothing sons all the way from Colony Junction. They were running away, the scoundrels ıey didn't even trust the superintendent.'

The aged lips fluttered with renewed life. She sat up. 'or a moment there was silence. Then two red-hot gems olled down and fell on Roopchandji's wrinkled hands.

Translated by Tahira Naqvi

. . . *and After*

Kanha Devi and her Family

Hasan Manzar

One of the houses in Memon Para belongs to Kanha Devi. The residents of the neighbouring houses are also Hindu. This Hindu enclave, created by the intersecting geometry of lanes and bylanes, looks like a tiny island surrounded by a sea of Muslim dwellings. These people, or the majority of them at any rate, have been living here for as long as anyone can remember. Once in a while, though, a relative from Bharat washes up on the tiny island like a wave, and then recedes. Life resumes its old rhythms, both inside Kanha Devi's household and out.

In the narrow bazaar, shy of daylight, wooden handicrafts are skillfully carved and sold. They also do some brasswork here, and the bazaar is always well stocked with homespun cloth from Sindhi villages. When people jostle about in the crowded bazaar, rubbing shoulders, it is impossible to tell their communal identity. Just about everyone here uses salaam, the Muslim greeting, and the Hindu custom of touching the feet of one older than oneself is so widespread among the locals that one never knows which of the two—the one touching the feet or the one affectionately placing his hand on the other's head—might be Hindu and which might be Muslim. Both may be Hindu; then again, they may just as well both be Muslim.

Certain items, though, are never sold here: miniature idols used in worship, copies of the Bhagavad Gita, and those big, coloured pictures, exquisitely printed on fine art paper, that the Hindu inhabitants of the neighbourhood use to decorate their homes. Some of these, in heavy gilt frames, hang on the walls of Kanha Devi's sitting room, and some, smaller in size, on the walls of the small prayer room directly behind the sitting room. A statue of Shiva and a brass oil lamp adorn a niche in one of the walls of the prayer room.

One step into these two rooms and you feel transported into quite another world—of long ago, inhabited by Krishna Gopal, the sly butter thief; Ganesha, the elephant god; Shiva and Parvati; and Duhshasana trying to disrobe Draupadi—but an unseen blue hand helping her, spinning Draupadi around, feeding out length after length of sari, like the hand of a kite-flyer in the heat of the contest, letting the string spin freely off the spool, causing his seemingly victorious opponent to give up the match in sheer exasperation . . . exactly what happened with Draupadi. 'Unless a woman is simply bent on a loose life—flitting around like a kite with a cut string—she always remains safe behind the folds of her sari, until such eager hands as those of Duhshasana are ready to admit defeat.'

And as she recounts all this, Kanha Devi herself becomes chastity incarnate.

And this picture here, it shows Bharat removing the wooden sandals from Ramchandarji's feet, so that he may install the sandals on the throne and rule by proxy until such time when Ramchandarji returned. One cannot even imagine such a thing today. Why would the proxy relinquish the throne once he's got it? Better yet, why would anyone give up the throne and go into voluntary exile in some forest in the first place? And leaving his sandals behind with his brother, at that!

Kanha Devi's sister fasts every Monday in honour of Lord Shiva. And Kanha Devi's brother-in-law—Persumal who is well only half the year and is seized during the other half by terrible fits which make him rant and rave, shout and scream—is in the habit of getting up before dawn and feeding the birds. At this time, the birds come in flocks and alight on the low wall around the roof of the house. Persumal feeds them and recites from the Bhagavad Gita somebody had brought for him from Bharat some eight or ten years ago.

This usually means that he is well these days, and the whole family can breathe a little. Which is not the case when he is in the throes of a fit, for then he begins to curse his *wanyas*—that is, his own caste people—up one side and down the other. It would seem that he recites the Bhagavad Gita when he is healthy; but it also seems that it is only during the bouts of anger and insanity that the sacred text actually begins to unravel its meaning to him.

Persumal calls his father and older brothers *wanyas*. These people lend money at terribly high rates of interest, unabashedly eat meat, liberally consume alcohol, and smoke marijuana—in other words, they do just about everything the Bhagavad Gita considers reprehensible.

When Persumal is giving them a tongue-lashing, Chandumal, Mirchumal, Dhumi, Sita, Ashok, even Kanha Devi herself—everyone feels terribly embarrassed. They touch the tips of their noses and then pinch their earlobes in repentance and say, 'Ishwar has given him so much knowledge, if only He had also put a brake on his brains!'

'By giving Persumal so much knowledge Allah has really made our life miserable.'

Now, who would say these are Kanha Devi's words? But they are.

Just as these people freely use the word salaam in their conversation, so they also use such other Muslim expressions as Allah and *insha'allah*. And nobody stops them. By having a different faith one doesn't also come to have a different creator!

Usually on such occasions, when Persumal is in a temper, the Muslim neighbours take him over to their homes and do everything to calm him down. One takes out a *tawiz*, a charm, and puts it on him, another wraps a black string around his thumbs and wrists, and some woman brings holy water from the sanctuary of one of the local saints and tries, by earnest entreaty, to make Persumal drink it. Persumal, otherwise a strict Vaishnava in dietary matters, finally drinks from her glass, and does not insist, 'No, I shall not drink from your glass because you people are meat-eaters.' Thus in madness, he manages to tell only what is truly blameworthy in man, never that which man has fabricated in order to put some above some others.

Their Bharati relatives, who visit them from time to time, have remained in the last thirty-odd years since Independence exactly where Manu had left them centuries ago: bound by caste differences and distinctions. The children of many such relatives now read and write only Hindi. During visits when these children play with their Pakistani relatives' Muslim neighbours, in Kanha Devi's inner courtyard no less, the older women from Bharat, unbending in religious matters, just gawk at this outrage with unbelieving eyes, though Kanha Devi herself finds nothing wrong with it. Children aside, even the adults in Kanha Devi's neighbourhood seem to have in one fell swoop scaled the restraining walls of untouchability and caste differences, and stepped into a refreshing open space where the son of the Brahmin Sri Ram is about to marry the daughter of the *wanya* Dhumi. Nobody loses any sleep over this glaring infraction of caste rules.

And not just that. Even the Shudras of this place freely participate in the Ram Lila festival. Every one of the last six or seven years, Okha's son has been playing the role of Raja Ramchandar in the Ram Lila play. Stranger still, at college, this fellow and the Brahmin and Muslim boys often drink unreservedly from the same glass, no different from the children playing in Kanha Devi's courtyard. In spite of her deference to Hindu customs, the thought never crosses Kanha Devi's mind to reserve separate glasses for the Muslim children, nor to serve her orthodox Hindu relatives in separate dishes.

So when Kanha Devi got her son married to a Bharati woman and brought the bride over to Pakistan, a strange tension swept across her home, although she remained unaware of it for quite some time. She had spent all her life rolling out papads, a daily staple in her family fare, doled out to the neighbours and served up as handy snacks to guests. Likewise, she would spend the whole year preparing achar, and on festival days make pancakes and other sweet dishes. Preparing two kinds of dishes was her responsibility: one a sort of poultry, seafood, and red meat combination, the other strictly vegetarian. In preparing the latter, she would be careful not to use the same ladle with which she had earlier stirred the meat gravy. It seems these chores had been her charge from as far back as one cared to remember, from when she lived at her father's.

Persu's wife was none other than Kanha Devi's own younger sister. Living with a crazy husband, she had become half-mad herself. Burn incense sticks or fast in honour of Lord Shiva, that's about all she knew. But nothing worked: she remained childless.

In that crazy environment, where the males in the family indulged in gambling throughout the rainy season and waited eagerly for the festivals of Holi and Diwali to get drunk, Kanha Devi alone knew what it took to run the house.

Kanha Devi had succumbed to the fatigue of old age by the time Damayanti, her daughter-in-law, had arrived. She had it all neatly worked out: 'The minute Damayanti sets foot in the house, I'll leave everything in her care and retire. All day I'll sit in my swing-seat and chat with the neighbourhood women, chew a paan maybe, or smoke a cigarette, and without so much as ever even lifting a finger be grandly served by her at meal times.'

Damayanti took over all right, but what she did not do was tell the old lady: 'Okay, I'll do the work, all of it, but you must promise to guide me. You must tell me exactly how many papads to roll, how much to spend and when, and what dishes to cook on what day.'

Only much later did Kanha Devi realize that Damayanti had already been stewing in her own juices for two, maybe three months. It had begun to annoy her that the neighbourhood children freely cavorted around in the courtyard. And yet if you sounded her out, you would know that Damayanti didn't really dislike children, though she did take umbrage with their barging in and out of the kitchen whenever they felt like it.

On the other hand, Damayanti didn't dislike visitors from Bharat. She would receive them with open arms, never mind the fact that they were driven to this country not because of any great love for their relatives, but by the desire to visit the sanctuary of their patron saint and offer up their votive dues, exactly as Kanha Devi herself had once gone to Ajmer in Bharat.

And visitors from Bharat brought gifts: colourful bindiyas and saris (which Damayanti was so accustomed to wearing herself, but which the other girls at her in-laws' did not wear), film magazines, and lots of gossip from over there.

That of course was understandable. But Kanha Devi had no idea that Damayanti should find the old acquaintances of the family so exasperating. Damayanti just couldn't bring herself to drink tea from the same cup used earlier by a Muslim guest, or, for that matter, a Hindu guest ignorant of the importance of caste differences. Then again, names such as Ramu, Shyamu, and Gopi were too fuzzy to indicate one's true caste origins. Worse still, just about anybody walked in uninvited, expecting hospitality.

Now not only did Kanha Devi herself visit her Muslim friends in their homes but also dragged an unwilling Damayanti along.

It seemed that true dharm—or at least as much of it as Damayanti could understand by her own lights—had all but vanished among the local Hindus, and the pictures of Sarasvati, Lakshmi, Krishna and the Gopis had been hung on the wall merely to invoke their blessing and protection. Absence of hatred for those outside the fold was as good a sign as any, Damayanti thought, that the local Hindu had gone slack in his faith.

Then again, she could lick any one of them hands down when it came to true religious knowledge. Didn't she know the Bhagavata by heart? And the correct meanings of Hindu names? It would seem that the myriad communal riots and clashes of high-caste Hindus with the Harijans, the untouchables, in her native Bharat, had quickened that religious nerve in her that feeds on hatred.

How many local Hindus had gone to Bharat on pious visits and pilgrimages? How many?

One night she asked Kishan Chand, her husband, 'Are

we going to rot here forever?'

Damayanti's question exploded like a bomb. Kishan Chand, who had just dozed off, was startled, and asked, 'Forever—what do you mean?'

'You *like* it here?'

'You don't?'

But Damayanti remained silent. Kishan Chand, sensing the palpable tension around him, tried to clear the air with a light-hearted joke. 'Don't you like me? Ah, I get it, you've got somebody over there.'

'I'm not talking about you. I'm talking about *here*.'

'Here is . . . here,' Kishan said. 'I'm from here. If I don't like it here, who will?'

Damayanti was sitting with her head tucked between her knees. She was uttering every word with the greatest circumspection, hesitantly, just as every girl does when she talks with her husband about some worldly matter for the first time, a matter which invariably ends up being the opinion of her in-laws.

'The fact is, the customs here are a little strange,' she said.

'And yours were different there?' Kishan asked.

'Yes. There we mixed only with our own kind, our equals. And nobody dared barge into the kitchen with their shoes on, as they do here. Nor did we cook meat.'

'But whenever I visited your folks, I always got to eat meat,' Kishan said.

'Not in our house. Maybe in other people's houses.'

'So where do the men in your family go to eat meat?'

'In restaurants,' Damayanti laughed.

'I get it. You'd rather we ate meat out in restaurants here too, is that it?'

Time and again Damayanti tried to get on with the

subject, but it seemed as though she and Kishan were talking on two different wavelengths.

Finally, Kishan Chand said, 'You know what I think? If you had been born here, then you too would be like mother: you'd obey your religion and not hate others for obeying theirs. Anyway, why would I want to abandon this country? This is a land of *opportunity*!'

'What's that?' Damayanti asked naïvely.

'Let's just say that I'm in no mood to emigrate to Bharat. I'm happy here. I've grown up among these people and consider them my own. Your misfortune is that you grew up in an environment full of instigators, people who keep themselves in business by stirring up members of one faith against members of another, and set one caste against the throats of another. Lucky for the politicians! Even in this day and age, they can find enough ignorant people to shore up communal unrest.'

Many times thereafter, when alone with the younger members of the household or with her husband, Damayanti would take exception to their use of the phrase *insha'allah*. She even set her cup apart. When forced to accompany Kanha Devi to a Muslim friend's house where they would be offered tea sent for from the neighbourhood restaurant, Damayanti would find some pretext or other to leave without drinking any.

One morning Kanha Devi's husband, a cotton merchant and moneylender, returned home unexpectedly early. When asked about it, he said that communal riots had erupted in some industrial town in Bharat.

Kanha Devi, as was her wont, said disinterestedly, 'Well, then, shall I start packing?'

In the kitchen Damayanti's hands suddenly stopped what they were doing. She didn't catch the note of sarcasm in Kanha Devi's voice.

And it had gone on this way in this household for the past thirty-odd years. For although Chandarmal did do business here, he always looked like a bird poised to take wing any minute. He thought it unwise to tie up his money. But the other *wanyas* carried on their business undisturbed: one ran a bakery, another a restaurant, another made movies, and yet another worked as a contractor. Chandarmal alone looked jittery, always in a big rush, as though he would miss the train. Whenever news arrived of a fresh communal riot in Bharat, he would hop on his swing-seat right away and start pulling nervously at the hair on his chin. People say that he too had in him a streak of the same illness which afflicted Persumal.

The same nervous tension gripped him that day. When he arrived at the bazaar, he found the others busy at their work. Only Lala Ram, the photographer, asked him in a hushed voice, 'Did you hear the BBC this morning?'

'No, why?' Chandarmal asked, worked up. 'Did you?'

'Communal riots . . . on a large scale.'

'Where?' Chandarmal asked, although he knew the answer.

'Bharat, Chacha. Where else?'

Each looked into the other's eyes.

A little later Chandarmal's ears began to buzz with the noise of the paper boy shouting the headlines: THREE HUNDRED MUSLIMS SLAUGHTERED IN HINDU-MUSLIM RIOTS! POLICE OPEN FIRE ON MUSLIMS!

Hidden behind these words were the sowers of dissension and chaos, those who turned communal riots into a roaring business. Hawkers were happy that they would be done early today. Chandarmal alone felt ill at ease. He walked to one end of the bazaar and then back to the other, hoping to gauge the people's mood. But people were preoccupied with their own worries: one had to take his polio-stricken child to the hospital, another had a court hearing to attend. Somehow the Hindu shopkeepers appeared more preoccupied with their work today than usual, deftly avoiding the eyes of others.

Deepak, the tailor master, was marking the material spread out before him with a piece of blue chalk, his head hung low, while his son busily took the measurements of a Baluchi youth.

Damayanti felt the night growing oppressively long. Kishan made no mention of the communal riots. He had gone to a movie with some friends, and when he got back, he went straight to bed.

In Kanha Devi's small two-storey house, crammed with some fifteen people, Damayanti was feeling herself perilously alone, expecting something terrible to happen any minute. Every whistle of the night watchman startled her.

At dawn when the sound of the *azan* arose from the neighbourhood mosque, Damayanti felt that fate had brought her into a cul de sac from which she couldn't possibly hope to escape. She was the animal tied to a stake and beaten to death. How different was her present from her past, when she still lived in her own country! Over there she wouldn't have given two hoots about the communal riots, she wouldn't have lost any sleep over them at all.

All minorities, like an orphaned child, fear the worst, even in their dreams.

When Kishan stirred in his sleep and said, 'What, up

already?', Damayanti quickly answered, 'I never really slept.'

Kishan, still in bed, threw his arms around a swollen-faced, groggy-eyed Damayanti who was sitting up in bed beside him, and asked, 'What's the matter? Don't tell me somebody drank from your glass again.'

'That happens every day. How much can one avoid . . .

'Then *don't*!' Kishan said, lifting a lock of her hair, and then added, 'Join the others. Mix with them.'

Damayanti freed her neck from his coiling arms and said, 'Come to Bharat with me. I will never be able to sleep peacefully in this country.'

'Why? Do beds have thorns here?'

'This isn't even your country. It's *theirs*.'

'Theirs—who?'

'Those who surround us. Who created this country in the name of religion.'

For the next few minutes Kishan strained as though trying to read some invisible writing on Damayanti's face. He said, 'Look at it this way: if a woman can be wife to one and mother to another at the same time, then why can't the same piece of land be held dear by some, because it was gotten in the name of religion, and be respected as a motherland by others? Tell me, when you become the mother of our child, will you stop being my wife? Or must we have two Damayantis? . . . Only then would it make sense to think of one as mother and the other as wife.'

Damayanti laughed. But her worried heart kept pounding in her chest. Never before had she heard the sound of the *azan* come from so nearby.

Early in the morning when her chores brought Damayanti to the rooftop, she found Persumal feeding the birds as usual. This was something he never failed to do not even when he was sick.

Everybody is crazy in this family, Damayanti thought, whether it was her mother-in-law, her husband, or his uncle Persumal. Why else would anyone worry about feeding the birds at this outrageous hour?

Instead of finishing her work and returning downstairs, Damayanti decided to stay a while and watch Persumal, who had meanwhile joined his hands to pray to the sungod.

When Persumal was done praying, he asked her affectionately, 'You want to ask me something?'

'As a matter of fact, I do,' Damayanti said. 'Yesterday there was a riot between Hindus and Muslims . . .'

'Where?' Persumal asked without much enthusiasm.

'In India.'

'So, what else is new?' Persumal uttered these words as though the occurrence was about as important and frequent as a common cold.

'Don't you ever think of moving over to India?' Damayanti asked.

'Your father-in-law—my brother—does. I don't.'

'Doesn't it scare you? What if somebody provoked these people? We're surrounded by them, you know. I'm so scared I stay awake the whole night long.'

Persu lifted his hand and pointed at something and asked, 'What is that?'

Damayanti looked into the distance and replied, 'Why, a minaret, of course.'

Persu shook his head and gestured toward the pigeons pecking at the grains in front of him. 'You know something?' he said. 'These pigeons roost in that minaret at night . . . More than this I shall not say; in fact, I'm not permitted to say.'

Damayanti wanted to ask who had prevented him, but

decided to keep quiet as Persumal had already become joyfully absorbed in his worship.

Downstairs Damayanti told Kanha Devi about it, who, instead of laughing at the matter, said with a feeling of profound respect, 'Let people call him what they will. But Persu is not mad. I say you can go through the whole city, let alone this neighbourhood, and never find a soul more enlightened than he.'

The Thaw

Muhammad Salim-ur-Rahman

An eerie hush swept over us just as Major Murad finished talking. In the ensuing long silence the only sound came from the gritty scrape of a match suddenly lighting up. Words seemed so inadequate to us all, or perhaps just to me, an affront to the overwhelming stillness. In the dim half light all round, the orange glow of Captain Haroon's cigarette had become the center of that heavy silence. Suddenly the rumbling sound of some army trucks arose far in the distance. It grew loud, dwindled, then faded away completely—like the resonance of a muddy fountain tearing out of the heart of silence and, just as suddenly, falling back down into it; or perhaps like a sound which conveys time past into time present. Engulfed by that noise, which came close and then receded into the distance, I sensed that cracks were about to open in the ring of silence which the Major's story had circumscribed about us. Captain Haroon started to say:

'I've heard this incident three times already. Each time I've felt as though the whole thing is beginning to jell for me. As though it's meant just for me. But Major, each time you are done relating it, I've felt strangely empty-handed. It seems I only have a right to its pain, to its body, while its life remains with you. In reality, though, I feel this story is as much mine as it is yours.'

What Captain Haroon meant was that just like Murad, he too had emigrated to Pakistan in the aftermath of the 1947 riots which had laid to waste his native East Punjab.

Murad said, 'Haroon, you're a little insensitive, and hasty to boot. Dying to understand the meaning right away, but too impatient to feel a thing fully, or move step by step through an incident and soak up its warmth. Certain things reveal their meaning right away, others merely go on throbbing in the heart for a long time. If you think I actually know what you don't, you are mistaken. I've thought long and hard about this incident and I feel, although I could be wrong . . . it was for the first time they sensed a glimmer of the truth, the idea for which they had died. For the first time!'

Lieutenant Nazir suddenly shuddered, started to say something but faltered. He was the youngest among the four of us. His hesitation irritated us: God knows what he wanted to say, and he might not be able to say it at all. Seeing us rapt with attention he felt somewhat confused. He quickly pulled out a pack of cigarettes from his pocket, removed one and stuck it between his lips. Then he took out a lighter and lit it. After taking a few puffs he said: 'Well, I didn't have to emigrate. I was just a kid back in 1947 and lived in a village on the banks of the Jhelum. I don't know why I suddenly have this tremendous urge to tell you about an event that occurred in my childhood. A slightly demented holy man came and stayed in our village mosque every once in a while. His haggard appearance, booming voice, delirious cries and flaming red eyes scared the daylights out of us kids. His clothes were always bloodstained and he carried a thick, coiled staff in his hand In those days we desperately prayed not to have to see him Once there was a wedding celebration, or some such event in the village. Gas lamps burnt the whole night long. Early the next morning I happened by there and saw our half crazy old man, diligently picking up moth wings and piling them up on an ochre sheet which he had spread over a platform freshly coated with a thin mud paste. There were thousands of tiny wings on the sheet. This struck me as so odd I forgot I used to be frightened of the man.

'I asked him, "Babaji what are you doing?" He stopped briefly, trained his flaming eyes on me and said in a heavy voice, "Child, you wouldn't understand what happened here last night; what these sinful eyes were made to witness. All that needs to be done now is pick up these souvenirs and put them to rest in the river. Come, you pick them up too! We don't have much time. The day's getting on." At that precise moment his voice sounded so compelling, I forgot all about myself and began picking up the wings. Who could blame me? Didn't it look like a fascinating game? Children, after all, are lured by such games. I kept picking up those transparent wings, covered with a mesh of almond-coloured veins, and piled them up on the sheet as my ears listened to the man hum away in some foreign tongue, his voice deep and resonant. I couldn't have known then what language it was. But when I grew older I surmised that it must have been Persian.

'This scene has stayed with me ever since. It returns every now and then. And when it does, it takes hold of me, even if for just a few seconds. I become drowned in its magical splendour and resonance and emerge from it feeling wonderfully fresh and full of vitality. The early morning hour, the two of us engrossed so fully in our chore, the ochre sheet, Babaji humming away and running about picking up those scattered wings—I feel that I alone dominate that scene, that it's filled only with my presence. I've never tried to fathom the meaning of that experience. Reliving it again and again, in its totality, provides its own justification. Well, I've heard you tell your event, or story, in exactly the same spirit. I've not insisted on understanding it. Instead, I have tried to participate in it with my whole being. For me it is filled with the same wonder which I found in the old man's gentle humming. This story of yours has now become part of me forever, the way that scene from my childhood has. It feels as though they are the two farthest ends of a single continuum, between which my consciousness—or blood if you will—will go on circulating forever: close to the fallen wings of moths in the first light of morning, and then to those returning during the night, and . . .'

He stopped abruptly. I'd never seen him talk like that before. He was not the man I knew. I began to understand, but only vaguely, his earlier hesitation. We were struck dumb. What else could we have done? Just then the orderly brought us a fresh round of tea, and Haroon, perhaps to break the silence, started telling us how he and his wife had made, in the time just before the war broke out, mistake after terrible mistake and endured great hardship in the seventeen or eighteen months it took to build their new house.

'On the night of 18th September, I and a band of some nine or ten infantry men went out on patrol near Asil Uttar. The battle front had been strangely quiet for some time, indeed so quiet we suspected that the Indian army was perhaps getting ready for a fresh assault. Precisely what, we wanted to find out.

'We proceeded gingerly, with the greatest caution. In many places along the way we spotted a rather large number of land-mines. So, we concluded, perhaps the enemy wasn't planning a frontal attack after all, not for now at least. Coming close to the Indian fortifications we moved, with utmost vigilance and care, to a safe place and lay down there, beginning to apprise ourselves of the enemy's strength and the deployment of its guns. Of course we couldn't have really seen much in the dark. But, as you know, one still can smoke out a lot by merely listening intently. I wanted to listen for the sound of enemy trucks hurtling off to the trenches up ahead, trying to ascertain if they were unloading their ammunition there, for this kind of movement most certainly would have foretold an attack. When we didn't hear any truck movement for quite a while, I felt reassured that an attack was not imminent. As for the strength, the enemy himself gave that away. Well, we'd just started to withdraw to our lines when an enemy guard suspecting something sounded the alarm. Immediately machine guns opened fire from two directions, along with a few rifles. The firing was totally random. It didn't hurt us at all. We just stayed put. The shooting continued haphazardly for some time. When we didn't return the fire, the enemy concluded that nobody was in the vicinity and that the guard had perhaps been mistaken. Well, the firing stopped, but it did give us a precise idea of their numbers and the locations of the two machine guns.

'Quietly we started back. Halfway through the trek the enemy guns erupted again, just as we were picking our way through an extremely narrow path, flanked on either side by barbed wire, between two mine fields. The firing was not aimed at us, but rather at our fortifications. It was totally random. So, by sheer accident, a couple of shells landed quite close to us and exploded and set off the mines. I felt somebody had pushed me with a tremendous force and wrenched my leg. My ears went numb. When I regained consciousness I noticed that my right leg was bleeding. Four of my men had also been injured; two didn't look good at all. Luckily my wound wasn't deep and the bone had been spared. The least one can say is that it would have been certainly difficult—if not entirely impossible—for me to get up and walk. After I had one of my men wrap a handkerchief tightly around my leg just above the wound, I told those who had escaped injury to carry or help their wounded comrades back to our position. "Look," I said, "my injury isn't serious, but these four men need immediate medical attention. You get going. I'll hide myself in the field up ahead. You can come back for me later." At first they hesitated a bit, but when I insisted they strode away with their wounded comrades. Slowly I crawled up to the sugarcane field and slipped into it.

'As a matter of fact I was quite safe in my hideout. Apparently the Indian soldiers wouldn't have come that way, and even if they had, there was little chance they'd know somebody was hiding there. True, I could have been hit by a stray shell, but that's something else again. By now, a few of our own guns had started firing back.

'Lying wearily in the field I was overcome by sleep. Exploding shells were shaking the ground, and others zooming overhead made me feel nervous. I was afraid I might be wounded or killed at any instant. And yet my eyes were closing from the accumulated fatigue of many days. One doesn't get the time to sleep at the front—does one? I kept quickly opening and shutting my groggy eyes. I was doing my damnedest to keep from falling asleep, but isn't it a fact, though, that only on waking does one discover that one had dozed off? I saw a place where a few women sat sewing by the dim light of two or three oil lamps. Presently an empty tonga, with a green lantern lit on one of its sides, pulled in. The tongawallah asked in a loud voice: "How far is Pakistan from here?" The women answered back in unison: "As long as it would take for us to finish sewing this." I felt as though I'd moved forward and seen that they were stitching something like a wedding wreath or a flag with flames and flowers. Flames were leaping out of the flag, as buds were snapping into blooms. I was surprised to notice that the illumination cast by the flames was dancing even over my own clothes. All of a sudden the horse fidgeted and began to stomp its hooves. Although it had been yoked to a very shabby looking tonga, it had a pair of immaculate bright wings. Because of those wings the tonga appeared to me quite unreal and, at the same time, because of the tonga, the horse so palpably real—as if all of us were part of some wondrous puzzle. I tried to touch the horse, but it neighed wildly.

'Just then I awoke with a start from my sleep. The first thing that crossed my mind was, God knows how long I have been sleeping? Could it be that my men had returned and, receiving no response to the signal I'd fixed with them, wandered off into the field looking for me? The silence around me was so deep that suddenly, for a moment, my heart was seized with terror. Such deathly silence right on the battle front—what could it portend? Misgivings, each more fearful than the other, assailed my heart. I started to think about my dream. The silence struck me as odd, as did the dream. Both were grossly out of place. But I'll say this though: if the silence struck fear, the dream seemed like an altogether refreshing fragrance.

'It was terribly close and muggy in the field. I was soaked to my skin in sweat. Soon the stuffiness and profuse sweating became unbearable. I felt beside myself and moved from my position until I reached the end of the field. Thinking that it would be hazardous just to up and go, I cocked my ears. I didn't hear a sound. The terror of absolute silence began to get to me. Even the most silent night is never entirely free of a vague, rustling sound. One can always feel the movement of silence: it breathes, snaps, and falls like dew. But now, strangely enough, it appeared shorn of all motion, even the slightest breath. I was feeling very uncomfortable and restless. So I got out of the field, wiping the sweat off my forehead. I sat down on the berm running along the edge of the field, pressed my eyelids tight and took a long, deep breath. A mixed smell of dirt and gunpowder, of objects charred and burning reached my nose. I opened my eyes wide and scanned the area. I lost my senses. My arms and feet went numb from a collision of uncertainty, confusion, and absolute bewilderment.

'Some forty or fifty yards directly in front of the cane field was a flat, open area with a narrow dirt road running across the middle of it. In spite of it being late at night, and the area being dangerously close to the battle line, I saw shoals of people coming along both on the open ground and the dirt road. From their appearance they seemed to be villagers. Their clothes were torn and coated with dust. The clothes of some appeared bloodstained, but I dismissed this as a mere delusion. Some of them walked in small groups, others by themselves. They came in droves: men, women, old and young, and children; some with cudgels in their hands, others with large bundles and chests balanced on their heads; a man walking with his child in tow, holding his hand, others carrying children in their arms or on their shoulders. A man passed in front of me walking his bicycle. He had a sewing machine tied to the bike rack and a bloodstained white burqa slung across the handlebar. I nearly stopped him.

'Most amazing of all, the crowd was absolutely

quiet—why, they weren't even looking right or left. Their eyes were trained on something straight ahead. I saw that quite a few of them had already gone ahead, others were passing by me, and still more made up a large crowd behind them. I stood frozen while they passed by me, like a silent scene without beginning or end.

'I bristled. It couldn't be! It's absolutely impossible! The thought occurred to me many times that I might be asleep, that this was all a dream, or perhaps I was already dead. But something told me irrefutably that I was neither dead nor sleeping, that I was instead wide awake. This was all outside of me and quite palpably real, though what was happening before me and why, I honestly couldn't tell.

'What with my bewilderment, I stood rooted there, glued to the spectacle as if by some invisible force. I was gaping at them passing by with the bewildered curiosity of a little boy who looks, for the first time ever, at a large procession, or at milling crowds and the exuberant gaiety of shops in a country fair or in a busy market; the way that boy feels overwhelmed by it all and wonders how, just how on earth so many people could come together in one place, or how there could be so many of them in the first place.

'My eyes fell on a man who was making his way along. Right away his gait struck me as oddly familiar. I even recalled his name. But I was feeling so rattled by it all that my mind refused to believe what it had so spontaneously remembered, nay, even recognized. My gaze became locked on that man, suspended between belief and disbelief.

'There could be no doubt that the man was Umar Din who lived in my native village. Once his leg had been run over by a cart, and because the bone hadn't been set properly he always walked lifting one foot quickly and letting the other sort of drag along slowly. So it looked as though he walked on one foot and merely dragged the other along. He also would shake his head with a quick, brisk movement as he walked. He had a grey, sparse beard. As a little boy I often mimicked his gait and teased him, just as the other village brats did. It was the same Umar Din who was now limping along before me, briskly shaking his head. I made an unsuccessful attempt to call his name; my throat had gone completely dry.

'In September 1947, when I reached my village near Hoshiarpur in Major Godfrey's jeep, escorted by an armed guard, the first person I spotted there was this Umar Din. A hundred yards outside the village limits he lay dead on a trail under a shisham tree. Rioters had slashed his throat. A couple of dozen yards from him lay the corpse of his orphaned niece Mehran.

'Umar Din had already trudged by me. But the thought of Mehran—who more than a name, represented for me a quiet little girl of tawny complexion and dark, frightened eyes, trailing behind her herd of sheep and goats with a stick in her hand, or like the faraway scene of dust coated wild jujube bushes and the desolate stretches of sunlit sand left behind by flash floods—made me turn around abruptly and look. Sure enough, there she was, coming along a short distance behind Umar Din. She too didn't bother to look at me and passed along.

'Suddenly my legs buckled and my heart began to pound. After Umar Din and Mehran, I knew somehow instinctively who I might expect to see next. I made a concerted effort to steel my heart. By now tears had welled up in my eyes. Up until that point I had been looking at these people with amazed though uninvolved eyes. There appeared to be no connection between them and myself except that they were in an entirely strange and incomprehensible way passing by me on their way to Pakistan, and I was merely looking at them. Now, though, in the time it takes to blink an eye, that indifference had changed into a feeling of deep attachment, indeed so deep that it tore at my heart. I knew, I just knew what more I'd have to see. Although I was hardly collected enough to fathom how and why this was happening, I still had enough sense to know that I couldn't hope to reach the essence of that experience by any rational or logical means.

'I recognized some, but only some of the people who passed by. As you know, I'd spent most of my time away from our village and could boast of only a handful of people there whom I knew well. The truth is, I've forgotten most of them now. Had I tried to look closely, I might have recognized a few more, but at that point my eyes were looking for somebody else.

'Then I saw them coming along from afar. I hobbled on and stopped right in the middle of the road. I stretched out my arms to stop them. Something dry and bitter caught in my throat and I began to cry.

'My mother walked ahead of them all; floral patterns painted in blood on her clothes, rosary in hand, followed a few steps behind by my three sisters. Water still dripped from the clothes stuck to the bodies of my two elder sisters. They had drowned themselves in the well. My little sister still held her Japanese doll in her hand. A big red scar, like a magnificent rose in bloom, flashed on her breast. Two or three small roses could be seen in her hair. Behind them came my twelve-year-old brother, the broken hockey stick with which he had tried to fend off the attackers still firmly in his hand. His clothes were streaked with blood and his neck looked like it had been wrapped with red silk lace.

'Behind them all came our old maidservant Rahmate—walking bent over, as she always did, her lily-white curls still scattered over her forehead. Accompanied by Major Godfrey, I had reached the front of our house through a long and circuitous route—burning houses had blocked the most direct path. The first thing besides the broken doors that had met my eye was the sight of blood. Trickling along the outer drain of the second floor room, it had now come all the way downstairs. Inside, Rahmate had barely a trace of life left in her. She could tell us but one or two things. Her only regret had been that my younger brother didn't have a gun in his hand instead of the hockey stick, so that he could have felled a few of them before he himself was felled. She had started to curse the Sikhs of Kapurthalla and Kartarpur, lapsed into delirium and then died. I have no idea how Godfrey had managed to get me out of there.

'Anyway, I was standing before my little clan, but my mother didn't so much as look at me, nor did my sisters nor even my brother or Rahmate. Their eyes were gazing elsewhere. I blocked my mother's way and said, crying: "To come now! Isn't it rather late, Mother?" I stretched out my hands to stop her, but she slipped out of my arms like a wisp of smoke. And yet I saw that her face was perfectly tranquil bathed in a soft green glow, as though someone walked ahead of her carrying a light. In fact they all had serene faces, suffused in the same gentle green glow. I didn't try to stop them; instead I turned around to see where the light might have come from. Maybe someone launched a flare from the Pakistani artillery position—I wondered.

'The people who had fallen behind were coming along now—in droves of hundreds and thousands, perhaps even more. Wherever I looked, I only saw a surging tide of humanity. For a moment I felt they were with me, that I knew them all, as surely as moths know where to look for light on a rainy night, and migrant birds know that they must fly to distant, warm climes before the advent of winter. I got in with these people and, like one sleepwalking, fell in step with them. I had scarcely taken a few steps when I felt as if I didn't have anything below my knees. I fell on the ground face first and lost consciousness.

'When I came to I found myself in a field hospital behind the Pakistani emplacements. One of our units had gone out looking for me at the crack of dawn. Luckily I lay unconscious right across a dirt road, and so somebody spotted me and carried me behind our position.'

Out on a stroll, Lieutenant Nazir and I wandered some distance away. It was quiet and dark all around. I felt I was imprisoned in a frightening night which would never again see the light of day. 'I wonder . . .' I began, but promptly stopped, thinking what exactly it was I wanted to say. Lieutenant Nazir asked, 'Do you doubt that . . .?'

'No, I don't!' I quickly replied. 'I only wonder why Murad even bothers to recount this event over and over again when it always reopens his wounds.'

After a brief silence Lieutenant Nazir said, 'You don't understand! I've seen him up close, even worked under him. I often feel that he has become sort of suspended somewhere. You know, like he isn't fully present. I'm not talking about readiness or ability. That's different. Murad is one of those people who are locked in time, unable to go forward or back. Time, which had long stood frozen, suddenly started to thaw for him in those days of the war. He felt it had again started to move, both ways, forward and backward, that perhaps in the future this could very well happen for him again, like a seed in a field left callow, where it lies in anguish, waiting impatiently to germinate. Then it starts to rain heavily and the seed sprouts. You know—don't you?—that a seed, with the intention of conveying the trust of a thousand past seasons to a thousand coming ones, grows in two directions, above ground, and beneath it as well. And this is how we are enabled to break out of the prison of time. But when Murad says that he tried to turn around and see where the light came from, I feel more than a little irritated. You see, he is annoyingly humble.'

We became silent. I looked at the stars that seemed to burn quietly across eons. Suddenly guns erupted up ahead at the battle front. The sound of the blasts tore through the darkness like a rude, awakening cry. And the reports of far-away explosions began to reach our feet through the earth. Yet another violation of the cease-fire—I wondered.

Of Coconuts and Bottles of Chilled Beer

Masud Ashar

Separated one sings doleful songs; but when love is near—well, there are a million things to do.

I remembered this adage when repeated requests failed to stir Husna Begum to sing a *bhatyali.* Has the moment of togetherness arrived, then?—I wondered. But whose union, and with whom? And who must sing a doleful song of separation: Husna Begum . . . or we?

Even though we were their guests, we couldn't have spent a more miserable night. True, we slept indoors under mosquito nets. What of it? The mosquitoes and other bugs got to us all the same. They kept us awake all night long. Then there was Rahman Sahib, who babbled on and on about all the different rivers of Bengal and about how sublime sunsets and sunrises looked over them.

The gentleman whom Husna Begum's husband had appointed as our guide was a certain Abul Kalam Muhammad Jaliluddin—a name which he had shortened to A.K.M. Jaliluddin. (At least that is how it appeared on his books.) During the introductions, however, when Husna Begum's husband pronounced the 'j' of Jaliluddin as a distinct 'z,' we had the hardest time suppressing our laughter. Later, aboard the cabin cruiser too, the memory of the outrageously funny pronunciation never failed to arouse laughter. The urge was so violent that only with the greatest difficulty did we manage to suppress it. We could neither laugh so brazenly in the presence of our hosts, nor stifle our laughter. So we used some pretext or the other to laugh, and sometimes we just pinched our noses and bent our heads. Chughtai had told us the trick about pinching the nose. He thought it helped suppress laughter. And it also, thereby, saved us from appearing rude to our hosts. Laughter, however, took its own time to subside, but meanwhile pinching the nose made our eyes water a lot. At such times, Rahman Sahib glowered at us, full of rage, and Jalil Bhai just looked away, pretending to be busy with something or the other, while we stepped out of the cabin into the open air and addressed one another as 'Zalil Bhai' and hurled coconut husks at flotsam in the river. In the evening, Jalil Bhai would spell out for our benefit—with statistics and all—how much we depended on the Bengalis for certain items and how we had made them depend on us for certain others. Then a raging thirst would parch our throats. While Jalil Bhai and Rahman Sahib slaked it with fresh coconut milk, Chughtai would take out some chilled beer from the bucket and pour three glasses for us. He would explain to Jalil Bhai, giving one proof after another why coconut milk, if taken during the afternoon, constituted a real health hazard, though it was quite harmless before sunrise or until about midday, and how 'Before sunrise, coconut milk is just like beer.'

But Jalil Bhai wasn't about to give in. Midway through an apparent altercation with Rahman Sahib (even when he talked normally, he appeared to be arguing), he would switch from English to Bengali. Yusuf Zai would take out a deck of cards and deftly divert us into a game of *canturi*.

At the Chittagong railway terminal, a hoary old man with a long lily-white beard, suddenly planted himself in our way. He was so dark it looked as though he had come straight from shovelling coal in a locomotive.

'Going north?' he asked us abruptly in Bengali. We didn't know Bengali; so we just gawked at Rahman Sahib, hoping that he would translate the old man's words for us. Instead, Rahman Sahib gruffly told the old man to clear off. But Chughtai, now in a playful mood, answered the old man, 'No, sir. We're headed south.'

'Stop slavery!' the old man yelled in English and, securing his tattered checked loincloth on the front of his hungry, incredibly flat stomach, shoved Rahman Sahib aside and fixed his penetrating gaze on Chughtai's pink, healthy face.

But Chughtai, missing the old man's drift, snapped, 'Listen Maulvi Sahib, don't try to make an impression by rattling off in your pidgin English . . .'

The hoary old man didn't let Chughtai finish. He sprang at him and dug his bony fingers into his neck. It all happened so fast we barely had time to react. Dazed, we thought it was some kind of a joke. But it couldn't have been a joke: the old man truly had sunk his fingers into Chughtai's neck, who was choking from the pressure, thrashing his hands and feet about.

Suddenly Yusuf Zai moved forward. He grabbed the old man by the waist and with a mighty tug tore him from Chughtai and tossed him in the air. The old man bounced like a rubber ball on the grass bank.

Just as Chughtai was also getting ready to pounce on the old man, a crowd suddenly materialized from God knows where and began to hem us in on all sides. The speed with which they scrambled to the scene made us believe that they were expecting a showdown—indeed they were spoiling for it. Instead of picking up the haggard old man from the ground, they moved ominously toward us.

'Get out of here! Quick! Or else, brace yourselves for a

riot!' Rahman Sahib whispered, pushing us to one side. But there was no getting away. The mob was steadily closing in on us. Rahman Sahib dashed to the side where the crowd looked thicker and began to jabber in Bengali.

But not one soul was listening to his words, which were dissolving into the air like a fine vapour. They were talking all at once and moving closer and closer toward us.

'Hitting a poor, old madman, huh? Don't you have any shame?'

'What? Madman? He is *not* mad!'

Suddenly the old man reappeared and installed himsel right in front of us again. 'Don't you know I am Lincoln? he screamed, 'Abraham Lincoln?'

'What did he say—Lincoln? . . . Of course!' In spite o the situation, we broke into ringing laughter.

Yusuf Zai quickly moved up close to the old man patted his hand and said in a perfectly serious voice, 'I an awfully sorry, Mr. President, I am truly sorry.'

Chughtai, too, had forgotten all about his aching neck and was laughing uproariously with us. But the old man didn't find it funny. He looked grave, and so did Rahman Sahib and the mob. The old man contemptuously pushed Yusuf Zai's hand away, waved his fist in the air and clamoured in English, 'No Slavery!'

We spotted an opening in the mob and began to slip away. 'What a weird fellow!' we exclaimed.

'What madman isn't weird?'

'But what the hell's he raving about? Slavery—wha slavery?'

'He's mad, after all. What are you getting so irritate about?'

Rahman Sahib didn't say a word. He just kept walkin along. This was his own city. He had lived here for the pa twenty-three years. And he had come to receive us at the railway terminal.

Rahman Sahib's little Fiat rounded the corner and we saw that the whole mob was now waving their fists ominously in the air along with the old man.

They called the joker the 'turtle'. And that woman with full fleshy lips got at least two jokers every deal. She would lick her lips with her blood-red tongue and coat them a deep red as well, as I brooded over the advantages of chewing betel leaf, so common in Bengal: it certainly made your lips look voluptuously red. Dangerous, too. And this 'turtle' was a strange creature: sensing the slightest danger, how it pulled its head back into its shell and froze on the spot. But why do these people call a joker a turtle?

Those full, fleshy red lips had managed to clean everyone's pockets, even Yusuf Zai's, who was otherwise known to be an accomplished card player. He just kept looking dumbly at us with his big, innocent eyes, as aghast as a sacrificial lamb. The Divisional Forest Officer was bursting with pride at his wife's smashing performance, breaking every now and then into loud applause: 'She's marvellous! Husna is simply terrific!'

'Endless rhapsodies about her delightfully tawny complexion, her incredibly melodious body. Bah! Propaganda, just plain propaganda and lies. You get so psyched up hearing those litanies, you begin to see the lousiest wench warbling a *bhatyali*.'

Yusuf Zai, who had for a whole fortnight not once seen the slightest ray of hope, finally vented his frustration on the much touted charms of Bengali women.

'Abject poverty and hunger—what else do you expect?

Give them enough to eat and then see how they blossom, how the deathly dark colour leaps into a vibrant tawny complexion.' Rahman Sahib had an answer for everything.

'Nonsense. Well, all right. So you can improve the complexion, but what about her features? How are you going to knock them into shape? Haven't you noticed: if the lips are beautiful, the nose is hideous; and if the eyes are lovely, the lips are weird-looking? Even her celebrated eyes aren't really all that beautiful, either. That is, if you cared to look closely.'

'You've got to jump into the river to see how deep it is.'

'Don't give me that. I've had quite a few jumps already.'

'Cross-breeding, that's the answer. That's it.'

'So you want us to marry them, is that it? Those shriveled mummies? Just for a pair of beautiful eyes? Forget it! Who wants to sire a whole generation of freaks?

'Who ever said anything about marrying them? But, I'd . . .'

'So what else is new?'

Rahman Sahib was very perturbed. Rahman Sahib, who was a Bengali, and then again not; one who backed us up, but who also backed up Jalil Bhai; who wished to offend neither us nor Jalil Bhai; who quarrelled with us, just as he quarrelled with Jalil Bhai; who looked to us for help, just as he looked to Jalil Bhai; and who, finally, understood neither our point of view nor Jalil Bhai's. Whenever a surge of love for Rahman Bhai swept over Yusuf Zai, he would pick up his diminutive body and waltz him all over the deck.

'When I set up a grand hosiery factory here, you know what? I'll make Rahman Sahib the General Manager.'

'Hosiery? But only yesterday you were talking about setting up a jute mill.'

'Well, you see, it's like this: none of the locals seem to

wear shirts; all they ever wear are undershirts. A hosiery business will do well. Don't you think? They'll profit from it, and so will we.'

'What about your plans for the bicycle factory?'

'That's good business, too. But where will I get the raw material for bicycles? Let bicycles come from West Pakistan. What do you think, Rahman Sahib?'

But Rahman Sahib didn't care to reply; he always preferred silence whenever the discussion veered to controversial matters. Only Yusuf Zai and Chughtai evinced a strong interest in them.

'Our people are very poor,' said Atiquzzaman Khan, pushing a mug of chilled beer toward his brother Amiruzzaman Khan in the Saqi—the bar in the Hotel Intercontinental.

'His pronunciation,' Chughtai whispered into my ears, 'it seems all right, doesn't it?'

It was afternoon. A young Bengali couple, beer mugs in hand, was talking in undertones at the table directly across from us.

'What I can't understand is . . .' Chughtai took a big gulp of beer and shut up.

'What don't you understand?'

'Nothing. Nothing at all.'

'You know why? Because you are perched up too high on your loft. How can you!'

'Or perhaps you don't try to understand it at all,' Amiruzzaman Khan was quick to remark in English.

Chughtai observed that the two brothers' pronunciation was atrocious after all.

'How can I? Yes, how can I?'

Amiruzzaman Khan had been asking me a great deal about the folk-songs of Multan and Bahawalpur regions; he had even promised to come to Multan to tape them. I just gazed quietly at the low ceiling of the Saqi and at the smart-looking bartender.

'Yes, our people are very poor,' said the Divisional Forest Officer of Khulna, who had, since Atiquzzaman was paying, already guzzled down two mugs of beer.

'And so are our people,' Chughtai shot back as he jumped a little from his chair and stared the Forest Officer full in the face. 'They are very poor, too.'

'*No*! We are poorer still. Really poor. No comparison.'

'In poverty,' Yusuf Zai tried to reconcile the two, 'we are all equals. We are one.'

'No! We are not *equals*. Nor are we *one*.'

'Dera Ghazi Khan, Mianwali, Sarhad, Baluchistan, Thar . . .'

But what are we fighting about? And why? The Forest Officer had offered to show us around Sundarbans. We must try to make him feel comfortable and happy. So I glared at Yusuf Zai, he at Chughtai, and the three of us shut up. But now the three of them had started to talk. And in Bengali at that. We felt isolated. We sat in their midst, but obviously we were not one of them. Suddenly a deluge of voices filled the entire hotel and bar. The mouths of Atiquzzaman Khan, Amiruzzaman Khan, and the Forest Officer began to open and shut with such frightening speed that I felt giddy and emptied the whole mug in one giant, nervous gulp.

Then, at last, we were on the river. We disturbed the waters hurling coconut husks at assorted targets, then aimed the husks at the butterflies and, somewhere along the line, got thirsty. Jalil Bhai picked out five coconuts from the bucket, took out a long, thin knife, and hacked one.

'Agh! Stop it, Jalil Bhai! It's sheer murder. Why are you

killing them in such cold blood?'

Jalil Bhai's hand froze. He looked at Chughtai with malicious eyes, but Chughtai gave an undaunted laugh and picked up a bottle of beer from the pail. Then he said, 'Khanji, go get a glass. Let's give Jalil Bhai something different for a change.'

But Jalil Bhai quickly mouthed the split coconut and downed all the milk in one hasty gulp. Rahman Sahib, to keep Jalil Bhai's morale high, picked out a coconut himself. Just as he was getting ready to slash it open, Yusuf Zai snatched the fruit from his hand and tossed it outside toward the Forest Guard. 'Here, catch!'

We had been cruising around in the boat from one river port to the next for two whole days and still we had hardly put a dent in the supply of beer and coconuts. The heap had hardly diminished; on the contrary, it seemed to be growing bigger.

'Why on earth did we have to haul these coconuts along?'

'To make you happy and to win over the hearts of Jalil Bhai and the Forest Guard, I suppose.'

'So?'

'So, nothing.'

'Well, then drink them!'

'We will, we will. After we've run out of the beer.'

But it seemed the beer would outlast us. Jalil Bhai's mood was getting worse. Was he upset because he couldn't get us to drink coconut milk or because he couldn't put up with Yusuf Zai puttering around in the engine compartment? We couldn't tell. Every time Yusuf Zai tinkered with the engine and sped up the boat, Jalil Bhai got jittery and shouted, 'Mr Yusuf Jai, let my men take care of the boat. Don't monkey around.'

'But Jalil Bhai, I can pilot a boat too. No big deal. In fact, I can pilot it even better . . .'

'No, mister, I won't let you mess around with it. No! Only my man will pilot it.'

'Huh? The hell he will!' Yusuf Zai would come over and sit beside us, still fuming, 'The son of a bitch hardly has an ounce of flesh left on his body. The hell he will! The bastard keeps dozing off the whole day long.'

When petty quarrels broke out over coconuts and beer, Jalil Bhai quietly withdrew to his cabin and immersed himself in his books. He had brought along quite a few and stuffed them into the small cabinet above his berth. In vain would I try to tell them that besides beer and coconut milk there was also such a thing as water; but they wouldn't listen. Jalil Bhai would quickly disappear behind his book and Chughtai would begin to warble a Nazrul song: '*Chol, chol, chal . . .*'

I believe it was Friday. The front of Bait al-Mukarram was filled with people who stood in sundry, large groups. The man who drew the biggest crowd was hawking amulets. He couldn't have been a smarter salesman. From one for ten paisa to one for fifty paisa—you name it, there was an amulet for everybody. And people were buying them with perfect humility and unswerving faith.

'What a paradox!'

'Paradox? What paradox?' Rahman Sahib couldn't understand any of it. For him this was nothing strange, nothing paradoxical at all. Everything was proceeding with perfect smoothness. Normal—period.

'All the same, it is a profitable business,' Yusuf Zai said. Moments later he plunged into the crowd, elbowing his way to the hawking peddler.

'Well, I'll tell you: on one hand you have a hoary old man shouting slogans to end slavery, and on the other slavery is being given a shot in the arm. That's the paradox.'

'You'll never understand *that*, you just can't.'

'Why can't I?'

'But Rahman Sahib, we thought every Bengali was a potential revolutionary?'

'Miyanji, do you sell an amulet for *inqilab*, too?' Yusuf Zai, who had probably caught Chughtai's remark, moved forward and asked the old vendor with studied seriousness.

By now Chughtai, Rahman Sahib and I had inched our way to the very first row and were directly facing the Pir Sahib. The Pir Sahib ignored Yusuf Zai's question and, his head bent low, went on selling amulets to people who sat squatting on the ground. Yusuf Zai repeated the question, only this time he didn't use the word '*inqilab*' but the English word 'revolution.' Still Pir Sahib didn't care to look up and continued to be busy in his work.

Rahman Sahib tried to nudge Yusuf Zai away from the scene, but the latter had dug in, and wasn't about to budge. A playful Chughtai was constantly egging him on, 'Come on, yaar, ask him again.'

'For God's sake, Chughtai Sahib, why must . . .'

'Oh, no, Rahman Sahib, I'm just joking. Can't the Pir Sahib see that? Surely, he can take a bit of sport.'

Frustrated in his third attempt also, Yusuf Zai tried to solicit Rahman Sahib's help. 'What is the word for "*inqilab*" in Bengali?' he asked.

But Rahman Sahib—whether because Yusuf Zai had

angered him with his antics or because he had become really scared of what might follow, we couldn't tell—quickly withdrew from the scene. Only I remained standing behind Yusuf Zai and volunteered, '*Kranti*.'

'What?' Yusuf Zai couldn't figure out the word.

'*Kranti*! *Kranti*!' I shouted, loud and clear, and before I knew it, the entire crowd had suddenly dropped their business with the Pir Sahib and was beginning to surround us. They were staring at us so hard it looked as though they would eat us alive. I turned around to locate Rahman Sahib. He had vanished without a trace.

And then it seemed as though suddenly all the bands of people from Jinnah Avenue to Bait al-Mukarram started to press in on us, trying to crush us with the weight of their collected bodies. I looked at the flight of stairs leading up to Bait al-Mukarram; maybe, just maybe, a single hand might rise in our defence. But the stairs only offered an unbroken view of a ferocious tidal wave of heads from which all hands had ominously disappeared.

A confused Yusuf Zai was looking sheepishly at the crowd and snickering to lessen his embarrassment, while Chughtai comically jabbered on in his pidgin Bengali, proffering a hand of friendship which nobody in the crowd seemed prepared to accept. The mob's eyes were glued, instead, on his big, jutting Pathan nose and broad forehead.

Suddenly my eyes fell upon the face of the Pir Sahib who had, God knows when, come and planted himself right in front of me. 'Chughtai,' I screamed, 'it's the same mad man we saw in Chittagong!'

Chughtai and Yusuf Zai, too, turned around to look at the man and let out a wild scream, 'Run!'

And we ran, tearing our way through the surging crowd. Chughtai had scrambled off towards Bait al-Mukarram. Yusuf Zai and I followed. But the stairs of Bait al-Mukarram seemed endless. Soon our legs buckled from fatigue and we crumbled on the steps.

I wanted to talk. I wanted to talk about many things, so many things that I wished everyone in the cabin cruiser would just stop their work and come over and listen to me, listen to what I had to say, to things whose oppressive weight was crushing my chest. I wanted to lighten this weight . . . and the weight of all the things that were weighing heavily upon the others as well. But they were preoccupied with their own work. They had no time for me. Rahman Sahib was getting the 'dispatch' ready for his newspaper; Chughtai was quarrelling with the Forest Guard over a suitably cool spot to store the pail of chilled beer; Yusuf Zai, having failed to interest anyone in playing rummy, had withdrawn to a quiet corner and occupied himself with solitaire; and Jalil Bhai was doing God knows what shut up inside the engine compartment.

Why don't these people ever sit together? Why are they so keen on keeping away from each other? Oh, how I wish this boat stopped for a while—even in the middle of the river! Perhaps then things might change. Or maybe not. Who knows? The waters of the river are muddy, the surface is riddled with *jal-kumri* plants. And the area is infested with crocodiles, they say. What if the *jal-kumri* were to spread over the entire river? How would the boats move, then? One could have asked all these questions of Jalil Bhai, if only he had been around on the deck. He couldn't have picked a worse time to worry about the engine.

Husna Begum won the hand again, and the Forest Officer's

unbounded adulation burst forth in cries of 'Marvellous! Terrific!' And then, all of a sudden, a naked, starving Bengali showed up from God knows where. They began to compare him to the starving and naked of Dera Ghazi Khan in West Pakistan. I just kept my eyes fixed on those juicy red lips which appeared totally motionless, while the others kept hurling question after blind question at one another. Whenever I took my eyes off those lips, it was only to look for a joker in the cards I held. But I didn't get a joker in a single hand. By now my tongue had become so dry and thick I could scarcely move it over my parched lips.

'Our man works for four annas. Imagine, just four annas. And yours for a whole *taka*—I mean a whole rupee.'

'A rupee? No. More like four.' Rahman Sahib quickly corrected the Forest Officer.

'Yes, yes, four rupees, yes,' the Forest Officer, who had travelled through West Pakistan, said. His wife, however, had only dreamed of Karachi and Lahore; so the very mention of those cities, along with a bare glance at our colourful, expensive clothes, was enough to set her eyes agleam.

'Husna Begum's eyes are truly lovely.'

'That they are. But in a different face they'd look even lovelier.'

After breakfast it was Chughtai who became impatient about the boat trip and asked, 'When will the damn thing get moving?'

'Mr. Zalil will be along soon. We'll leave as soon as he comes. In the meantime, you get ready.'

This was the first time when this pronunciation of 'Jalil Bhai' had brought us to the verge of laughter; Chughtai had quickly pinched his nose to keep from laughing—the sudden onrush of blood colouring his eyes a deep red—and

Rahman Bhai whirled around and glowered at us in irritation.

Finally, Jalil Bhai arrived. Introductions followed. We started to pack the things we were bringing along: three suitcases, a huge burlap sack stuffed with coconuts, and a wooden case of bottled beer. The coconuts were a gift from the Forest Officer and his wife. ('You won't get drinking water on the river, so use them when you get thirsty,' the couple had said.) The beer was the common property of Yusuf Zai, Chughtai, and myself.

'Look fellows, this isn't proper,' said Rahman Bhai, who was lounging in a cane chair inside the room watching us pack for the trip ahead.

'What isn't proper?' Chughtai asked, flabbergasted, as he affixed a pair of expensive cufflinks to his silk shirt.

'That you keep mocking these people all the time.'

'For God's sake Rahman Bhai, just tell us who we've mocked?'

'Then there is such a thing as a sense of humour, too.'

'Khan Sahib,' Rahman Sahib began with some irritation, 'you are now in Bengal. You must really try to accept its ways.'

'Are you going to tell me that you have?' Chughtai shot back, emerging from the bathroom.

'Yes. I have.'

'You mean there is no difference between how you live and how the average Bengali lives?'

Rahman Sahib became speechless. He looked out of the window for a while, picked his way to the door, but then stopped short. 'When we were new here,' he began, lighting the cigarette pressed between Chughtai's lips, 'an amusing thing happened to us. We employed a young Bengali girl to help us out with the house work . . .'

'A young girl—wow!'

'Yes, about seventeen or eighteen years old.' Rahman Sahib sank back into the cane chair. 'She never wore a blouse, though . . .'

'No blouse?' Yusuf Zai cut in, jumping up. 'You mean altogether nude? God be praised!'

'Well, she'd just wrap herself in a gauze-like muslin sari . . .'

'How much of her could she possibly have wrapped in a sari.'

'That's just it. It bothered us a lot, especially my wife.'

'I bet it did, you being a strapping youth and all that. Your wife had to . . .'

'Anyway, my wife got her a few blouses and ordered her to put one on.'

'What a pity! She should've left her alone.'

'Yes, what a pity. She somehow endured the blouse for a day, but the very next day she ran away.'

'Ran away? You mean she quit?'

'Yes, she quit. Nobody in her entire family had ever even dreamed of wearing a blouse.'

'Makes sense. She didn't want to be cooped up inside a blouse.'

'Oh, there was more. Her family thought it plain indecent to wear a blouse. It meant that the girl was whoring around.'

'My goodness!'

'You didn't look for another servant girl?'

'Oh yes, we did.'

'One without a blouse?'

'Wow! Rahman Sahib, you must've had lots of fun.'

Suddenly there was a loud crash outside, followed by the screams of the Forest Officer. We were so shocked we just stood staring dumbly at one another for some time. Rahman Sahib then shot out of the room. We followed. In the veranda we all came to a sudden halt.

A beer bottle lay shattered on the floor, and in the middle of a pool of spilled beer stood a hoary old man wearing nothing except a rag of checked cloth wrapped around his waist. He stood with his back to us, supporting the wooden case of beer on his left shoulder, as rivers of sweat ran down the upper half of his body. His head was hung very low, and with his right hand he was rubbing his cheeks embarrassedly. Nearby the Forest Officer was wringing his hands and shouting at the old man in Bengali.

'Never mind,' Yusuf Zai said, moving a bit forward. 'He just broke *one* bottle.'

'No, sir. These lazy bums never do anything well. They'd rather die of starvation than work. And when, for a change, they do work, they always botch it.'

The Forest Officer screamed again at the old man. Rahman Sahib and even Husna Begum, who had meanwhile walked in, started saying something to the old man in Bengali.

The scrawny old man shifted the case from his left to his right shoulder, turned around and looked at us. Suddenly we, who weren't Bengalis, cringed with shame.

'Oh, no! He's here, too!'

'Be quiet!'

We remained silent until we had boarded the boat and Yusuf Zai had dealt out the cards for a game of rummy.

'Bengal is truly a land of magicians!'

'Huh! We shall never accept the slavery you force upon us, though we wouldn't mind being mistreated by one of our own . . .'

'We want the right to slap *our* people with *our* own hands.'

'Bravo!'

We sailed past one quay, then another; downed three beers, then six; split coconuts and gave their milk to the Forest Officer, Jalil Bhai, Rahman Sahib, and the Forest Guard; and tossed some coconuts into the river.

Suddenly it hit me with brutal clarity that all these people were somehow drifting farther and farther away from me; as if there were two separate boats, not one; that they were aboard one and we aboard the other; and the two boats were headed in opposite directions.

I was afraid. I was afraid of being left alone. I did not want to be left alone. I looked at all those very busy people once again and picked my way to the small cabinet above Jalil Bhai's berth in search of an understanding companion. Why not talk to books? Yes.

But those books, too, did not know my language. Tagore, Madhusudan Das, Nazrul Islam, Munir Chaudhury, Shahidullah Qaisar—all neatly lined up before me but unable to understand me. Of course I recognized these authors from their pictures on the dust covers; they, too, perhaps, recognized me by my face. I couldn't understand what they were saying; I was just looking over the titles, leafing through the pages, dumbly. It was all useless; no one knew my language, no one could talk with me. Then my eyes fell upon a book that knew me, that also knew Jalil Bhai—indeed it knew us both at the same time. It was *The Spy Who Came in from the Cold*.

I left the cabin.

Evening mist blurred the edges of the river, as a weary sun slipped into its waters. Or, was it perhaps rising from the river? Was it evening? Morning? Sunrise? Sunset? I couldn't tell.

Husna Begum's voice was assaulting my ears. Was she also on the boat, then? I heard the voices of Atiquzzaman Khan and Amiruzzaman Khan as well. And of the Forest Officer, too. It seemed they were all aboard the boat—indeed it seemed all of Bengal had scrambled aboard the boat, which was rocking perilously.

'Rahman Sahib . . . Rahman Bhai . . . Where have you run off to? And you, too, Jalil Bhai? How on earth have these people managed to jump aboard right in the middle of the river? Didn't the *jal-kumri* block their way? And the crocodiles—millions of crocodiles, who rule the river waters—didn't they scare them off? Rahman Sahib? Rahman Dada?'

Rahman Sahib was nowhere to be found. Somehow I knew—as certainly as I knew that I existed—that Jalil Bhai was lurking somewhere nearby. Had Rahman Sahib been around, he surely would have responded to our urgent pleas and rushed to help us.

The entire boat was filled with people: swarthy, cadaverous Bengalis crowding in the engine compartment, cabins, the small deck, everywhere. It was impossible to tell them apart. I quickly hid Chughtai and Yusuf Zai behind me and desperately looked around in the crowd for the benign faces of Husna Begum and Atiquzzaman Khan, but couldn't find them. They, too, had become lost in the crowd—or, perhaps, become part of it. I could only hear their voices, which were so distant I couldn't make out what they were saying.

'Where in the hell has Rahman Sahib run off to?' And then I screamed, pulling all the strength out of my lungs: 'Rahman Sa-a-hib!'

'The boat had become too damn heavy,' came the answer from someone standing close by, who spoke ominously and with slow deliberation.

I turned around to see who it was. 'My god!' I shrieked, 'You, again?'

' . . . and still *is*.'

The Wagon

Khalida Husain

In a rush to get back to the city, I quickly crossed the dirt road and walked onto the Ravi bridge, looking indifferently at the blazing edge of the sun steadily falling into the marsh. I had a queer feeling, as though I had seen something. I spun around. There they were, three of them, leaning over the guard rails and gazing straight into the sunset. The deathly concentration made me look at the sunset myself, but I found nothing extraordinary in the scene; so I looked back at them instead. Their faces, though not at all similar, looked curiously alike. Their outfits suggested that they were well-to-do villagers, and their dust coated shoes that they had trudged for miles just to watch the sun as it set over the marshes of the receding Ravi. Impervious to the traffic on the bridge, they continued to stare at the marshes which were turning a dull, deep red in the sun's last glow.

I edged closer to them. The sun had gone down completely now; only a dark red stripe remained on the far horizon. Suddenly the three looked at each other, lowered their heads, and silently walked away, toward the villages outside the city. For some time I stood watching their tired figures recede into the distance. Soon the night sounds coming to life in the city reminded me that it was getting rather late and I'd better rush home. I quickened my pace and walked on under the blue haze of the night sky, pierced here and there by the blinking lights of the city ahead.

The next evening when I reached the bridge, the sunset was a few minutes away. I suddenly recalled the three men and stopped to watch the sunset, even though I knew Munna would be waiting on the front porch for sweets and Zakiya, my wife, would be ready for us to go to the movies. I couldn't budge. An inexorable force seemed to have bound me to the ground. Through almost all the previous night I'd wondered what it was about the marsh and the sunset that had engrossed those strange men so entirely.

And then, just as the blazing orange disc of the sun tumbled into the marsh, I saw the three walk up the road. They were coming from villages outside the city limits. They wore identical clothes and resembled each other a lot in their height and gait. Again they walked up to the bridge, stood at the same spot they had the previous evening and peered into the sunset with their flaming eyes, filled with a mute sadness. I watched them and wondered why, despite their diverse features, they looked so alike. One of them, who was very old, had a long, bushy snow-white beard. The second, somewhat lighter in complexion than the others, had a face that shone like gold in the orange glow of the sunset. His hair hung down to his shoulders like a fringe, and he had a scar on his forehead. The third was dark and snub-nosed.

The sun sank all the way into the marsh. As on the previous day, the men glanced at each other, let their heads drop and, without exchanging a word, went their way.

That evening I felt terribly ill at ease. In a way I regretted not asking them about their fascination with the sunset. What could they be looking for in the sun's fading light?—I wondered. I told Zakiya about the strange threesome. She just laughed and said, 'Must be peasants, on their way to the city to have a good time.'

An air of mystery surrounded these men. Zakiya, of course, couldn't have known it. One really had to look at them to appreciate it.

The next day I waited impatiently for the evening. I walked to the bridge, expecting them to show up. And they did, just as daylight was ebbing away. They leaned over the bridge and watched the sun go down, indifferent to the traffic around them. Their absorption in the scene made it impossible to talk to them. I waited until the sun had gone down completely and the men had started to return. This would be the time to ask them what it was they expected to find in the vanishing sun and the marshes of the receding river.

When the sun had sunk all the way, the men gave one another a sad, mute look, lowered their heads and started off. But, instead of returning to the village, they took the road to the city. Their shoes were covered with dust and their feet moved on rhythmically together.

I gathered my fading courage and asked them, 'Brothers! what village do you come from?'

The man with the snub nose turned around and stared at me for a while. Then the three exchanged glances, but none of them bothered to answer my question.

'What do you see over there, on the bridge?' I asked. The mystery about the three men was beginning to weigh heavily on me now. I felt as though molten lead had seeped into my legs—indeed into my whole body, and that it was only a matter of time before I would crumble to the ground reeling from a spell of dizziness.

Again they did not answer. I shouted at them in a choking voice, 'Why are you always staring at the sunset?'

No answer.

We reached the heavily congested city road. The evening sounds grew closer. It was late October, and the air felt pleasantly cool. The sweet scent of jasmine wafted in, borne on the breeze. As we passed the octroi post, the old man with snow-white hair suddenly spoke, 'Didn't you see? Has nobody in the city seen?'

'Seen what'

'When the sun sets, when it goes down all the way?' asked the hoary old man, rearranging his mantle over his shoulders.

'When the sun goes down all the way?' I repeated. 'What about it? That happens every day.'

I said that very quickly, afraid that the slightest pause might force them back into their impenetrable silence.

'We knew that, we knew it would be that way. That's why we came. That other village, there, too.' He pointed toward the east and lowered his head.

'From there we come . . .' said the snub-nosed man.

'From where?' I asked, growing impatient. 'Please tell me clearly.'

The third man peered back at me over his shoulder. The scar on his forehead suddenly seemed deeper than before. He said, 'We didn't notice, nor, I believe, did you. Perhaps nobody did. Because, as you say, the sun rises and sets every day. Why bother to look? And we didn't, when day after day, there, over there,' he pointed to the east, 'the sky became blood-red and so bright it blazed like fire even at nightfall. We just failed to notice . . .' He stopped abruptly, as if choking over his words. 'And now this redness,' he resumed after a pause, 'it keeps spreading from place to place. I'd never seen such a phenomenon before. Nor my elders. Nor, I believe, did they hear their elders mention anything quite like this ever happening.'

Meanwhile, the darkness had deepened. All I could see of my companions were their white flowing robes; their faces became visible only when they came directly under the pale, dim light of the lampposts. I turned around to look at the stretch of sky over the distant Ravi. I was stunned: it was glowing red despite the darkness.

'You are right,' I said, to hide my puzzlement, 'we really did fail to notice that.' Then I asked, 'Where are you going?'

'To the city, of course. What would be the point of arriving there afterwards?'

A sudden impulse made me want to stay with them, or to take them home with me. But abruptly, they headed off on another road, and I remembered I was expected home soon. Munna would be waiting on the front porch for his daily sweets and Zakiya must be feeling irritated by my delay.

The next day I stopped at the bridge again to watch the sunset. I was hoping to see those three men. The sun went down completely, but they didn't appear. I waited impatiently for them to show up. Soon, however, I was entranced by the last magical glow of the sunset.

The entire sky seemed covered with a sheet soaked in blood, and it scared me that I was standing all alone underneath it. I felt an uncanny presence directly behind me. I spun around. There was nobody. I was wrong. I couldn't have looked behind my back. How can anyone? All the same, I felt sure there was someone, standing behind me, within me or, perhaps, somewhere near.

Vehicles, of all shapes and sizes, rumbled along in the light of the street-lamps. Way back in the east, a stretch of evening sky still blazed like a winding sheet of fire, radiating heat and light far into the closing darkness. I was alarmed and hurried home. Hastily I told Zakiya all I'd seen. But she laughed off the whole thing. I took her up to the balcony and showed her the red and its infernal bright glow against the dark night sky. That sobered her up a little.

She thought for a while, then remarked, 'We're going to have a storm any minute, I'm sure.'

The next day in the office, as I worked, bent over my files, I heard Mujibullah ask Hafiz Ahmad, 'Say, did you see how the sky glows at sunset these days? Even after it gets dark? Amazing, isn't it?'

All at once I felt I was standing alone and defenceless under that blood-sheet of a sky. I was frightened. Small drops of sweat formed on my forehead. As the evening edged closer, a strange restlessness took hold of me. The receding Ravi, the bridge, the night sky and the sun frightened me; I just wanted to walk away from them. And yet, I also felt irresistibly drawn toward them.

I wanted to tell my colleagues about the three peasants who, in spite of their distinctly individual faces, somehow looked alike; about how they had come to the city accompanying this strange redness, had drawn my attention to it, and then dropped out of sight; and about how I'd searched in vain for them everywhere. But I couldn't. Mujibullah and Hafiz Ahmad, my colleagues, had each borrowed about twenty rupees from me some time ago, which they had conveniently forgot to return. And, in the bargain, they had stopped talking to me, too.

On my way home, when I reached the bridge, a strange fear made me walk briskly, look away from the sun, and try to concentrate instead on the street before me. But the blood-red evening kept coming right along. I could feel its presence everywhere. A flock of birds flew overhead in a 'V' formation. Like the birds, I too was returning home. Home, yes, but no longer my haven against the outside world; for the flame-coloured evening came pouring in from its windows, doors, even through its walls of solid brick.

I now wandered late in the streets, looking for the three peasants. I wanted to ask them where that red came from. What was to follow? Why did they leave the last settlement? What shape was it in? But I couldn't find them anywhere. Nobody seemed to care. Life moved on as usual.

A few days later I saw some men pointing up to the unusual red colour of the evening. Before long, the whole city was talking about it. I hadn't told a soul except Zakiya. How they had found out about it was a puzzle to me. Those three peasants must be in the city, I concluded. They have to be.

The red of the evening had now become the talk of the town.

Chaudhri Sahib, who owned a small book shop in Mozang Plaza, was an old acquaintance of mine. People got together at his shop for a chat every evening. So did I, regularly. But for some time now, since my first encounter with those mantle-wrapped oracular figures, I had been too preoccupied with my own thoughts to go there. No matter where I went, home or outside, I felt restless. At home, an inexorable urge drove me outdoors; outdoors, an equally strong urge sent me scrambling back home, where I felt comparatively safe. I became very confused about where I wanted to be. I began to feel heavy and listless.

All the same, I did go back to the book shop once again that evening. Most of the regulars had already gathered. Chaudhri Sahib asked, 'What do you think about it, fellows? Is it all due to the atomic explosions, as they say? Rumour also has it that pretty soon the earth's cold regions will turn hot and the hot ones cold, and the cycle of seasons will be upset.'

I wanted to tell them about my encounter with the three villagers but felt too shy to talk before so many people. Just then that ominous moment arrived:

A pungent smell, the likes of which I'd never smelled before, wafted in from God knows where. My heart sank and a strange, sweet sort of pain stabbed at my body. I felt nauseous, unable to decide whether it was a stench, a pungent aroma, or even a wave of bitter-sweet pain. I threw the newspaper down and got up to leave.

'What's the matter?' asked Chaudhri Sahib.

'I must go. God knows what sort of smell that is.'

'Smell? What smell?' Chaudhri Sahib sniffed the air.

I didn't care to reply and walked away. That offensive smell, the terrifying wave of pain, followed me all the way home. It made me giddy. I thought I might fall any minute. My condition frightened Zakiya, who asked, 'What's the matter? You look so pale.'

'I'm all right. God knows what that smell is.' I said, wiping the sweat off my brow, even though it was November.

Zakiya also sniffed the air, then said, 'Must be coming from the house of Hakim Sahib. Heaven knows what strange herb concoctions they keep making day and night. Or else it's from burnt food. I burnt some today accidentally.'

'But it seems to be everywhere—in every street and lane, throughout the city.'

'Why, of course. The season's changed. It must be the smell of winter flowers,' she said inattentively, and became absorbed in her knitting.

With great trepidation I sniffed the air again, but couldn't decide whether the sickening odour still lingered on or had subsided. Perhaps it had subsided. The thought relieved me a bit. But there was no escape from its memory, which remained fresh in my mind, like the itching that continues for some time even after the wound has healed. The very thought that it might return gave me the chills.

By the next morning I'd forgotten all about that rotten, suffocating smell. In the office, I found a mountain of files waiting for me. But Mujibullah and Hafiz Ahmad were noisily discussing some movie. I couldn't' concentrate on the work and felt irritated. So I decided to take a break. I called our office boy and sent him to the cafetaria for a cup of tea. Meanwhile I pulled out a pack of cigarettes from my pocket and lit up.

Just then I felt a cracking blow on my head, as if I had fallen off a cliff and landed on my head, which fused everything before my eyes in a swirling blue and yellow stream. It took my numbed senses some time to realize that I was being assaulted once again by the same pain, the same terrible stench. It kept coming at me in waves, and it was impossible to know its source. I found myself frantically shutting every window in the office, while both Mujibullah and Hafiz Ahmad gawked at me uncomprehendingly.

'Let the sun in! Why are you closing the windows?' asked Hafiz Ahmad.

'The stench, the stench! My God, it's unbearable! Don't you smell it?'

Both of them raised their noses to the air and sniffed. Then Hafiz Ahmad remarked, 'That's right! What sort of stench . . . or fragrance is that? It makes my heart sink.'

Soon, many people were talking about the waves of stench that came in quick succession and then receded, only to renew their assault a little while later. At sundown they became especially unbearable.

Within a few weeks the odour had become so oppressive that I often found it difficult to breathe. People's faces, usually lively and fresh, now looked drained and wilted. Many complained of constant palpitation and headaches. The doctors cashed in. Intellectuals hypothesized that it must be due to nuclear blasts, which were producing strange effects throughout the world, including this foul odour in our city, which attacked peoples' nerves and left them in a mess. People scrambled to buy tranquilizers, which quickly sold out. Not that the supply was inadequate, but a sudden frenzy to stock up and horde had seized people. Even sleeping pills fetched the price of rare diamonds.

I found both tranquilizers and sleeping pills useless. The stench cut sharper than a sword and penetrated the body like a dagger. The only way to guard against it was to get used to it, I thought; and people would do well to remember that. But I was too depressed to tell them myself. Within a few weeks, however, they themselves came to live with the stench.

Just the same, the odour struck terror in the city. People were loath to admit it, but they could not have looked more tense: their faces contorted from the fear of some terrible thing happening at any moment. Nor was their fear unreasonable, as a subsequent event showed a few weeks later.

On a cold mid-December evening, I was returning home from Chaudhri Sahib's. The street was full of traffic and jostling crowds. The stores glittered with bright lights, and people went about their business as usual. Every now and then a wave of stench swept in, made me giddy, and receded. I would freeze in my stride the instant it assailed my senses and would start moving again as soon as it had subsided. It was the same with others. An outsider would surely have wondered why we suddenly froze, closed our eyes, stopped breathing, then took a deep breath and got started again. But that was our custom now.

That December evening I'd just walked the bridge when I felt as if a lance had hit me on the head. My head whirled and my legs buckled. Reeling, I clung to a lamppost and tried to support my head with my hands. There was no lance, nor was there a hand to wield it. It was that smell—that same rotten smell—I realized with terror. In fact, it seemed that the source of the oppressive stench had suddenly moved very close to me, between my shoulder blades, near my back, immediately behind me—so close that it was impossible to think of it as separate from me.

It was then that my eyes fell on the strange carriage, rambling along in front of me. It was an oversized wagon pulled by a pair of scrawny white oxen with leather blinders over their eyes and thick ropes strung through their steaming nostrils. A ribbed wooden cage sat atop the base of the wagon, its interior hidden behind black curtains. Or were they just swaying walls of darkness?

Two men, sitting outside the cage enclosure in the front of the wagon, drove the two emaciated animals. I couldn't make out their faces, partly because of the darkness, but partly also because they were buried in folds of cloth thrown loosely around them. Their heads drooped forward and they seemed to have dozed off, as if overcome by fatigue and sleep.

Behind them the interior of the curtained wagon swelled with darkness, and from the heart of that darkness emanated the nauseating stench that cut sharper than a sword. Before I knew it, the wagon had moved past me, flooding my senses with its cargo of stench. My head swirled. I jumped off the main road onto the dirt sidewalk, and vomited.

I had no idea whether the people in the city had also

seen the eerie wagon. If they had, what must have they endured? I had the hardest time getting home after what I had seen. Once inside the house, I ran to my bed and threw myself on it. Zakiya kept asking me what had happened, but a blind terror sealed my lips.

A few days later a small news item appeared in the local papers. It railed against the local Municipal Office for allowing garbage carts to pass through busy streets in the evening. Not only did muck-wagons pollute the air, they also hurt the fine olfactory sense of the citizenry.

I took a whole week off from work. During those seven days, thought hardly fit to go out and observe firsthand the plight of the city, I was nonetheless kept posted of developments by the local newspapers. Groups of concerned citizens demanded that the municipal authorities keep the city clear of muck-wagons or, if that was impossible, assign them routes along less busy streets.

On the seventh day I ventured out. A change was already visible. Wrecked by insomnia and exhaustion, people strained themselves to appear carefree and cheerful, but managed only to look painfully silly. Suddenly I recalled that in the morning I had myself looked no different in the mirror.

About this time, the number of entertainment programmes and movies shot up as never before. People swarmed to the movie halls—often hours before a show—formed long lines, and patiently waited to be let in, only to file out later looking still more pale and ridiculous.

In the office, no matter how hard I tried, I couldn't concentrate on my work. Intermittently, the image of the muck-wagon lumbering down the streets flashed across my mind. Was it really one of those municipal dump-carts? No. It couldn't be. Municipal dump-carts never looked like that eerie wagon, with its sleepy drivers, a pair of blindfolded, bony oxen, black curtains and the outrageously nauseating smell. What on earth give off such an odd smell, at once fragrant and foul?

An insane desire suddenly overwhelmed me: to rush up to the wagon, lift up those swaying curtains, and peek inside. I must discover the source of the stench!

Coming to the bridge, my feet involuntarily slowed down. There was still time before sunset and the waves of the pain-filled odour came faster and stronger. I leaned over the bridge, an unknown fear slowly rising in my throat. The bottomless swamp, its arms ominously outstretched, seemed to be dragging me down toward it. I was afraid I might jump into the swamp, sink with the sun and become buried forever in that sprawling sheet of blood.

I became aware of something approaching me—or was I myself drawing closer to something? Something awaited by all men, those before and those after us. My whole body felt as though it were turning into a piece of granite, with no escape from the bridge, the miasma, the sun. For now they all seemed inseparable from my being. Helplessly, I looked around myself and almost froze.

The three men were coming towards me from the direction of the countryside. As before, they were wrapped in their flowing white robes and walked with their identical gait. I kept staring at them with glassy eyes until they walked right up to me and stopped. The hoary old man was crying, and his snow-white beard was drenched with tears. The other two couldn't look up; their eyes were lowered mournfully, their teeth clenched and their faces withered by a deathly pallor.

'Where were you hiding all these days?' I said between gasps and stammers. 'I searched for you everywhere. Tell me, please, what's happening to the city?'

'We were waiting. Trying to hold ourselves back. We had tied ourselves with ropes. Here, look!' They spread their arms before me and bared their shoulders and backs, revealing the deep marks of the rope.

'We did not want to come,' the old man said, drowned out by a fit of sobs.

'But there was no choice,' the second man said. Before he had finished, he doubled over. His companions also doubled over, as if unable to control a sudden surge of pain. The same wave of pain-filled stench stabbed the air about us, cutting us into halves, flooding our senses as it scrambled past us.

'There! Look!' said the old man, pointing in the direction of the distant villages and turning deathly pale.

In the distance, I saw the wagon come up the road from behind a cloud of dust. The drowsing coachmen had wrapped their faces because of their proximity to the cutting stench.

A cold shiver ran up my spine. The eyes of the three men suddenly became dull. They were approaching their end perhaps.

The wagon rumbled close—the stench from it draining the blood from our bodies—and then passed us. Its sinister jet-black curtains, fluttering in the gentle breeze, appeared oddly enough, entirely motionless.

The three men ran after the wagon, caught up with i and lifted the curtains. A split second later, a non-humar scream burst from their gaping mouths. They spun arounc and bolted toward the distant fields.

'What was it? What did you see?' I called, running afte them. But they did not reply and kept running madly. Thei eyes had frozen in a glassy stare.

I followed them until we had left the city several miles behind us, then grabbed the old man's robe and implored, 'Tell me! Please tell me!'

He turned his deathly gaze toward me and threw open his mouth. His tongue had got stuck to his palate.

All three had become mute.

My head whirled, and I collapsed. The three men continued to run, soon disappearing in the distance behind a whirling cloud of dust. Slowly the dust settled and I returned home.

For months now I have searched in vain for those men. They have vanished without a trace. And the wagon—from that fateful evening, it too has changed its route. It no longer passes through the city. After crossing the bridge, it now descends onto the dirt trail leading to the villages in the countryside.

The cityfolk are no longer bothered by the cutting stench. They have become immune to it and think it has died, like an old, forgotten tale.

But it continues to torment my body, and day and night a voice keeps telling me, 'Now, your turn! Now you shall see!' And this evening I find myself on the bridge, waiting for the wagon . . . waiting.

The Rogue

Syed Muhammad Ashraf

The sun had long set, or perhaps just minutes ago, when a van slowed down and exited to the right of the highway, onto the sloping road that led to the forest. It had not yet rounded the curve and picked up speed again when a woman in an overcoat standing near the small foot-bridge with a young boy in tow beckoned them to stop.

Nadim slammed on the brakes. The van jerked to a halt, sending up a thick cloud of dust which obscured the woman's and the boy's legs.

Nadim, in the time it took for the dust to settle and the engine to die down, heard three sentences inside the van and felt embarrassed by each.

Dr Vaqar grabbed the hunting rifle from the seat and said in a tone at once sharp and instructional, 'Why did you stop, yaar? We're late as it is. Back at the Ranger's complex the DFO sahib must have already dried up waiting for us.'

Asif slid the window down and peered out at the woman and the boy. Pulling his face back in, he laughed, 'Out hunting the rogue elephant, but one glance at a woman, and they start acting all macho.'

And Rashid, thinking of something, said with unwarranted apprehension, 'Let's at least get down and find out. Who is she? What does she want?'

Nadim flung the door open. Outside a December wind was blowing. He stepped out and walked over to the woman.

'Fool! It's cold! At least he could have shut the door,' D

Vaqar said, as if to himself. 'Vicious cold. I bet it even snowed again.'

Nadim climbed back into his seat, shut the door, turned around and was about to speak to them when he suddenly realized something and threw the door open again.

Rashid noticed how the woman's face, which had tensed up as the van door closed, slowly relaxed again when Nadim opened his door the second time.

'Actually, she has ten thousand rupees on her . . .' Nadim stopped short, perhaps realizing that the sentence sounded strange without some sort of explanation.

'What do you mean? Whose money? Why would she have so much money on her in the first place . . . along a forest road?' . . .

Nadim interrupted Dr Vaqar and confidently reeled off the whole story: 'She got the money from the catechu merchant Agarwal of Baroli Village. She lives in Canada and is here on a visit, but she's originally from Lucknow. She herself gave Agarwal the money in Canada, so that he'd return it to her when she visited here. She has to be in Lucknow by evening. The boy in tow is her nephew. His name is Raju. The buses are on strike today. This she found out only after she'd already left the village. She doesn't want to go back to the village, because in the entire village there isn't a single house . . .'

He stopped short, just then sensing the presence of Ramesh, the Doctor's pharmacist, who sat quietly in the rearmost seat, hugging his single-barrelled shotgun.

It's amazing how sometimes the entire situation becomes absolutely clear in just an instant.

'Let's give her a ride to the Ranger's complex. There we'll have the DFO sahib escort her to Bahraich, I mean we'll ask him to drop her off at the Bahraich bus terminal.'

Dr Vaqar spoke as though he were soliciting an endorsement.

This dispelled the tension that had descended on them from the moment the van had stopped, and everyone began to look hugely relieved.

Dr Vaqar picked up his rifle and moved to the rear seat and sat down beside Asif.

Grabbing the steering wheel with one hand and reaching for the open door's handle with the other, Nadim leaned out and called to the woman, 'Climb aboard. Why are you standing there? We were making room for you.'

The lie satisfied everybody's heart.

Nadim leaned over and opened the passenger door of the van. The woman first helped the boy get in and then stepped on the running board and hopped in herself. She was wearing a pair of full boots. In the time it took her to climb in and settle down in the seat, they had given her a close look, but back when she was standing some distance away at the edge of the road, they had felt it unseemly to turn their heads and look at her.

She was a young woman, attractive and quite tall. The taut skin of her face and its soft glow hinted that she had long fed herself on a diet especially rich in succulent fruit—at least that's what Nadim thought. The others may have thought something similar.

The woman put her hand gently on her overcoat pocket and felt for something. She grasped the boy's shoulder and pulled him closer and without turning her face said 'Thank you' to everybody in a low voice. After a moment's thought, she added, 'Thank you all very much.'

Fields stretched out on either side of the road, but it had grown so dark by now that one couldn't tell what crops were growing in them.

The barrier of the forest guard's checkpoint appeared up ahead. The van had just slowed down when the guard in a dark coloured outfit strode in front of it, raising his hand to shield his eyes from the glare of the headlights. Screwing up his face he managed to recognize the van and raised the barrier. The van moved on. It had barely gotten going again when Asif said, 'Nadim, could you stop . . . just for a minute?'

'Again? . . . It's the smell, isn't it?' Dr Vaqar asked.

'Yes,' Asif replied in a soft voice.

When the van stopped, Dr Vaqar also got out along with Asif. The breeze that rushed in through the open door seemed to come from another world. The van had entered the forest.

Leaning against the van, both Asif and Dr Vaqar stood breathing in the forest air. Nadim too had flung open his door. He faced the woods in front of him and quickly took a series of long deep of breaths, trying to take in the primeval fragrance with complete concentration. Blended in it, he thought, were the smells of teak leaves, as big as elephant ears, of pungent plane bark, of myriad wild grasses, and the strong odour emitted by the skin and fur of countless wild creatures. And since it was now dark, and their vision now disabled, the forest was spilling itself deep into their bodies through their sense of smell alone. Its deep stillness, he wondered—how it sometimes endows life with perfect meaning, and how, just as often, it renders it utterly meaningless; how when the dark quiet of the forest is broken by the sleepy twitter of a bird, or the sound of a beast grazing or fleeing, or the growl of some predator, how that part of the forest suddenly seems to light up. There are times when sound becomes light.

The boy looked at them first with indifference, then

with growing interest, and then with excitement.

Just as sound sometimes becomes light—Nadim followed his train of thought—so too could light sometimes also become sound? He wanted to carry this train of thought to some logical conclusion, but before he could, Dr Vaqar threw himself on the seat, slammed the door shut, and declared, 'Absolutely breathtaking! So serene! Damn the rogue elephant, it's wrecked everything.'

The mention of the rogue elephant made the woman and the boy shift uncomfortably in their seats.

'How we used to enjoy spending days on end here, Vaqar Bhai,' Rashid said. 'You could stroll freely in any direction you wanted without the slightest fear. Last season, remember how we walked from the Ranger's complex all the way up to the Gerva River in the moonlight? And the great fun we had lying there on the sandy beach watching the alligators? We even saw a leopard. In fact, two of them.'

'And now one can't even set foot in the forest after sundown,' Ramesh chimed in from the back seat.

When Nadim shut the door and turned on the ignition he noticed that the boy had clung to the woman in an attempt to hide. He might even have been crying.

'What's the matter?' he asked the boy; but he was looking at the woman.

'All your talk about the elephant has scared him,' she said, tucking the boy ever closer to herself. 'I mean about the rogue elephant. Has some elephant gone rogue here or something?'

'Yes. One has gone rogue just recently. We're on our way to destroy him.'

The boy, clutching the woman's waist tightly and looking over his shoulder, was now listening to Nadim.

By the time they reached the Ranger's complex, Nadim had filled the woman in on all the details about the notorious rogue. It had already taken many innocent lives; one of its tusks was broken, and there was a gunshot wound on its abdomen left there by a peasant's bullet. The District Forest Officer had sent a report to the Chief Wildlife Warden and had had it declared rogue; Dr Vaqar and Asif had been granted official permission to kill it. At first the incidents had remained few and far between, but over time the elephant started to kill as it pleased. People protested. The matter moved from the village council to the block level, then on to the district level, and from there it was introduced in the Provincial Assembly, but since matters pertaining to forests and wildlife also had to do with the Central government, it had provoked heated discussion in the national parliament. When asked by the woman, Nadim also told her that one of the reasons why this mad elephant couldn't be destroyed earlier was perhaps that it was proving difficult to pick him out from the herd. Then again, official matters usually dragged on, because for such a vast territory, the bureaucratic system, by its very nature . . .

Because the Ranger's complex was far, because there was plenty of time, and because the woman in the front seat was quite attractive, Nadim also held forth about how government resources were always limited, but especially so during such crises, which often compelled it to delegate some of its duties to private institutions or individuals. For instance, the original permission to kill the elephant was still granted to the DFO sahib, who was a government functionary, and not very reliable to boot. So it was no secret to all such high functionaries, and even to some members of the government itself, that the permission, in fact, was intended for Dr Vaqar and Asif Bhai, and DFO sahib's name had been stuck there only as a formality.

In the course of their discussion, the woman, addressing herself to Nadim but intending all to hear, informed them that she had lived in Canada for the past ten years. Her husband was a doctor there. Every other year she came to Lucknow to visit her parents. When she first left for Canada, Raju was only a year old. Now he was in the sixth grade. Further, she could have travelled alone from Lucknow to Baroli in Bahraich District, but the idea didn't go down well with her parents, who sent this little 'man' along to escort her. When she uttered the word 'man', she looked at her nephew with affection and smiled. Raju too, in spite of the fear provoked by the talk about the rogue elephant, smiled back, and even blushed some. She also said that her parents had strongly urged her to be back by sundown, because this whole region nowadays . . .

She was forced to stop talking, however, because hearing all this Dr Vaqar started to call Ramesh loudly by name and yelled to him something totally unrelated to the situation.

Ramesh, in the meantime, confessed that ever since the disturbance in the Tarai region, he too had been feeling afraid and tried to avoid travelling on the highway at night, because just last week near Puranpur in Pilibhit, a bus was forced to stop and . . .

The woman, during all this, tried to explain something to the boy now and then in a soft, reassuring voice. And Nadim, in order to relieve her a bit, proceeded to take the boy into his confidence. The more the boy began to trust him, he happily noted, the more it relieved and pleased the woman. The realization prompted Nadim to talk to the boy even more animatedly.

'We may end up needing several rifles to kill this beast,'

he told the boy.

'How many rifles do you have?'

'One. But we also have two shotguns. However, shotgun slugs are usually less effective on elephants. One really needs a high-calibre rifle for that.'

'Are there different kinds of rifles?' the boy asked.

'Yes, there are. And each kind is determined by the size and velocity of the cartridge, such as .30 Springfield, .315 carbine, and so on.'

Perched on the back seat, Rashid sensed that although Nadim was talking to the boy, it was really the woman's ear he was trying to catch. Perhaps he was trying to impress her with his vast knowledge.

Nadim continued: 'The rifle we intend to use on this elephant is a .375 magnum. Its cartridge is unmatched in the world for the balance of its weight and velocity.'

'What do you mean by balance?' the boy asked.

'Balance . . . balance, that is, ratio.'

'But ratio is part of arithmetic,' the boy said.

'Yes, all right, boy, so it is. But it's found in other things, too.' The inadequacy of his explanation irritated Nadim.

'What if the rifle fails just when one fires at the elephant? . . .' the boy continued.

'Don't even say such things,' Asif interrupted.

'In that case, we could fire in the air and scare him away,' Nadim said.

'Suppose it didn't scare him away. What then?'

'We could light a big fire and chase him off.'

'Is he scared of fire?' the boy asked.

'At night the light would scare him,' came the reply, but from Rashid, not Nadim.

'You've got something to light the fire with?' the boy asked.

'Of course. This, here.' Dr Vaqar smiled as he showed the boy a box of matches, then proceeded to light a cigarette for himself.

Raju stared at the matches.

During this exchange, the woman informed Nadim that back in Lucknow her parents had also warned her, among other things, about the abject backwardness of the area, about the bandits and highwaymen who took people by surprise all along the way, and that, therefore, she must on no account spend the night there, since she would be carrying such a large amount of cash.

A sense of shame gripped Nadim. He rummaged through his memory as he steered the van and recalled the impressions he had picked up browsing through English language magazines. He said to the woman, 'The thought of our people now settled in Canada often worries us. Those skinheads, they are out to make trouble for the Asians, to humiliate us.'

He emphasized the word 'humiliate'. The woman saw through Nadim's ruse. But aware that she was in a tight spot, she said gently, as if merely offering information, 'Places like London are troubled much more by such gangs. Canada has other problems.' She then proceeded to spell out those problems at length.

For a while Nadim felt embarrassed by the deficiency of his knowledge. Then he changed the subject and began to enumerate the disadvantages that invariably resulted when an elephant went rogue in the forest. First off, all normal forest activity came to a halt. Labourers fled, abandoning their work on the dirt roads. Women hired to sweep up leaves quit going into the forest. The forest grass went unmowed, for who in their right mind would want to put their lives in harm's way just to cut some grass? Honey contractors stayed away. The forest officers were unable to call in their lumber-thieving cohorts during this period, so they didn't get their cuts either. We can't even do any poaching on our own, either, for who knows when, or from behind what tree, or tall grass, or brush the trumpeting rogue might charge, eyes blood red and brandishing its trunk, looking only to crush somebody?

A little ways from the Ranger's complex the headlights fell on a sign in Hindi, nailed to a wooden post: CAUTION: ELEPHANT CROSSING.

Raju too read the sign and huddled even closer to the woman.

Nadim quickly turned off the headlights and cut the engine. The van lurched forward and stopped with a jolt, knocking everyone off balance, and throwing the eerie forest stillness into sharper relief.

'Up ahead,' Nadim said slowly, 'elephants are crossing the road.'

With baited breath everyone looked at the train of ponderous dark spots that paded across the road with spongy steps. A ringing stillness continued both outside the van and inside.

A little later Nadim restarted the engine and practically raced the van to the Nishan Gara Ranger's complex, where he stopped. He looked first at the woman and then at the frightened boy. Before stepping out, he told the boy that a rogue elephant never stays with the herd. Herd elephants are usually harmless. A rogue always keeps to himself. Only when the boy saw the bonfire in the Ranger's complex compound—around which some men were warming themselves—did the pallor on his face begin to subside. He asked, as he was stepping down from the van, 'Suppose several rogue elephants got together, wouldn't that make a herd?'

He talks nonsense, Nadim thought as he got out of the van and closed the door.

The Ranger sahib, outfitted in full uniform, was shaking hands with everyone. 'Your son?' he asked Nadim.

'No, yaar. We ran into them in Baroli.' He then explained the whole matter, including the part about having the DFO escort the woman to Bahraich.

'That'd be difficult. The DFO sahib has already left for Nepal via Motipur. One of our men has been apprehended at the customs post there.'

Despair swept across the woman's face. She stared at them one by one.

'I can easily wireless Lucknow to let your folks know that you're OK. Shall I?'

'But how will that solve her problem? How will she get there?' Dr Vaqar asked.

Nadim walked over to the woman and said, 'You could stay here at the Ranger sahib's. His wife is a very nice person. She considers us her own brothers.'

The woman was still thinking it over when the Ranger sahib informed her that his family had already left for his in-laws two days ago, on account of the terror the rogue had struck throughout the forest community. Actually, the children's grandfather had himself come to fetch them.

Standing by the bonfire in the middle of the old red Ranger's complex buildings enclosed by a barbed-wire fence, the entire forest staff, two motorcycles, the van, the hunters from Bahraich and the woman and the boy—they all looked like so many phantoms. When the flames leapt up, they caused their shadows to lengthen, and when they subsided, they made them shrink back. The forest, stretching far and wide on all sides of the Ranger's complex, with its towering, stout teaks, planes and shishams, stood stock still under a thick blanket of fog. At this hour in the forest, nearby or far away, many of the animals would be dozing off, or quietly grazing, or drinking water, or just standing within their herd. Many would be gently touching their female's horns, or licking their young ones' bodies, or pouncing on their victims, or scurrying on hungry stomachs from one part of the forest to another in search of food.

The woman was looking at all of the men in utter helplessness. She felt she was about to cry.

'It's getting late,' Dr Vaqar broke the silence. 'Any news today?'

'Yes, there is.' The Ranger sahib stepped forward. 'We found some scratch marks today near teak plot no. 1955 in the Guest House forest in Motipur Block.'

'Talking like a lion hunter today, eh?' Asif remarked, smiling.

'No. Actually, everyone's so frightened, if anyone even saw the rogue, he'd drop dead right in his tracks. All the families have already fled the area. And all this since the day the beast broke into the Ranger's compound and trampled the watchman to death. You really have to get him today.'

'We'll see.'

'So what have you decided?' Dr Vaqar asked as he strode to Nadim and the woman.

Nadim just stood there quietly watching Raju light a tiny fire with a match stick.

The woman answered, slowly but confidently, 'Please wireless my family and let us ride along. Please don't leave us here at the Ranger's office.'

'Well, think about it. You've got a child with you. Rogues can be pretty frightening.'

'We'll take it as it comes. Animals don't scare me easily . . . After I got married, my husband and I took a hunting trip . . . to a jungle in Africa . . . in Zimbabwe . . . on our honeymoon . . . I myself shot a bison.'

Nadim heard this with both wonder and relief. 'But Raju . . .?' he asked.

'He'll just sit beside me quietly,' the woman said.

They filled up the van's petrol tank and sat around the bonfire eating sandwiches, sipping tea and smoking cigarettes. They used the rest rooms and once again checked the shotguns and the rifle.

'Same strategy, OK? Shoot from close range, but if that's not possible, fire in the air and scare him away,' Dr Vaqar gave the instructions to Asif, Rashid, and Nadim. 'If you don't bring him down right off,' he explained, 'he'll only be wounded, and then God only knows what he'll do.'

The Ranger's office staff and Ramesh took some rags and were vigorously trying to scrub off the frost that had covered the windows of the van. But it was so cold that within minutes the windows were covered again.

'You've checked the spot light, haven't you?' Dr Vaqar asked.

'Yes,' Ramesh replied as he shook out the rag.

'The frost's going to give us trouble,' Dr Vaqar expressed his fear. 'And with the windows rolled up, the moisture will also fog up the inside.'

'Not much you can do about that,' Nadim mumbled. 'Damn, why did it have to be so cold and frosty today!'

A light appeared far ahead on the dirt road leading into the Ranger's complex, followed by the slow drone of a motorcycle . . . The motorcycle drew near and stopped. Two men, one holding a gun, hurriedly got off.

'Which one of you is the Ranger sahib?' the man without the gun asked.

'I am.' The Ranger sahib nervously walked over to the men. His forehead was covered with sweat from the heat of the fire. He looked very ill at ease. 'Has the rogue . . . again?' he asked.

'No . . . A message came in from Bijnor that the railroad car your father-in-law and family were riding in . . .' His voice dropped almost to a whisper.

The Ranger sahib began to scream, calling his children by name.

Dr Vaqar feigned anger and yelled at him, trying to get him to come to his senses and to think with a cool head. 'At least hear them out, whether there have actually been any casualties . . .'

'We couldn't hear everything clearly on the phone. The line was bad, and the voice was choppy,' the older of the two men said.

'It's about bandits, isn't it?' the woman edged closer to Nadim and asked in an anxious voice.

'I don't know. They say the phone line was bad.'

'*That* kind of thing is happening around here too frequently these days,' Asif said softly.

'Maybe it's the same thing that happened in Tarai,' Rashid said, as if reminded of something.

'But, yaar, Tarai is a long way from here,' Nadim said.

'May be. But the actual scene of the incident isn't. It's quite close.'

'No use speculating. You all talk too much,' Dr Vaqar remarked, but his voice suddenly seemed fearful. Everybody just looked at him.

But he quickly gained control over himself and said to

the Ranger sahib, 'You should get on the motorcycle and leave immediately. Go to Bahraich first and call Bijnor to find out, and only then think of taking the trip. Take one of the staff with you. And don't drive the motorcycle yourself.'

A long silence followed the Ranger sahib's departure, broken only now and again when a piece of wood crackled in the leaping fire.

'The heart of the matter is this,' Dr Vaqar said, facing the fire and warming his hands over it. 'That nowadays everywhere . . . I mean in every region . . . I mean among all the people . . .'

After a pause he said, 'Let's get on with the work we've set out to do. Come on, everybody into the van.'

Dr Vaqar settled in the front seat beside Nadim; Asif, the woman, Raju, and Rashid took the next seat back; and Ramesh sat in the rearmost seat, shotgun in hand.

Rashid sensed that the woman stole side-glances at Ramesh and his gun every so often. A thought flickered through Rashid's mind and he smiled, but the smile had barely crept to the corners of his mouth when deep lines appeared on his forehead. He, too, began to steal side-glances at Ramesh and his gun.

God, how red Ramesh's face got when the Ranger sahib was being told about the attack on his family!—Asif thought, and then vaguely recalled: And just then somebody among the staff had whispered to Ramesh that the same kind of incidents were also going on in the Bijnor region these days. Who had said it? One of the staff? Or Nadim? Or both? Or perhaps neither had, and I merely thought it to myself. Or said it out loud . . . Asif's mind went numb.

The van started. Dr Vaqar loaded the magazine, pushed the bolt shut, and sat down with his rifle at the ready. Asif loaded some slugs into his shotgun and took his position by the window. Rashid grabbed the handle of the spot light and gazed out intently through the windshield. The woman tied her overcoat tightly and pulled Raju close beside her. And Ramesh loaded only one of the chambers of his double-barrelled shotgun and planted himself firmly beside the window.

'Please, all of you, don't make a sound,' Dr Vaqar said in a hushed voice. 'Elephants have very keen ears.'

'But we're not there yet,' Nadim said.

'All the same, it won't hurt to be quiet.'

Nadim took a rag from the dashboard and wiped the windshield from the inside, only to find out that the frost had formed again on the outside. He turned on the wipers. Only after the blades had swept quickly across the length of the windshield a few times did he realize that the inside had fogged up yet again. Outside, everything looked fuzzy; only the two beams of the headlights were clearly visible.

'If we opened the window it'd at least clear up the inside,' Nadim said.

'I wouldn't recommend it. I mean, not now. It would be dangerous,' Dr Vaqar said softly.

'Well then, it'll just stay fogged up inside,' Rashid said in an anxious voice. 'We won't be able to see anything.'

'Can't help it,' Dr Vaqar said with an air of finality.

Asif looked around the inside of the van and said, 'Can't see a thing through the side or rear windows.'

'There's no *light* there, either,' Rashid said. 'I mean the headlights don't help any to the sides or in the rear.'

'The fog outside will get worse the closer we get to the Gerva River,' Nadim mumbled.

'Keep the wipers on, Nadim,' Dr Vaqar instructed.

'That'll drain the battery,' Nadim mumbled again.

The van was moving along at a snail's pace. Outside, in the dim glow of headlights, the fog was drifting in big curls. Nothing in the forest stretching out on either side of the road could be seen clearly beyond the dim glow of the headlights and the wisps of drifting fog.

'Is that a spotted deer crossing?' Nadim, fixing his gaze on the road ahead, asked Dr Vaqar.

Dr Vaqar looked closely and then said, 'No, yaar, it's a rabbit. Nothing's clear in the fog, it all looks bigger than it really is.'

The rabbit, hearing the sound of the approaching van, had stopped in its tracks. As soon as the headlights fell on it, two blue bulbs seemed to light up in its head.

'Wow . . . look how its eyes are shining!' Raju shouted.

'Be quiet!' Dr Vaqar scolded him. Then, stretching one of his hands over the seat in back, he patted the boy on the shoulder.

At that moment Ramesh sensed everybody except Raju's eyes on him; there was in them something of an ill-concealed uncertainty. And he looked back at them, one by one.

Everybody except Raju sensed that Ramesh was looking at them strangely. It was dark inside the van, but their eyes had become accustomed to it.

And everyone except Raju was swept up by a strange uneasiness.

Raju lifted his face and asked, 'So Aunty, who killed the Daroghaji and his wife and children?'

Suddenly, Nadim hit the brakes. The van stopped with a jolt. He quickly turned off the headlights. 'The rogue . . . up ahead,' was all he could say.

An icy chill ran down everybody's spine. 'Where?' Dr Vaqar, turning the rifle's safety to on, asked in a soft voice so soft that even he doubted if Nadim would've heard it.

'Crossing to the left, I think . . . or maybe coming straight on . . . I'm not sure . . .' Nadim said.

'Lights, Nadim, the lights!' Dr Vaqar said. 'How else do you expect us to see him?'

Nadim was about to turn on the headlights when Ramesh said nervously, 'He's behind the van, right behind it!'

Everyone turned and looked to the back of the van. There definitely was something on the dark road.

Suddenly Asif reached out with his hand and pressed Dr Vaqar on the shoulder . . . 'He's here, by my window . . . right next to it.'

Everyone peered through Asif's window and sensed something like a shadow standing in the fog. Their hearts raced.

'He just now put his trunk on my window,' Rashid whispered.

Something long appeared to be twisting in the air outside Rashid's window.

Nadim gestured them to be quiet and told them, 'The rogue I saw on my side earlier is perhaps still standing there.'

'Can you see him clearly? Do you think you can get a shot at him?' Dr Vaqar asked.

'Not so clearly. The window has fogged up. Should I lower it?'

'No! . . . he'd hear us breathing then.'

The woman looked at the boy, whose face had turned white with terror. Nestled into her side, he was constantly craning his neck to see out all the windows.

The woman closed her eyes, passed a hand over her face wet with cold sweat, and wiped it on her overcoat.

'He's slowly coming this way—no doubt about it,' Ramesh said apprehensively. He was sitting dead still, his nose actually pressed up against the window.

Asif and Rashid confirmed it, looking out through their windows.

Dr Vaqar, in a state mixed with uncertainty, fear, and agitation, said, 'Watch for the one with the broken tusk. He's the one we want. He's the real rogue. And only he is dangerous.'

Everyone strained their eyes into the darkness, and each of them felt that one of the tusks of the elephant standing by their window did appear to be broken.

'Are there several rogues?' Dr Vaqar asked, as though to himself. Questioningly he looked at the woman, who had just now peered out the window with dread mounting in her heart. She nodded. Her eyes were dilated with fear. Dr Vaqar thought he heard a thump outside his window, or maybe it was just his heart, or perhaps his rifle butt had knocked against his shoe. He stared into the thick darkness outside.

In the darkness the rogue's eyes looked red to them, one of his tusks broken, his trunk drawn up and waving in the air. 'We won't fire,' Dr Vaqar said in a choking voice. 'We can't get so many of them at one time. We're surrounded. But we're safe as long as the windows are shut; they can't hear us. Otherwise, they would have trampled us to death already.'

'So what do we do now?' Nadim asked in a weak and sinking voice.

Everyone was gripped by a strange mixture of fear, impotence and shame.

'We can . . . wait till morning, can't we?' the woman said in a low voice, choking on the words.

This would have put them all at ease, but for the boy who pulled something out of his pocket and fell unconscious, still clutching it in his hand . . .

Nadim turned around and, without looking at anybody, reached out with his hand and pried open the boy's fist. He looked at the thing, thought for a moment, and closed the boy's fist again. He turned back and, like everyone else, sat quietly with his head hung low.

A Sheet

Salam Bin Razzack

He was standing behind the window looking out onto the street, which, as far as one could see in the distance, was shimmering in the sun as if somebody had magically stopped a flowing river. It was the same street on which traffic flowed uninterrupted well into the night, where crowds of people milled about like crawling ants right up to midnight. Morning and evening, the noise from the traffic and the people gave the sidewalks the atmosphere of a carnival. But at the moment, both the street and its sidewalks were completely deserted. Not a soul anywhere, not even a sound.

His mind too was as empty as the street in front of him. Now and then, though, a whirlwind of some inarticulate anxiety or fear did sweep over him. Dread and despair had begun to thicken around him like a gloom, and he felt smothered by it. He picked up the packet of cigarettes from the table near him, lit up, drew a deep breath, and exhaled the smoke out of the window. There was no wind at all. The smoke dissolved slowly, like life ebbing away from a dying patient. He longed for home. The image of his beautiful wife Salma, the innocent pranks of his sons Sajid and Majid, and the deep affection in the eyes of his old, paralytic mother flashed before his eyes. Salma had told him as he was leaving, 'It doesn't look good at all in Bombay. I'm worried.'

But he had tried to allay her fears. 'Riots are common in big cities like Bombay. Nothing to get so worked up about. They usually don't affect business there at all.'

'But you said you were going to Dadar. Dadar is one of the places affected by riots. The newspaper said so.'

'Oh, come on now. After all, Vidyacharan also lives there. I'll go to his house first. I'll meet the party with him.'

'What if you went after a few days?'

'You don't understand. Vidya told me that these people are absolutely genuine. The supermarket under construction there in Bhawani Peth belongs to that party. Two or three local interior decorators are bending over backwards to somehow clinch the deal for themselves, but Vidya wants me to get the contract. He's the chief engineer. It's a big contract, worth several lakhs. Such an opportunity's not likely to come my way again in a long time. I'll take the bus straight from Dadar after the deal and will be back home in Pune by the evening. Don't you worry.'

Salma didn't say anything further, but the cloud of worry still didn't quite leave her face.

He tossed the cigarette butt out through the window, stepped back and half-stretched out on the sofa. The ceiling fan was whirring away, making a muffled sound, like someone trying to let something out but held back by a nagging fear. Even though he was perfectly safe here, he still could feel fear surge up inside him like a wave. Vidya, Vidya's father, Vidya's mother—they all tried to fortify him with reassuring words. Vidyacharan's wife Sushma and his sister Arti kept piling more puris and servings of vegetable on his plate, and Vidyacharan's younger brother Shyam kept inviting him to games of carrom. In short, the entire household was doing its best to draw his heart away from the thoughts that troubled him. All the same, he could feel his heart weighed down deeper with anxiety with every passing moment.

It was around one o'clock in the afternoon when he got down from the Ashiyad bus at the Dadar terminal. He strode over to the sidewalk and stood there, his smallish briefcase in hand, looking for a taxi. But he spotted none. There was very little traffic on the street. Most of the stores had their shutters pulled down. The sidewalk had only a few pedestrians, who walked on swiftly with a purposeful gait, looking cautiously around, as though they were in a big rush to get somewhere. There was a strange but palpable tension in the air. He suddenly remembered what Salma had told him in the morning as he was leaving. An anxious thought reared up inside him, which he quickly shrugged off with a light jerk of his neck. Just then he saw a taxi approach from the right, carrying no fare. He stepped down from the sidewalk and waved, but the taxi just zoomed past him without stopping. The driver didn't even so much as look at him. He was sitting behind the steering like a statue, his hands frozen on the wheel. Afterwards a couple more taxis came along, but not one stopped. 'OK,' he thought. 'I can just walk. Vidyacharan's house isn't all that far anyway. It'll take at most ten minutes to get there.'

He set out, briefcase in hand. After crossing the main street, when he entered a passageway under the street, he felt even more acutely the sense of gravity in the air. The entire passageway was infused with an eerie silence, and the sound of his footfalls was making his blood freeze in his veins. The passageway ended in a series of buildings, but most had their gates closed. Some four or five young men stood in a group in front of one of the buildings, heatedly discussing something or other. Seeing him approach, one of the young men said something to his companions. They all fell silent and looked over their shoulders at him. He lowered his eyes and took long strides past them. He didn't turn around to look at them, but he could hear that they had resumed talking. He entered the gate of Building 11 and took the stairs to the third floor, where he pressed the bell to Vidyacharan's apartment.

Vidyacharan himself opened the door. The moment he saw him, he said, '*Arey*, Anwar! Come on in. We were waiting just for you.'

Inside, Vidyacharan's father was sitting in a wooden swing-seat poring over a fat tome. He closed the book as soon as he saw him and said, 'We were quite worried about you, son! You didn't have any problem on the way, did you?'

'No, Uncle. But I did feel a strange tension in the air. The streets are deserted, shops are closed, and I couldn't even get a single taxi to stop.'

'Yes, it's been like this for the last two or three days. Today, though, the atmosphere appears to be even more grim.'

'I called your house this morning,' Vidyacharan said. 'Bhabhi said that you'd already left about an hour earlier. If I'd caught you on the phone, I'd have told you not to come today.'

'What's the matter? Is it really serious?'

'Seems that way. Police cars are out patrolling. And there are rumours everywhere. About a hundred huts were torched last night in Dharavi. We could see the smoke even from here in the morning. I just heard on the telephone that several chawls have been set on fire in Jogeshwari as well.'

Now his heart began to sink even deeper, like a heavy stone in water. He could feel a faint restlessness squirm inside him. His silence prompted Vidyacharan to comfort him, 'There's no reason for you to worry. Everything is OK Here, give me your briefcase.'

Vidyacharan took the briefcase from him and he sat down on the sofa. Meanwhile Sushma appeared with a glass and jug of water. After greeting him, she set the glass and the jug on the tea-table, smiled and asked, 'How are Bhabhi and the children?'

'They're fine,' he responded, smiling formally.

In the meantime both Vidyacharan's mother and sister walked in. 'Vidya!' the old lady said to her son, 'Take Anwar to wash his hands. Lunch is ready.'

Shortly thereafter low wooden stools were set on the floor and everybody took their seats. Thalis were placed in front of everyone, and Sushma and Arti dutifully served the food. He took a look around and said, 'I don't see Shyam. Where is he?'

'He's gone to college. He'll be back soon.'

After the meal he picked up a piece of betel nut from the saucer and put it in his mouth. Then he said, 'Vidya, shouldn't we go now and take care of the job? I'll take the bus home right after.'

'But the office is closed today. Because of the riots. I called you this morning to tell you just that.'

'Oh.' Anxiety deepened in the lines on his forehead. 'In that case, allow me to leave. I should return right away. Otherwise Salma and Mother will start worrying.'

'All right. But I think you should take the train instead. Let me walk you to the station.'

'Uncle, I'm leaving now,' he looked at Vidyacharan's father.

'OK, son. Given the situation, we can't even ask you to stay over. But be careful. Give us a call as soon as you've arrived in Pune.' His voice was full of concern.

Just then the bell rang. Vidyacharan opened the door and in walked Shyam. The minute he saw him, he said, '*Arey*, Anwar Bhaiyya! When did you arrive?' He then came over and sat down right next to him.

'About an hour ago. Tell me, how are your studies?'

'A-1. And I mean A-1 . . .'

'How is it outside?' Vidyacharan inquired.

'Bhaiyya, it isn't good. Somebody was knifed outside the railway station just a little while ago. Police cars are patrolling everywhere. A curfew's been declared in the area around the station.'

Abruptly everyone fell silent. He looked up, only to see that everyone else was looking just at him. Vidyacharan cleared his throat and said, 'Let me call Inspector Rana and find out.'

Vidyacharan got up and dialled the number. He talked with someone briefly, hung up and returned to the sofa.

'What did the inspector say?' he asked feeling impatient.

'He said that the trains are running all right, but the situation isn't at all good. A curfew is expected in the entire area any time. News has just come that a terrible riot's broken out in Mahim as well.'

'But, Vidya, I have to return today. If I don't, they'll be worried sick.'

Once again everybody fell silent. After a while, Vidyacharan's father said, 'Anwar, son, listen to me and stay here today. You can go back tomorrow after the work. It's possible that the situation will have become normal by tomorrow. Call bahu and let her know that you'll be staying here tonight.'

'But, Uncle, if I start right away, I can make it to Pune

by evening. If the situation doesn't improve by tomorrow . . .'

Just then a police siren blared outside. The police van was announcing the curfew.

'There, they've imposed the curfew. Didn't I say that they would, pretty soon?' Shyam said, suppressing his excitement. Then he got up, walked over to the window, and peered outside.

Vidya's father chided him: 'Shyam, shut the window and sit down quietly.' Then he ordered his elder son, 'Vidya, see to it that the windows in all the rooms are securely shut.'

Vidya got up and started to close the windows like a dutiful son, while his mother, Sushma, and Arti stood quietly inside the inner room.

Vidya's father got up and aimlessly started to pace. Shyam, somewhat miffed, went over to the sofa and plopped down in it. The room became dark with the closing of the windows. Vidya's seven-year-old boy Pappu asked his grandmother, 'Dadi, Dadi, what is a curfew?'

But nobody gave him a reply. In the semi-dark room they all looked like so many quiet, immobile shadows. The only movement came from Vidya's father, who was still walking restlessly with his hands folded behind his back. He was bare chested above the waist. The sacred thread hung over his shoulder. His head was clean shaven except for a tuft of hair which hung over his back like a squirrel's tail. He had vibhuti painted between his eyebrows, and he was clad in a white dhoti.

Anwar had often seen him in just this garb. In fact, he had seen him like this for many many years. A devout, religious man, he was nevertheless quite secular in his thinking. He was well read, not just in his own religion, but lso in many others. Anwar respected him a lot, and the old nan always treated Anwar with affection. Every time he net him, every time he spoke to him, he had the feeling of itting in the shade of some ancient peepul tree and istening to an old, dread-locked Sadhu expound on the neaning of contemplative life.

Today, however, he appeared to be an altogether lifferent man. A stranger, who never had anything to do vith him at all. And not just the old man alone—even 'idya's mother, Sushma, Arti, Vidya himself, and Shyam, eemed strangers.

Anwar felt he would suffocate. His throat went dry and e longed for water. But, at this moment, asking for water vould have amounted to an admission of his weakness. So e satisfied himself by running his tongue over his parched ps.

The darkness intensified the heaviness inside the room. Vhy didn't anyone turn on the light? Just then 'idyacharan, as if sensing his friend's wish in some occult vay, got up and did just that. The moment the room lit up, current of animation swept through it. Vidya's father esumed his place on the swing-seat, which began to sway ently like a houseboat. Shyam got up and turned on the 'V. Pappu ran up to the rocking swing-seat and stood upon , clutching the bar for support. Sushma and Arti retreated the inner room. Vidya's mother edged up to Anwar and aid softly, 'Son, think of this as your own house. And don't t yourself worry too much. Nobody's going to harm you ere. Now get up and call bahu. She must be out of her wits vith worry. Give her a few words of assurance. Tomorrow, s soon as the situation improves, you can return.'

He peered into the old lady's eyes: bonding and otherly affection was all he could see there. The unknown fear that had taken hold of his mind relaxed some, and the feeling of being in the midst of strangers that had tormented him a while ago slowly began to disappear. Fear had raised a wall of suspicion. As the fear itself lessened, the wall too crumbled away. He took out his handkerchief from his pocket, wiped the sweat off his forehead, got up and went over to the phone.

Sure enough, it was Salma who answered. The moment she heard his voice, she was overcome with emotion, on the verge of tears. 'How are you?' she inquired. 'Vidyacharan Bhai called right after you left. Where are you calling from? Come home quickly, please. I feel terribly afraid.' She said it all at one go, without seeming to take even a breath.

Fighting back his own emotion, he tried to say in as normal a voice as he could possibly muster, 'Don't worry, Salma. I'll be back tomorrow. I'm calling you from Vidyacharan's house. Ordinary skirmishes, that's all. Nothing big. It'll all return to normal by tomorrow.'

'But why do you want to stay on overnight? Why not return this evening, if your work's finished?'

'That's just it. The work isn't finished. The office of the party we want to meet is closed today. I'll take care of the paperwork first thing tomorrow morning. I'll be back in Pune by the afternoon. Tell Mother not to worry. Vidyacharan is here with me. Kiss Sajid and Majid for me.'

'Give your mother my namaskar,' Vidya's mother instructed him in a loud voice.

'Aunt is sending Mother her greetings. I'll call you back again in the evening. And now I'll hang up. Khuda Hafiz!'

Salma, too, from the other end said in a drained voice, *'Fi amani 'l-Lah!'*

'It's good that you didn't tell Bhabhi about the curfew,

Vidya said.

'All the same, she'll find out. Tomorrow. In the papers. She'll know everything. And she will feel miserable . . .'

He wiped the sweat off his forehead once again and sat down on the sofa. Then Vidyacharan grabbed his hand and brought him into the other room, with a bed, a couple of couches, a writing table and a few books. 'This is my room,' Vidyacharan said as he opened the window and slid the curtain to one side. 'I had it built only recently. You can rest here.'

He didn't reply.

'Pitaji worries too much. But really there's no need to close the window. You keep it open. Nothing will happen.'

He peered down from the window. It opened onto the main street. But it was completely deserted at the moment.

'The bathroom's over there. Take a shower if you like. You'll feel fresh. But just rest now. We'll meet again over tea at four o'clock.'

He then stepped forward and put his hand on Anwar's shoulder. 'Don't think that I don't know what you're going through. But don't you worry. Everything'll turn out OK. You'll get back to Pune in one piece—I promise.'

He looked at Vidya with a withered smile and stretched out on the sofa. 'I'm OK, Vidya. Don't worry about me.'

'Just yell if you need anything.' Vidyacharan left the room.

The evening news on TV showed a few glimpses of the riots in the city. The dreadful scenes left no doubt that rioting had spread through the entire city, and a curfew had been imposed in several areas. Towards the tail end of the news, the police commissioner was shown repeating the same asinine assurance: 'But the situation is under control.'

His restlessness grew worse. Even before the news ha
ended, he quickly got up and dialed his number at Pune
but couldn't get through. He tried again and again. Perhap
there was a problem with the line itself. A bit irritated, h
returned to his seat.

'What happened?' Vidya's father asked.

'Looks like the line is out of order.'

Later, Vidyacharan himself tried a few times but had n
luck. They'd already had their supper and were now
commenting on the news.

Vidya's father said: 'What's gotten into people that the
are slaughtering others just like them as though they wer
goats and sheep? I can't understand how a man can hat
another so much.'

'God knows where these riots will take the country
Vidyacharan wondered in a voice full of anxiety.

Vidya's mother joined both her hands against he
forehead and said, 'May Ishwar protect us all.'

Suddenly they were all looking at him. He too wante
to say something, but just couldn't get it out. Not a singl
word. Thoughts were swirling in his mind like a whirlwinc
but the corresponding words, before they so much a
reached his tongue, perished like bubbles on the surface c
water. The feeling that he had been caught in thorn
bramble took hold of him. If he stirred even slightly
countless sharp needles would prick him all over his body
Never before had he felt himself so helpless. Just the
Shyam got up, brought the carrom board over, and saic
'Anwar Bhai, how about a game or two?'

A sense of relief washed over him, as if somebody ha
pulled him from the water just as he was drowning. H
agreed right away.

The board was laid out. Arti and Vidyacharan sat opposite each other as partners, with Shyam and he as partners against them. The game began.

The round black and white pieces were arranged in the circle in the middle of the board and were then struck with the striker, which scattered them all over the board. For a long time, the striker kept hitting the pieces, sending them in the corner pockets.

He was playing well enough, but his thoughts were elsewhere, as scenes of the rioting replayed in his mind—houses going up in flames, women running out screaming and crying, children weeping bitterly, old men stumbling along, young men brandishing swords and spears, and rising above them all the loud body-shaking cries of 'Allahu Akbar!' and 'Har-Har Mahadev!'

'What are you thinking about, Anwar Bhai?' Shyam alerted him. 'Take the queen! It's just within reach!'

'Where is it?' he asked, with a start.

The queen was within easy reach of him. He hit it with the striker. The piece banged against the edge and bounced back, fluttering on the board for a while before dropping dead.

Once, seven or eight years ago on Baqar Eid, he had sacrificed the goat with his own hands. But before the knife had completely slit the throat, the animal thrashed violently and got away from him, running to one side, blood gushing from the gaping wound. People ran after it and grabbed it. But he was unable to finish the job. Somebody else had to do it for him. Never again since that day was he able to slaughter an animal for sacrifice. Looking at the queen, now, as it writhed on the board, he suddenly recalled that goat with its throat only half-slit.

'Come on, Anwar Bhai, what's this? You could've

pocketed the piece so easily,' Shyam said, showing his regret.

'I'm sorry, Shyam. I'm just tired.' He leaned back in his chair and closed his eyes.

'Shyam, you play with Arti. Let Anwar rest.' Vidyacharan then grabbed Anwar's hand and made him get up.

'Let's try to call again,' Anwar said.

'Yes, sure.' Vidya dialled the number. He dialed again. And again. He shook his head in disappointment and said, 'I don't think it'll work. Looks like the line's dead.'

He quietly went into the other room and lay down on the bed face down. His heart was sinking. If only he had gotten some news of Salma and the children, perhaps it would have helped ease his worry. The thought of his helplessness hit him hard. He felt like breaking down in tears, crying his heart out. But even crying wasn't easy. What will these people think—people who were doing their best to comfort him? If he cried, not only would he humiliate himself, but he'd also hurt their confidence. Perhaps the limit of helplessness is the inability to cry when tears alone might help. Just then he heard a click and the light was turned off in his room. He turned over with a start.

'Nothing! It's just me. Go to sleep!' Vidyacharan said, closing the door gently behind him on his way out.

After his departure a deathly stillness swept over the room. Not even the sound of a dog barking somewhere. Perhaps even the dogs had withdrawn to their shelters, cringing with fear. Only the sound of some policeman's whistle rose now and then, or that of a siren. Meanwhile, he fell asleep.

God knows what hour of the night it was when a sound woke him up. The same darkness and stillness was around him once again. But no. Small cracks had begun to appear in the wall of silence. He heard the muffled screams of hundreds, no, thousands of people coming from afar. He got up from the bed, quietly opened the window and peered out. The street lay just as quiet and deserted as it had been earlier during the day. But he did see what he thought was smoke rising far on the western horizon. The sky, too, looked reddish. Perhaps there had been an immense conflagration there. The noise too seemed to be coming from there. Just then he heard the rumble of a truck on the street. It too was coming from the same direction. He couldn't see clearly because of the darkness, but he did see that several people sat huddled inside the truck, with weapons flashing in the hands of at least a few of them. A tremor shot through his entire body. Just then he heard a faint clatter outside his room, which set his heart pounding. An unknown fear reared up in his mind like the hood of a cobra. God knew what was about to happen! Could it be that the neighbours had found out that Vidya's family was harbouring an enemy, and so now were insisting, even this late at night, that they hand him over to them? He imagined himself being dragged out by a group of young men with saffron head-bands. He would be gagged and, try hard as he might, just wouldn't be able to get a sound out. He groped for the light switch and turned it on. The room brightened. Shortly thereafter the door opened and Vidyacharan entered.

'You turned on the light—what's the matter?'

'Nothing. I just woke up suddenly.'

Vidyacharan stared and then said as he sat down on the sofa, 'I peeked in earlier, but you were sleeping.'

'How come you aren't in bed?'

'I can't fall asleep.'

'How come?'

'I keep thinking that you don't feel safe here.'

'No, it isn't like that at all. You wouldn't let me be harmed in any way—I know that, Vidya. But given the conditions, it's hard not to feel at least a little bit alarmed.'

'I understand. But remember this: no matter how volatile it may be all around, all it'll take is a phone call, and a whole battalion of policemen will show up. The Police Commissioner is my friend. If you'd like to talk to him, I can arrange that right away.'

'No, no. There's no need. Vidya, please don't misunderstand me. I trust you completely.'

After a brief silence, Vidya abruptly asked, 'Want some coffee?'

'I suppose I could do with a cup.'

'Wait. I'll go and fix some.'

The entire household came together again in the morning at breakfast. The situation outside remained unchanged. The curfew, though, was lifted for two hours. It was back in effect at ten o'clock.

Vidya called the railway station, police station, S.T. bus depot, Ashiyad bus terminal, taxi stand—just about everywhere to get some idea of the situation. Everywhere he got the same answer: 'The situation doesn't look good. Better not travel.'

The telephone line to Pune was still dead. Inquiries were made at the telephone exchange, but no satisfactory explanation was offered. His anxiety was growing worse by the minute. But deftly hiding what was eating away at him inside, he kept talking to Vidya, his father, his mother, Shyam, and Arti as normally as he possibly could. He had

Pappu recite two poems for him, and told him the story of the triple-horned demon, in which the prince hacks off each of the three horns one after another with his sword. Pappu was extremely pleased. He clapped and laughed for a long time. For his own part, though, he wondered: how could a six-foot-tall prince possibly exterminate a giant six times his size? But children are so gullible. How easily they believe everything in a story. It's only when they grow up that they sink into the quagmire of doubt, suspicion, skepticism, and lack of trust. Seeing Pappu clap so joyously, he remembered his sons Sajid and Majid. He quickly bent over Pappu and kissed him on the forehead. Once again he started to feel anxiety tug at his heart. He got up and returned to his room.

Standing at the window he gazed into the desolate street for the longest time. All looked clear in the direction where he had seen that terrible smoke rising last night. A few young men stood talking inside the compound wall of the building directly in front. A police van drove in, moving at a snail's pace, and slowly inched farther and farther away. Suddenly a noise erupted to his left. He poked his head out to see. A scrawny young man ran out of a narrow alley. His wrists were bound behind him and his clothes were on fire. 'Help! Help!' he was shouting. 'Water! Water!' Perhaps his clothes had been doused with kerosene, because the fire was spreading very fast. His screams prompted the windows of the buildings around to open one by one. A few people craned their necks to look at him. The emaciated young man was jerking his head, all the while screaming for help. 'Untie my hands! What will you get by killing me? Water! . . . Water!'

He ran toward the compound where the group of

young men stood talking. But the moment he came near the gate, they quickly closed it. The man kept begging them for water. But they turned around and went inside the building.

By now the flames had completely enveloped the youth, who looked like a single flame in motion. Running, he fell, and started to roll in the middle of the street, still screaming in sheer torment.

The tied hands finally broke free. All at once, charged with a sudden surge of energy, he got up and started madly to tear off his burning clothes from his body. But once again he stumbled and fell down, and began to writhe and thrash on the ground. His screams subsided into moans, his convulsions getting progressively weaker. His clothes had turned to ashes that stuck to his body, which had itself become as charred as a piece of charcoal. His moans too died down. Only one or another part of his body twitched as the fire began to die down.

He gazed into the scene like it was a frightening nightmare, his hands clutching the frame of the window. His temples pounded as though he had been stuffed into the belly of an endlessly beaten kettle-drum. He was shaking . . . slowly.

Down below, the body of the youth had by now become completely charred. The fire too had died, giving off a few stray curls of smoke. Just then a police siren blared. People peering out quickly shut their windows, though some left just a crack from which to peek. He too backed up, closed the window with his tremulous hands, and looked out from the chink. The police van stopped a little ways from the charred body. Four or five constables got down from the van, and the inspector from the front seat. The inspector walked over to the body with perfect composure. He had covered his mouth and nose with his handkerchief. The constables too held their noses between their thumbs and index fingers and followed him. They stood around the body. The corpse was now naked and had been rendered grotesque by the fire. The inspector said something, and one of the constables, still holding his nose, bent over and poked the corpse with his long stick. Then, shaking his head 'No,' he stood up straight. The inspector lifted his head and gave a sweeping look at the neighbouring buildings. Heads peering from behind the slim openings in the windows instantaneously withdrew like turtles.

The inspector thundered: 'Who burnt him? Tell me, who burnt him? Answer me!'

The openings in the windows further narrowed. Waving his stick the inspector walked to the corner of the alley on the left, peered into it, then walked back to the corpse. Once again he raised his head to the windows and yelled, 'At least throw down a cloth to cover the body. Have you lost all sense of humanity?'

A painful silence swept over the scene for a while. Then a window on the first floor of the building in front opened and an old man, leaning half-way out, tossed a white bed sheet down to the street. Then another window opened. A woman poked her head out and she too threw a folded white bed sheet down to the street. And then another window opened, and then another. Seven sparkling white bed sheets were tossed out within a few minutes. The inspector shouted, 'That's enough charity! Now stop it!'

Two constables stepped forward. Picking up one of the sheets, they unfolded it and spread it out over the corpse.

Anwar closed his window and sat down on the bed. Suddenly he felt the whirlwind of dread starting to subside in his mind, replaced by a terrible emptiness.

Astonishingly, all at once, he had risen above every fear, every apprehension.

The Vultures of the Parsi Cemetery

Ali Imam Naqvi

It was all so unexpected. They were stunned. They put the stretcher down abruptly, gawked at the dead body, and then looked at each other with a million questions stirring in their eyes. Their eyeballs moved dumbly in their sockets for quite some time, and when they stopped, the two shrugged their shoulders uncomprehendingly. Then, simultaneously, they grimaced, severely straining their necks and letting their gaze hover over the dense trees of the Parsi cemetery. Not a single vulture! Not even as far as one could see! This was absolutely the first time it had happened. The bell had gone off two hours earlier to put them on alert. And sure enough, a quarter-of-an-hour later the attendants of *bagli* no.2 were handing the corpse over to them. The two had pulled the corpse into the *bawli* area and closed the doors behind them. Later Pheroze Bhatina, after he had opened the small window in the door and questioned the funeral attendants outside about the relatives of the deceased, asked one of them, 'How about the tips—did they give any?'

The attendant had smiled and flashed two ten-rupee notes at Bhatina, who promptly snatched them, stuffed one in the pocket of his *dagla* and gave the other to his companion, Hormoz. Then they shut the window.

'Good Lord,' Hormoz lifted his head and thankfully looked at the stretch of sky peeping in from the thick foliage of tall trees. Then he motioned to Bhatina with his eyes. The two bent over, picked up the stretcher, and started to walk toward the *bawli*.

'Pheroze,'Hormoz addressed his companion, walking along.

'Yes.'

'How long . . . I mean how long will we go on doing this sort of work?'

'Cut it out.'

'Yaar, is it the only thing we're good for?'

'So what do you think.'

'Nothing, really. I was merely asking.'

'That's all?'

'That's all. I swear by Zaratushtara.' He looked up at the sky.

After a brief silence Bhatina said, 'Look, Hormoz. The Parsi Council took care of us, didn't it? Let's just say we were the unlucky ones. Right? What do you say?'

'Same story. Not much difference. But the truth is, I'm fed up. I'm just fed up.'

Their conversation was cut short, as they had reached the *bawli* enclosure. A single kick of Hormoz's foot opened the door and the very next instant they took their places by the corpse, one standing by the corpse's head, the other by its feet. The corpse's face, which had been smeared with yogurt, was absolutely white. Hormoz lifted the head a little and Bhatina quickly pulled the shroud clean out from under it. By turns they reverentially touched the corpses feet, touched their hands to their eyes and chests as a sign of respect, and got up. A handkerchief had been put around the waist with the ritual *kasti*-string to cover the corpses nakedness. They left it alone. Then they came to their quarters in the corner of the *bawli* compound and sat down at a table. After some time Hormoz set a wine bottle on the table and the two filled their glasses. Pheroze Bhatina popped a piece of arvi roll into his mouth and said, 'Hormoz.'

'Yes, what?'

'What a life!'

'What's the matter?'

'*Bagli* No. 1, 2, 4, . . . the bell, . . . son of a bitch, . . . and . . .'

'And?'

'Yeah, and . . .'

'And—what?'

'Corpses . . . still more corpses . . .'

'I don't understand.'

'Just look. Look at the life of a Parsi.'

'Life?'

'Yes.'

'What about it?'

'His youth runs super fast but his old age merely crawls along like a freight train.'

'True, brother, absolutely true.'

'Yes, absolutely true.'

They kept up the litany of 'true, true' for quite a while as they continued to drink, breaking somewhat later into fits of sobs. After an hour or so the bell went off again. This time the corpse was coming from *bagli* no. 4.

'There, Lord Zaratushtara's provided for more wine.'

'Come on, yaar, let's get going.'

They made their way over to the *bawli's* main gate. The door opened a second time. They slid the empty stretcher out. Moments later it was pushed back in with the corpse from *bagli* no. 4. One of the attendants tossed two ten-rupee notes at them once again. But this time Hormoz stepped forward to collect the money. Then they closed the door, picked up the stretcher and started off toward the *bawli*.

'Hormoz?'

'Yes, what?'

'One day we too will end up dead, just like this, no?'

Hormoz stopped, turned his head to look at Pheroze Bhatina, and then asked him rather harshly: 'Now what makes you ask a question like that?'

'Everyone has to die.'

'True. But I'm not planning on dying quite yet.'

'Planning? What the hell do you mean?'

'Shut up, fool. What have we seen in life so far? Dead bodies, more dead bodies, and vultures. At the most, a little wine now and then from that fucking Sitara Road liquor store . . . crude, mixed with ammonium chloride . . ten-rupee notes. I ask: is this what you call life?'

Pheroze didn't answer, he just kept looking at Hormoz

'Come on, brother, is it life?'

'What can I say. All I know is this: when the call comes I must go. Somebody else will take my place. When you go somebody else will take your place too.'

'Shut up, fool! Bastard! Pig!' Hormoz shouted.

'Don't make so much noise. Stop talking about life Look, we've got a corpse to take care of.'

They shut up. Walked over to the *bawli* in silence. And when they opened the door . . .

It was all so unexpected. They were stunned. They put the stretcher down abruptly, gawked at the dead body, and then looked at each other with a million questions stirring in their eyes. Their eyeballs moved dumbly in their sockets for quite some time, and when they stopped, the two shrugged their shoulders uncomprehendingly . . . And then they let their gaze hover over the dense trees of the Parsi cemetery. There was not a single vulture anywhere in sight

This was absolutely the first time it had happened. Corpses, but no vultures in sight anywhere. Usually though, after Hormoz and Pheroze had dragged a corpse to the *bawli*, the vultures made short work of it within minutes. As they saw the vultures return, they would come back to the *bawli*, douse the skeleton with acid, which would then crumble like fine dust into the depths of the *bawli*—gone forever, who knows where? Sometimes no dead body was brought in for days on end. But on such occasions the Parsi Council would buy a goat and have it delivered to Hormoz and Bhatina who would then feed it to the vultures, lest hunger drive them away for ever. But this? Corpses—a shoal of them, so to speak—ready but no vultures around to finish them off!

Both gawked at each other with peeled eyes. After they had stood there dumbly for some time they put the second corpse on the netting as well, then they covered the mouth of the *bawli* and gave each other a deep questioning look.

'What do you think? Shall I go and let Keqabad know?'

'Yes. Go!'

Bhatina went into his room and pressed the emergency button. The red bulb on the wall of the office of the Parsi cemetery began to blink. The clerks scampered out—confused, shocked. Similar bulbs also went on in the *baglis*. The clerics stopped the holy recitation from the *Avesta*. Dogs wandering about in the *baglis* were suddenly gripped by fear and slunk into corners. Mournful relatives accompanying their dear departed stepped out of the *baglis* in a state of prodigious nervousness. Everywhere there was a single question: What's happened?

Keqabad bounded out, looked at the sky closely and promptly went back in. People hemmed him in, noisily asking the same question, 'What's happened?' In response

Keqabad announced, 'The vultures have gone away!'

'Vultures've gone away?'

'But why?'

'Something's bound to happen!'

'But what?'

The secretary of the Parsi Council received Keqabad's phone call. His forehead began to wrinkle. After he had heard it all he returned the receiver to its cradle, turned on the intercom and informed the director of the matter. Right away an emergency meeting was called. The matter was presented before the board of directors. But the question persisted: Where did the vultures disappear to?

'What did you say, the vultures have disappeared?' the police commissioner asked with a trace of surprise in his voice.

'Yes, our vultures have disappeared,' the chairman of the Parsi Council confirmed, stressing each syllable. In rapt attention he listened to all that the police commissioner had to say, his face turning one colour after another. He listened to him for a long time. After the commissioner had hung up, the chairman too had returned the receiver to the cradle and looked at the directors and found their gaze intent upon him with a single question. He apprised them of the substance of his talk with the commissioner. Each of the participants left the meeting with prodigious worry and only a slight feeling of reassurance. The secretary rang up the cemetery. Then Keqabad briefly summed up the substance of the exchange between the police commissioner and the chairman to the revered clerics and others present. From the clerics the news travelled down to the attendants of the *Baglis* and from them ultimately to Pheroze Bhatina and Hormoz. Bhatina listened to the whole thing very carefully. He then looked at the sky, clearly visible from random openings in the dense foliage: there was not even a crow anywhere, or a kite, let alone a vulture!

All of a sudden they flinched. The bell had gone off again. A corpse was being sent from *bagli* no. 3. Once again they were standing at the door. The corpse arrived. This time, though, the attendant thrust two fifty-rupee notes at Bhatina. After Bhatina and Hormoz had pulled the corpse inside, the latter grimaced and said 'Hormoz!'

'Yes, what is it?'

'Why in hell have all the Parsis decided to die only today?'

Hormoz didn't answer. He just went on looking at the sky.

'To start with, no vultures in sight; then corpse after corpse comes our way.'

'Where have the vultures disappeared to?'

'The police commissioner said the vultures, all of them, are flocking to the Kharki, Raviwar Peth and Somwar Peth neighbourhoods.'

'What for?'

'Oh these idiot Hindus and Muslims are at each other's throats again. There's been a riot. The bastards, they've torched everything: houses, shops, even ambulances and hearses, the whole lot. The street is littered with corpses. One right on top of the other. Piled high. Our vultures—well, they're having a field day there. And that police commissioner . . . he said that after the street's been cleaned up, the vultures will come back on their own accord.'

'Even if the street's cleaned up—so what? What makes you think the vultures will return? This fucking India . . . there is a riot every day here, every day a fire, every day people die. The vultures'll come back? The hell they will!'

A Land Without Sky

Ilyas Ahmad Gaddi

I

I, Rifat Jahan, also known as Raffu, want to finish this story of my brother Kalim Khan—a story which has been left unfinished, who knows why. There sometimes comes a point in a story when the writer's hand begins to shake, his pen burns, and everything becomes altogether too difficult to bear. This often troubles the writer so much that he gives the story an unexpected twist, or he takes the reader to some profound subtlety, and then hurriedly wraps things up. Few have the courage to cross over this river of fire.

Such has been the fate of Kalim Bhai's story too. It's been left in a state of suspension. Let alone its ending, even the portrayal of life within and without the house—the fire of hatred and insult which smouldered slowly within our family and suffocated us with its thick, heavy smoke, and which often sent Kalim Bhai scrambling outside for some fresh air—has been treated perfunctorily. Maybe such narrative caution was foisted upon the writer by some great emotional pressure, or maybe by his fear simply of over-heating. This happens when the story of another starts to become one's own; the writer finds himself seared by the unbounded fire of truth. But it is precisely here that a writer's endurance, his spunk, his guts are tested.

But I'm not a writer. I'm only Kalim Bhai's sister. I've lived with him, in fire as much as in smoke. As many blisters as he had on his body, I have had on mine too. As much as the thick smoke suffocated him, it has suffocated me too. As much indignity as he had to put up with, I've had to suffer too.

I do not regret his death. Death couldn't be such a bad thing, after all, compared to the kind of life he'd had to live. Why then die a little each day? Why not just spit at the world, at this life and be done with?

Don't jump to conclusions. No, he didn't commit suicide. He was not such a coward. He was not one to throw in the towel. He couldn't have spat on life, either. If anything, he loved life. Always. Like an innocent child, life's every glitter filled him with immeasurable excitement. He'd rush toward it. He'd want to grab it in his hand. That every glittering object turned out to be fire in the end and burnt his hand, well, that's something else again. For days afterwards he would smart from the sting, the sensation of burning.

I know what I say is difficult to understand, because you can't see him the way I do. If you could, you'd easily understand my drift, these allusions would have sufficed.

Our house . . .

Well, a Muslim middle-class home, with three rooms. One for Kalim Bhai, another for us children, the third for Abba and Ammi. If a house guest arrived, Kalim Bhai's room would be requisitioned. He'd have to switch to ours. This meant all kinds of restrictions on us: Don't laugh! Don't make so much noise! Don't play the tape recorder! And all so that Kalim Bhai could study undisturbed.

In families with little or no tradition of education, if a boy takes to studies, he pulls a lot of weight, like some big officer. His clean and tidy uniform and bright face make his parents feel fulfilled. The entire household snaps to attention at the sound of his approaching footsteps. Guests are especially informed of the boy's school and the class he is in.

Kalim Bhai pulled just such weight. His commanding, imposing manner used to rub both Sajid and me the wrong way. We dared not slap him, or tug or snatch at him, even in jest, which would guarantee us not only a beating from Ammi, but also such awesome scolding and yelling by Abba that we would head cringing with fear to our beds for the evening.

Efforts were made to educate Sajid too, but his heart was so given over to play and amusement that he always managed to flunk his exams. He had a special camaraderie with the lowlives of the neighbourhood. He'd leave the house with his school bag and invariably end up in the park playing cricket. He'd also picked up smoking and going to the movies. Finally, Abba just gave up. He had an acquaintance give Sajid a job at his garage.

Returning home from work, Sajid would be covered with motor oil and grease. Not just his clothes, but his hands and even his face would be covered with black grime, his hair full of grit and dirt. His sorry figure sometimes prompted Abba to recite a couplet with touching humility:

> Twin pearls from a single oyster, yet how different their fates:
> One ground to dust in the mortar, the other set in the royal diadem.

He affected not just Abba alone; his proximity made even Ammi quickly cover her nose with her dupatta and remark, 'For heaven's sake Sajid, you stink. I can't even breathe.'

Being an unemotional man, Sajid rarely took offence at

this; instead, he'd just shrug it off with a hearty laugh. He apparently liked the path he had chosen for himself. The twenty rupees a week he made at the garage had put some spending money in his pocket. He started to go to the movies once a week, openly, and helped himself to half a dozen cigarettes a day. And for none of this did he have to beg from Abba.

Kalim Bhai passed all his exams with distinction, including his B.A. But by then we had hit bad times. Abba had lost his job at a private firm because of his deteriorating eyesight. He tried out several pairs of eyeglasses, one after another, all purchased from the Iranian sidewalk peddlers, but none worked. When he finally consulted an ophthalmologist, he found out that one of the blood vessels had burst due to his high blood pressure, and the escaping blood had clouded his vision.

Abba took it in stride, however. Twenty years of uninterrupted work had left him so exhausted, so fed up that he rather liked his new leisure. Kalim Bhai had finished his B.A. after all; he'd find a job before long. And besides, Sajid was now making six hundred rupees a month. It wasn't much, but we were managing somehow.

This was the time for sending out job applications. Kalim Bhai's desk drawers had become full of newspaper clippings—ads for the banks, the railway, Coal India, Oil India, you name it. A fresh application by registered mail went out every week. In the end he was thoroughly tired. He turned to large private companies. Disappointed even there, he concentrated on finding a job, any job, with a private firm.

For years he chased after shadows, until all the brightness had disappeared from his eyes, and repeated failure had sucked all the freshness from his face. He stood immobile in his defeat—broken, vanquished.

Abbu, seeing him so stricken, sometimes let out, 'There are no jobs for Muslim boys in India. Discrimination is rampant everywhere. And why not? Just about every department is filled only with communalists.'

'No, Abbu,' Kalim Bhai would interrupt. 'It's not like that at all. Actually . . .'

'Oh, come on. How would you know? This hair you see, it hasn't turned grey in the sun. I speak from experience. The end of the Angrez Raj means the end of the Muslim Raj. When the Angrez ruled, they trusted Muslims, not *these* people. That's why all their chefs and cooks used to be Muslims.'

Kalim Bhai would immediately counter, 'It's not like that at all, Abbu. They did it to protect their power. Only two religious groups in India had sizable numbers. Hindus and Muslims. It was imperative that they keep one of them on their side. They opted for the Muslims. Why? Because feudalism still survived among Muslims. They could easily be used. Divide and Rule—that was the British policy.'

Kalim Bhai would fall silent; he could hear in all this a ring of the feudal hangover which still persisted in some people. Abbu was one of them. He considered Muslim rule the golden period of history. Perhaps that's why, still under its affect whenever he felt in the mood, he proudly recited this line from some old stage play: 'The grandeur of the Sultanate lives on no matter what the guise.'

Those who have lived all their lives in poverty are seduced by such dreams of monarchical grandeur. But Kalim Bhai would simply smile at the recitation and keep quiet. One day, though, he said to me, 'Just look at Abba. Doesn't it look like he too came straight from Samarkand and Bukhara, wielding a spear to conquer India? Really though, I doubt if his relatives going back seven generations ever had anything to do with ruling. Who knows what our original lineage is?—Banya, Dusadh, Kayasth. But it takes so little: rattle off the *kalimah*, embrace Islam, and push your claim to Sultanhood.'

Kalim Bhai was not given to bitter talk, although at times he did boil over. He was generally a very cool-headed and mild-mannered person. Even when he disagreed or protested, he did so with such gentleness and courtesy that he failed to win his point. Then again, gentleness didn't work with my folks. What did work with them was the harsh, aggressive manner of Sajid, to which he resorted frequently. Now and then when Ammi pressed Sajid for more money, he'd flare up and snap, 'Where do you expect me to get the money from? You want me to steal? Rob a bank? If you can't manage, just smash the cooking pots!'

Once during Ramzan Abbu called Sajid and had him sit near him. After talking about casual things he came down to business: 'Ask your boss to give you a thousand rupees this time. We need new clothes for Eid.'

Sajid, who was following Abbu's drift, flatly refused. 'I can't,' he said. 'I've already taken an advance from him for the Ramzan expenses. I can't ask him for more again so soon.'

'But, Miyan, we can't very well do without new clothes. Maybe not for us old people, I mean your Ammi and I, but there is your Brother Sahib, big Mr. B.A. degree, then there is Raffu, then there is the customary *fitra* that must be offered, etc., etc.'

Sajid stood up in a huff and fired, 'You're wrong if you think I'll go begging for all of you. Since when do I provide for everyone in the house? You brought them into the world, you take care of them!'

The exchange was so loud that just about everyone heard it. Abbu was absolutely stunned. Such a gross thing to say! And coming from a mere handful of a brat!

Abbu remained dazed for the entire time Sajid was in the house, but the minute he went out, he started to thunder: 'Haramzada! Now that he's started earning a little, he's forgotten his manners! Ask him, who took care of him when he was small? Who trained him for his job? I'm unemployed and disabled today, so he can say with impunity, "You brought them into the world." All right, I brought them into the world, and I'll take care of them. I *will*, even if I have to beg!'

Ammi didn't say a word but wept a lot. Indeed she wept intermittently throughout that whole day. Kalim Bhai stayed quiet. A melancholic silence had fallen over the entire household.

The silence didn't dissipate for the next few days. Nobody talked to anybody. Kalim Bhai stayed away from home as much as he could. Ammi found one reason or another to get upset with me. 'Fit only for animals, is this how you cook!' she would yell, tasting a dish I'd fixed. 'Tomorrow when you go to your husband's, they'll grab you by your braid and throw you out.'

A breath of spring wafted through the house a week later when Sajid placed a thousand rupees in Abbu's hands. A smile came to Abbu's lips, a current of animation livened Ammi's step, and satisfaction washed over Kalim Bhai, who said to me later that evening, 'Money's a very powerful thing.'

Just how powerful? He knew well, and so did I. Unemployment was slowly pushing him ever deeper into humiliation. The hopes Abbu had pinned on him, the dreams he had, all began to slowly vanish. Attention began to shift away from Kalim Bhai: whether he had eaten or not, when he went out and what time he returned, how many job applications he'd sent out, which ones were likely to get him a position—all this disappeared, and Kalim Bhai was tossed aside like an unusable—and now unnecessary—utensil.

An argument broke out between Sajid and his employer over the Eid advance. Sajid quit the job. After hard work and plenty of running around, he managed to set up his own garage. It started poorly, but in the end the situation improved as the business picked up.

This coincided with the time when Kalim Bhai started working gratis for a newspaper. After some time the owner, taking pity on Kalim Bhai, added him to the payroll. Seven hundred rupees a month.

The value of money is always relative to the total earnings of a family. If Sajid didn't have his garage, Kalim Bhai's seven hundred rupees would have seemed like a considerable amount. But the family was experiencing something like a glut now. Sajid was raking in four or five thousand rupees a month—a sum Abbu had not even dreamed of. As a result, Abbu felt pretty overwhelmed and cowed down by Sajid. Perhaps he had even come to fear him. He never asked Sajid for anything directly; instead, he asked through Ammi. And Sajid turned out to be so dutiful that whatever Ammi asked, he gave without question.

In less than a year the house itself got a tremendous face-lift. Curtains were added to the doors and windows. Old charpoys, their frayed batting sagging with exhaustion, were replaced with regular beds and folding cots. Taking meals upon *daris* and *chatais* began to seem uncivilized, so now we sat grandly at a huge dining table, including even Ammi, who had until recently taken her food squatting on the bare floor of the dingy, dimly-lit kitchen.

So the value of Kalim Bhai's seven hundred rupees suddenly shrank before this affluence, and he, as a result shrank even further. Nobody felt the need to talk to him any more. Abbu too no longer cared if anyone sent him a letter offering an interview. Ammi scarcely ever ventured into his room to exchange even a few words.

His insignificance reached a low point when, suddenly one day, the matter of his marriage was broached. It wasn' that Abbu and Ammi were eager to see their elder son married, rather they feared that since Sajid now had plenty of money and was behaving so independently, he migh start heading down the wrong path. Ammi tried to cover i up, but the plain fact was that Sajid occasionally returned home quite late at night, and sometimes also drunk. So they thought they world rein him in with the ties of matrimony But there was a problem: Kalim Bhai was older, and marrying the younger brother first was awkward. They thought if they could get Kalim Bhai to marry first, it would open the way for Sajid.

That, however, didn't happen. Kalim Bhai flatly refused, giving his small salary as the reason. He could hardly provide for a wife with his paltry earnings. Abbu and Ammi insisted that the family already had quite a few members, so one more person's needs wouldn't make such a big difference. And Sajid would never shy away from providing for his bhabhi, just as he did for everyone else But Kalim Bhai wouldn't go along.

The first time I ever saw Kalim Bhai protest openly was the day when both Abbu and Ammi tried hard to trap him somehow as they all sat at the dining table. Ammi started with marked gentleness: 'The thing is, Kalim, that I'm well along in my years. My sight is getting weaker. I can hardly see. How long do you expect me to mind the kitchen? To blow into the fire? If I could just have a bahu, I could see some relief.'

'In that case, maybe you should consider getting Sajid married.'

'How can I? How can I marry off the younger one before the older one? This is just not done.'

'I don't see what difference it makes, since all you want is a bahu.'

Abbu, so far content merely with listening to the exchange, blew up. 'Don't talk like idiots. What will the world say about me?'

'The world will shout for a few days and then shut up.'

Abbu frowned and said, 'Why are you opposed to getting married? Don't you think you're old enough?'

'It's not a question of being old enough or not, my situation just isn't . . .'

'Well, what is your situation? Let's hear it.'

'Not until I can stand on my own two feet financially. How could I even dream of marriage on a salary of only seven hundred rupees?'

'I can't see you making much more. Ever! So, am I to understand that you'll never marry?'

'Yes, maybe.'

'Which means none of my other children will get married either?'

'I never said that. By all means, marry Sajid. When I have found a regular job with a decent income, you can certainly think about my marriage then.'

Abbu lost his patience. 'You've been running after jobs for five years now! And what do you have to show for it? You'll never get married, if you wait for a job.'

Kalim Bhai got up and left. Abbu went on fuming and frothing.

Finally it was decided to marry Sajid first.

Kalim Bhai participated eagerly in Sajid's wedding. He did a lot of running around to make it come off nicely. He took care of sending out the wedding invitations; he arranged for the music, lighting, and the *walima* banquet; and he even ran back and forth several times to the florist's for Sajid's wedding *sehra*. God knows how he had become charged with so much bustling energy—Kalim Bhai who was otherwise so given to a quieter existence. Needless to say, his performance pleased Abbu mightily.

As is customary for weddings, a suit of clothes was also ordered for Kalim Bhai from the tailor's. But he refused to accept it, preferring to appear in his everyday clothes. This not only burnt up Abbu, but also made Sajid feel insulted. They had both become quite status-oriented now, in need of a demonstration of their wealth and grandeur. Kalim Bhai's plain clothes offended them precisely in this area. Perhaps. Anyway, Abbu babbled about the affront for some weeks after the wedding and then moved on. But Sajid never did forgive Kalim Bhai for it. It turned into enduring hate.

Another obvious change also occurred after Sajid's wedding. Kalim Bhai, who usually returned from work around 11 p.m., now started to return past midnight. He would rap on the door. Earlier Ammi would get up and open it for him. Now, finding it a bother, she'd let him rap for a while, then wake me up to go open it. 'Hey, go see,' she'd say. 'Must be our bread-winner, returning at midnight with a big haul.'

This late-returning had apparently begun to bother Sajid—perhaps even his wife. So early one morning he exploded at Abbu. 'You call this home? All this banging at the door at midnight? Just when one has finally dozed off? Others can sleep through the day, but I've to work like a mule the whole day long. Exhausted, when I finally can get some rest and am just about to doze off, the door latch begins to rattle.'

Abbu was frightened. He frequently feared Sajid now, afraid, somehow, that he might take his wife and move out. So he became hugely worried. Late in the day when Kalim Bhai got up, he came after him.

'Where do you go until midnight?'

'I'm held up at the office.'

'Held up at the office—huh! Get this straight, you don't have a servant waiting to open the door for you halfway through the night and serve you your dinner. You wreck everybody's sleep!'

'In that case, tell Ammi to leave my dinner in my room.'

'But who's going to open the door for you?'

'I'll ask Rifat, she'll open it.'

'Perhaps you don't know, but Sajid and his wife don't like your pounding so late at night.'

Kalim Bhai had no answer for this. He bowed his head and walked out. He knew Sajid's importance, and now he also knew his wife's.

Thereafter Kalim Bhai only tapped at the door very softly, while I, fearing Sajid and his wife's displeasure, stayed awake in bed. The moment I heard the tap, I'd dart out to open the door for him. Usually Kalim Bhai stayed away from talking at that hour. If he had something to say, he spoke very softly, almost in whispers, so that it wouldn't disturb anyone. This fear of his was the limit of humiliation, where a man begins to suffocate.

A month later, Kalim Bhai brought a silver necklace and

gave it to Ammi—his wedding gift for dulhan bhabhi. It turned out that just to make the money for this gift he had taken on an additional two-hour job at another newspaper as a translator.

Ammi looked at the necklace and frowned so hard that a dark shadow instantly descended on Kalim Bhai's happy face. When Abbu saw the gift, he said, 'Why bother now? The time for gifts was right after the *walima* banquet. Now, it'd sound like an untimely tune. And what makes you think Sajid's wife would care for a silver necklace?'

Clearly the disparagement was aimed not at the gift but at Kalim Bhai himself. He knew it; but more than him, I knew it. A terrible humiliation swirled about him, as he seethed with disgust. He probably realized, for the very first time, that one relationship was held over and above all others: the money relationship.

In the evening before leaving for the office, Kalim Bha said, 'I'll be back early tonight. I've quit that extra job as translator.'

'Why?'

'Oh, I had to stay out late, which meant I bothered all o you.'

Outwardly there wasn't anything in this sentence of his but perhaps inwardly there was. Some pain, lament complaint, a sense of one's utter helplessness, of degrada tion, of ignominy. I looked at his face. None of these coulc be seen clearly, but it was nonetheless etched with a web-work of lines no one could see. Of that I'm sure Suddenly he took a step toward me, patted me lovingly or the head, and asked softly, 'If I gave you a gift at you wedding, would you too . . .'

I didn't have the strength to listen any further. A tida wave, held back for ages, broke through the dikes. I put m head against his chest and broke down in tears. He didn't say anything. He didn't even try to console me. He only said this, 'Money counts for a lot these days.' He then lifted up my face, wiped my tears with his cool, thin fingers, and said, 'You're crazy. Coward! Don't you see how I've been fighting for years? How can you be so faint-hearted, Sister? Look at me, do I let all this bother me?'

I don't know whether you have ever seen a man with no tears in his eyes, and only a smile on his lips, but who's still crying. I've seen Kalim Bhai in just such a state often enough. How this sort of inner grief wrings your heart and frays your nerves! One can understand something of this grief only when one is all alone.

I left him briefly to go inside. When I returned I found him gazing at a stain on the wall, his face fast becoming dark, beads of cold perspiration glistening on his forehead and nose. He was breathing hard, as if joined in a fierce battle deep inside, which he had begun to lose.

II

Kalim Bhai had announced that he'd give up the supplementary job as translator, but apparently he didn't. He continued to return late at night. I tried to quiz him about it several times, but he light-heartedly evaded the issue, although once he did say: 'The wedding gift for Sajid's wife was still something within our own family. So one could get away even with a silver necklace. But you'll be going to another man's home. Nothing less than gold would do there. Well, let's just say I'm collecting money for that.'

His words uttered in cheerfulness somehow still left a scratch on my heart. I felt the urge to tell him straight out:

Even a pinch of dust from a brother like you would be worth a fortune! But I couldn't. And even if I had, he wouldn't have believed it. The bonds of family relationships had so often betrayed him, and he had seen them break and disintegrate so often—even the sacred bond of motherly love—that he no longer had any confidence at all in them.

Right about then the atmosphere in the city suddenly took a turn for the worse. The air echoed with communal slogans. Shops began to close early in the evening. The otherwise bustling and noisy city fell into silence. People were consumed by anxiety, fearing that the impossible might just come to pass.

Our house was located in a non-Muslim neighbourhood. Only two Muslim houses, both surrounded by thousands of non-Muslim houses, and yet it never occurred to us that we were alone, defenceless, or in any kind of danger. We mixed freely and were so assimilated with our non-Muslim neighbours that it was difficult to distinguish between us. During Holi, our men participated in the festival, as they went scaring everybody dressed up as ghosts. And we celebrated Diwali by lighting lamps and setting off fireworks just like everyone else. And on Baqar Eid, it looked like a veritable bhoj. Entire contingents of guests arrived at our house. These included Sajid's friends, Abbu's acquaintances, and Kalim Bhai's colleagues from the newspaper office.

Among Kalim Bhai's co-workers, the closest to him was Parkash, Parkash Shrivastav. Both had been, as Abbu put it, wasting their time at the same newspaper for the last so many years. They also had their desks in the same hall at the office. In the daytime, he often showed up with Kalim Bhai at our house. And the minute they came in, Kalim Bhai would call out at me, 'Raffu, tea!'

The colour on Ammi's face would change a bit, but she actually never said anything. Abbu, on the other hand, often muttered, 'The layabouts are back in business.'

The two would start talking, about everything and anything—poverty, wealth, society, politics, American and Russian policies, violence in Africa, oppression of the Palestinians, you name it. Sometimes the discussion got so heated it seemed the two would come to blows. But they never did. As soon as the heat had escaped their heads, they would start gossiping cheerfully. When I arrived with the tea, Parkash Bhai, affecting the high-flown manner of Urduwallahs, would spread out the newspaper and say patrionizingly, 'Set it right here, Bibi. Oh, we've troubled you for no reason.'

Subsequently he'd ask, in the same patronizing manner, 'How are your studies coming along, Bibi?'

'Just fine,' I'd answer respectfully.

'If you ever come across a difficult spot in your studies, let me know. This brother of yours has always gotten the highest marks, from the fourth class all the way up to B.A.'

Kalim Bhai burst out laughing. 'That's why the "highest marks" makes a salary of only seven hundred rupees a month!'

Parkash Bhai would get testy and snap, 'What, you judge ability by salary? You know . . .'

Another heated discussion would get going, in which all the current injustices and exploitation would come in for a heavy thrashing. I'd quietly slip out.

Ever since the marked deterioration in the city's civil life, worry had taken hold of everybody. Kalim Bhai's fear stemmed from the feeling of insecurity, Parkash Bhai's from his inability to do anything about the tide of undesirable conditions. The strife and unrest was getting out of hand.

Abbu had now only two, maybe three friends left. They, along with dozens of Sajid's friends, Parkash Bhai and Kalim Bhai's other colleagues, visited us now and then, doing their best to boost our morale, assuring us that nothing untoward would happen, at least not as long as they were around, while uncertainty and weakness showed in their faces even as they said these words. One could hardly doubt their sincerity; they really didn't want us to get hurt. But it was also clear that they lacked the wherewithal to stem the tide of events. Their condition, in a manner of speaking, was even worse than ours. For if our lives were in danger, they had their faith at stake.

Ammi was perhaps the most apprehensive of any of us. Every minute she feared that a stampede, killing and carnage would begin. Somebody had told her that women were also raped during riots. Ever since, she'd started to look at me as though I was going to be the principal victim. She'd look at me and sigh, sometimes even cry. Several times she even asked Abbu to take me to stay with our Khalu at Ranchi, but he didn't go for the idea. How could he shoo a young girl away to somebody else's house. For better or for worse, we'd face it together.

At least on the face of it, Abbu showed a lot of courage. He comforted everyone with reassuring words. 'Don't worry at all,' he'd say. 'They're no lions, that they'd come and gobble you up. Even today, if a Muslim resolved to fight, he'd be the equal of ten of them.'

This, of course, was just a lot of hot air, a delusion. A lie which even Abbu didn't believe. What gave him particular worry was if ever rioters did barge into our house, we didn't have a single weapon to defend ourselves with. The time when lathis and dandas sufficed was long gone. And it was not possible to keep bombs and handguns.

Yet another fear dogged him: that people might surround Sajid on his way to or from work. His garage was in a Muslim neighbourhood. So that was one worry less; at least nobody would touch him during the day. But on the way, what if somebody shot him or knifed him? If Sajid didn't return by early evening, Abbu would start feeling restless. He'd walk out to the intersection and look down the street that ran to Sajid's garage, returning disappointed minutes later. Then he'd climb to the rooftop, and unable to stem his anxiety, he'd walk out of the house again. He remained restless and apprehensive until Sajid actually returned.

Surprisingly, nobody was worried for Kalim Bhai, even though he returned late at night and was in the greatest danger of all the family members. Once or twice when I mentioned this to Abbu, he evaded the issue, saying, 'He works for the press. Nobody, Hindu or Muslim, ever touches press people.'

His reply never allayed my fears. After all, nobody carried a tag reading 'newspaper man' on his forehead. I.D. card, yes. But who'd search someone's pockets for it? So if I worried at all, it was not on my own account—despite Ammi's constant reminders—but rather on Kalim Bhai's account. He was a somewhat careless man, who in spite of all the trouble that had already occurred still believed that nothing would happen, and that conditions would gradually return to normal. Consequently, he kept returning late at night, and I kept praying for his safety, spending the entire time in great mental stress. The moment his familiar tap came at the door, I felt that a calamity had been averted. Perhaps Abbu too was beginning to worry about his late returns, or perhaps it was the fear lodged deep inside him that kept him restless until late in the evening. Whatever it was, he called Kalim Bhai to his room one day and asked, 'Could you possibly return a bit earlier—I mean, say, by seven or eight o'clock?'

'Seven o'clock is when the work actually begins to pick up at the newspaper office.'

'Well then, maybe ten o'clock.'

'It's difficult. I have to provide the headlines for all the local and PTI news. I have more or less to put together the first two pages. Given the country's present situation, an important news item can come in at any time. So I have to wait until quite late. After all, we have to give our readers the latest news.'

'But at least you could ask your editor to let you go a bit earlier, as long as the conditions are bad.'

'As a matter of fact, I did ask, but the answer was "No" They aren't as afraid as we are.'

'What is there for them to be afraid of? How could they know the torment we're going through? Quit the job, I'd say. It won't be such a big loss, after all. The five hundred you contribute toward the household expenses isn't so much. It won't matter even if you don't give it.'

Kalim Bhai fell silent. The question of money had once again come into the picture. Those five hundred rupees didn't mean much to Abbu, but the remaining two hundred and fifty meant a great deal to Kalim Bhai. This was his entire estate, his need, his dignity and self-respect, the palpable sign of his being a person in his own right. So he didn't stop coming home late, and perhaps he didn't give up his extra job as translator, either.

The atmosphere around us got even more heated and precarious. Demonstrations took place daily. Slogans and cries went up in the middle of the night, and cassette tapes full of inflammatory rhetoric, played over loudspeakers in the middle of intersections, blared well into the night, setting off a storm of fear and apprehension in people's hearts.

As soon as one of these cassettes would start to blast, Abbu would walk into the room, out of his wits with worry. 'They're playing the same cassette at the Bata corner again.'

Nobody would respond. We would look at each other with a feeling of despondency, which made Abbu's tension even worse. 'Isn't Sajid back yet?' he would ask.

Again, nobody would answer. Bhabhi, busy knitting a sweater, would look up at him briefly and then busy herself with her knitting once again.

We were neighbours to Mukul Babu and Sudhir Ghosh for a long time, twenty years, maybe even longer. From childhood on we'd socialized with them and grown up together, and felt as close to them as we did to our relatives. Mukul Babu's bahus called Abbu 'Babuji' and Kalim Bhai, 'Jethji'. Sudhir Ghosh's old mother called Abbu 'Dada', i.e., 'older brother', which often prompted Ghosh Babu to joke about it with Abbu. His five-year-old granddaughter practically lived with us. His ties with us were so strong that they didn't waver at all during this temporary storm. Now and then, when Abbu's worry reached its limit, Ghosh Babu would try to reassure him in his endearing Bengali manner, 'Sala Babu! Why do you keep worrying so much? Nobody's going to come and kill a simple, decent man like you. And if ever you suspect such a thing, come straight over to my place, and let me see who this tiger is who's coming after you.'

In spite of the assurances, our insecurity only grew worse. Even though we hadn't taken a firm decision to move out by then, it had become increasingly apparent that staying further in the area amounted to absolute insanity—for which we may have to pay dearly.

Then one day a veritable stampede broke out. Nobody had any idea what actually happened in the bazaar, but everyone was fleeing in whatever direction seemed open. When you stopped a fleeing person and asked him about the matter, he scarcely had the time to respond. Yes, one fleeing person did manage to respond, 'It's finally happened!'

Happened—what had happened? Rioting? No, it wasn't that. Two bulls had collided with each other in the Sabzi Mandi, knocking over a few fruit-sellers' pushcarts, which set people running every which way. Muslims were bolting from fear, but surprisingly, the Hindus from the villages and small towns who had come to make purchases were also bolting.

The stampede lasted only a short while, because the police quickly arrived on the scene, followed by the military. All the same, the city had become deserted. Faces, turned dark from fear, lit up, but nerves still felt raw and quivering. How heavily these few moments weighed on Abbu only I knew. Ammi half fainted and fell over on the takht as soon as the noise of the stampede was heard. She hurriedly started repeating in a loud voice as many Quranic verses as she could recall. It seemed that if, God forbid, the unspeakable did happen, she'd lose her mind immediately. Abbu rushed throughout the house, closed the main door, the doors to all the rooms, and then the windows. He emphatically told Bhabhi and me several times to shut ourselves inside the inner room, and repeated Sajid's name as many times: 'Why isn't he back yet? He should be back by now. I hope they haven't surrounded him on the way. Please, God, keep him safe!'

Nowhere did Kalim Bhai's name once crop up in these

anxious words. No one remembered him once, for even a second. Both Ammi and Abbu were worried sick on account of Sajid. Bhabhi was praying for the safety of her husband. In my mind alone Kalim Bhai's name had jelled palpably like a frozen drop.

Kalim Bhai returned quite late that night too. The brief commotion earlier in the day had kept us all awake. When he knocked at the door, I got up to open it, but Abbu stopped me and said, 'Wait, I'll open it.'

Unexpectedly seeing Abbu behind the door, Kalim Bhai was jolted. 'Is everything all right?' he asked anxiously. 'Raffu isn't sick, is she?'

'Why would you care, whether we live or die! You go right along, having fun till midnight!'

It was all so unexpected that Kalim Bhai couldn't think of anything to say. Nor was Abbu expecting to hear anything. He just kept pouring out: 'What a terrible stampede! What a riot! But the thought never crossed your mind that you have a home, parents, a young sister.'

'But I did hear about the riot! Lots of people called the newspaper. And I did think to rush back home. But when we found out that it was all a misunderstanding, I decided to stay on at work.'

'Rush back home—the hell you will!' Abbu was enormously angry. 'Yes, you will come, but only to identify our corpses. And why not? To collect on the compensation. After all, it'll set you up nicely.'

Kalim Bhai suddenly turned red with anger, as though all his blood had been pumped to his face. He got up, turned his eyes from Abbu and looked at Ammi, at me, at Bhabhi, and then said, 'Money is just a pile of filth for me. I consider it beneath my dignity even to spit at it. But I've seen people, one more distinguished than the other, wallow in just this filth.'

Abbu was so enraged it seemed that he would hit Kalim Bhai. But by then Kalim Bhai had gone to his room.

The entire house was suddenly thrown into deathly silence. Abbu's face turned dark. Ammi stood dazed with anger. Just then Sajid sauntered out of his room. Apparently he'd heard the entire exchange. He sat down, lit up (he now smoked openly before Abbu and Ammi), then said angrily, 'Throw him out for a month, then we'll see what he's got to say about money. It doesn't take much to shoot your mouth off like this anyway, especially when you're a freeloader. In four days he'll forget all his fancy talk.'

Nobody said anything. Sajid's timely harangue gave Abbu's spirits a boost, and Ammi's flushed face too softened a bit.

I was out of my wits. These quarrels worried me a lot, and even frightened me a little. I knew how vulnerable Kalim Bhai was. One can't go down life's gritty road driving nothing but a beat-up old seven hundred rupee car. Numberless people had been buried alive under these shifting sand dunes. The house, for better or for worse, did provide a kind of support. What if that support too was pulled down?

It hurts even to think how those words would have torn at his heart, made him feel small and utterly humiliated. I felt the same degradation which he must have felt. That a man could be standing so alone and so distant among his own parents and siblings defies imagination. He needs a little love, a little sympathy, a little bonding and motherly affection, a little protection. And, yes, a little bit of happiness too, without which life appears to be nothing but a gaping darkness.

The fear on my face must have been obvious to

everyone as I stood there dazed by the argument. Ammi saw the condition I was in and said, 'What are you doing here? Go to your room and sleep.'

I got up like a dutiful little girl, glanced at Kalim Bhai's door which was shut, and moved on toward my room.

I couldn't fall asleep, not for a minute the entire night. When you see a fellow human being so brutally disgraced, without any reason, your inner anger, your pain becomes keener, more trenchant, razor-sharp. It flows like a liquid fire all the way to the edges of your eyes, and those burning pathways keep you awake. But this pain, this sensation of burning is nothing compared to what Kalim Bhai must be feeling. What could I do? And what could he? Nothing! Because in this market a man's weight is determined by his worth, and both he and I knew how little he weighed.

When Kalim Bhai didn't get up the next day until late, I went into his room and found him sound asleep, lying in his day clothes, his shoes still on, and his dinner untouched. I could well imagine how he had spent the night. Indeed I was well aware of many such nights.

There is a plaza, ordinarily called the Chowk, up beyond our house. One can access it either through the main street or through a narrow side lane, which itself fed into the street from which the plaza could be seen clearly. The hub of all kinds of demonstrations and rallies, it became the site of temporary publicity centers for all the political parties during elections. General meetings and mourning assemblies following the deaths of prominent leaders also took place here. Earlier the Congresswallahs had almost monopolized the Chowk. But recently it had passed into the control of another party—a party that had laid minefields through the length and breadth of India in the name of religion. Just that handful of people was responsible for all the civil unrest and disorder, and they would not have it any other way. Dead drunk, they sallied forth past ten o'clock in the evening daily, mouthing obscenities and making a racket with their loud inflammatory slogans, which instantly flew to Muslim neighbourhoods and spread as rumours.

'They're shouting slogans in the bazaar!'

'Obscenities are hurled at Muslims in the bazaar!'

'Such-and-such cab driver was forced tonight to run from his vehicle so that they could shoot him down.'

Maybe these rumours pained and angered the residents of Muslim neighbourhoods. In our family though, they created fear. Nobody dared walk to the Chowk past 10:00 p.m. Abbu or Karani Babu would only go as far as the main street, cast a sweeping glance at the Chowk and then come back. Only Kalim Bhai walked through it in a leisurely manner past midnight, on his way home from work, his khadi bag dangling from his shoulder. Nobody ever harassed him, nor did he himself ever feel any kind of apprehension. Whenever Abbu pleaded with him to return early, underscoring the nature of the times and the current conditions, he replied with perfect composure, 'Abbu, you worry for no reason. All this mischief is the work of just a few goonda types. None of the decent people are with them. The common man isn't in favour of all this fighting and rioting.'

Quick would come Abbu's response: 'Miyan, they're peas from the same pod, good men or bad. Think of them as garlic cloves. Down below, they're all connected to the same root. If a riot broke out today, you'd see how they all come together.'

Of course Kalim Bhai knew how the atmosphere had become more heated lately. But he didn't believe that it would lead to a major rioting incident or to bloodshed. One reason was that most people here were businessmen, who had come from different parts of the country. Then again, this area had traditionally been peaceful. Not even a ripple of unrest had risen when after independence all of India was witnessing general bloodshed and killing. Kalim Bhai felt that people here were basically peace-loving and didn't care for bloodshed. Now and then Kalim Bhai had explained all these things to Abbu. But he always felt that none of it did any good for Abbu's sagging confidence. Abbu, for some reason, always appeared apprehensive to him, cringing from some nagging, inarticulate fear. A slight cry at the Chowk, or even the sound of two men squabbling was enough to put his nerves on edge.

'You hear it, don't you, Sajid's Mother?'

This displeased Ammi and she'd snap at him, 'You're worrying your head over nothing. What is in our fate will happen.'

'O Fortunate One, it's not a matter of fate,' Abbu too would become irritated. 'I'm not worried about my life. I'm worried about our children, most of all Rifat.'

Abbu wasn't really worried about my life, he was worried only about my honour, my virtue—something which worried Ammi too. This was why she would periodically remind me how, back in the olden days, just before a Muslim attack, funeral pyres were set up, and how with the first news of defeat at the battlefront, young unmarried girls eagerly threw themselves into the fire.

Kalim Bhai too laughed at the examples Ammi gave. Once he told me, 'Did you notice, Ammi has to get her examples from Hindus, of all people. And at a time no less when Hindus constitute her greatest enemies. You know why? Because somewhere deep down our cultures stem from a common core. We're inextricably linked with one another at some point farther back. But today, religion rides roughshod over those links. Hence the oppression all around. But tyranny is no more Hindu than it is Muslim. It's just itself—tyranny. And its victims are always those who have nothing to do with disturbing the peace. And if you cared to go deeper still, you'd know that the perpetrator of tyranny too is neither Hindu nor Muslim. Rather it is the politics that places the weapon of religion in the hands of ordinary innocent people, inflames them, and turns them loose in the battlefield.'

This was more than I could fathom. But I did understand one thing well enough: Abbu's fear and Ammi's examples were intended to incite me to a similar sacrifice of my person, should the situation ever demanded it.

Cries went up suddenly one night around one o'clock. Abbu woke up with a start. So did Ammi. Sajid and Kalim Bhai came out of their rooms. Everybody at Mir Sahib's—that is, at Karani Babu's—also woke up. A commotion set in. Everyone fidgeted and ran about. Bhabhi quickly started to stuff all her jewellery into a handbag. Ammi harshly ordered me to go hide myself in the inner room. Meanwhile slogans continued in the Chowk. Not one, not two, but hundreds of men were shouting slogans in unison, as if gearing up for an attack. All of a sudden the cries stopped and an eerie hush fell over the neighbourhood. Abbu said anxiously, 'What was it? Why aren't they shouting any more?'

Nobody answered him. Meanwhile Karani Babu arrived with all his womenfolk in tow. He said, 'Bhai, together we just might be able to defend ourselves. At least for a while. You've even got boys. But I'm the only man in my house.'

Nobody answered Karani Babu either. Everyone was thinking of only one thing: What is one to make of this sudden hush after so much clamouring and noise? Are they thinking of a surprise attack? An ambush?

A while back Sajid had brought home a locally-made handgun from one of his friends. He'd put it in a cellophane bag and buried the bag under the courtyard floor. At the moment, he dropped everything and hurried to the spot, dug out the handgun and returned. He wiped it clean, loaded it with a single shell, and got ready.

Sajid only had three bullets. The handgun—never mind if it was cheap and made locally—and the three bullets did much to restore everybody's sagging spirits. They knew well enough that an entire mob couldn't be stopped with just this much fire power; all the same, it was like a straw to a drowning man. How ridiculous one becomes sometimes.

When nothing happened for quite some time, when no other slogans were heard, Kalim Bhai said softly, 'I'll go out and have a look around.'

Sajid stopped him. 'No, you stay. I'll go.'

Sajid threw a sheet around himself, hid the handgun inside the sheet, and was about to go out, when suddenly Abbu got up and said, 'Hold on! Let me go. You stay here and look after the family. I'm an old man. If something happens to me, well, it won't be much of a loss.'

He too was told to stay put, but he walked out anyway, repeating the *Darud Sharif*.

He was gone for a few minutes. We all spent those few moments in a state of extreme tension and anxiety. Sajid scouted the corner of the street again and again, his handgun at the ready.

Finally, Abbu returned, his face looking peaceful. 'It was just a send-off party for some party volunteers. All that clamouring and shouting was in their honour too. They're gone now. And so are all the people.'

The terrible tension which had taken hold of us began to slowly relax. Just as Karani Babu's family moved to leave, Abbu suddenly remembered. 'Where's Raffu? I don't see her.'

I was right there. I'd never left. Somehow I didn't like the idea of hiding myself in some dark room. Abbu spotted me and said, 'Daughter, some tea for Karani Babu.'

Karani Babu kept excusing himself but Abbu insisted.

'Bhai,' Karani Babu began, sipping his tea, 'to stay in this area any longer would be plain idiocy. We're just two houses. Not much we can do, can we?'

'But where will we go,' Abbu said. 'We've been living here for generations, haven't we? Where will we go now in our ripe old age?'

Leaning toward Abbu, Karani Babu said furtively, 'Bhai, I've got three grown-up girls. You see that, don't you? If something unseemly happened, I'd die of shame. I see no way out, other than to pack and leave, just anywhere. We'll eat half a loaf of bread, but at least we'll sleep peacefully. This all-night vigil, night after night in mortal fear, hiding like common thieves in this corner and that, day after day—we'll be spared that at least.'

For some time now, cracks had already begun to appear in Abbu's resolve, but he had shied away from taking a decisive step. Karani Babu's decision today gave him the required nudge. He said, 'Karani Babu, if you move out, we'd be left totally alone. Don't think that I haven't thought of *hijrat*. But that son of mine, with a B.A., he has this crazy notion that absolutely nothing will happen, even though a lot already has. Even these days he returns home from his newspaper past midnight.'

Karani Babu did move out. Our Hindu neighbours tried to reason with him, bent over backwards to assure him that nothing would happen to him here, but he couldn't be persuaded to stay on. Every day in the area weighed heavily on him. He ignored all reassurances and moved out.

The day Shilaniyas took place, the entire bazaar remained closed. Muslims didn't open for business out of fear, indeed they didn't even venture into the city from their localities. But surprisingly, even the Hindus felt so afraid that day that they didn't open their shops. The streets were empty of taxis, autorickshaws, even tractors—vehicles which played a prominent role in the city's noise, frenzied pace, and bustle—so that their absence now made it look even more deserted. A horrible dark cloud of fear hung over the entire city. Adding to the sense of utter eeriness were the faces of people, pale with some unknown fear. People looked at each other as if for the last time.

About eleven o'clock news arrived that Shilaniyas had taken place without incident. Both Hindus and Muslims breathed a sigh of relief: thank God, the calamity had been averted. But then the sound of the conch shell suddenly boomed from all the city temples, large and small, followed by small explosions of firecrackers, so many of them that those set off during Diwali paled in comparison. The din made it impossible to hear any other sound, not even one poured straight into your ear. A handful of Muslim shopkeepers and spectators who had somehow ventured out, took flight once again.

The loud boom of firecrackers really disturbed Abbu.

Maybe it had scared even Sajid, for he said, for the first time ever, 'It's useless to stay in this area anymore.'

Sajid was nothing if not extremely practical. Within three days he rented a house in Shernagar neighbourhood, and the night of the fourth day had a truck come out and start loading. A veritable crowd of our Hindu friends gathered outside the house. Kalim Bhai's local friends, Sajid's buddies, our neighbours—all were feeling terribly distressed at Abbu's decision to leave. They were reasoning with him, pleading with him not to leave, assuring him that nothing would happen. But, obviously, the time for assurances was long past.

I saw that Ammi was crying, even as she pointed to the items to be hauled over to the new place. She would glance at the house, the courtyard, the kitchen, and break into tears. God knows how many of her memories were associated with this house, this courtyard! It must have looked terribly empty when she'd first set foot into it. Little by little she'd put it together and settled it. She'd laughed and cried here, brought three children into the world, fought with the neighbours, and then in their bleak moments gone over to them for night-long vigils of sympathy, support, and commiseration. She had joked with Ghosh Babu here, and greeted Mukul Babu bowing reverentially like a bahu, her ghunghat drawn low over her face. She must have splashed coloured water during Holi, and on weddings she must have sung songs with her Hindu friends all night long. Of course none of this was on her lips today; it rather bubbled forth in her tears, which she wiped every now and then.

Abbu was running about like a crazy man, between the house and the truck, making sure that none of the stuff got lost in the moving, so he was dumping even those soap cases in the truck that had long ago lost their lids.

When I stepped into Kalim Bhai's room to pick up an item I had inadvertently left there, I was surprised to see him there. All the stuff from the room had already been loaded on the truck, but he just stood there, staring at the empty walls, utterly lost in the world of his thoughts. It was impossible to locate him precisely in that world, but it was obvious from his anguished face that he had sunk quite deep into it. Seeing me he started, took a sigh, and said with a terrible feeling of loneliness, 'An old bond's broken today.'

I couldn't figure out what he meant. All the same, I had no difficulty reaching to the inconsolable pain which squirmed in the space of this little sentence.

Glossary and Notes

abjad: arrangement of the Arabic according to the numerological value of letters.

Abu Jahl: literally, 'Father of Ignorance'; he was an uncle of the Prophet Muhammad who resisted the spread of Islam and treated Muhammad very harshly.

ai bi: *'ai'* is an emphatic exclamation, used to draw attention or show surprise; 'bi' short form of 'bibi,' lady.

Akhfash Square: *'akhfash'* means day blind, hemeralopic; weak-sighted, afflicted with defective vision; 'Mr. Blind.'

Akhand Hindustan:'Undivided India'; Hindu slogan demanding to keep India undivided.

al-Hamdu-o Lillah; see 'Sura Fatiha.'

Aligarh College: refers to what was originally called the Muhammadan Anglo-Oriental College, founded for the political revival of Indian Muslims by Sir Saiyid Ahmad Khan (1817-1908) at Aligarh, UP, India. In 1920 it was raised to the status of a university, and its name become the Aligarh Muslim University. A large number of the intellectual and political leaders of Muslim India in the last decades of the nineteenth and the first half of the twentieth century were educated at Aligarh.

Allah-o-Akbar!: 'Great is God!'—a Muslim cry frequently used to express admiration, surprise, or denial; a war-cry.

anar: pomegranate.

andarsas: a kind of sweetmeat; fried and sugared rice-and-flour balls.

Ansar: helpers; applied technically to the Muslims of Medina who helped the incoming Meccan Muslims following their migration to Medina in 622 CE; here, original Muslim residents of those parts of India which became Pakistan in 1947; those who didn't have to migrate.

Aqa-e-Namdar: *'aqa,'* lord, master; *'namdar,'* well-known, distinguished, respected.

arvi: a sticky, root-vegetable; *arvi* roll: spicy stuffing in rolls of *arvi* leaves, which are then deep fried and served as a snack, *hors d'oeuvres*.

Ayaz: was a dear slave of Mahmud Ghaznavi who conquered India; their mutual regard and affection has become proverbial in Muslim literature.

Ayyub: the Prophet Job.

azan: Muslim prayer-call cried from the minaret of a mosque five times a day just before the commencement of the ritual prayer.

bagli: one of the several rooms in a Parsi mortuary where the corpse undergoes it final rites before being handed over to the caretakers for its ultimate disposal.

bahu: daughter-in-law.

bakri: she-goat, ewe.

binaut; binot: club-fighting; an indigenous South Asian form of martial art that requires tremendous skill and agility.

barah-mahs: same as *barah-masa;* literally, twelve months of the year; a kind of verse of twelve stanzas each of which corresponds to one of the twelve months of the year and its characteristics, which expresses the theme of separation of a wife from her husband.

barkhurdar: a son; often used patronizingly; something like 'Boy'.

batasha: sugar drop; a kind of confectionery.

Befarma'id, Befarma'id: Persian for 'Very well,' 'Yes, of course.'

bhatyali: a popular Bengali folk song.

bhatyaran: wife if a *bhatyara* (innkeeper); often used pejoratively to indicate someone's coarse and uncouth manner and low social standing; something like a 'country bumpkin.'

bigha: a measure of land equal to about five-eight of an acre.

bismillah: 'In the name of God'; a formula uttered frequently by Muslims before commencing any activity.

bodi: a small tuft of hair left on shaven head by Hindus as a sign of religiousness and piety.

canturi: a kind of card game.

chata'i: a mat.

chauka: a low, wooden platform; also the kitchen area.

chauki: a low, wooden stool.

chutiya: same as *bodi* above; also a [woman's] braid.

dakshina: an offering; gift.

dagla : a knee-length garment, like a long coat, made of a goshtsamer material called *malmal*, worn by Parsis on special occasions such as weddings and funerals.

dahi-bare: fried *mung* or *urad* (lentils) balls served in a spiced yogurt sauce.

dal-roti: lentils and bread; food indicative of poor status and prowess; contrasted with *gos-roti*: meat and bread.

Darbar Sahib, Data Sahib: refers either to Ali ibn Usman Jullabi—also Hujwiri—commonly known as Data Ganj Bakhsh, or to his tomb-sanctuary in Lahore.

Darud Sharif: 'The Noble Blessing'—applied to short Muslim prayer of benediction, blessing, praise, and salutation to the Prophet Muhammad.

Dauji ke bachche!: 'You son of a Dauji!'; spoken in irritation.

devrhi: threshold, porch, antechamber, entrance, door.

din: (pronounced *deen*) a Muslim term for faith.

din ba-din: day by day.

din par din: day by day.

Domni: a woman or girl of the *dom* caste; a gypsy; a dancing and/or singing girl.

Dulhan Bhabhi: dulhan: bride; bhabhi: sister-in-law.

Dusadh: a caste of Hindus, very low in standing; its members keep pigs, work as night watchmen, and are often called upon to remove carcasses.

Eidgah: a large space (may or may not be enclosed) where the prayer on the two major Muslim festivals of Eid takes place.

Far-far: lickety-split; immediately.

Fi amani 'l-Lah: 'In the protection of God,' used by Muslims in the sense of 'Good-bye.'

fitra: alms required by every able Muslim to be given to the needy at the end of the Ramzan fast and prior to the Eid prayer.

gali: curse; swear word.

Gama: a famous South Asian wrestler who remained undefeated for nearly thirty years.

ghori: a mare.

ghoriyan: wedding songs at the arrival of the groom's party.

ghunghat: a covering or mantle for a woman's face as a sign of modesty.

gol-mol: roly-poly.

Golu: from *'gol'*, meaning round and chubby.

gos-roti: gos (meat); *roti*: (bread); see *'dal-roti'* above.

Granthiji: one learned in the sacred scriptures of the Sikhs (short moral poems by Guru Nanak and other gurus).

Haramzada!: Bastard!

hazrat: a term expressing regard and respect for a religious or learned person.

Hazrat Maulana: best rendered as 'Lord and Master.'

hijrat: migration; the spiritual experience of the Prophet Muhammad's migration from Mecca to Medina in 622 CE.

Ibrahim: Abraham.

ikka: open, single-horse carriage.

iktara: single-stringed musical instrument.

iman: Muslim word for 'faith.'

I.N.A.: Indian National Army, founded by Subhash Chandra Bose.

insha'allah: 'If God wills'; used principally by Muslims.

Isa: Arabic name of Jesus.

isa-e a'zam: the sublime name.

ism fa'il: active participle.

Jalil Bhai: 'Illustrious Brother'; *jalil* means glorious and high in dignity, and is often used to underscore God's majesty; Bengali people pronounce 'j' as 'z,' which turns *jalil* into *zalil*: a word which means wretched, despicable, contemptible, low, ignominous.

jal-kumri: water-weeds; algae.

Jan-e-Pidar: 'jan' (life) and 'pidar' (father): 'Life of your Father'; used endearingly when addressing a son or daughter.

jethji: husband's elder brother.

jhatka: slitting an animal's throat with one stroke, as opposed to sacrificing it by uttering God's name and slitting the throat half-way to let the blood flow out; roughly equivalent to unkoshered meat.

jijaji: brother-in-law.

jinn-bhuts: ghosts; evil spirits.

Jamhurnama: an epic or story of the common people.

kachcha: shorts; knickers, usually worn by Sikh boys.

kaharis: female of the Hindu caste of Kahars

(palanquin-bearers; dooley-bearers; water-carriers).

kalimah: Muslim profession of faith ('There is no god but Allah; Muhammad is the Prophet of God'); this is the major *kalimah*, but there are a number of others in which a Muslim testifies to his faith and belief in all other Prophets, revealed books, angels, and the Day of Judgment.

kara: a bracelet which all Sikh males are required by their religion to wear.

kasti: a child is formally initiated into the religion of Zarathushtara in the ceremony of Navjote which takes place in the fifth or seventh year of life, but never past the ninth.

Henceforward, the Parsi must always wear the *kasti*-string or cord around the waist as a token of his/her faith.

kes: hair; Sikhs are not permitted by their religion to cut any hair on the body.

khaddar: coarse home-spun cotton cloth.

Khala: mother's sister.

Khalsa: a Sikh.

Khalu: mother's sister's husband.

Khele Khub: a Persian expression denoting something like 'Very well.'

khes: a sheet: shawl.

Khuda Hafiz: 'May God Protect You'; spoken by Muslims when leaving; same as *'Fi amani 'l-lah,'* above.

Khudavand-e Ta'ala: 'God, the Most High (Sublime).'

kirpan: a dagger; worn by Sikh males as a token of their religion.

'Ko'i mare, ko'i jiye, Suthra Ghol batashe piye': 'Outside it's a matter of life and death, but the Suthra only cares about his sweets'; Suthra: a particular ascetic group.

kot, *patloon*, and *ta'i*: coat, pants, and tie; somebody dressed formally in suit and tie.

kotah qismat mujawwizah: one short on luck or fortune.

kufr: infidelity (resulting from ascribing partners and associates to God); the greatest and only unforgivable sin in Islam.

La-haul: short for the Arabic expression *'La haula wa la quwwata illa bi 'l-Lahi 'l-alliyi 'l-azim'* ('There is no strength nor power but in God, the High, the Great'); expressed mostly to ward off real or presumed evil or to neutralize fear.

lajwanti: the touch-me-not plant; a bashful woman.

lallah: son; boy.

Leagies: Leaguers; a member or supporter of the Muslim League, which rallied for the creation of Pakistan.

Lord of Bat'ha: allusion to the Prophet Muhammad; *bat'ha* stands for a basin-shaped valley or flatland (Mecca).

Madiyan: a mare.

Mahasabhai: a member or supporter of the Hindu Mahasabha.

Mahmud: see 'Ayaz' above.

mahris: same as 'kaharis' above.

makiyan: a hen.

maktabs: schools, to be distinguished from madrasas (religious schools).

Malihabad: a place twenty miles north west of Lucknow and 250 miles south east of Delhi; it's famous for its mangos.

matra: a vowel symbol or mark.

Maulvi Sahib: one learned in Islamic religion; a distinguished, respected individual; one who instructs children in Quranic lessons and elementary writing and reading.

mazhab: Muslim word for religion.

Mazhar Jan-e Janan: name of a prominent mystic and a noted Persian poet (1699-1781).

milad: celebration of the Prophet Muhammad's birthday; among South Asian Muslims a gathering, mostly of women, at which religious poetry is chanted, offered as an act of piety.

Mir Munshi: the head of an administrative department or office.

Mister Hawannaq: 'Mr. Clueless.'

moh-maya: earthly and creaturely attachments; love of materialism.

momin: strictly a Muslim believer.

morni: a peahen.

Muhajir: those who migrate; immigrants; here, those Muslims who migrated to Pakistan on Partition.

Mullaji: a Muslim religious tutor who teaches young children the Quran.

Mumani Bi: Mumani: wife of one's mother's brother; Bi: title of respect applied to Muslim women.

'Munh-carhi Domni': Spoilt gypsy.

Munshi: a scribe; one who writes applications and petitions for others for a fee.

Murshid: preceptor; spiritual director.

Musalla; Musla; distortion of 'Muslim'; indicative of dislike and disgust.

na'in: wife of a barber.

namaz: Muslim ritual prayer; offered five times a day at specified times.

nambardar: village revenue collector.

Nazrul song: a song by Nazrul Islam, the second major Bengali poet after Tagore.

Pandata, jai Ramji ki!: 'Oh Pundit, Victory to Ram!'—here spoken with sarcasm.

Pansari: a vendor of herbs, grains, spices, and groceries; a provisions merchant.
pari-churels: fairies and witches.
Pir Sahib: a Muslim saint.
qasba: small town.
qawwali: a devotional song sung at the tomb-sanctuaries of Muslim Sufi saints.
qa'ida: a primer.
Qarun: he was a cousin of the Prophet Moses; in the Muslim lore he is represented as an exceedingly rich and equally stingy person; the idea here is that even a proverbially large treasure cannot last forever.
Qul huwa 'l-Lahu Ahad!: 'Say, God is One'; 112th chapter of the Quran comprising only four lines; considered the essence of monotheism; frequently repeated by Muslims.
Rabbul Alamin: Lord and Master of the Worlds; a Muslim epithet for God.
rakhi: a thread bound round the wrist on the Hindu festival of Saluno.
raksha-bandhan: tying of an amulet of protection (rakhi) on the wrist of another.
R.M.O.: Resident Medical Officer.
roz ba-roz: day by day.
ruku: kneeling; a posture in the Muslim ritual prayer.
Salaam : Muslim greeting offered by raising the right hand to the forehead and uttering *'as-salamu alaikum'* ('Peace be on you').
Salé: from *sala* (wife's brother, but never sister's husband), a term of mild-abuse; here, the nearest equivalent would be: 'You bastard.'
Saluno: see rakhi above.
samdhi: son-in-law's father.
sara'e: inn.

saut: the other wife; a term indicative of jealousy, unhappiness, anger.

sehra: flower worn by a bride and bridegroom at the wedding ceremony.

ser: a weight of about two pounds.

Shahnama: an epic or story of the kings.

shakistah: broken; a longhand style of calligraphy.

she 'r-geet: she 'r (a couplet in poetry), *geet* (song).

Shila Niyas: literally, 'laying of the brick'; refers to the movement that preceded by roughly two years the destruction of the Babri Mosque in 1992. The Hindu nationalist groups jointly referred to as the Sangh Parivar, (Sangh Family) asked people to send bricks, ceremoniously sanctified, to Ayodhya to lay the foundations of the proposed Rama Temple. The bricks, with the name of Rama on them, were sent from all over the world and were usually carried in long processions to Ayodhya.

shisham: the tree Dalbergia sisu; its dark reddish-brown hard wood is used for making furniture.

sifat-e mushabbah: predicate adjective.

sijdah: prostration, a posture in Muslim ritual prayer.

Sikhra: a derogatory term, a distortion of 'Sikh' to indicate one's dislike and disgust of them.

siparah: *si* (thirty), *parah* (piece, part); the chapters of the Quran divided into thirty parts so that the entire Quran could be recited over a month.

Subedar Sahib: a junior commissioned officer in the British Indian army.

suhag: the happy and auspicious state of wife-hood.

'*Sura Fatiha*': the opening chapter of the Quran, also called '*al-Hamdu li'l-Lah,*; with which it begins; the chapter ends with the expression : '*dallin, ameen*.'

taka: the unit of currency used in Bangladesh.
takht: an all-purpose square or rectangular low wooden platform.
Tanpura: an Indian string instrument used as a drone to accompany other instruments; it typically has a large, round 'belley.'
ta'wiz: an amulet, charm to ward off evil.
Taya: father's older brother; one's older uncle.
taziyas: In the South Asian Muslim context, replica of the mausolea of Prophet Muhammad's grandsons Hasan and Husain, his son-in-law Ali, and daughter Fatima at Karbala in Iraq. The *taziyas* are constructed from wood, bamboo and paper work. On the tenth of the Islamic month of Muharram, they are carried in Procession along city streets, followed by crowds of devoted Shi'ites reciting elegies and self-flagelating. At the end of the day these replicas are released into the river, where they sink and disappear.
Thakurs: a feudal nobleman or landholder; the head of a tribe or village; a person of rank and authority.
thanedarni: wife of a thanedar (officer in charge of a thana—police station); one who struts about banking on the position of her husband.
Thanewale: the police.
Tilka 'r-Rusul: name of the third *siparah* (see above) of the Quran.
Tipu Sultan: eighteenth-century ruler of the state of Mysore. He is famous for his efforts to check the growing power of the British East India Company. He was killed in 1799 fighting the British at Seringapatam.
'Ulloo ki patthi!': literally, 'daughter of an owl'; fool; an owl is considered a foolish and inauspicious bird in South Asia.
Umm-e Jahileen: Mother of Fools.

Vehguruji (Vaheguruji): 'the Guru is great,' 'salutations to the hornourable Guru'; a Sikh expression.

Vaishnava: name of the one of the three divisions of modern Hindu sects; a worshipper or follower of the Hindu god Vishnu; a strict vegetarian.

Voh sachchi sarkar: 'The truthful Lord.'

walima: a wedding feast or banquet given the day after consummation of marriage.

wanyas: a variant of the more commonly used bania, a Hindu cast; in literature and common parlance stands for moneylenders, with a propensity for ruthlessness and exploitation in collecting.

wuzu: ritual ablutions before Muslim prayers.

Ya Ali: 'O Ali!'; a Muslim (especially Shi'ite) cry uttered before commencing a difficult or arduous act.

Yunani: Ionian, Greek.

Zalil Bhai: see 'Jalil Bhai,' above.

Contributors

ASHFAQ AHMAD was born in Ferozepur District in 1925 and was educated at Government College, Lahore. He started writing fiction in the 1950s and quickly established himself as a major short story writer. *Ujle Phool*, from which 'The Shepherd' is taken, and *Ek Muhabbat Sau Afsane* are among his more famous short story collections. He has also written a short novel and a volume of Punjabi plays. He was the editor of the tastefully produced literary magazine *Dastan-go* and the weekly *Lail-o-Nahar*. Today his fame rests chiefly on his travelogues, radio features, and TV plays. He worked as Director General, Urdu Science Board, Lahore, for a number of years.

UPENDAR NATH ASHK was born in Jallandhar in 1910 and worked for some time for All India Radio, Delhi. He started as an Urdu writer, but concentrated on writing in Hindi after Partition. He has published several novels and collections of short stories. He was also well known as a major Hindi playwright; his contribution in this area was recognized in 1965, when he received the Sangeet Natak Akademi Award. He died in 1996. 'Tableland' is taken from *Fasadat ke Afsane*, compiled by Zubair Rizvi.

MASUD ASHAR is the pen name of Masud Ahmad Khan, who was born in 1931 in Rampur. He emigrated to Pakistan in 1952 and became a career journalist. After working for sundry Urdu newspapers, he finally joined, in 1958, the influential *Imroz*. His quarter-of-a-century-long association with this paper suddenly terminated when, in 1983, he was fired for supporting a petition demanding removal of Martial Law and the restoration of democracy in Pakistan. But when the government changed in 1988, he was reinstated. 'Of Coconuts and Bottles of Chilled Beer' is taken from his collection *Ankhon par Donon Hath*, which also includes a number of his other short stories about the social and political situation of East Pakistan on the eve of its separation in 1971. His entire fictional output until the mid-1980s has been collected in *Sare Fasane*, which appeared in 1997.

SYED MUHAMMAD ASHRAF, who is among the youngest generation of Urdu writers of India, was born into a Sufi family of UP. He was educated at Aligarh Muslim University and is now a Deputy Commissioner in the Income Tax Department, Bombay. He has published two collections of short stories and his first novel is to be released soon. 'The Rogue,' included in the present anthology, is taken from his first collection, *Dar se Bichhre*. A short story of his, 'Man,' was the recipient of the Katha Award for Creative Writing.

RAJINDAR SINGH BEDI was born in Lahore in 1915. He first worked as a clerk in the postal department; later he joined the Lahore station of All India Radio and wrote many successful plays, having meanwhile established himself as a highly nuanced fiction writer, with the publication of *Dana-o-Dam*, his first collection of short stories. On Partition he moved to India. After working for a short period as station director, Radio Kashmir, he joined the Bombay film industry, producing and writing scripts for a number of successful films. His Urdu novel, *Ek Chadar Maili Si*, translated into English as *I Take This Woman*, published by Penguin India received the Sahitya Akademi Award in 1965. Bedi, who died in 1984, is regarded as the second most prominent Urdu fiction writer after Saadat Hasan Manto. 'Lajwanti' is taken from his collection of the same title.

ISMAT CHUGHTAI, counted among the earliest and foremost women Urdu writers, was born in Bạdayun, UP in 1915 and was educated at Agra, Aligarh, and Lucknow. She worked as a headmistress first in Jawra State and later at Bareilly. Her literary career started in 1938 with a play. Subsequently she wrote short stories which appeared in the renowned literary magazines of the time, such as *Saqi* and *Adabi Dunya*. A major voice in the Progressive Writers' Movement and an outspoken champion of women's causes, she moved to Bombay, married writer, producer, and director Shahid Lateef, and wrote for films and the radio. She died in Bombay in 1991. Her published works include several collections of short stories, three novellas, and a novel, *Terhi Lakir*, which has been translated into English as *The Crooked Line* (Heinemann, 1995). 'Lihaf' ('The Quilt') is considered her most controversial work, as it deals with the plight of a married woman thirsting for her husband's love and embrace which, when denied, drives her to the affections of another woman. 'Roots' is taken from her collection *Chhu'i-Mu'i*.

ALTAF FATIMA was born in Lucknow. Her ancestors hailed from Kherabad, known after the 1857 War of Independence as Patiala State. On Partition she migrated to Pakistan and settled in Lahore, where she took an M.A. and a B.Ed. from the University of Punjab and started teaching

Urdu literature at Islamia Girls' College. She is counted among the second generation of women Urdu writers. She has published several collections of short stories and novels, all of which have been very well received, but her second novel, *Dastak na Do*, translated into English as *The One Who Did Not Ask* (Heinemann, 1993), is considered her best so far. 'Do You Suppose It's the East Wind?' is taken from her collection *Voh Jise Chaha Gaya*.

ILYAS AHMAD GADDI, novelist and short story writer, was born in Jharia, Bihar, in 1932. He made his literary debut in 1948 with his short story 'Afkaar'. He published two collections of short stories, two novellas, and a novel, *Fire Area*, which portrays life and its moral conflicts in the coal fields of Bihar. With its rootedness in the soil of Bihar, ts effective exploitation of the local idiom and its powerful plea for social justice and humanism, this novel was hailed as a significant addition to Urdu fiction and won Gaddi the prestigious Sahitya Akademi Award in 1996. He also received awards from the Urdu Academies of Bengal, Bihar, and UP. He was the owner of a small business in his native Jharia, where he died in 1997.

AMILA HASHIMI was born in Lyallpur (now Faisalabad) in 1929. She received a Master's degree in English literature and taught in a school for a number of years. 'Banished,' counted among her best short stories, is taken from her collection *Aap-biti, Jag-biti*. She is the author f several collections of short stories and a number of novels, of which *Talash-e Baharan*, with which she began her literary career, was the recipient of the Adamjee Literary Award in 1960. She also received great critical acclaim for her novel, *Dasht-e Sus* (1983), which is based on the life of the nineteenth century martyr-mystic Mansur al-Hallaj. She died in 1988.

INTIZAR HUSAIN was born in Dibai near Bulandshahar in UP (India) in 1925. He was educated in Meerut and, after migrating to Pakistan in 1947, in Lahore as well. A creative writer, critic and translator, he has published seven volumes of short stories, four novels, and a novella. *The Journal of South Asian Literature* (East Lansing, Michigan, USA) devoted an entire issue to him in 1983, and his second novel, *Basti* (town), for which he was offered the Adamjee Literary Award in 1982, but which he declined, has appeared in English translation. He was the recipient of the first Yatra Award (1994), instituted by Rupa & Co. with assistance from HarperCollins, Calcutta. He makes his home in Lahore where he resigned from his job as a columnist with the daily Urdu newspaper *Mashriq* (The East), a job he had held for a quarter of a century. He now writes a weekly column for the Karachi-based English newspaper *Dawn*. *The Seventh Door and Other Stories*, a collection of his short stories in English translation, was recently published by Lynne Rienner (U.S.A.). 'An Unwritten Epic' appears in his first collection *Gali Kuche*.

KHALIDA HUSAIN was born in Lahore in 1938. She started writing fiction in 1963 under her maiden name Khalida Asghar. After half a dozen brilliant short stories she dropped out of the Urdu literary world altogether. Married in 1965, she moved to Karachi in 1967. After a twelve-year silence, she staged a comeback in 1977—wiser, more experienced, somewhat less willing to take risks. The subconscious compulsions of a pained psyche, so powerfully captured in her earlier work, appear mor muted in the stories spanning the second phase. She has published four volumes of short stories, some of which have been translated into Hindi. Currently she is working on her first novel. She is now settled in Islamabad where she teaches English in a girls' college. 'The Wagon,' Which first appeared in *Savera* 35 (Lahore) in early 1960s, is generally regarded as her crowning achievement.

SAADAT HASAN MANTO is regarded as the subcontinent's pre-eminent modern Urdu short fiction writer. He was a brilliant and prolific innovator. Born in Sambrala (Ludhiana district) in 1912, he passed away in Lahore in 1955 at the age of 43. Of all Urdu fiction writers, he was the one who contributed the largest number of consistently high-quality and equally controversial creative work to the Partition corpus. In pre-Partition India, he worked for a while at All India Radio, Delhi, and later moved to Bombay to work for the movie industry. On Partition, he opted for Pakistan, and at Lahore, for a time, co-edited, with Muhammad Hasan Askari, who was then promoting the idea of a distinct Pakistani literature, the literary periodical *Urdu Adab*. Manto's prolific writing, which includes plays, short stories, personality sketches, Partition vignettes, and articles have recently appeared in four huge volumes from Lahore. He was tried in court for his short story "Thanda Gos,' which is set against the rioting and bloodshed of 1947. Roshan Dhunjibhoy made a film on Manto for German TV in 1990, which includes the dramatizations of three of his stories. In 1987, another of his Partition stories, 'Toba Tek Singh,' was made into a feature film by Bandung Films, London, with Saeed Jaffrey, Roshan Seth, and Zia Mohyeddin as actors. 'Sahae' is taken from his collection *Khali Botlen, Khali Dibbe*.

HASAN MANZAR is the pen name of Syed Manzar Hasan, who was born in 1934 in Hapur and raised in Gorakhpur (India) before migrating to Pakistan in 1947. After finishing his medical studies in Lahore, he joined the Dutch Merchant Navy as a surgeon and subsequently worked in different medical capacities in Saudi Arabia and Nigeria. He later decided to study psychology at Edinburgh University. After taking additional degrees from the Royal College of Surgeons, Edinburgh, and Royal College of Physicians, Glasgow, he took up a teaching position at Malaya University, Kuala Lampur. He is now settled in Hyderabad (Pakistan), where he runs a psychiatric clinic. He has so far published four collections of short stories and is currently working on a fifth, as well as a novel. A volume of his stories in English translation, *Requiem for the Earth,* has been published by Oxford University Press as part of its Pakistan Writers' Series.

ALI IMAM NAQVI was born in 1945 in Bombay, where he received his early education at Ismail Beg Muhammad High School. He has published two collections of short stories and a novel. He makes his home in Bombay, where he works for the Iran Council.

AHMAD NADIM QASIMI is the pen name of Ahmad Shah, who was born in 1916. A prolific writer, his fictional works alone comprise fourteen published volumes, of which *Sannata, Kapas ke Phool, Neela Patthar,* and *Aas Paas* are among the most famous. He is also a major poet, with several collections to his credit. He was an ong the leading members of the Progressives Writers' Association and after Partition, when he opted for Pakistan, worked as its

Secretary. He was frequently jailed, the last time in 1958, following the takeover of the government by Field Marshal Muhammad Ayyub Khan, when he was working for the weekly *Lail-o-Nahar*. He is Director of Majlis-e Taraqqi-e Urdu, Lahore, and has been editor of the literary magazine *Funoon* since its establishment over thirty years ago. 'Parmeshar Singh' has been taken from *Bazaar-e Hayat*.

MUHAMMAD SALAM-UR-RAHMAN was born in India in 1934, and is an eminent Urdu poet and critic. He started his literary career with an Urdu translation of Homer's *Odyssey*. He has worked as the editor of one of the best modern Urdu literary journals, *Savera*, and was also an associate editor of the weekly *Nusrat*. Since 1963 he has been writing book reviews and literary columns for many English newspapers. He has published poems, half a dozen short stories, and numerous translations from English into Urdu and vice versa; three of his English poems once appeared in *Poetry North West*. The first volume of his critical work on ancient Greek literature was published a few years ago.

SALAM BIN RAZZAQ it the pen name of Shaikh Abdussalam Abdurrazzaq, who was born in 1941 in Panvel in Maharashtra, India. He finished high school in 1960 and published his first short story two years later in the literary magazine *Sha'ir*. He is the author of three collections of short stories, two in Urdu and one in Hindi; he has also translated Marathi fiction into Urdu. Currently he is putting together for the Maharashtra State Urdu Academy a two-volume selection of Marathi writing from the last twenty-five years, which he is also translating. He lives in Bombay where he teaches in a school run by the Municipal

Corporation. 'A Sheet' appeared in *Saughat* 11 (Bangalore) early this year.

Abdussalam Abdurrazzaq, who was born in 1941 in Panwil in Maharashtra, India. He finished high school in 1960 and published his first short story two years later in the literary magazine *Sha'ir*. He is the author of three collections of short stories, two in Urdu and one in Hindi; he has also translated Marathi fiction into Urdu. Currently he is putting together for the Maharashtra State Urdu Academy a two-volume selection of Marathi writing from the last twenty-five years, which he is also translating. He lives in Bombay where he teaches in a school run by the Municipal Corporation. 'A Sheet' appeared in *Saughat* 11 (Bangalore) early this year.

READ MORE IN PENGUIN

In every corner of the world, on every subject under the sun, Penguin represents quality and variety—the very best in publishing today.

For complete information about books available from Penguin—including Puffins, Penguin Classics and Arkana—and how to order them, write to us at the appropriate address below. Please note that for copyright reasons the selection of books varies from country to country.

In India: Please write to *Penguin Books India Pvt. Ltd. 210 Chiranjiv Tower, Nehru Place, New Delhi, 110019*

In the United Kingdom: Please write to *Dept JC, Penguin Books Ltd. Bath Road, Harmondsworth, West Drayton, Middlesex, UB7 ODA. UK*

In the United States: Please write to *Penguin USA Inc., 375 Hudson Street, New York, NY 10014*

In Canada: Please write to *Penguin Books Canada Ltd. 10 Alcorn Avenue, Suite 300, Toronto, Ontario M4V 3B2*

In Australia: Please write to *Penguin Books Australia Ltd. 487, Maroondah Highway, Ring Wood, Victoria 3134*

In New Zealand: Please write to *Penguin Books (NZ) Ltd. Private Bag, Takapuna, Auckland 9*

In the Netherlands: Please write to *Penguin Books Netherlands B.V., Keizersgracht 231 NL-1016 DV Amsterdom*

In Germany : Please write to *Penguin Books Deutschland GmbH, Metzlerstrasse 26, 60595 Frankfurt am Main, Germany*

In Spain: Please write to *Penguin Books S.A., Bravo Murillo, 19-1'B, E-28015 Madrid, Spain*

In Italy: Please write to *Penguin Italia s.r.l., Via Felice Casati 20, I-20104 Milano*

In France: Please write to *Penguin France S.A., 17 rue Lejeune, F-31000 Toulouse*

In Japan: Please write to *Penguin Books Japan. Ishikiribashi Building, 2-5-4, Suido, Tokyo 112*

In Greece: Please write to *Penguin Hellas Ltd, dimocritou 3, GR-106 71 Athens*

In South Africa: Please write to *Longman Penguin Books Southern Africa (Pty) Ltd, Private Bag X08, Bertsham 2013*